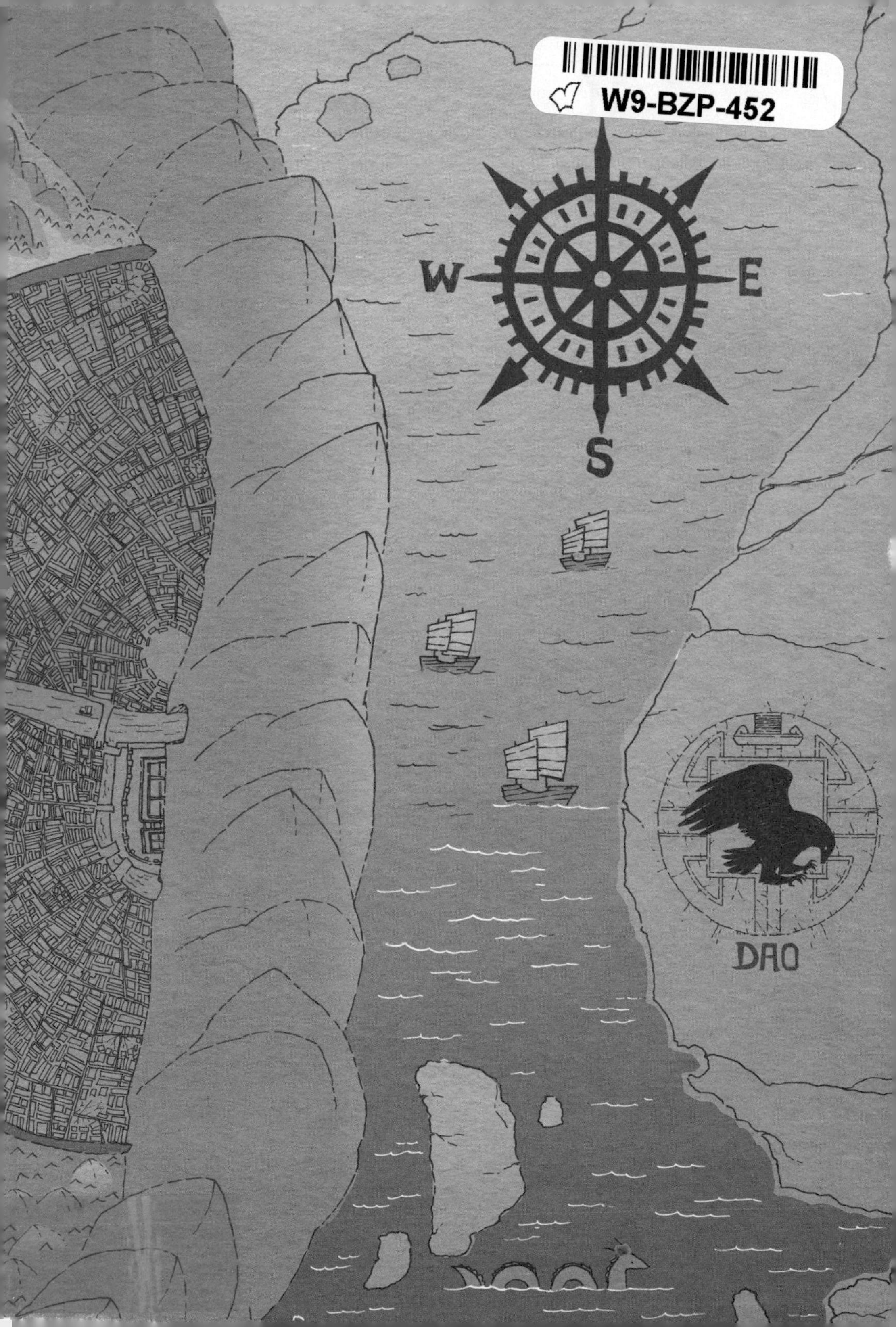
W
E
S
DAO

THE STONE HEART

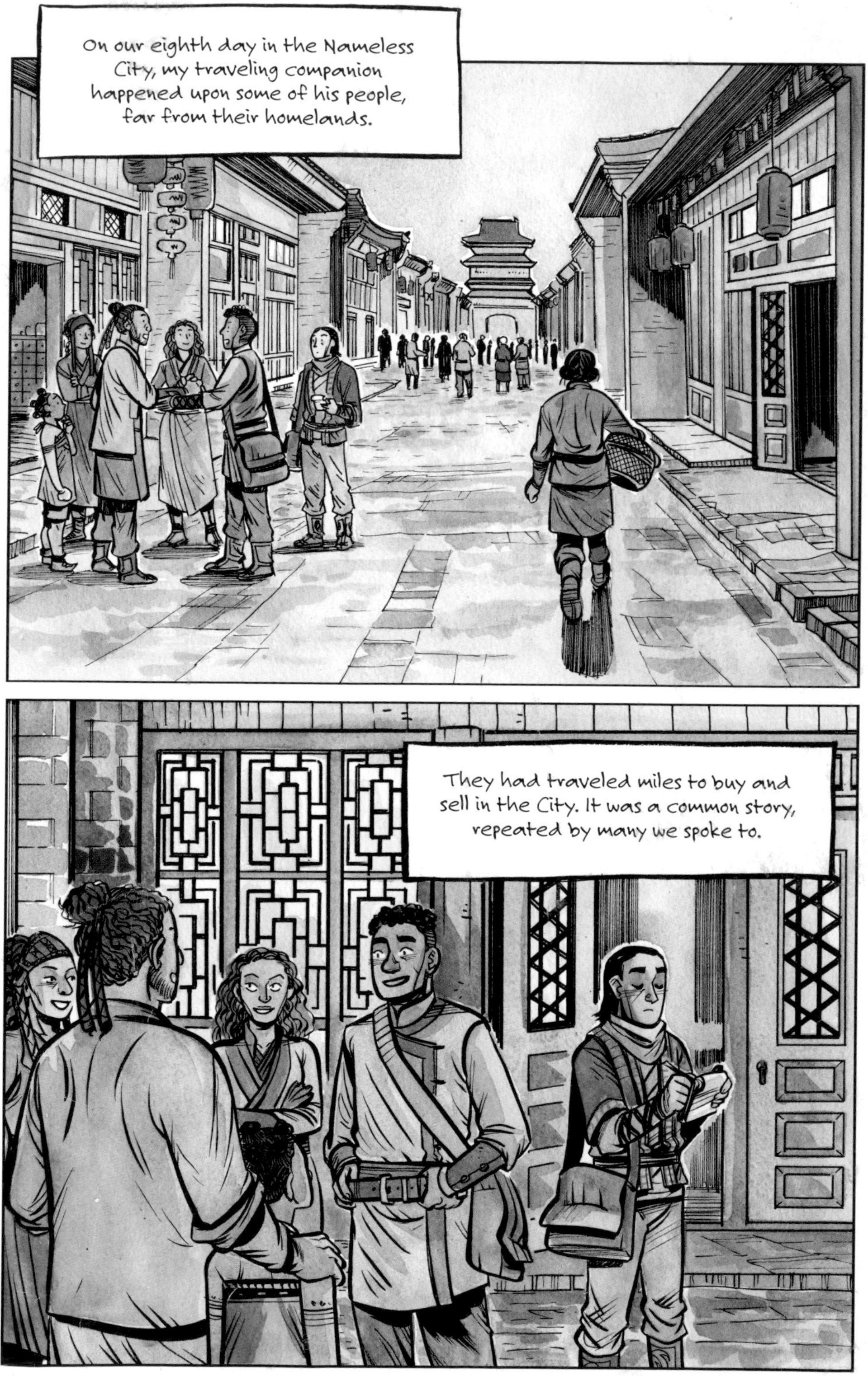
On our eighth day in the Nameless City, my traveling companion happened upon some of his people, far from their homelands.
They had traveled miles to buy and sell in the City. It was a common story, repeated by many we spoke to.

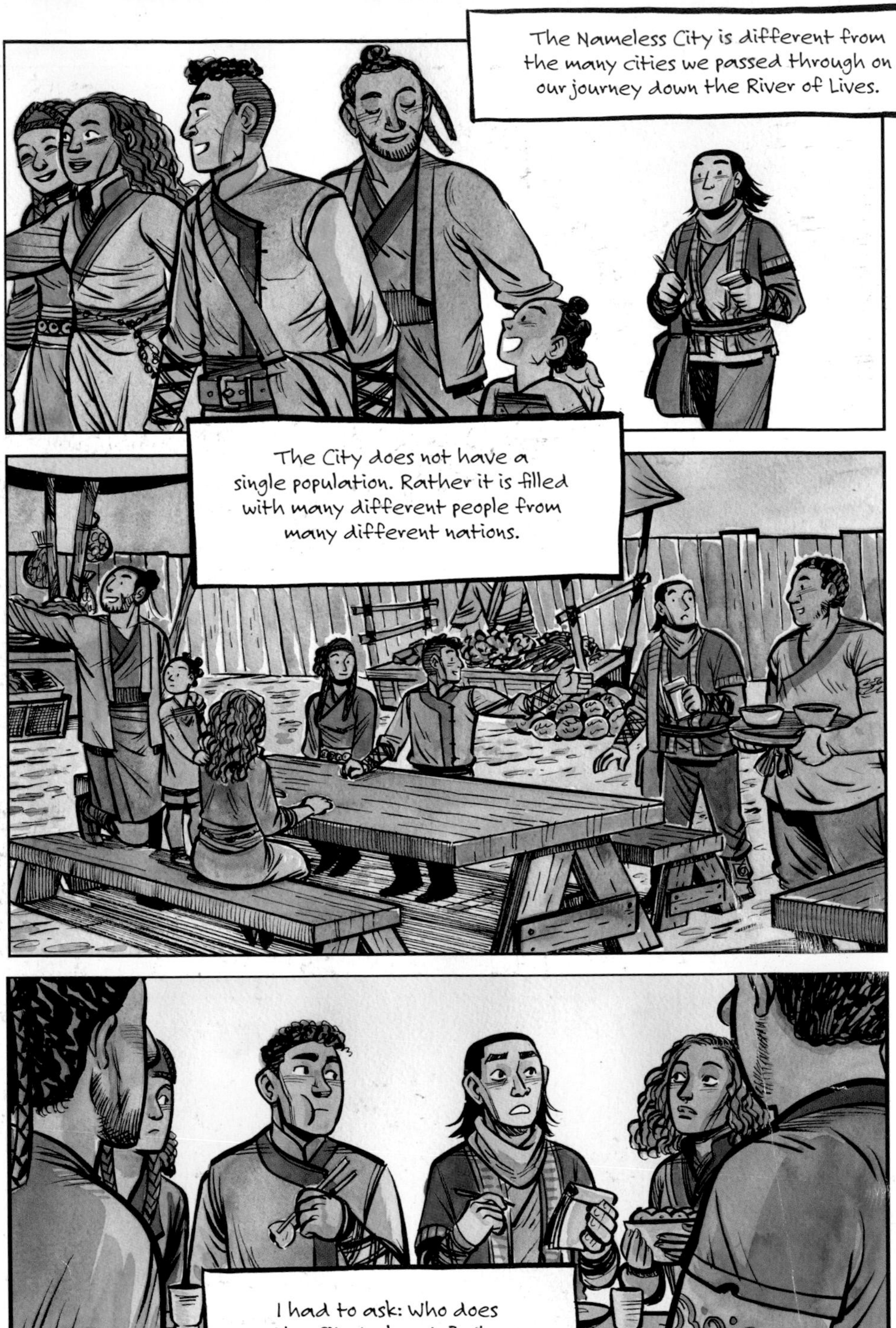
The Nameless City is different from the many cities we passed through on our journey down the River of Lives.
The City does not have a single population. Rather it is filled with many different people from many different nations.
I had to ask: Who does the City belong to? Who are its rightful people?

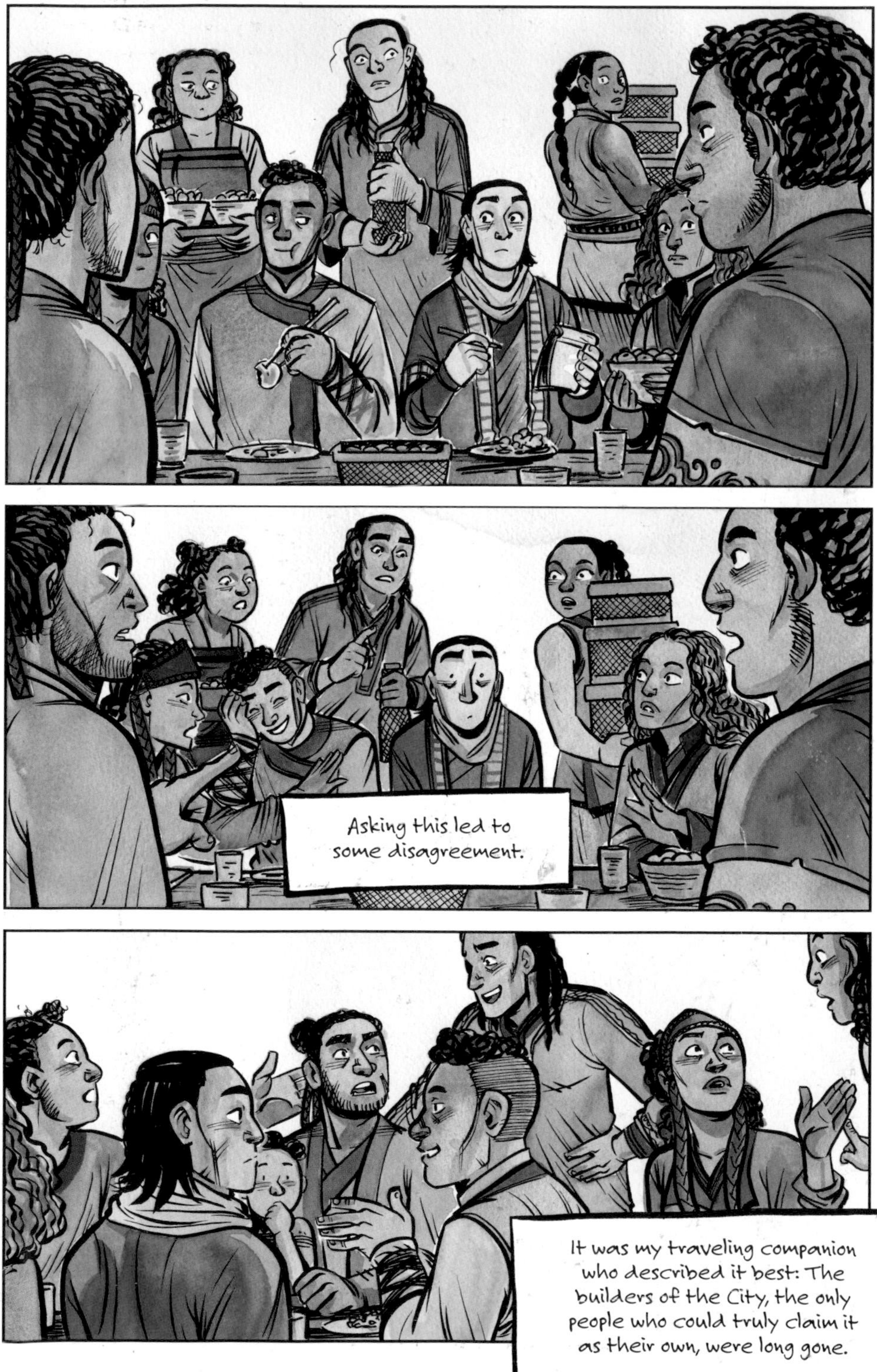
Asking this led to some disagreement.
It was my traveling companion who described it best: The builders of the City, the only people who could truly claim it as their own, were long gone.

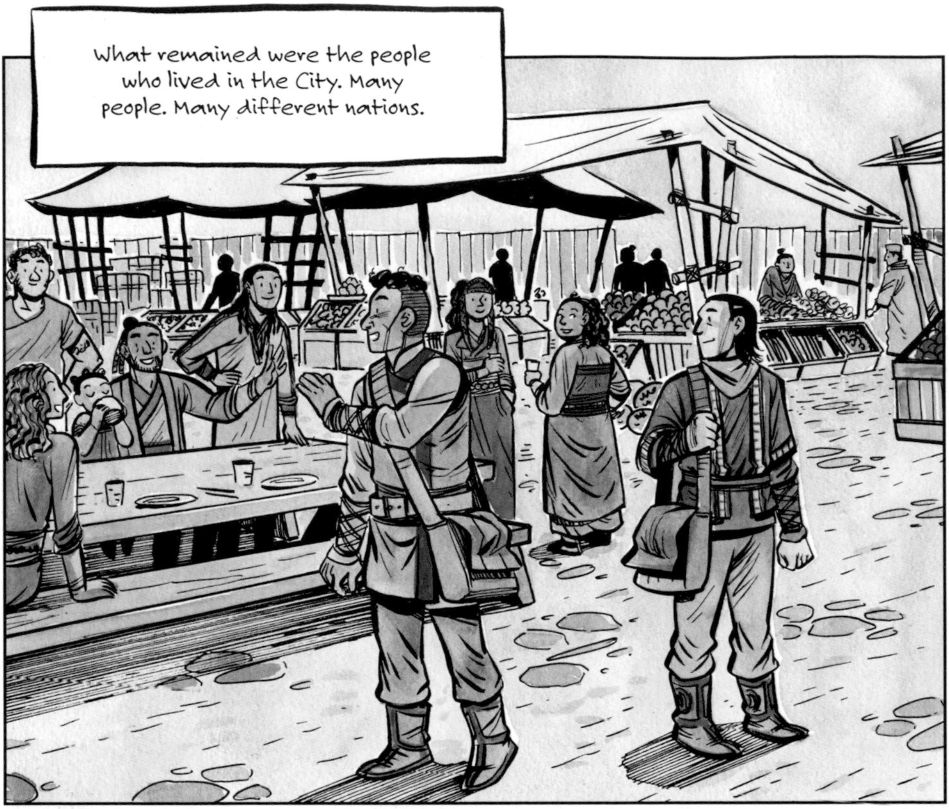
What remained were the people who lived in the City. Many people. Many different nations.

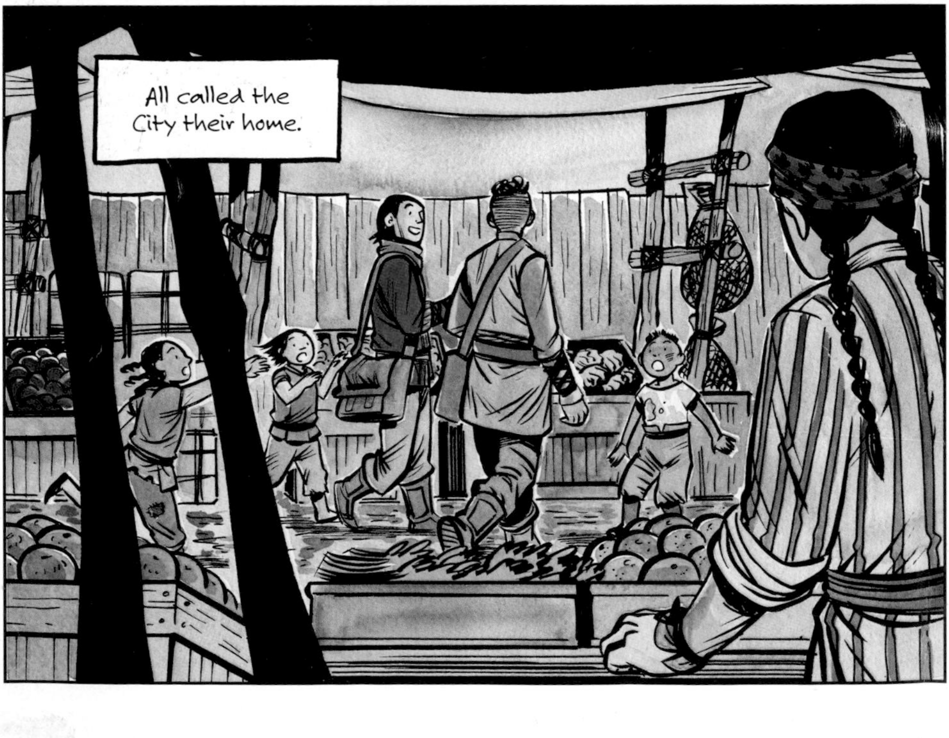
All called the City their home.

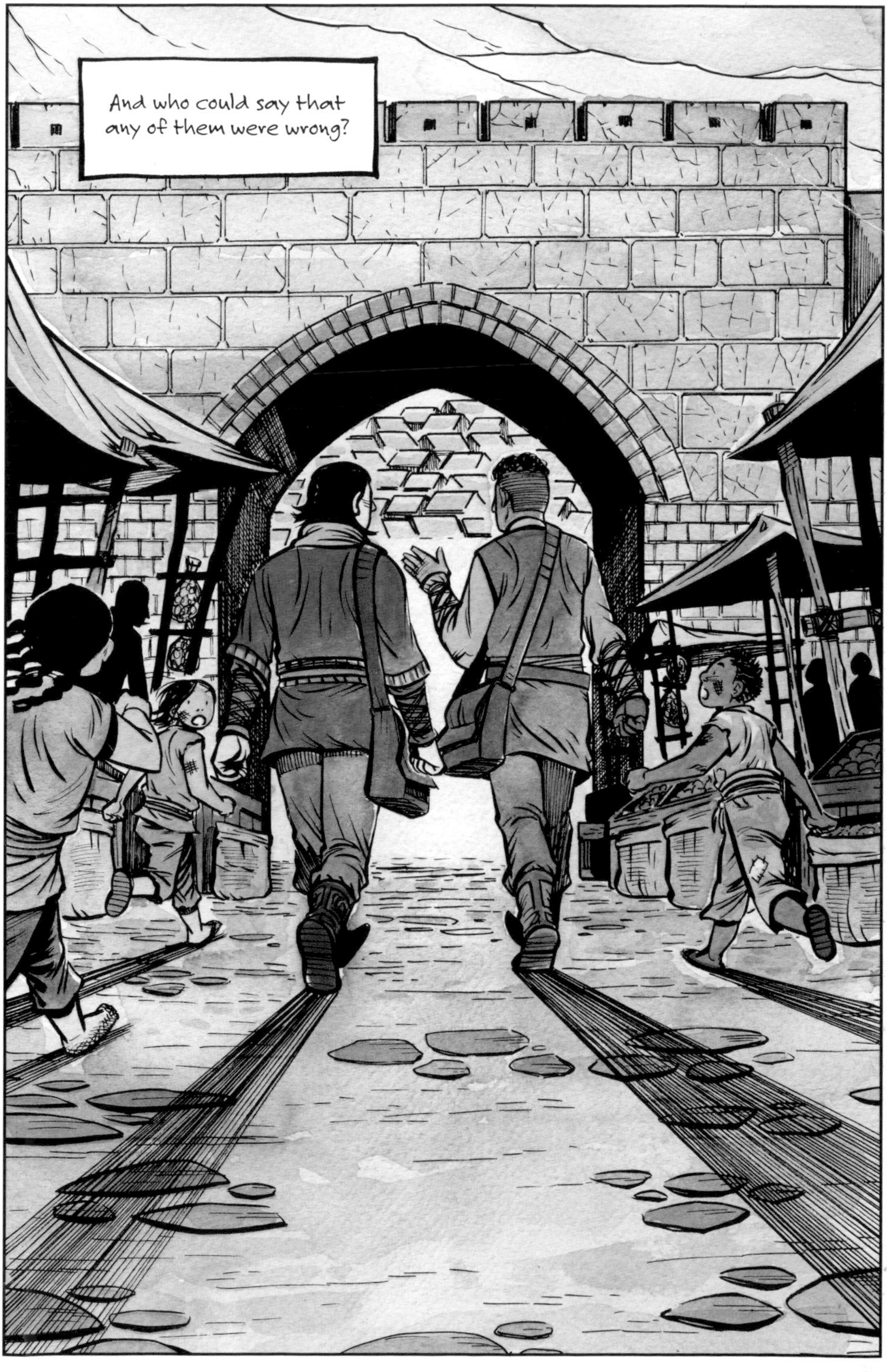
And who could say that any of them were wrong?

THE STONE HEART

THE NAMELESS CITY

FAITH ERIN HICKS

COLOR BY JORDIE BELLAIRE

:01

First Second

NEW YORK

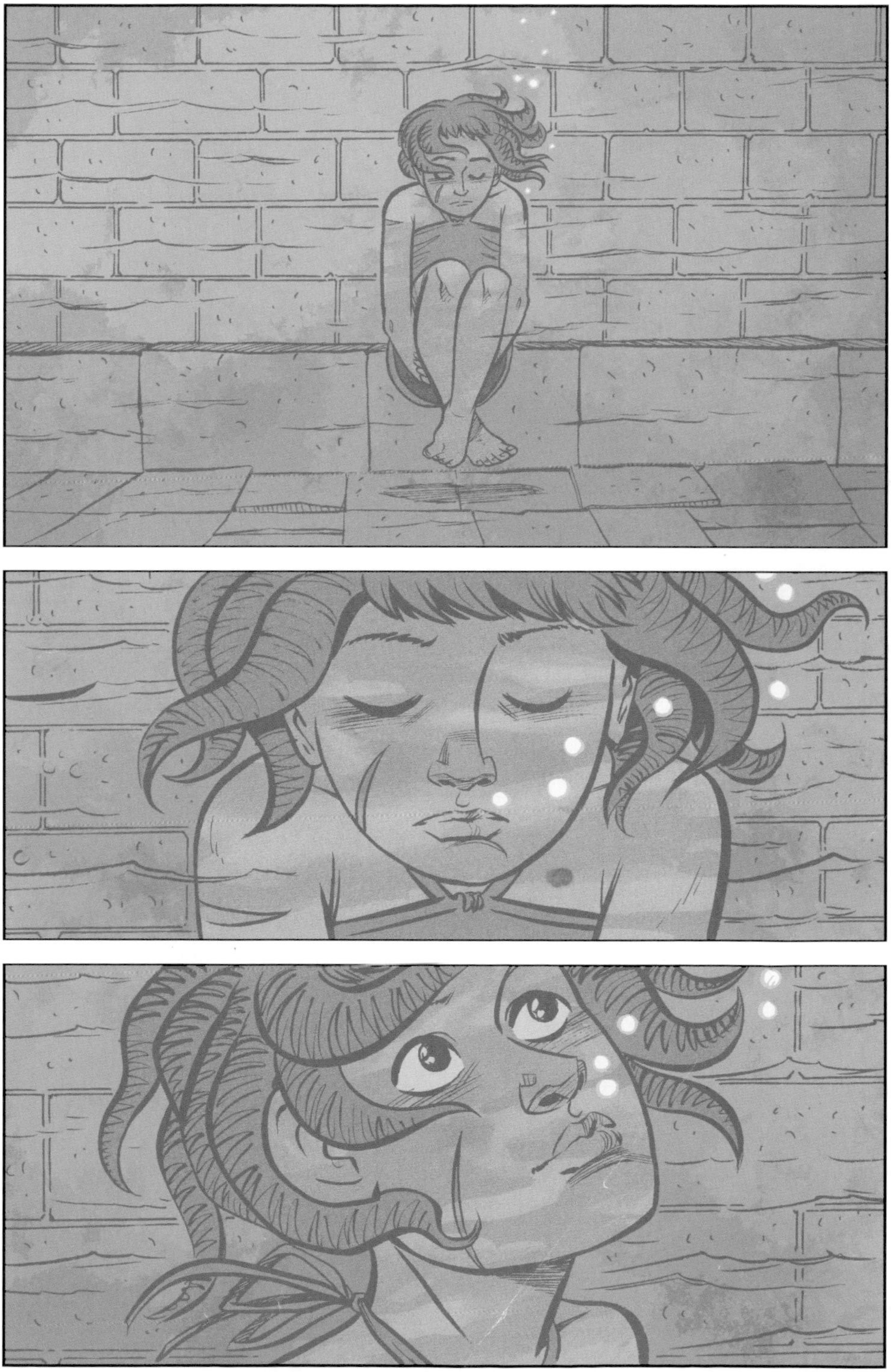

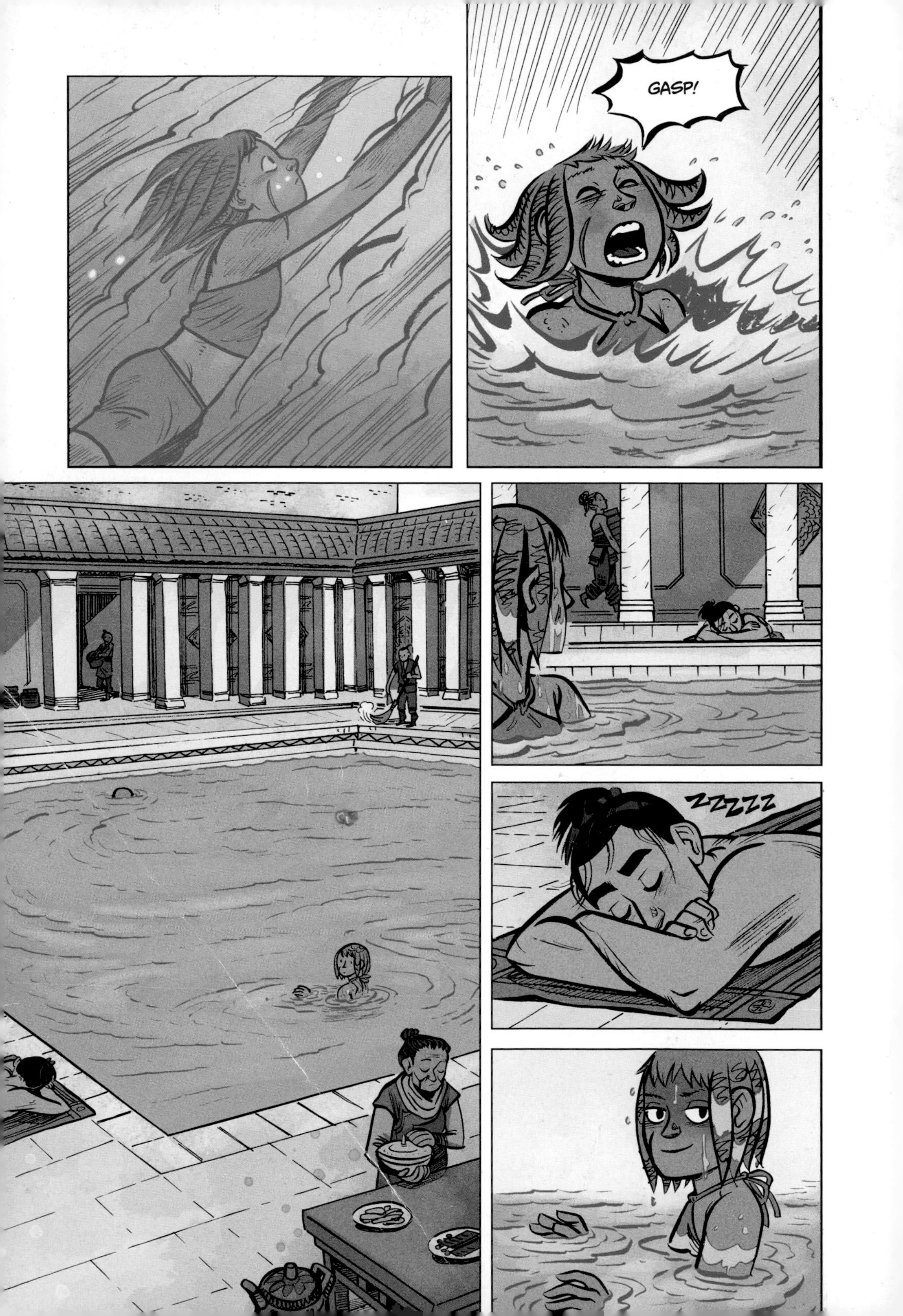
GASP!
ZZZZZ

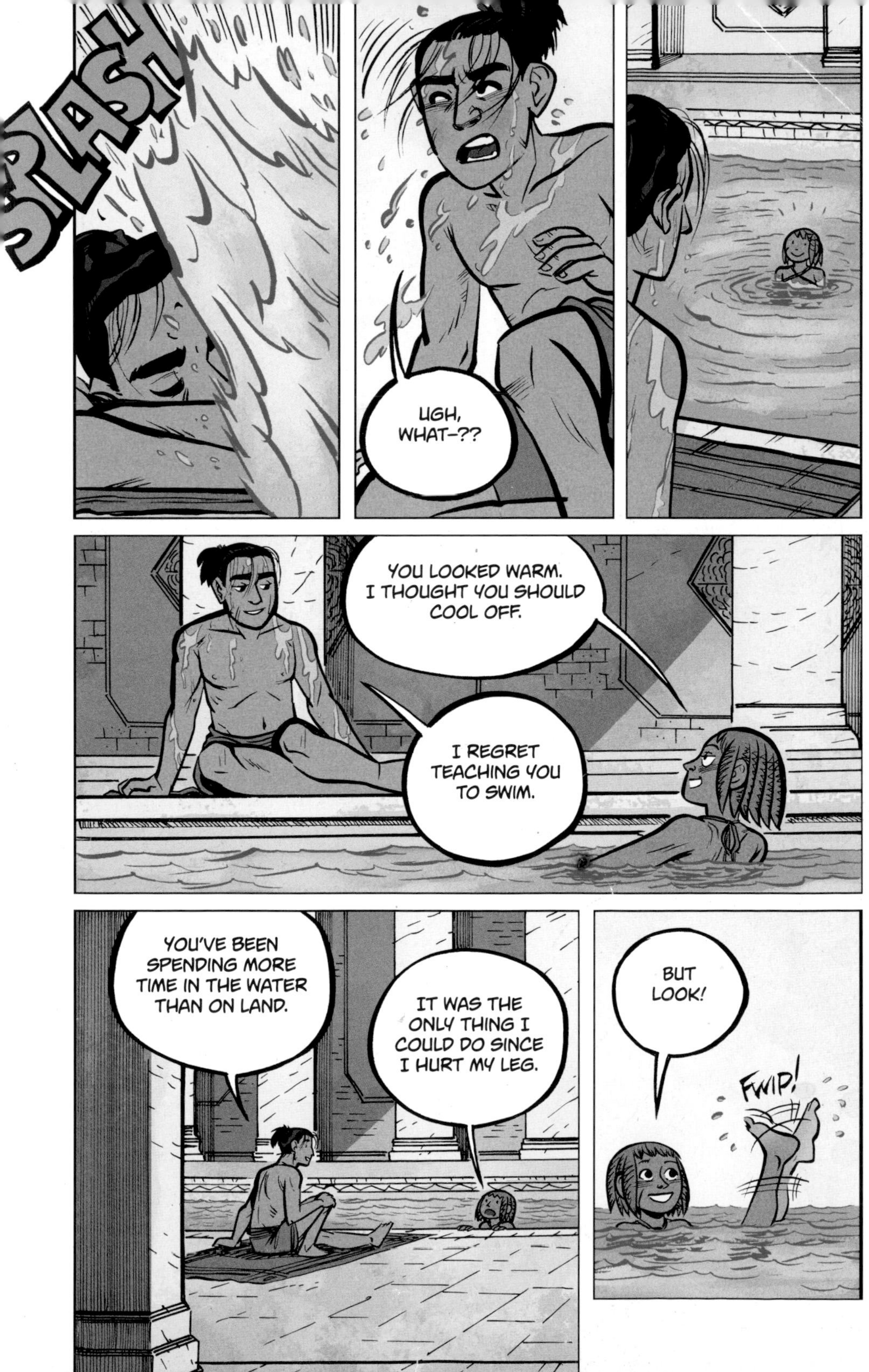
SPLASH!
UGH, WHAT-??
YOU LOOKED WARM. I THOUGHT YOU SHOULD COOL OFF.
I REGRET TEACHING YOU TO SWIM.
YOU'VE BEEN SPENDING MORE TIME IN THE WATER THAN ON LAND.
IT WAS THE ONLY THING I COULD DO SINCE I HURT MY LEG.
BUT LOOK!
FWIP!

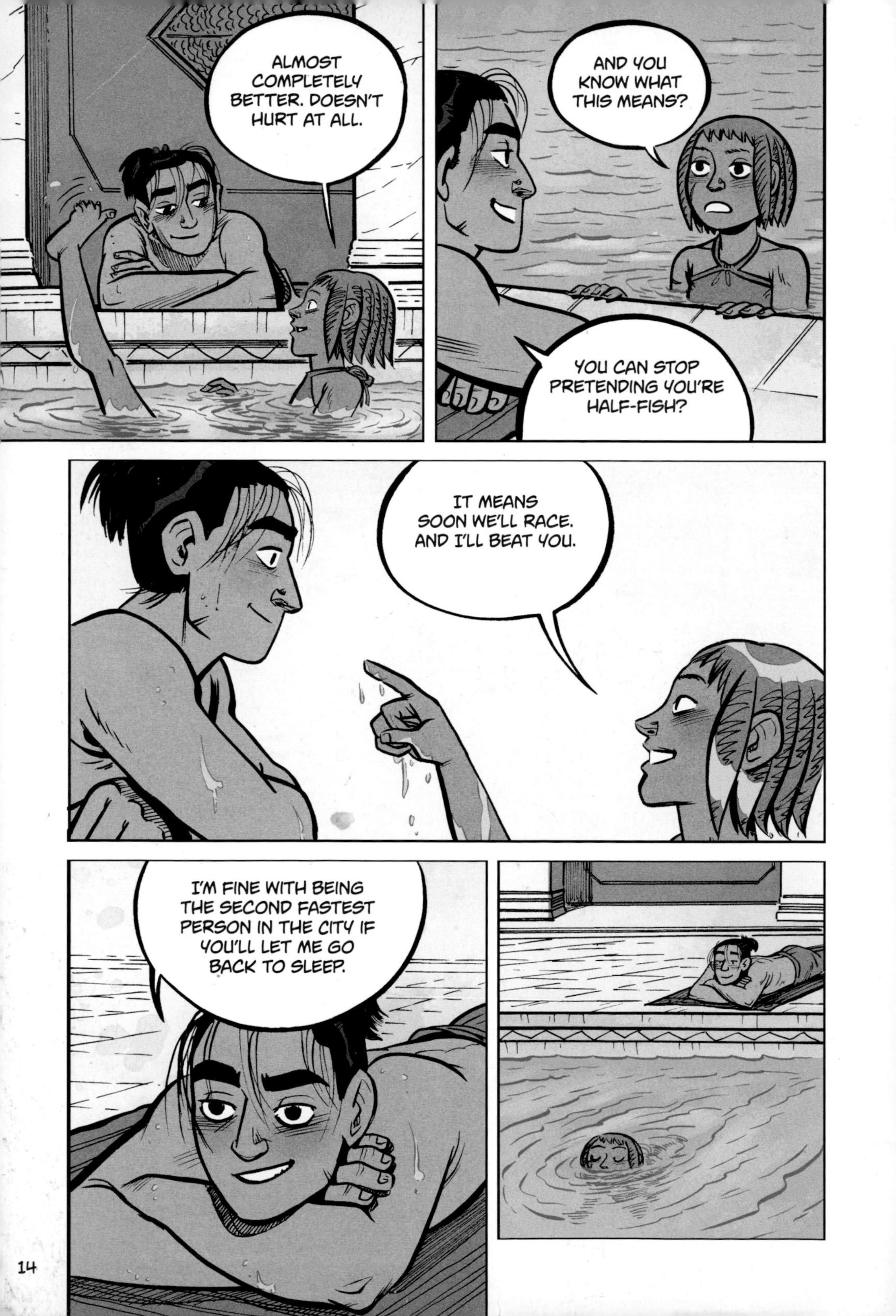
ALMOST COMPLETELY BETTER. DOESN'T HURT AT ALL.
AND YOU KNOW WHAT THIS MEANS?
YOU CAN STOP PRETENDING YOU'RE HALF-FISH?
IT MEANS SOON WE'LL RACE. AND I'LL BEAT YOU.
I'M FINE WITH BEING THE SECOND FASTEST PERSON IN THE CITY IF YOU'LL LET ME GO BACK TO SLEEP.

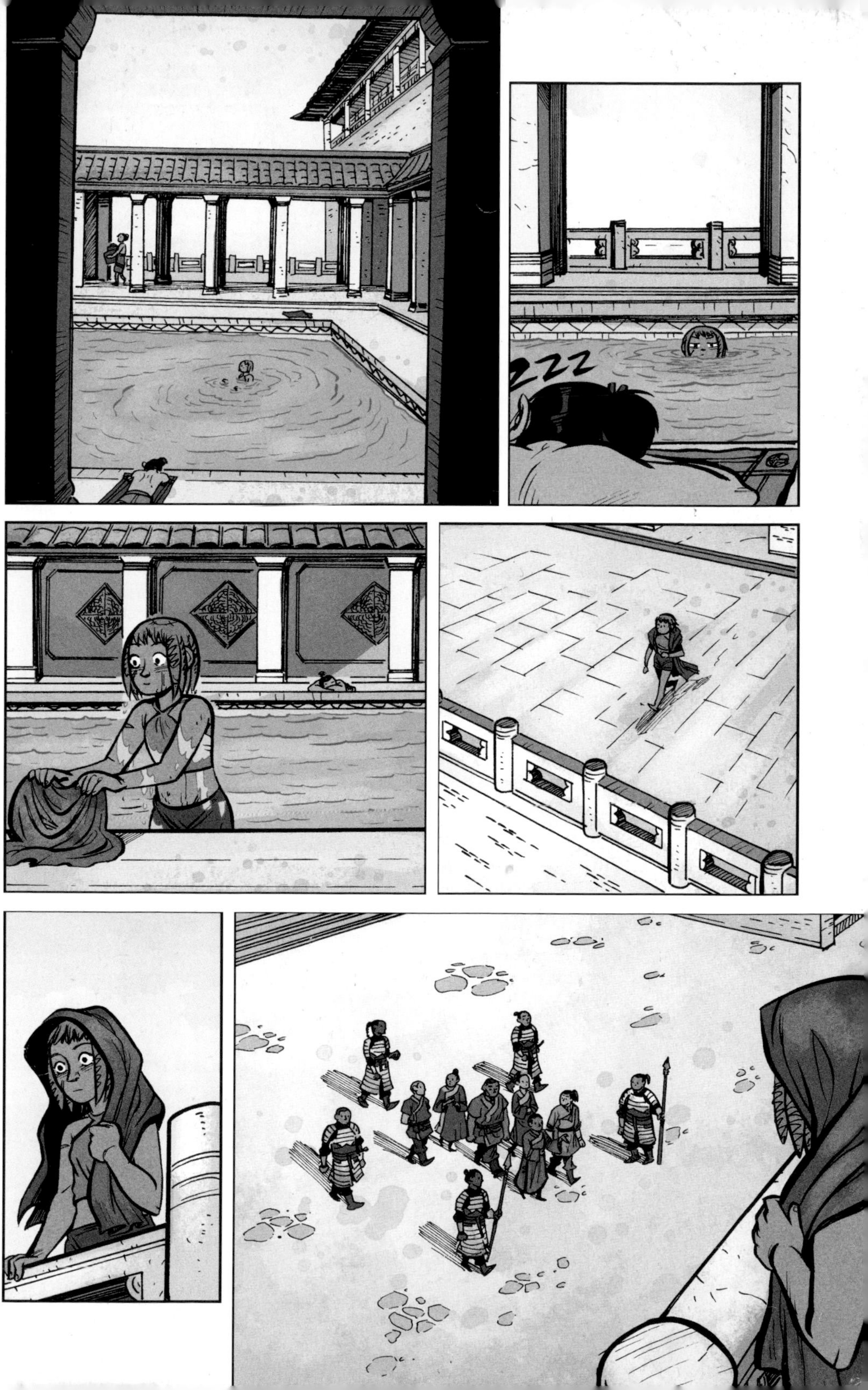
ZZZ

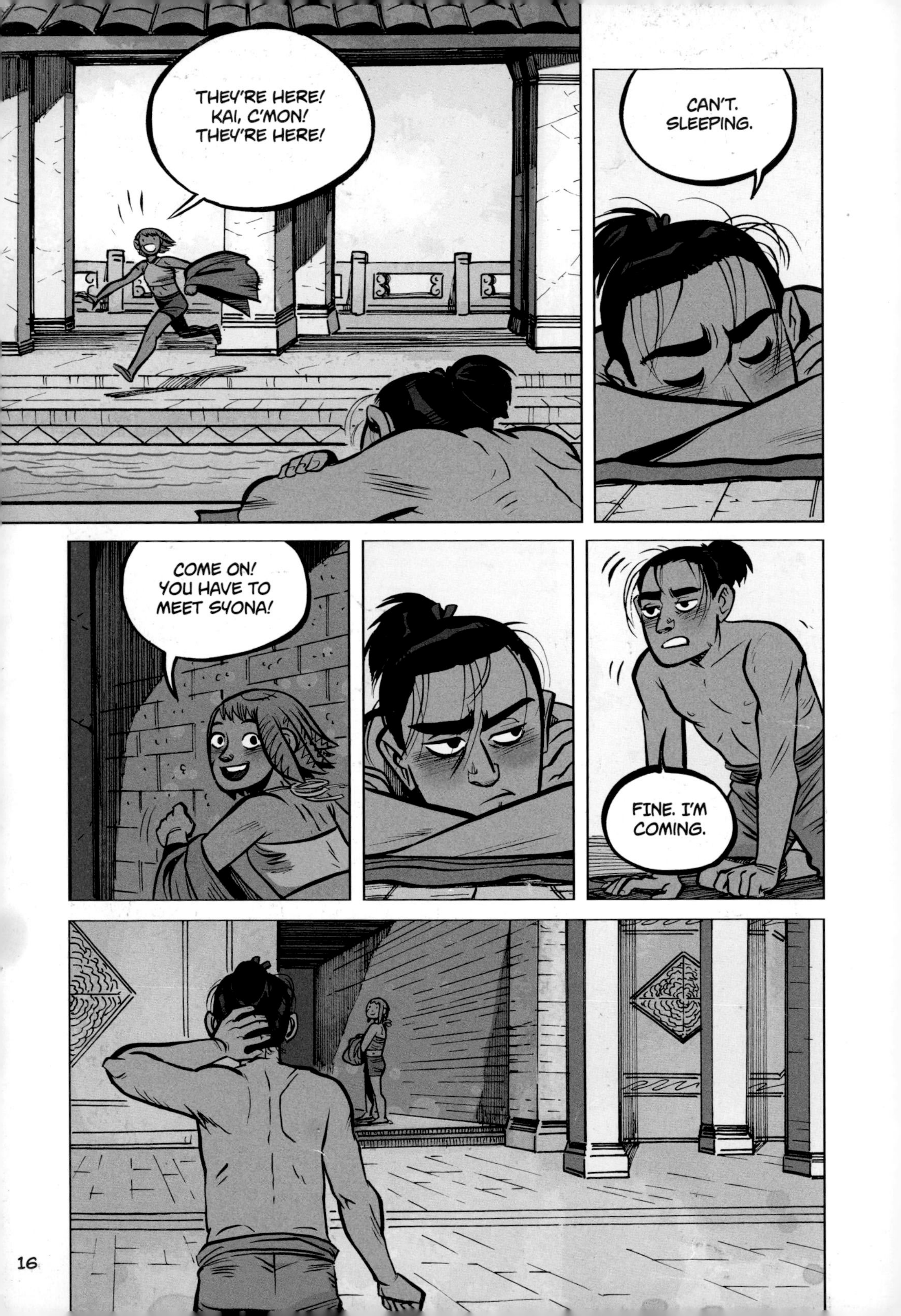
THEY'RE HERE! KAI, C'MON! THEY'RE HERE!
CAN'T. SLEEPING.
COME ON! YOU HAVE TO MEET SYONA!
FINE. I'M COMING.

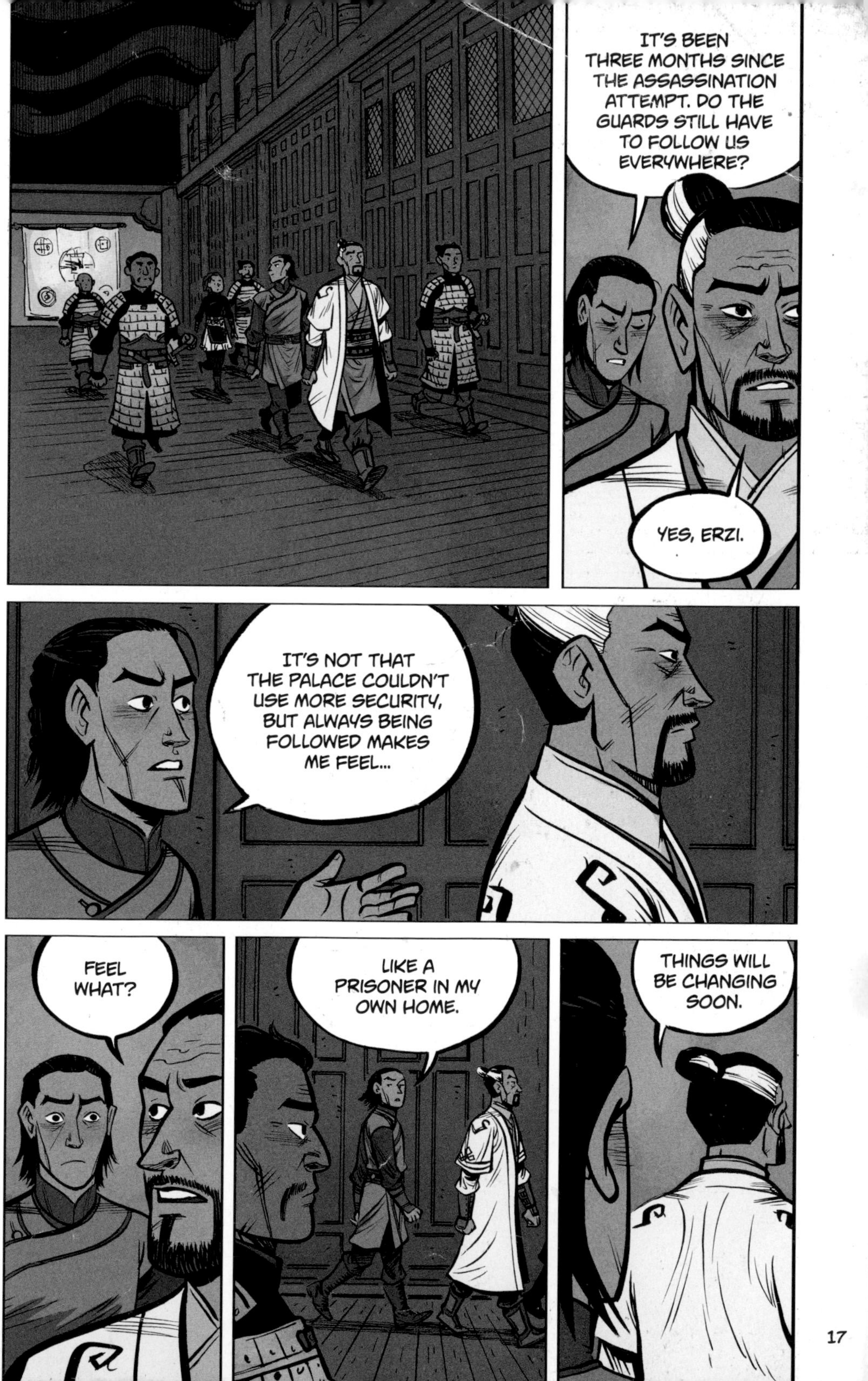
IT'S BEEN THREE MONTHS SINCE THE ASSASSINATION ATTEMPT. DO THE GUARDS STILL HAVE TO FOLLOW US EVERYWHERE?
YES, ERZI.
IT'S NOT THAT THE PALACE COULDN'T USE MORE SECURITY, BUT ALWAYS BEING FOLLOWED MAKES ME FEEL...
FEEL WHAT?
LIKE A PRISONER IN MY OWN HOME.
THINGS WILL BE CHANGING SOON.

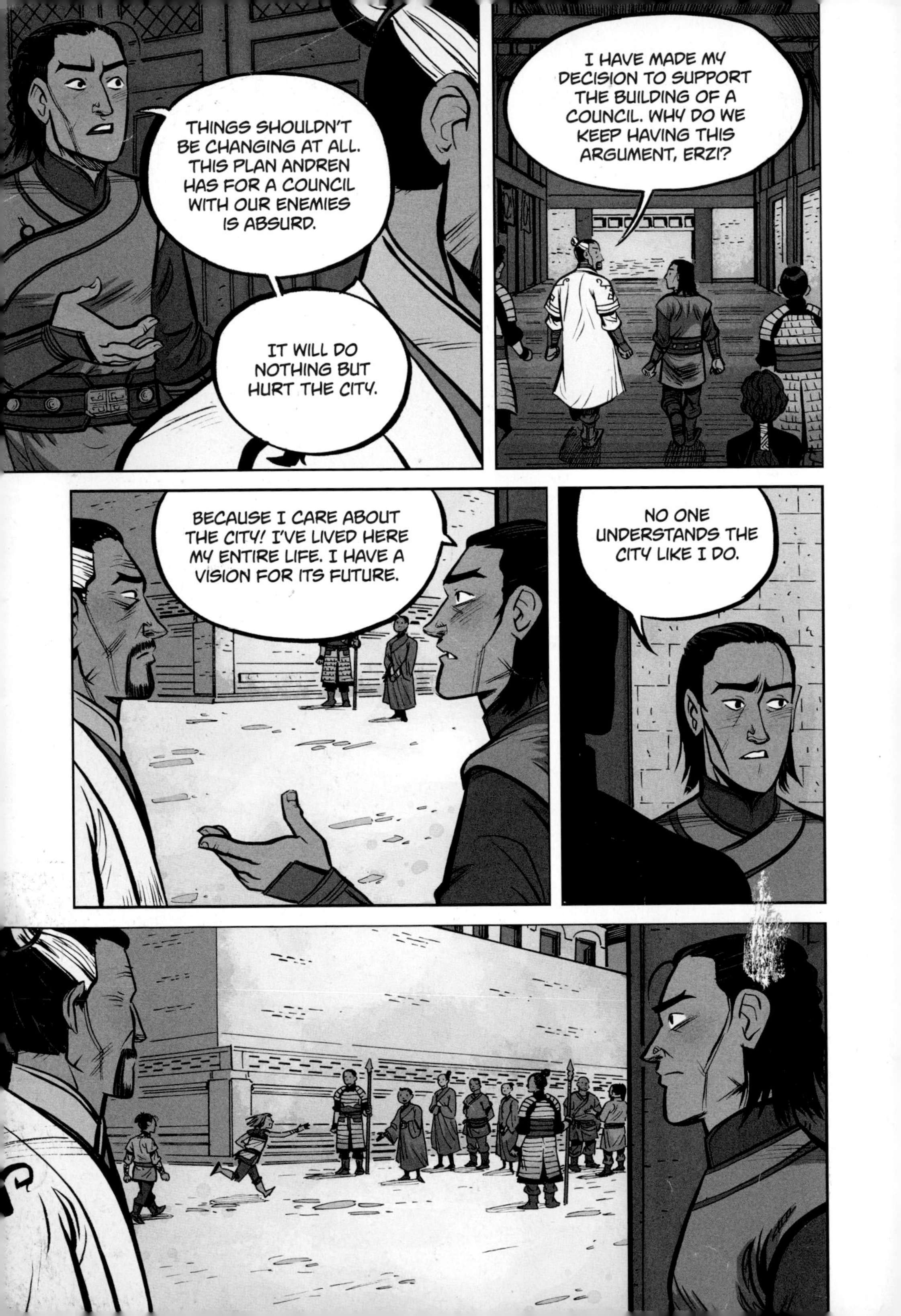
THINGS SHOULDN'T BE CHANGING AT ALL. THIS PLAN ANDREN HAS FOR A COUNCIL WITH OUR ENEMIES IS ABSURD.
IT WILL DO NOTHING BUT HURT THE CITY.
I HAVE MADE MY DECISION TO SUPPORT THE BUILDING OF A COUNCIL. WHY DO WE KEEP HAVING THIS ARGUMENT, ERZI?
BECAUSE I CARE ABOUT THE CITY! I'VE LIVED HERE MY ENTIRE LIFE. I HAVE A VISION FOR ITS FUTURE.
NO ONE UNDERSTANDS THE CITY LIKE I DO.

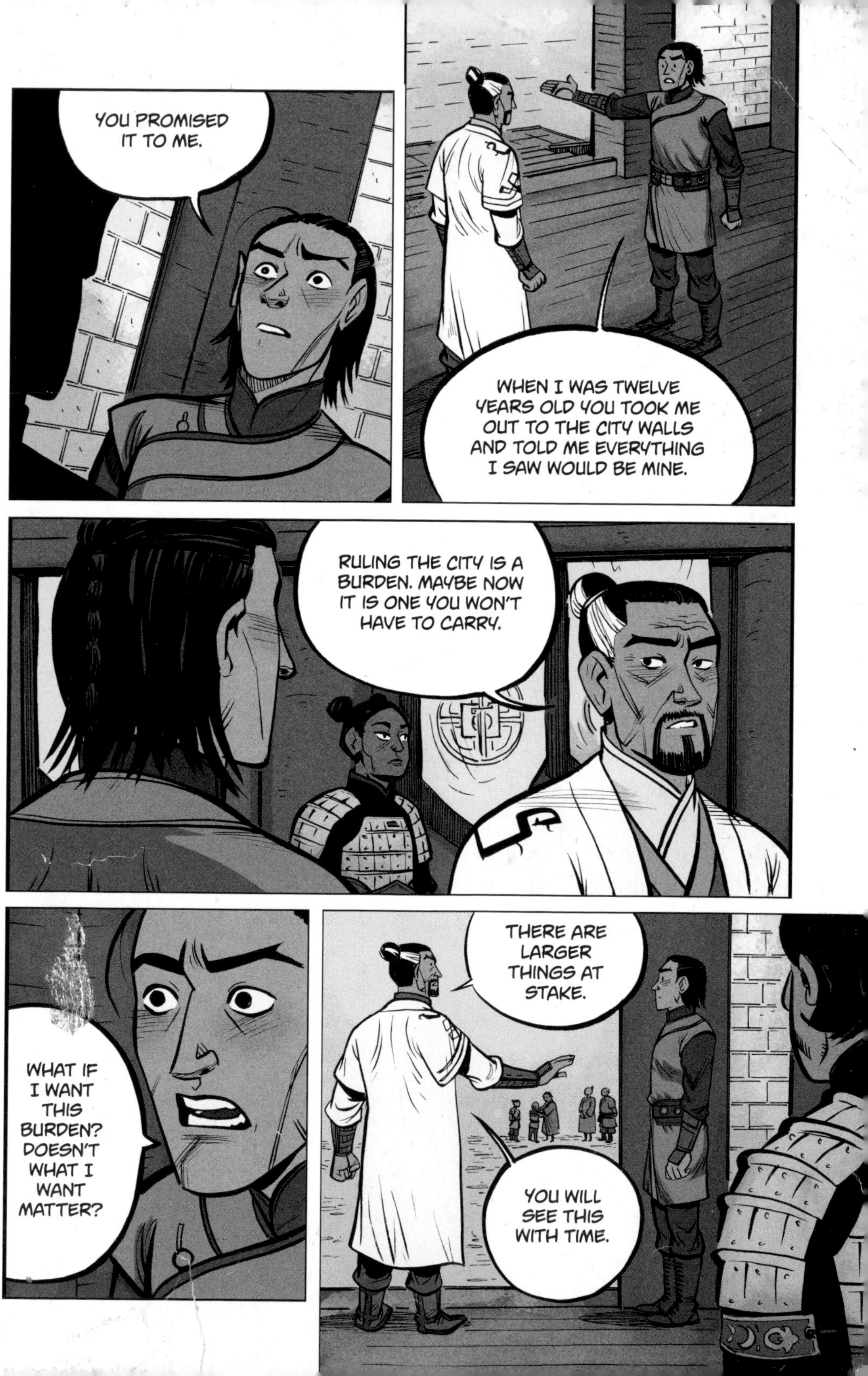
YOU PROMISED IT TO ME.
WHEN I WAS TWELVE YEARS OLD YOU TOOK ME OUT TO THE CITY WALLS AND TOLD ME EVERYTHING I SAW WOULD BE MINE.
RULING THE CITY IS A BURDEN. MAYBE NOW IT IS ONE YOU WON'T HAVE TO CARRY.
WHAT IF I WANT THIS BURDEN? DOESN'T WHAT I WANT MATTER?
THERE ARE LARGER THINGS AT STAKE.
YOU WILL SEE THIS WITH TIME.

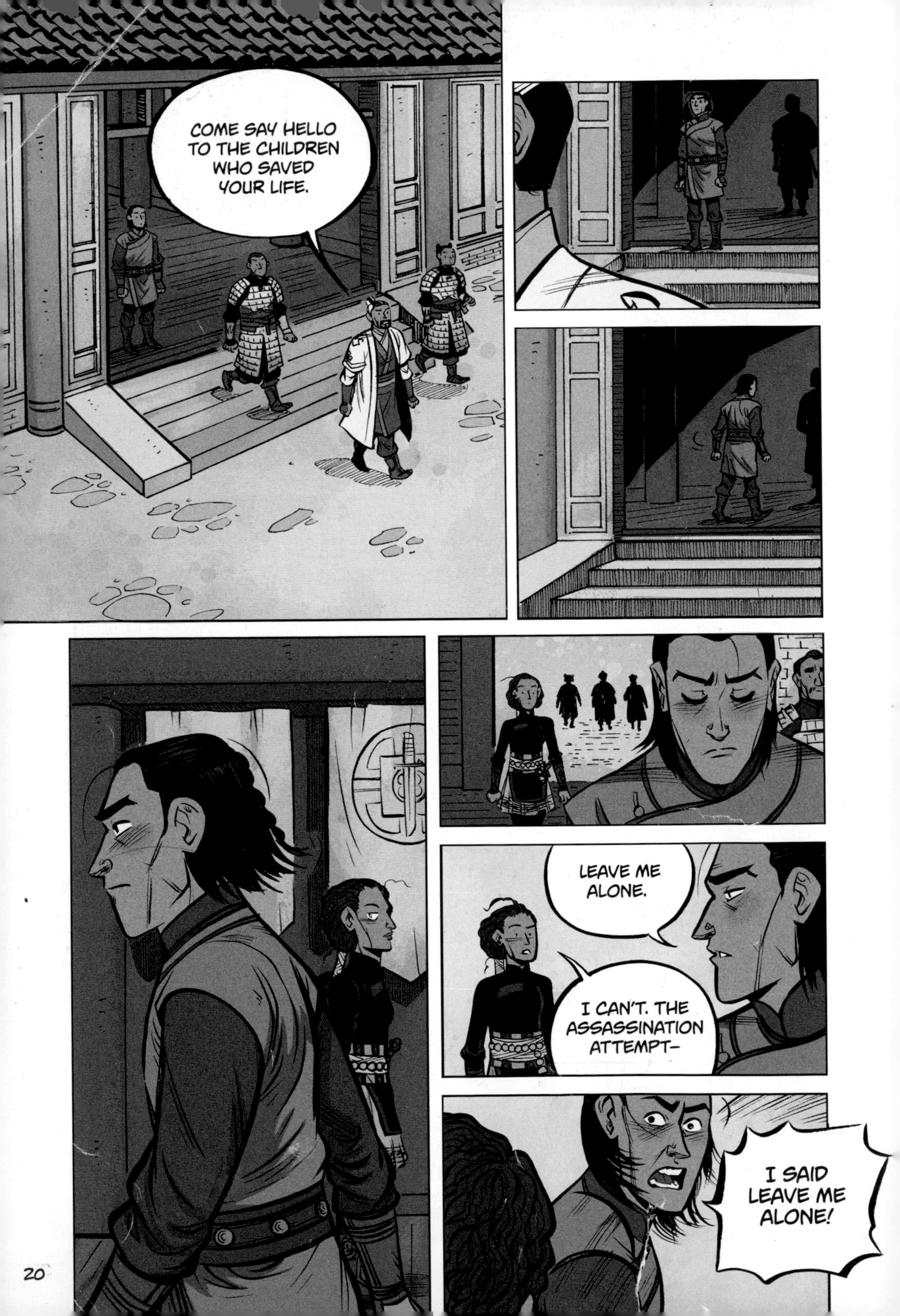
COME SAY HELLO TO THE CHILDREN WHO SAVED YOUR LIFE.
LEAVE ME ALONE.
I CAN'T. THE ASSASSINATION ATTEMPT-
I SAID LEAVE ME ALONE!

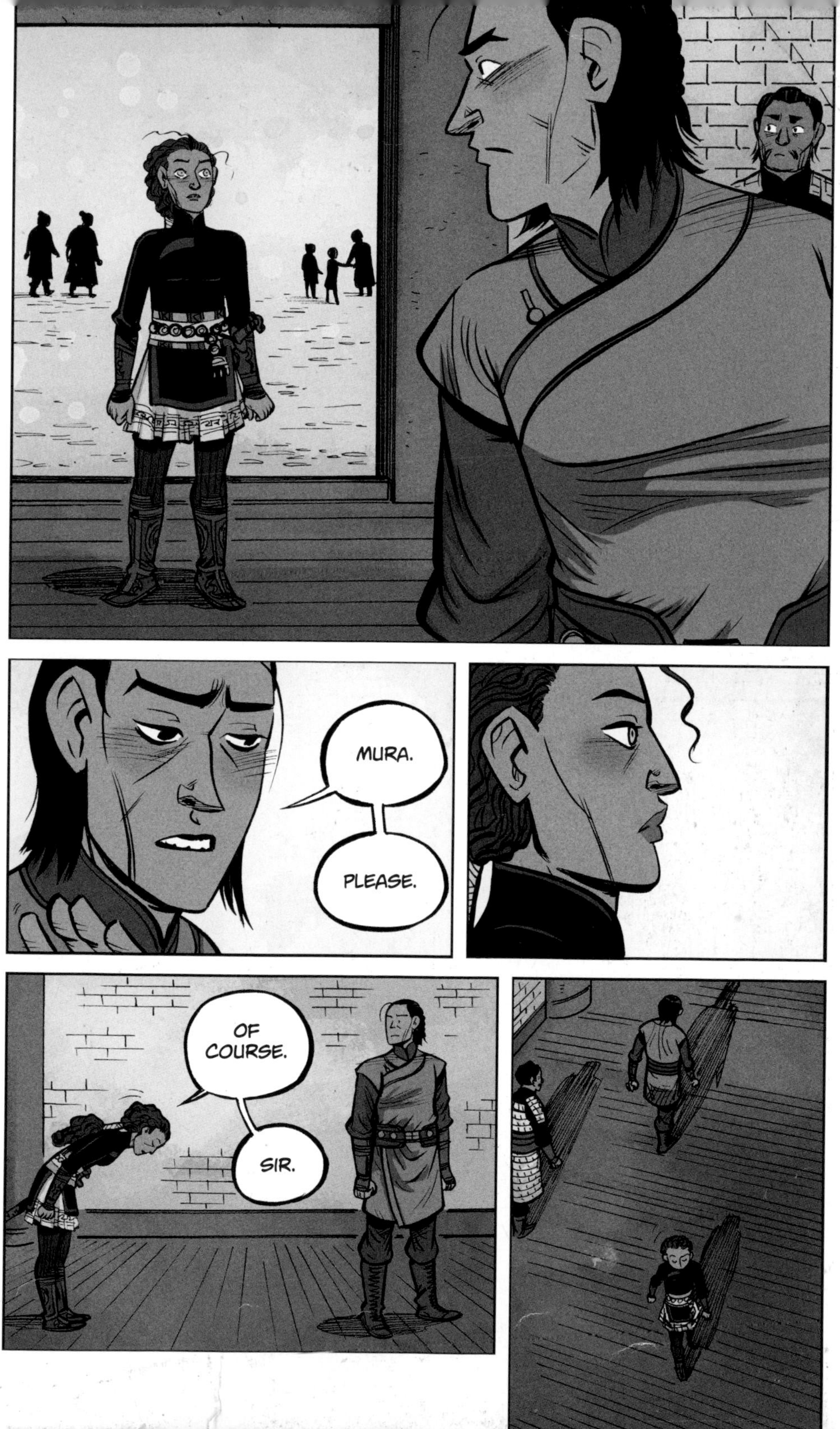
MURA.
PLEASE.
OF COURSE.
SIR.

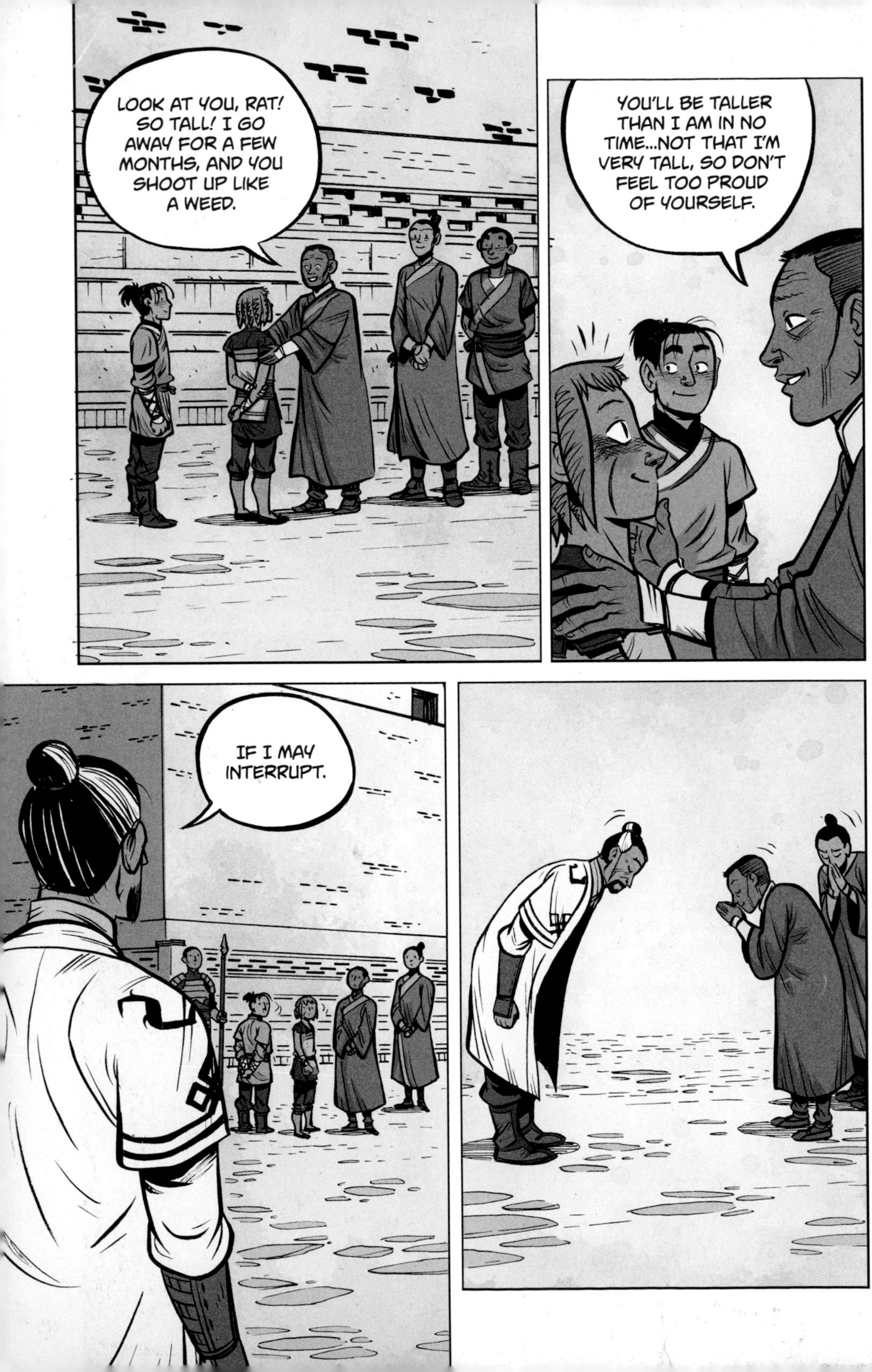
LOOK AT YOU, RAT! SO TALL! I GO AWAY FOR A FEW MONTHS, AND YOU SHOOT UP LIKE A WEED.
YOU'LL BE TALLER THAN I AM IN NO TIME...NOT THAT I'M VERY TALL, SO DON'T FEEL TOO PROUD OF YOURSELF.
IF I MAY INTERRUPT.

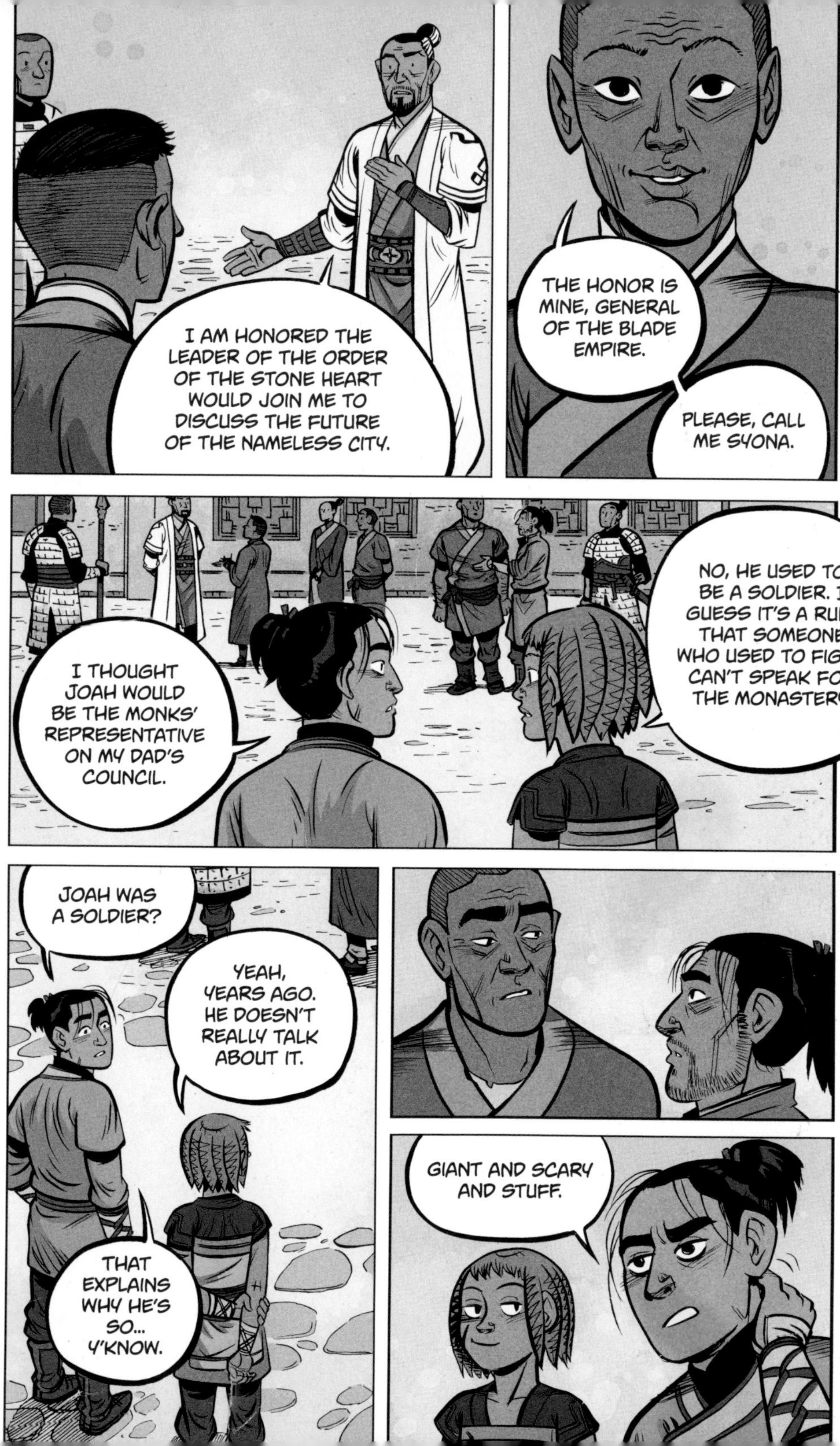
I AM HONORED THE LEADER OF THE ORDER OF THE STONE HEART WOULD JOIN ME TO DISCUSS THE FUTURE OF THE NAMELESS CITY.
THE HONOR IS MINE, GENERAL OF THE BLADE EMPIRE.
PLEASE, CALL ME SYONA.
I THOUGHT JOAH WOULD BE THE MONKS' REPRESENTATIVE ON MY DAD'S COUNCIL.
NO, HE USED TO BE A SOLDIER. I GUESS IT'S A RULE THAT SOMEONE WHO USED TO FIGHT CAN'T SPEAK FOR THE MONASTERY.
JOAH WAS A SOLDIER?
YEAH, YEARS AGO. HE DOESN'T REALLY TALK ABOUT IT.
THAT EXPLAINS WHY HE'S SO... Y'KNOW.
GIANT AND SCARY AND STUFF.

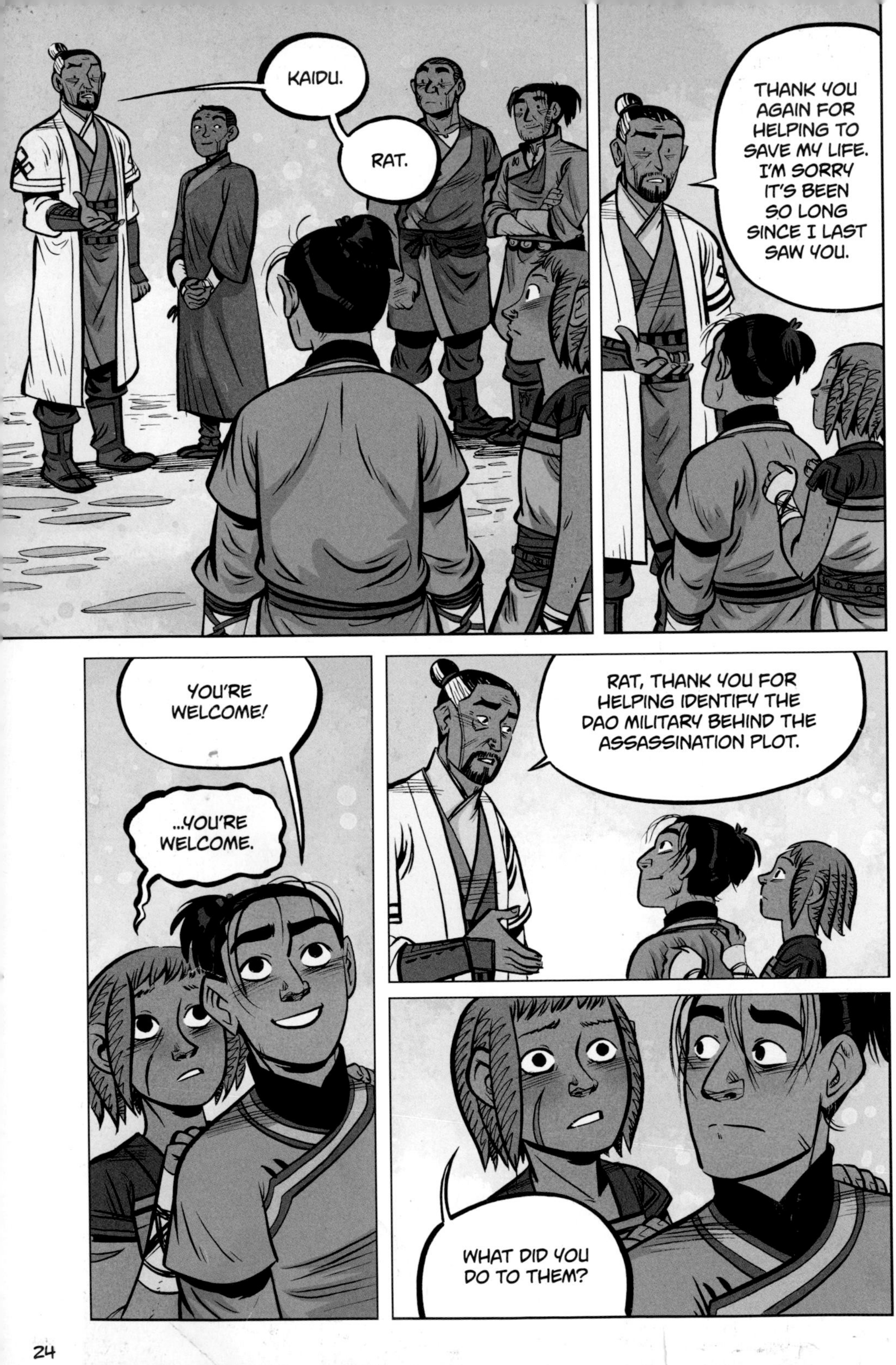
KAIDU.
RAT.
THANK YOU AGAIN FOR HELPING TO SAVE MY LIFE. I'M SORRY IT'S BEEN SO LONG SINCE I LAST SAW YOU.
YOU'RE WELCOME!
...YOU'RE WELCOME.
RAT, THANK YOU FOR HELPING IDENTIFY THE DAO MILITARY BEHIND THE ASSASSINATION PLOT.
WHAT DID YOU DO TO THEM?

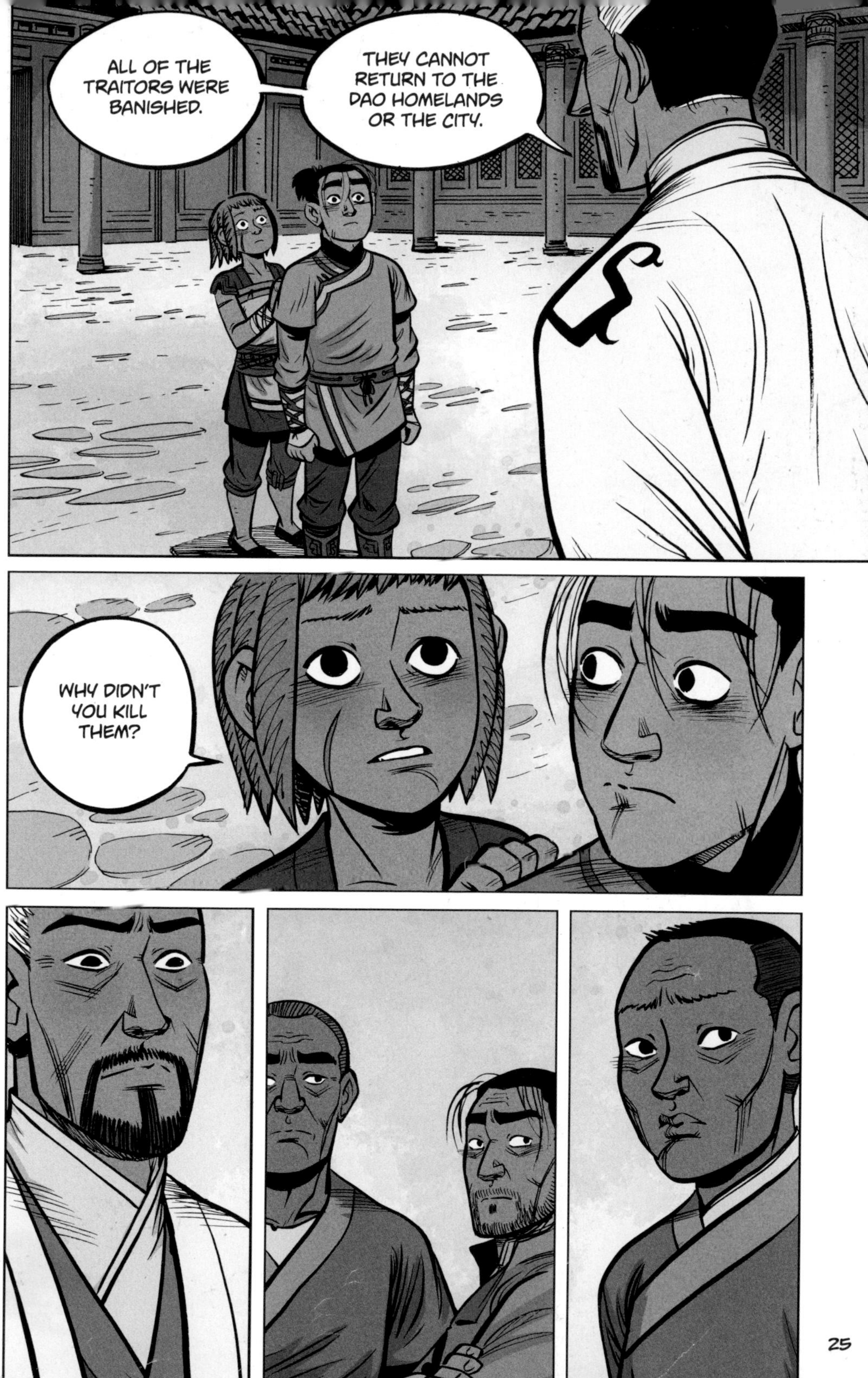
ALL OF THE TRAITORS WERE BANISHED.
THEY CANNOT RETURN TO THE DAO HOMELANDS OR THE CITY.
WHY DIDN'T YOU KILL THEM?

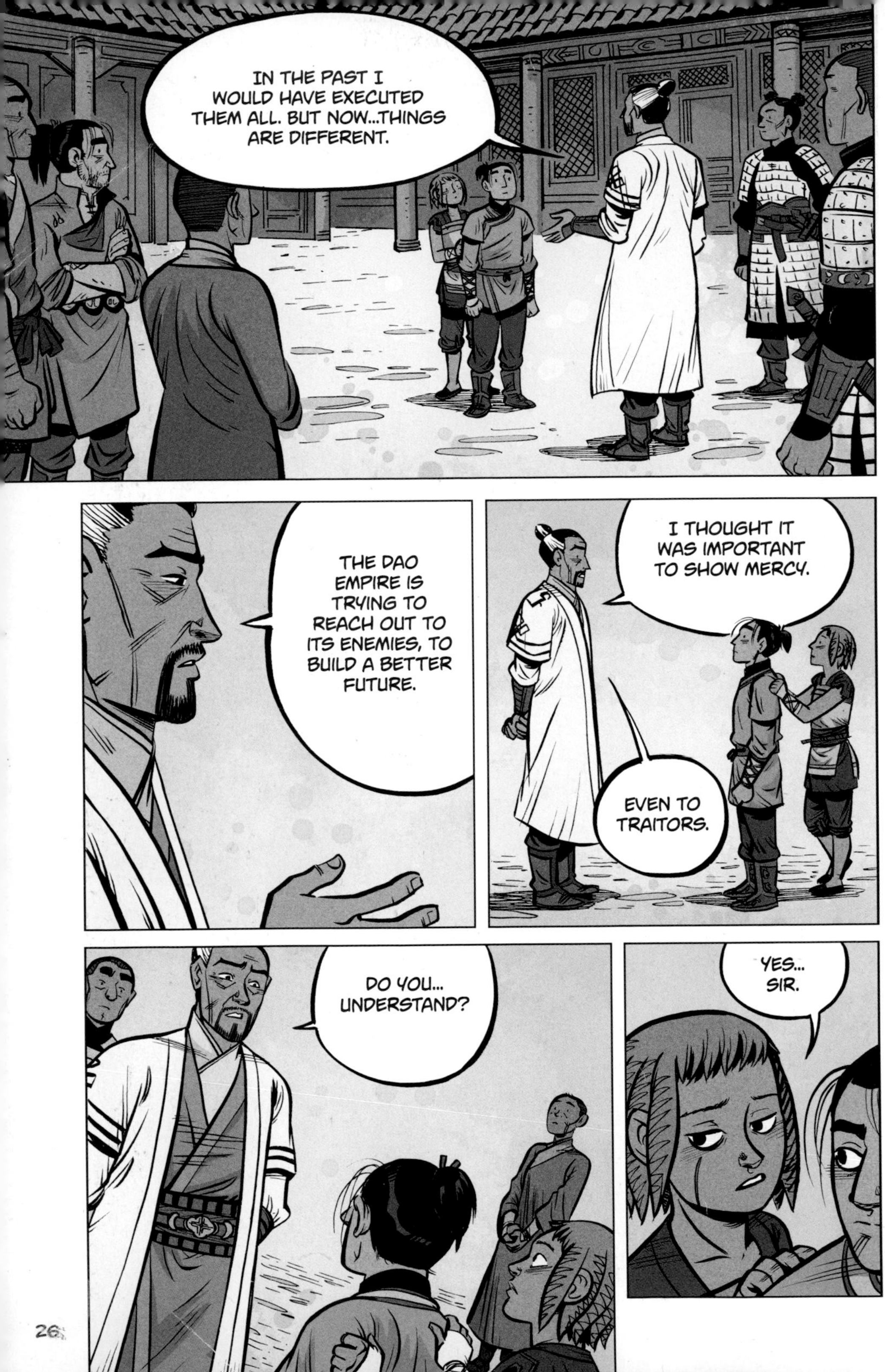
IN THE PAST I WOULD HAVE EXECUTED THEM ALL. BUT NOW...THINGS ARE DIFFERENT.
THE DAO EMPIRE IS TRYING TO REACH OUT TO ITS ENEMIES, TO BUILD A BETTER FUTURE.
I THOUGHT IT WAS IMPORTANT TO SHOW MERCY.
EVEN TO TRAITORS.
DO YOU... UNDERSTAND?
YES... SIR.

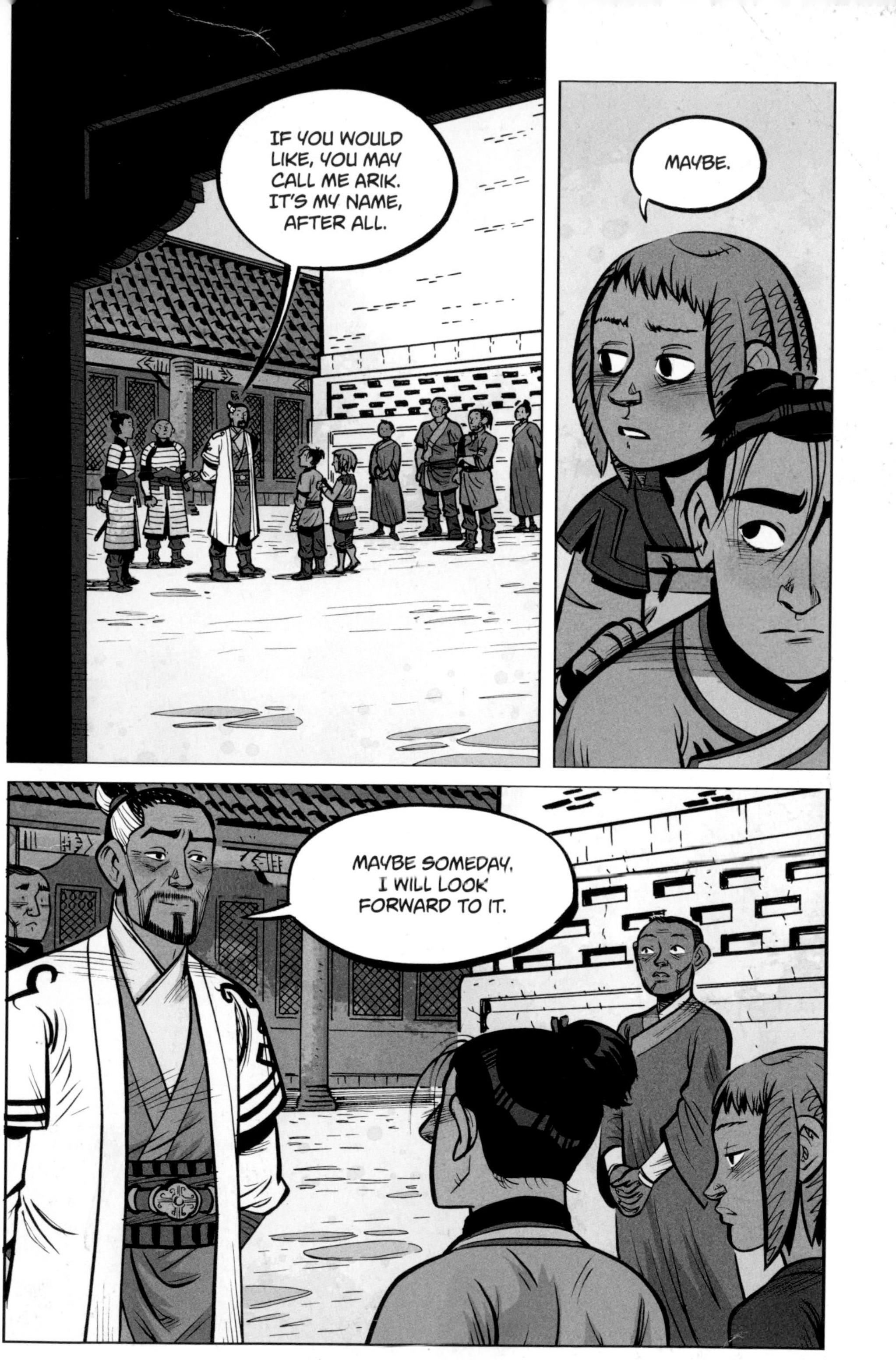
IF YOU WOULD LIKE, YOU MAY CALL ME ARIK. IT'S MY NAME, AFTER ALL.
MAYBE.
MAYBE SOMEDAY. I WILL LOOK FORWARD TO IT.

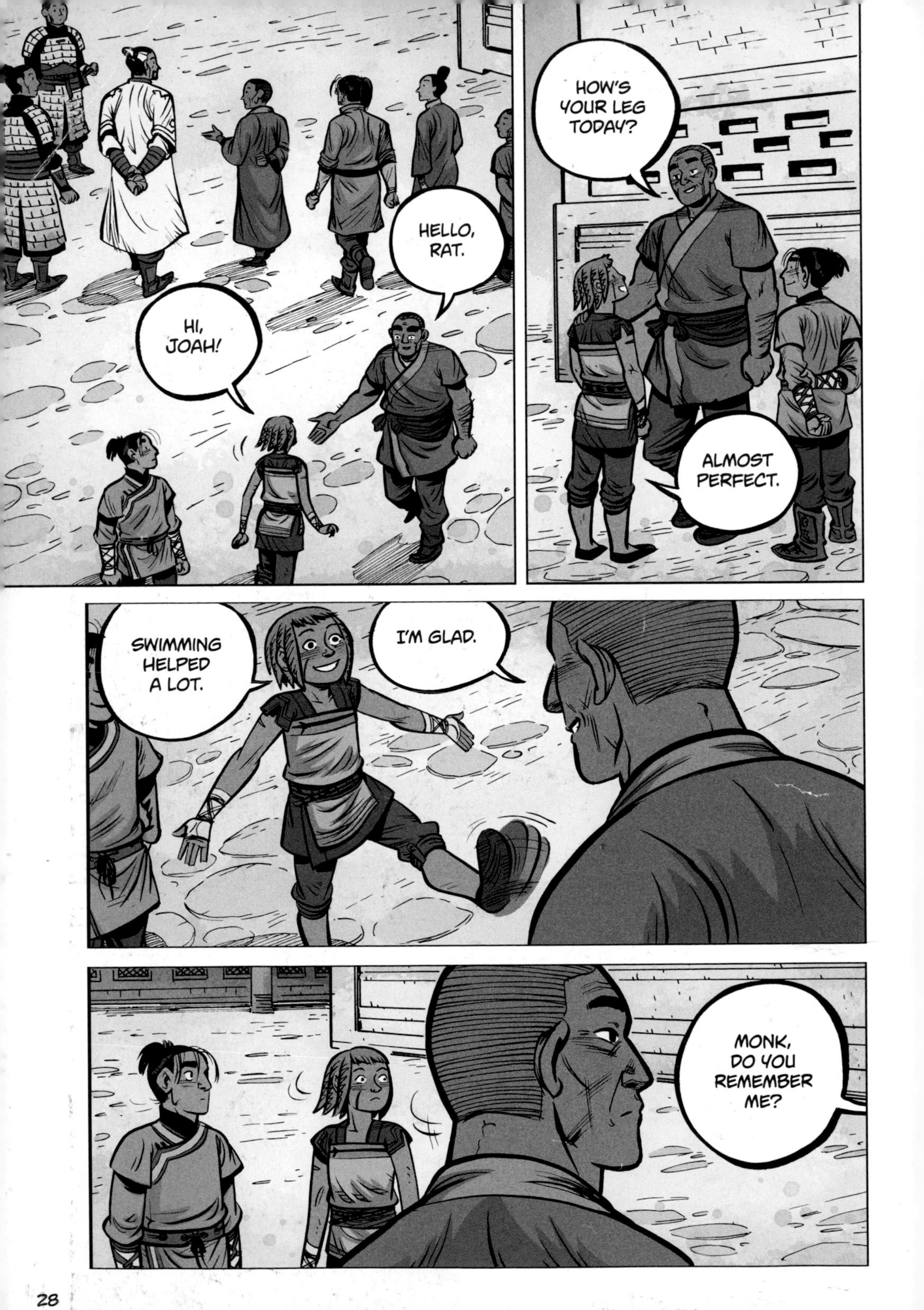
HELLO, RAT.
HI, JOAH!
HOW'S YOUR LEG TODAY?
ALMOST PERFECT.
SWIMMING HELPED A LOT.
I'M GLAD.
MONK, DO YOU REMEMBER ME?

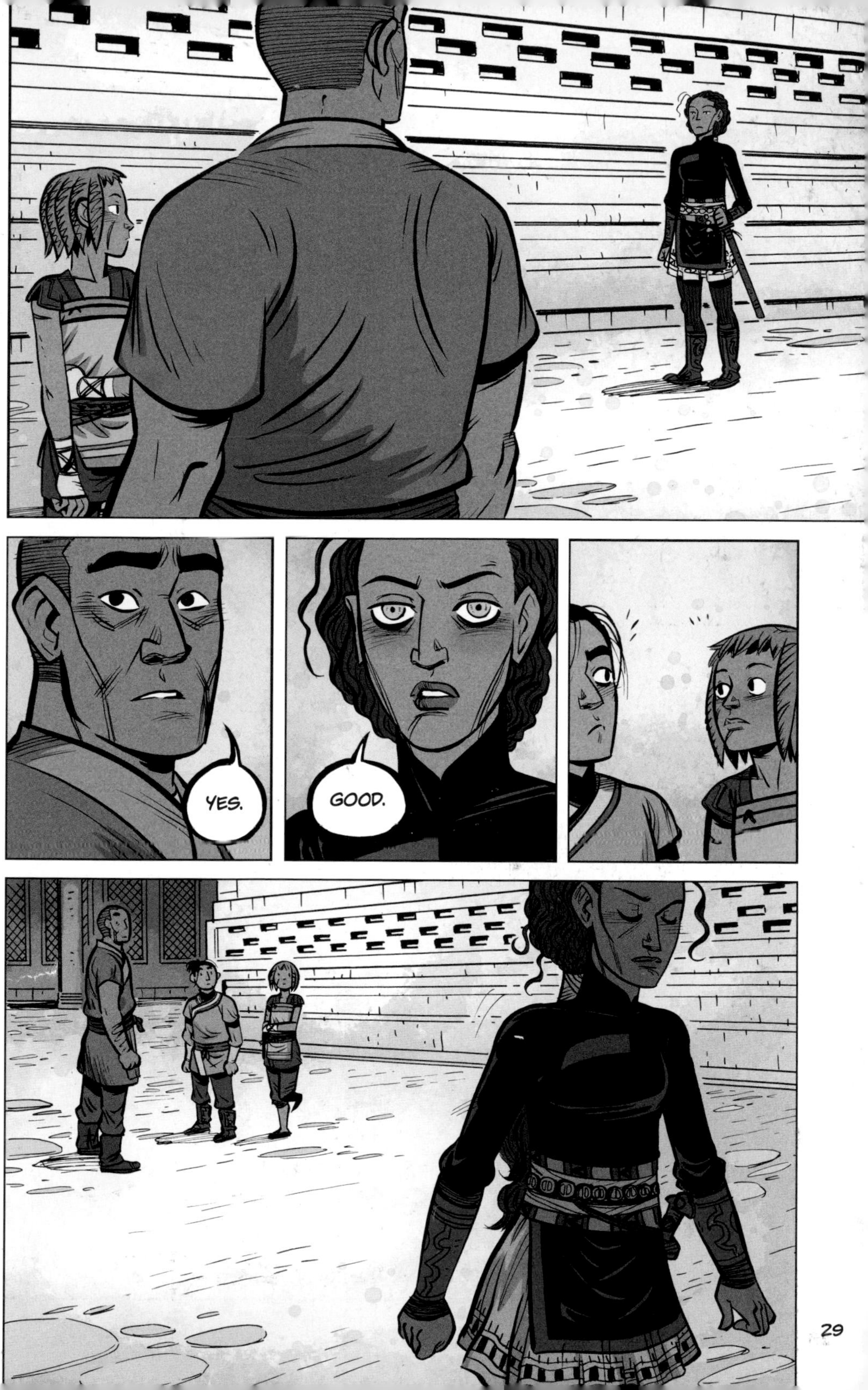
YES.
GOOD.

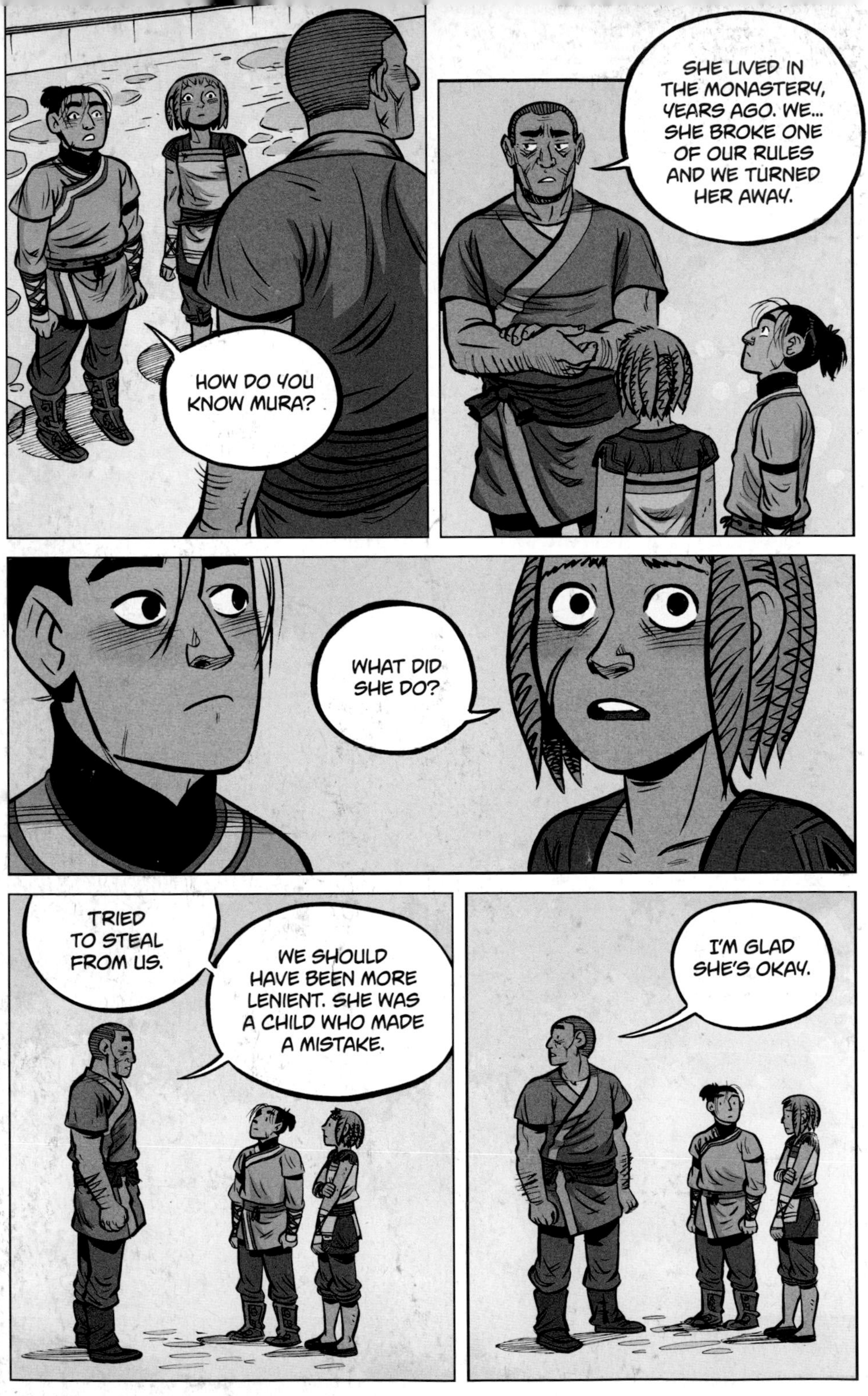
HOW DO YOU KNOW MURA?
SHE LIVED IN THE MONASTERY, YEARS AGO. WE... SHE BROKE ONE OF OUR RULES AND WE TURNED HER AWAY.
WHAT DID SHE DO?
TRIED TO STEAL FROM US.
WE SHOULD HAVE BEEN MORE LENIENT. SHE WAS A CHILD WHO MADE A MISTAKE.
I'M GLAD SHE'S OKAY.

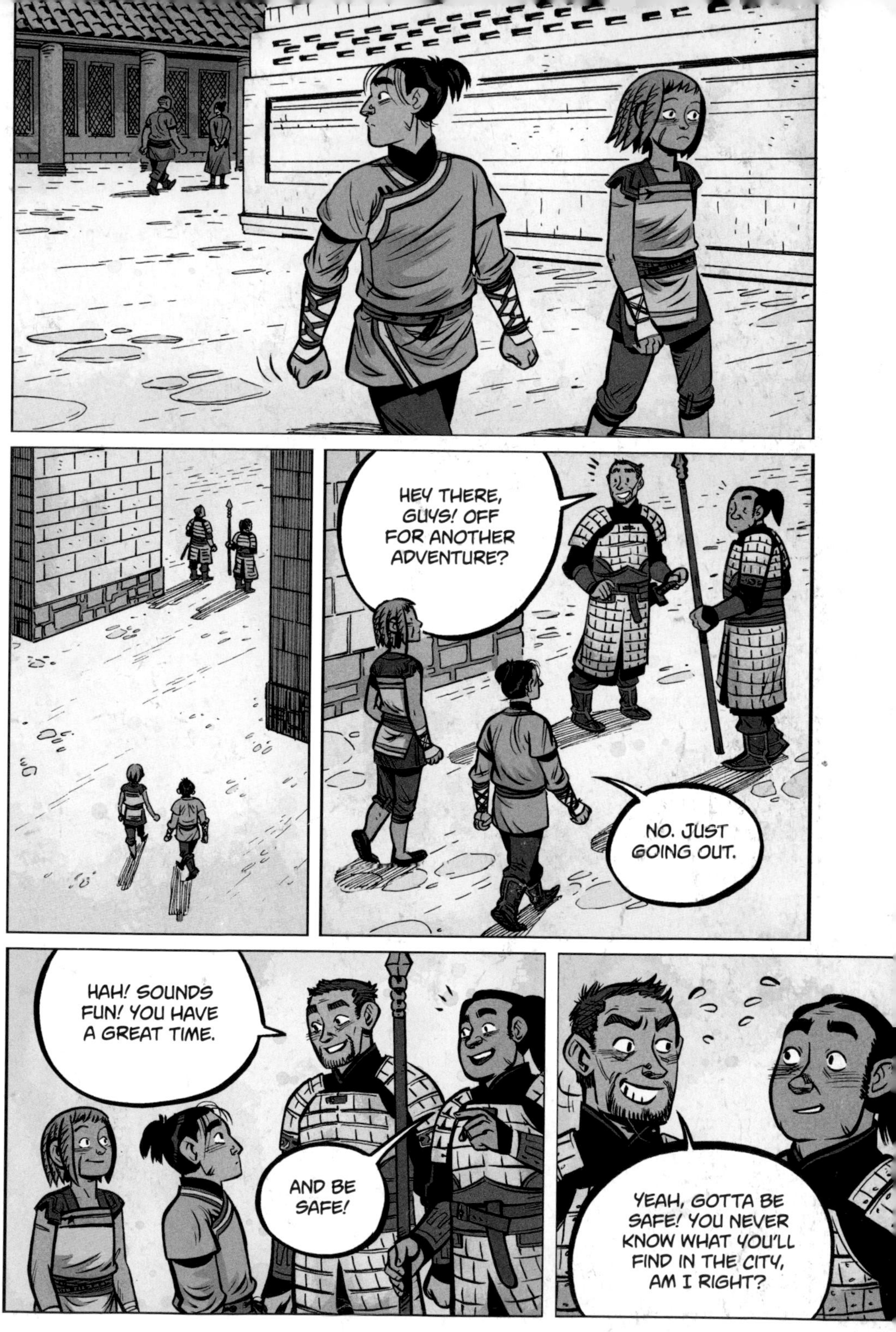

HEY THERE, GUYS! OFF FOR ANOTHER ADVENTURE?
NO. JUST GOING OUT.
HAH! SOUNDS FUN! YOU HAVE A GREAT TIME.
AND BE SAFE!
YEAH, GOTTA BE SAFE! YOU NEVER KNOW WHAT YOU'LL FIND IN THE CITY, AM I RIGHT?

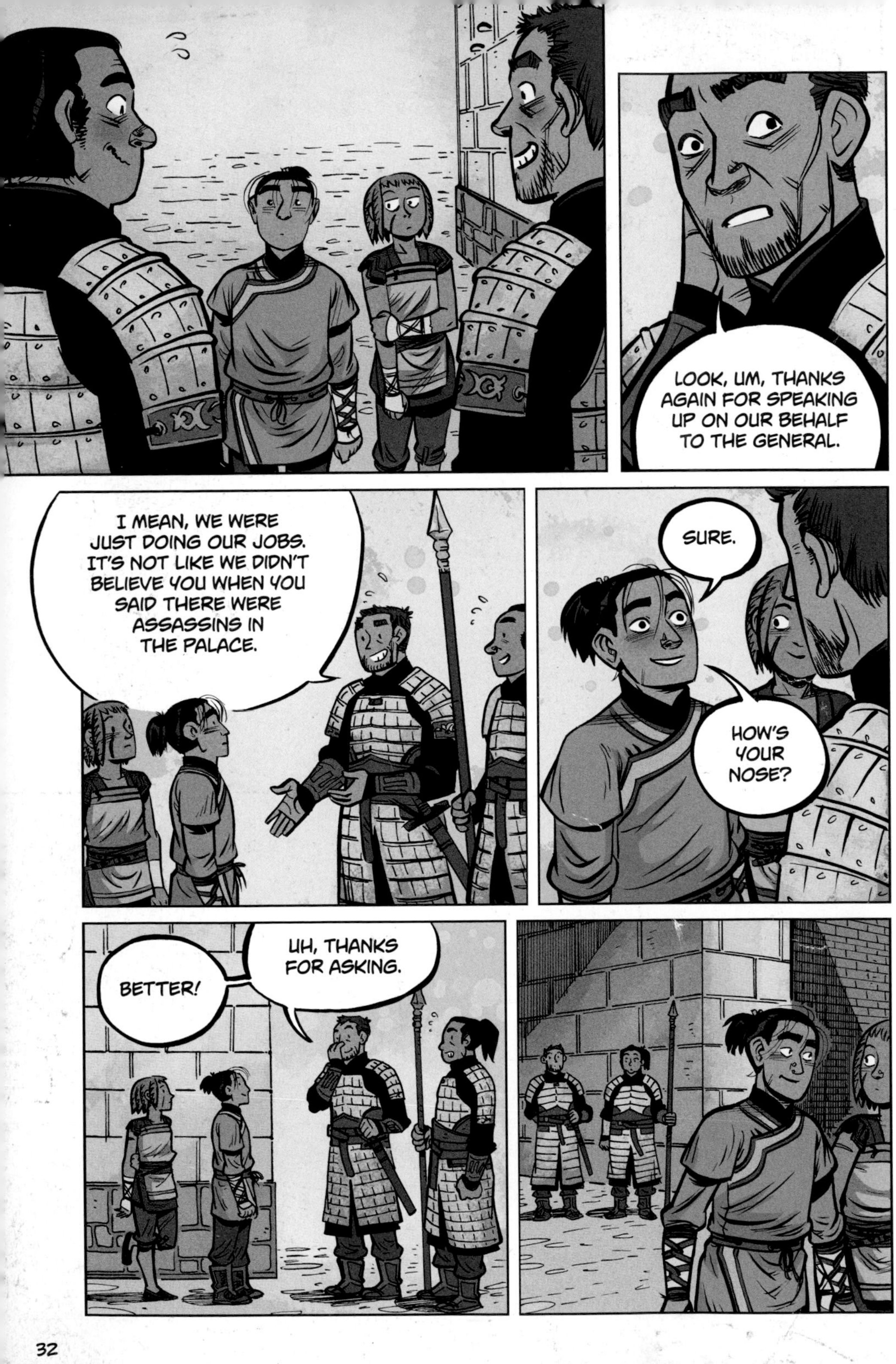

LOOK, UM, THANKS AGAIN FOR SPEAKING UP ON OUR BEHALF TO THE GENERAL.
I MEAN, WE WERE JUST DOING OUR JOBS. IT'S NOT LIKE WE DIDN'T BELIEVE YOU WHEN YOU SAID THERE WERE ASSASSINS IN THE PALACE.
SURE.
HOW'S YOUR NOSE?
BETTER!
UH, THANKS FOR ASKING.

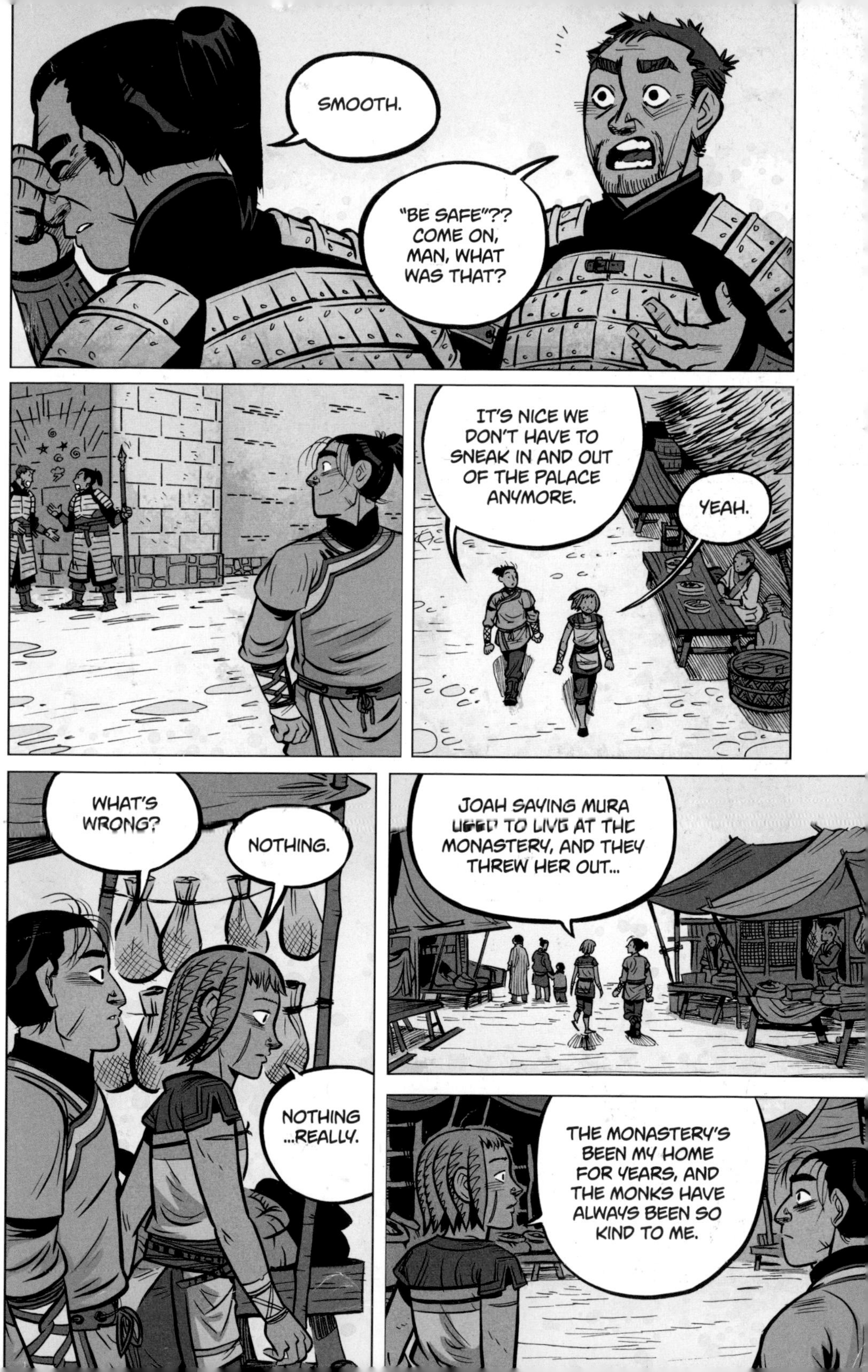
SMOOTH.
"BE SAFE"?? COME ON, MAN, WHAT WAS THAT?
IT'S NICE WE DON'T HAVE TO SNEAK IN AND OUT OF THE PALACE ANYMORE.
YEAH.
WHAT'S WRONG?
NOTHING.
NOTHING ...REALLY.
JOAH SAYING MURA USED TO LIVE AT THE MONASTERY, AND THEY THREW HER OUT...
THE MONASTERY'S BEEN MY HOME FOR YEARS, AND THE MONKS HAVE ALWAYS BEEN SO KIND TO ME.

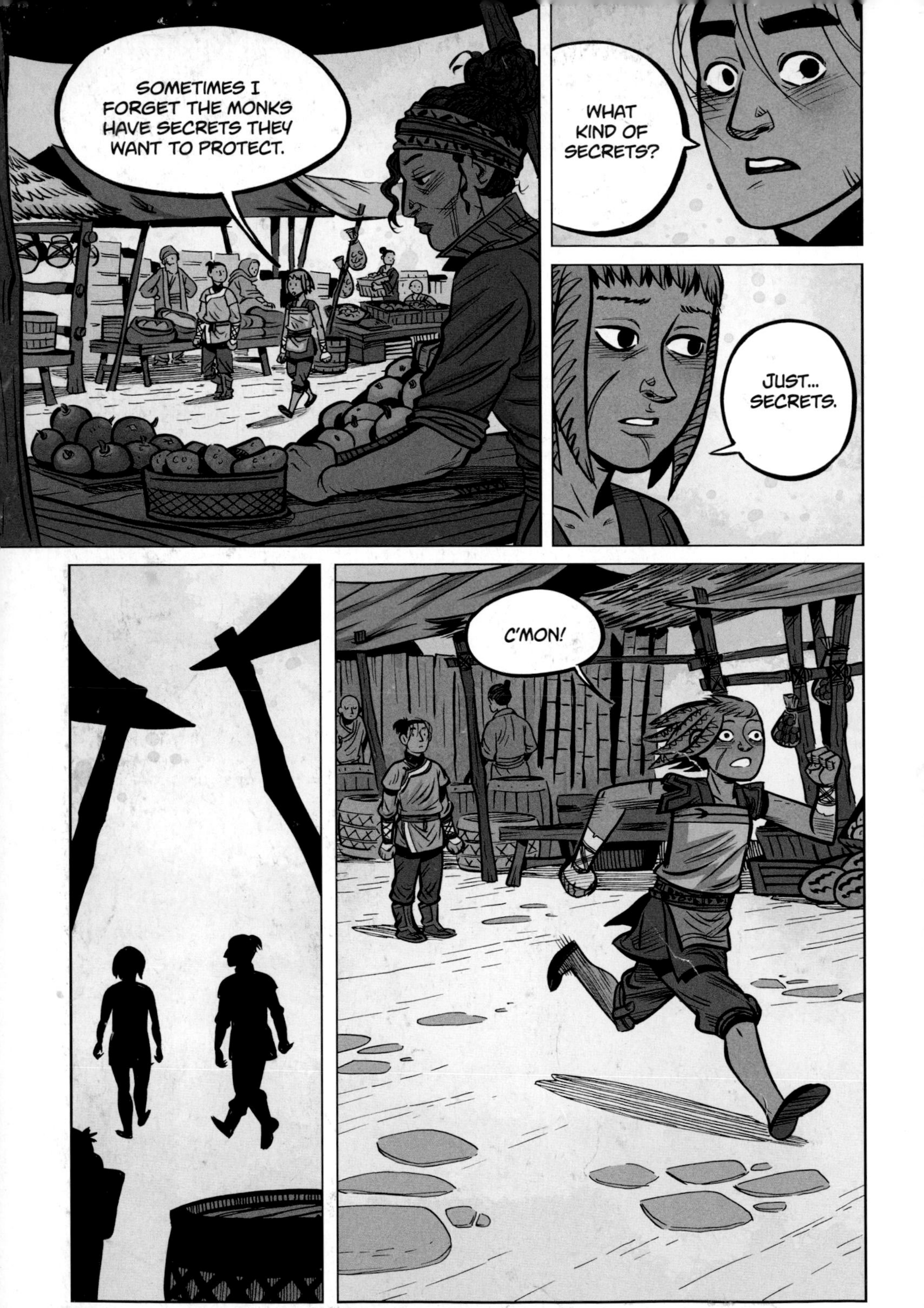
SOMETIMES I FORGET THE MONKS HAVE SECRETS THEY WANT TO PROTECT.
WHAT KIND OF SECRETS?
JUST... SECRETS.
C'MON!

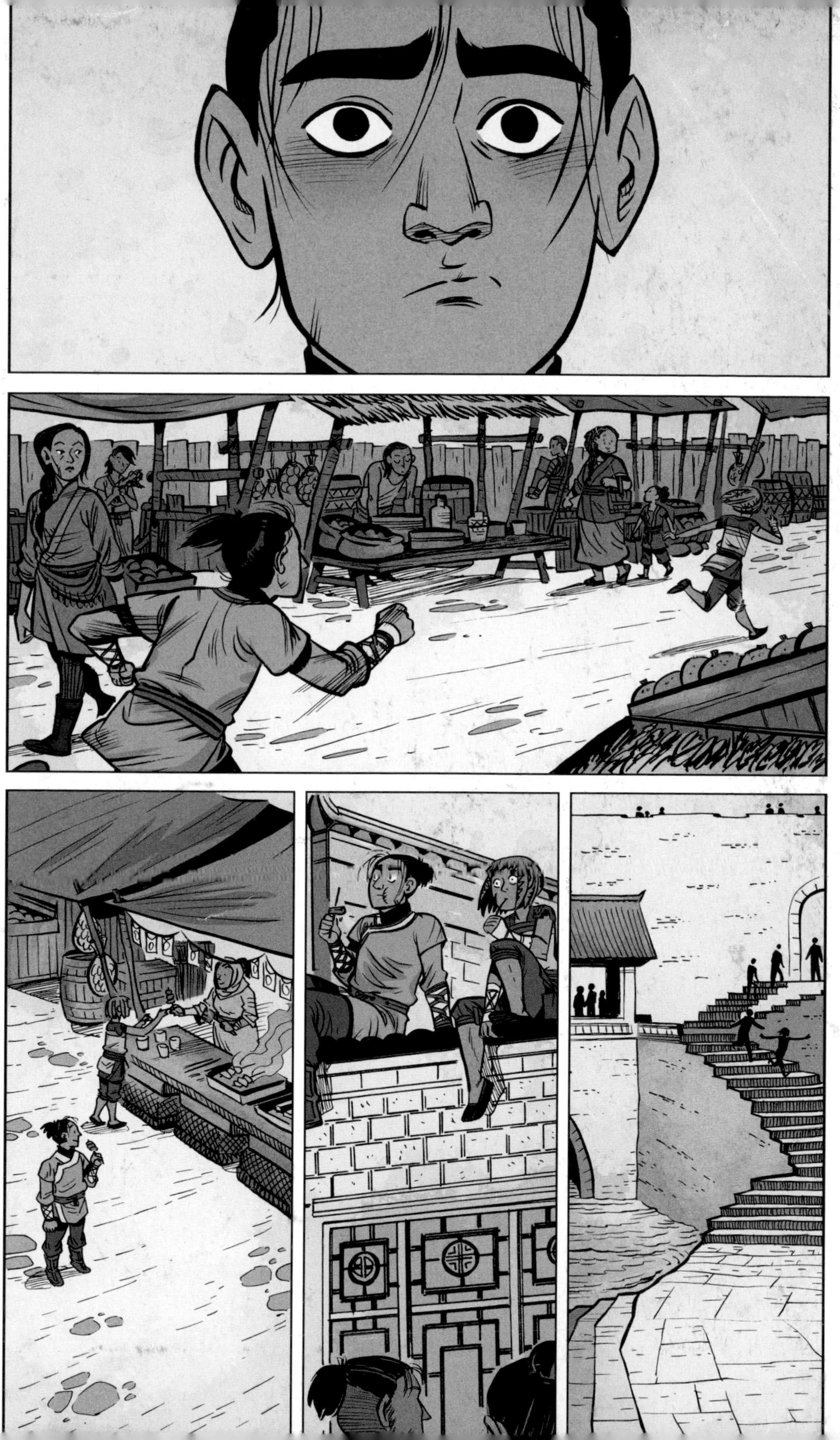

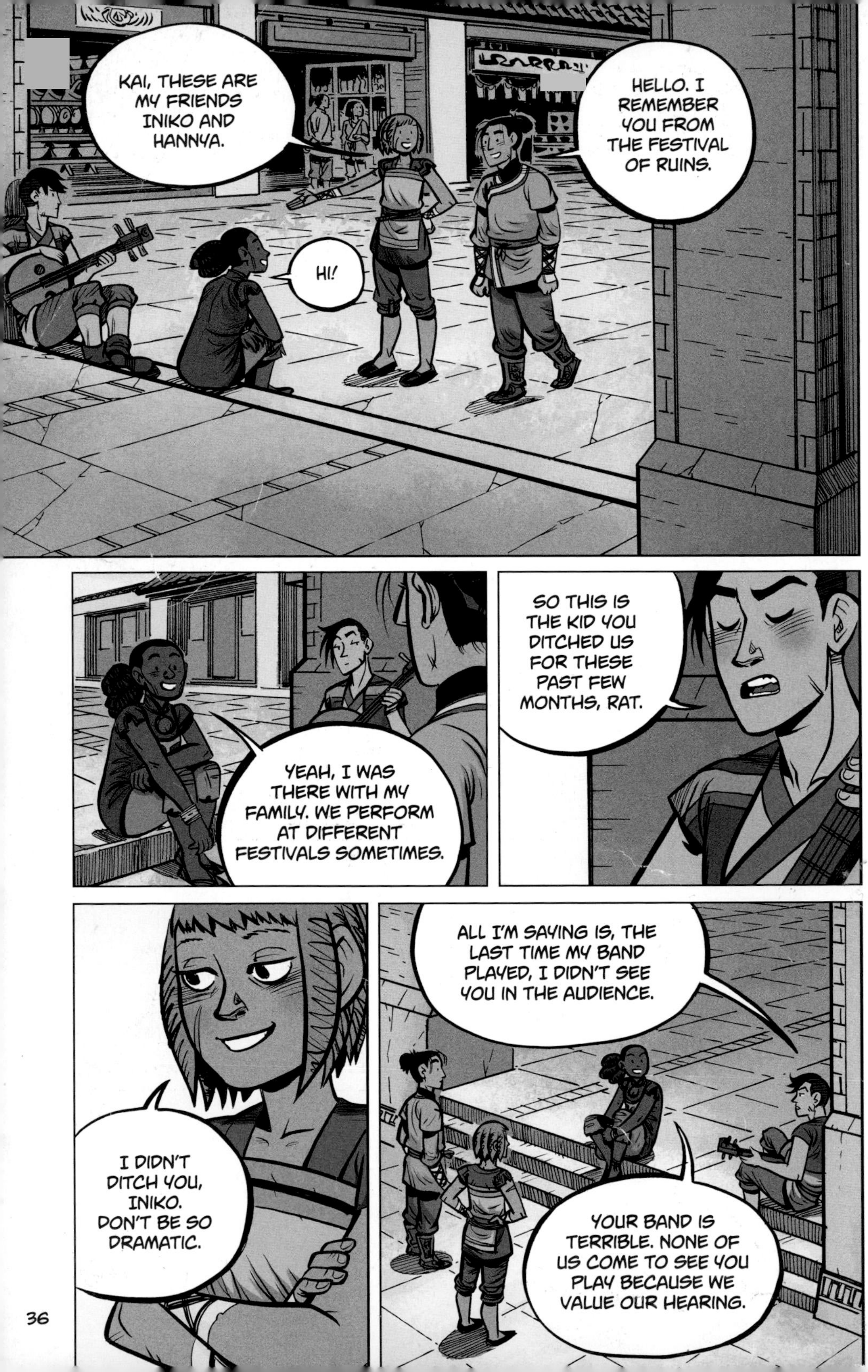

KAI, THESE ARE MY FRIENDS INIKO AND HANNYA.
HELLO. I REMEMBER YOU FROM THE FESTIVAL OF RUINS.
HI!
YEAH, I WAS THERE WITH MY FAMILY. WE PERFORM AT DIFFERENT FESTIVALS SOMETIMES.
SO THIS IS THE KID YOU DITCHED US FOR THESE PAST FEW MONTHS, RAT.
I DIDN'T DITCH YOU, INIKO. DON'T BE SO DRAMATIC.
ALL I'M SAYING IS, THE LAST TIME MY BAND PLAYED, I DIDN'T SEE YOU IN THE AUDIENCE.
YOUR BAND IS TERRIBLE. NONE OF US COME TO SEE YOU PLAY BECAUSE WE VALUE OUR HEARING.

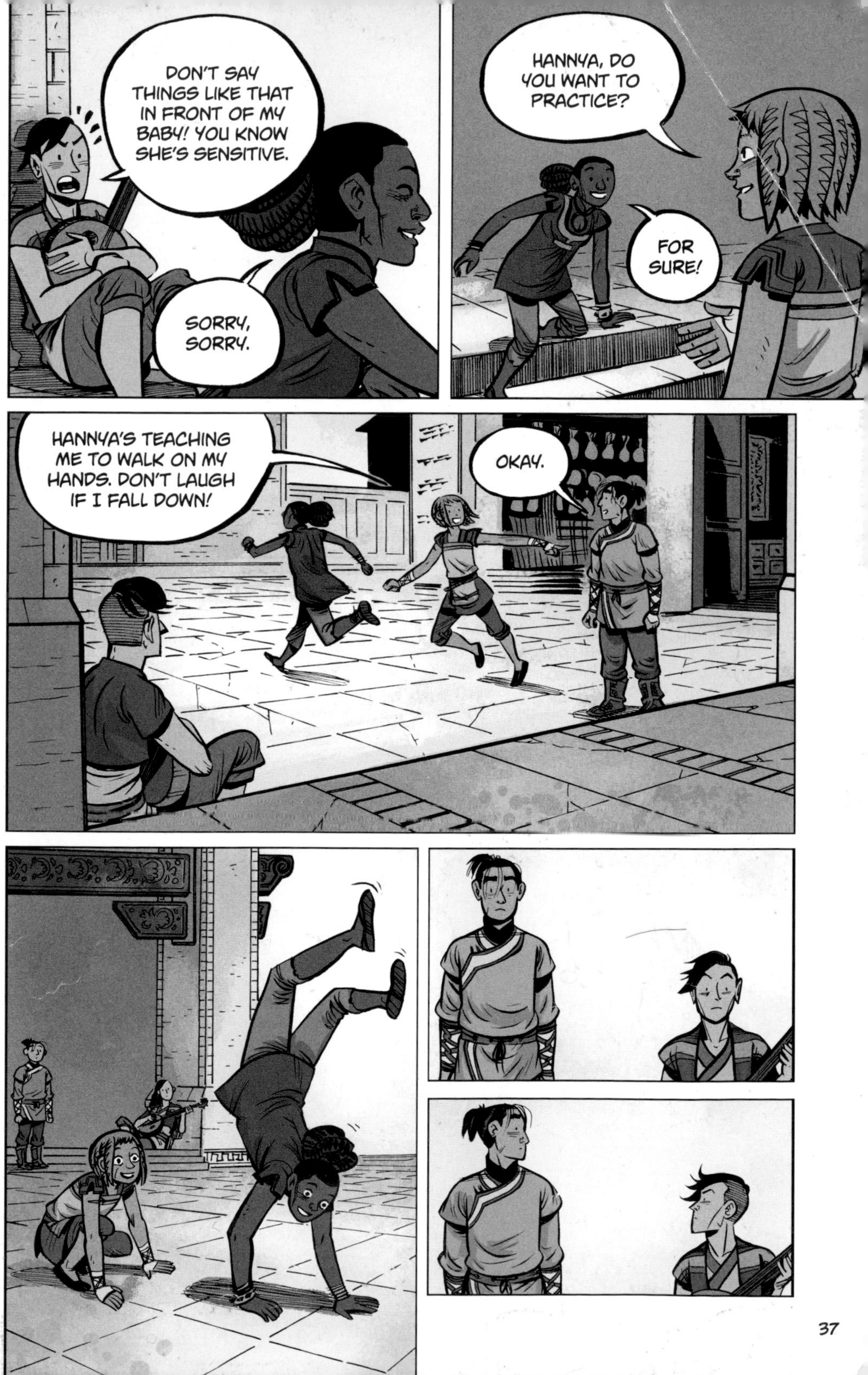
DON'T SAY THINGS LIKE THAT IN FRONT OF MY BABY! YOU KNOW SHE'S SENSITIVE.
SORRY, SORRY.
HANNYA, DO YOU WANT TO PRACTICE?
FOR SURE!
HANNYA'S TEACHING ME TO WALK ON MY HANDS. DON'T LAUGH IF I FALL DOWN!
OKAY.

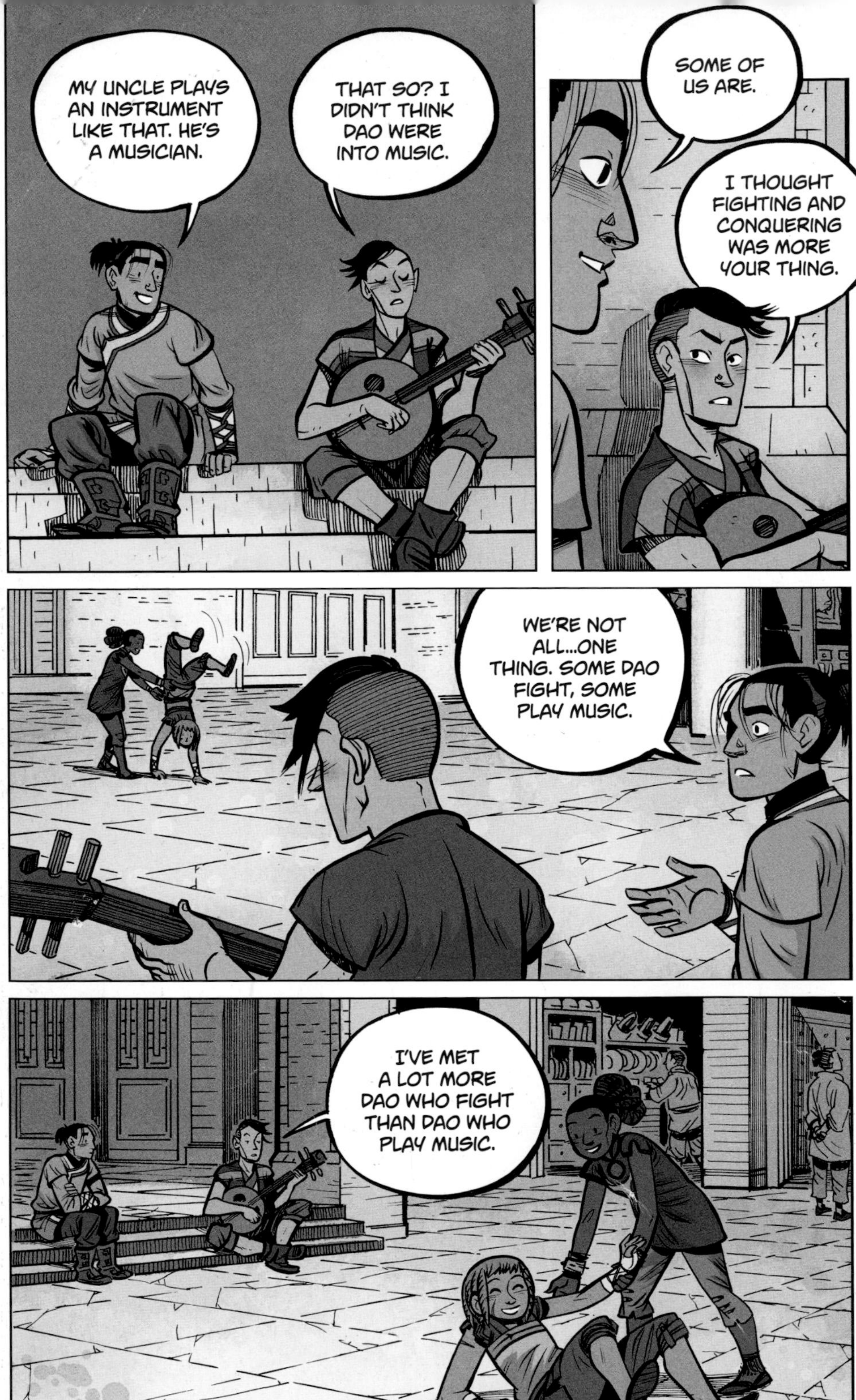
MY UNCLE PLAYS AN INSTRUMENT LIKE THAT. HE'S A MUSICIAN.
THAT SO? I DIDN'T THINK DAO WERE INTO MUSIC.
SOME OF US ARE.
I THOUGHT FIGHTING AND CONQUERING WAS MORE YOUR THING.
WE'RE NOT ALL...ONE THING. SOME DAO FIGHT, SOME PLAY MUSIC.
I'VE MET A LOT MORE DAO WHO FIGHT THAN DAO WHO PLAY MUSIC.

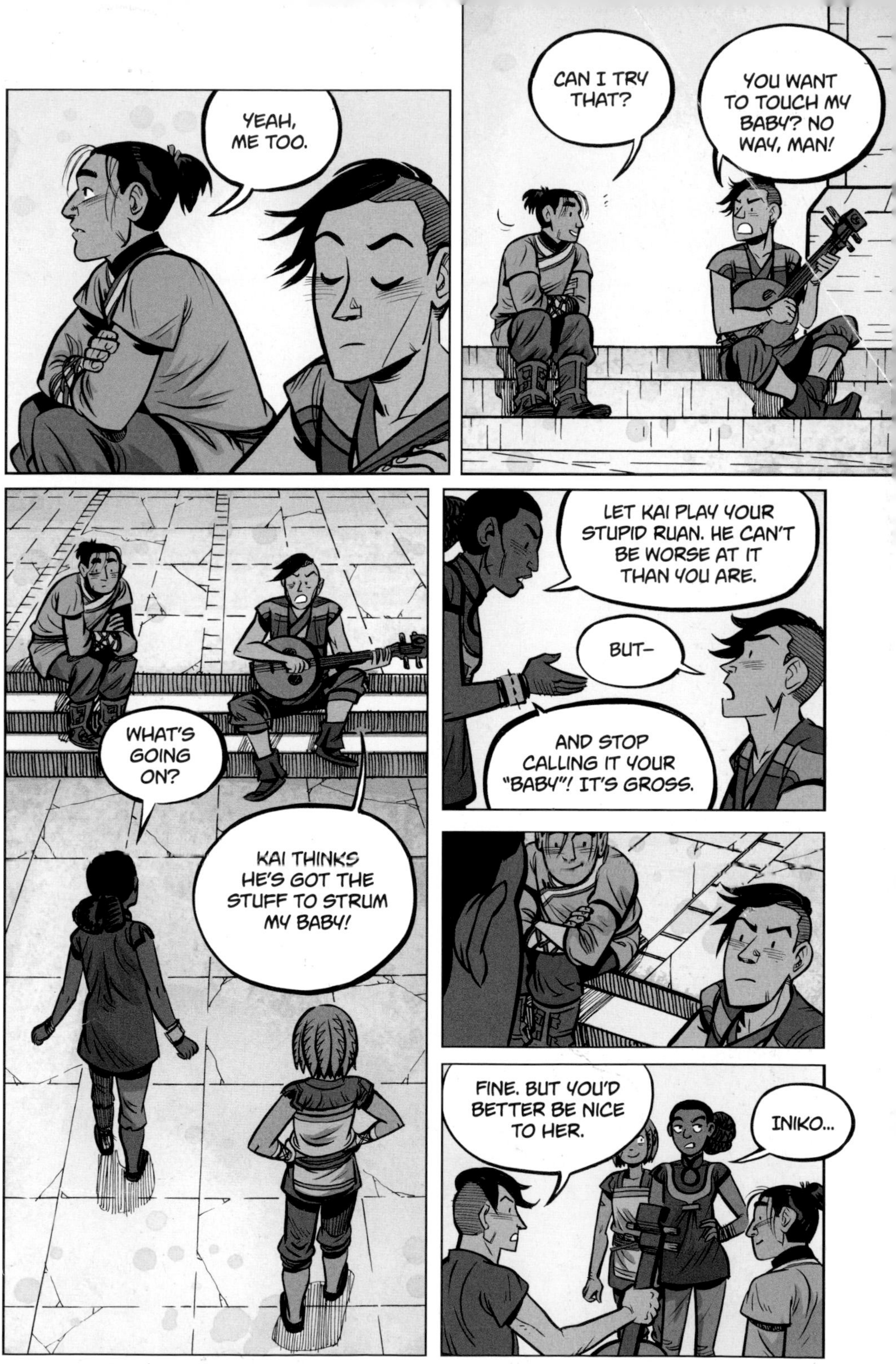
YEAH, ME TOO.
CAN I TRY THAT?
YOU WANT TO TOUCH MY BABY? NO WAY, MAN!
WHAT'S GOING ON?
KAI THINKS HE'S GOT THE STUFF TO STRUM MY BABY!
LET KAI PLAY YOUR STUPID RUAN. HE CAN'T BE WORSE AT IT THAN YOU ARE.
BUT–
AND STOP CALLING IT YOUR "BABY"! IT'S GROSS.
FINE. BUT YOU'D BETTER BE NICE TO HER.
INIKO...

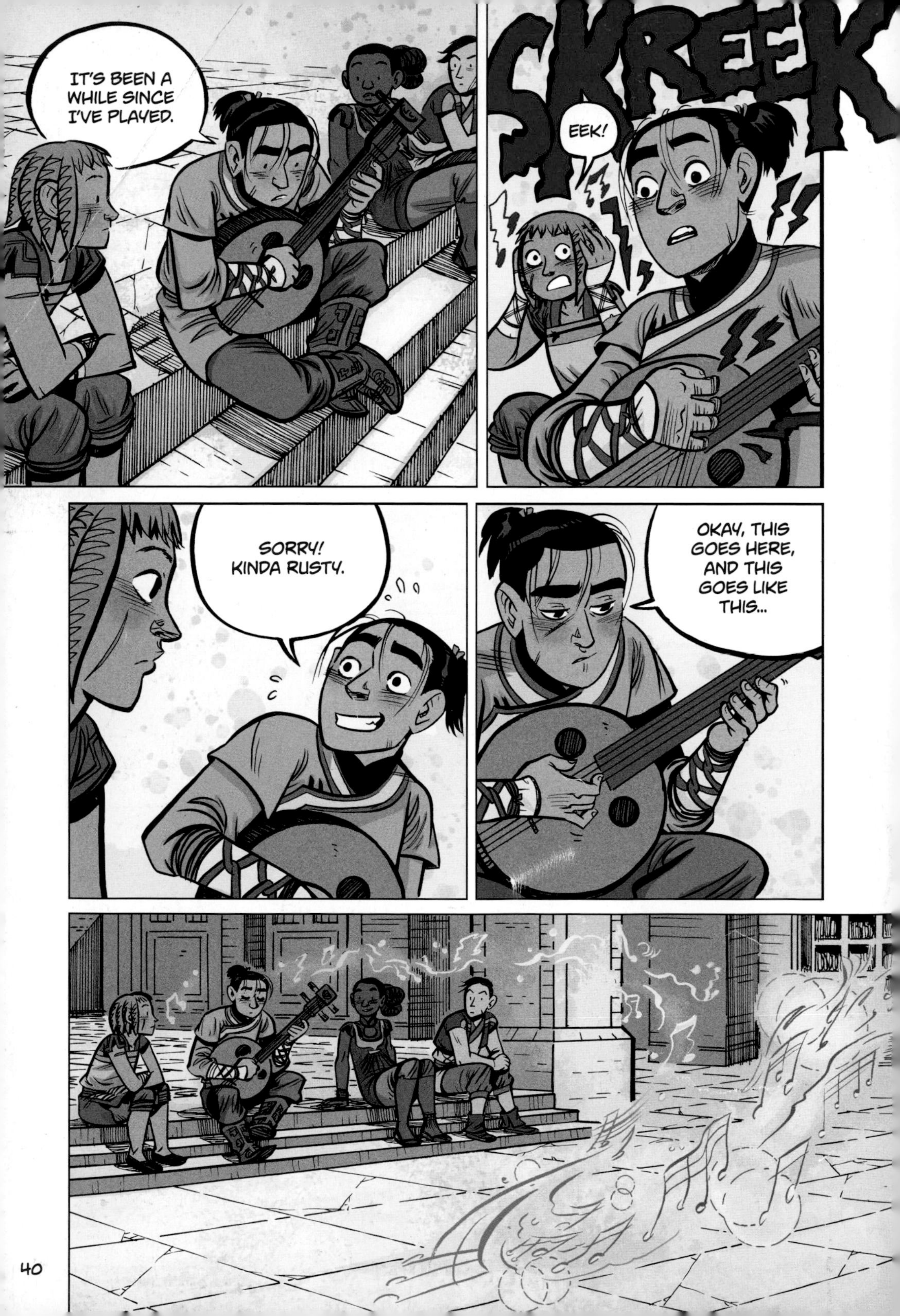

IT'S BEEN A WHILE SINCE I'VE PLAYED.
SKREEK
EEK!
SORRY! KINDA RUSTY.
OKAY, THIS GOES HERE, AND THIS GOES LIKE THIS...

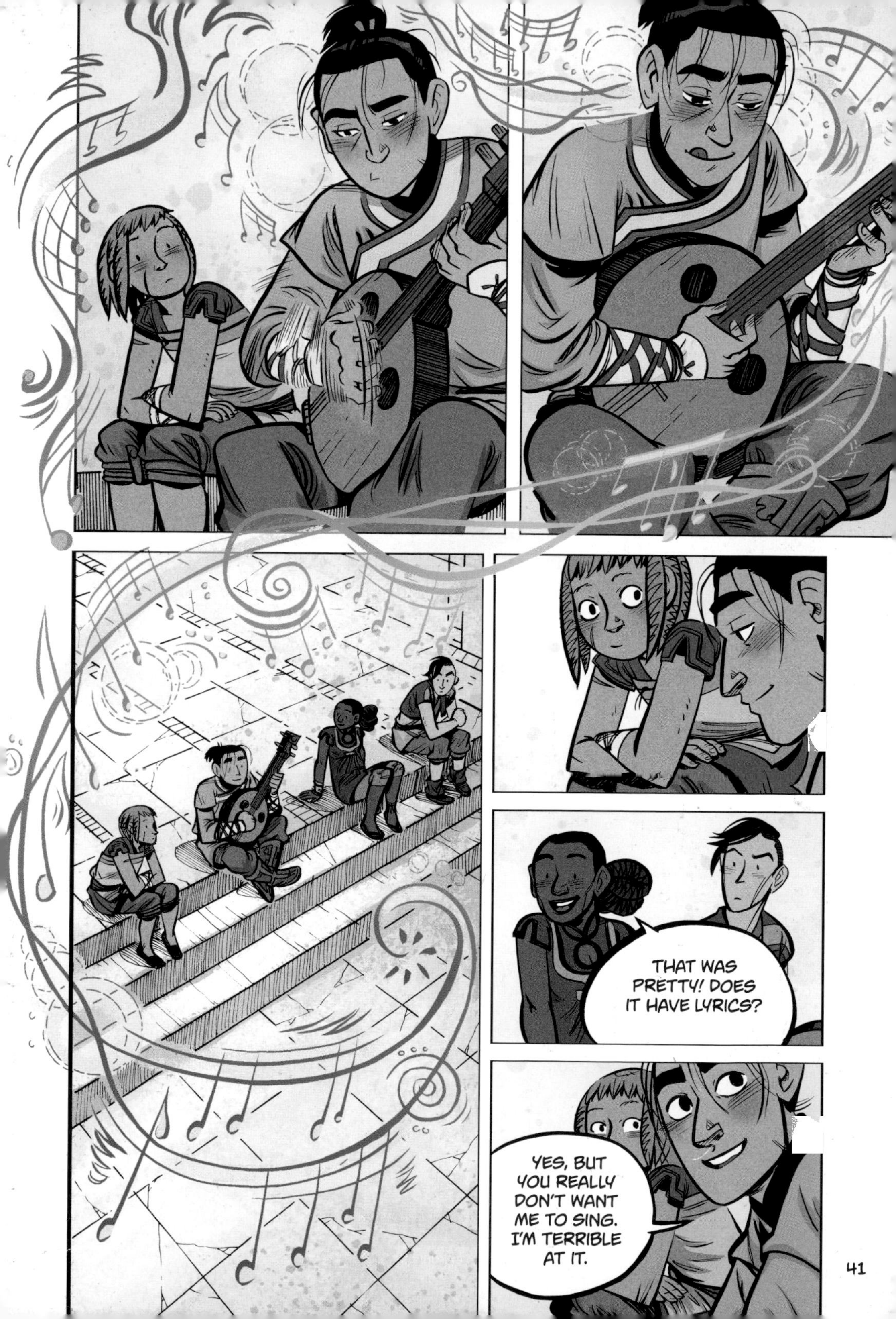
THAT WAS PRETTY! DOES IT HAVE LYRICS?
YES, BUT YOU REALLY DON'T WANT ME TO SING. I'M TERRIBLE AT IT.

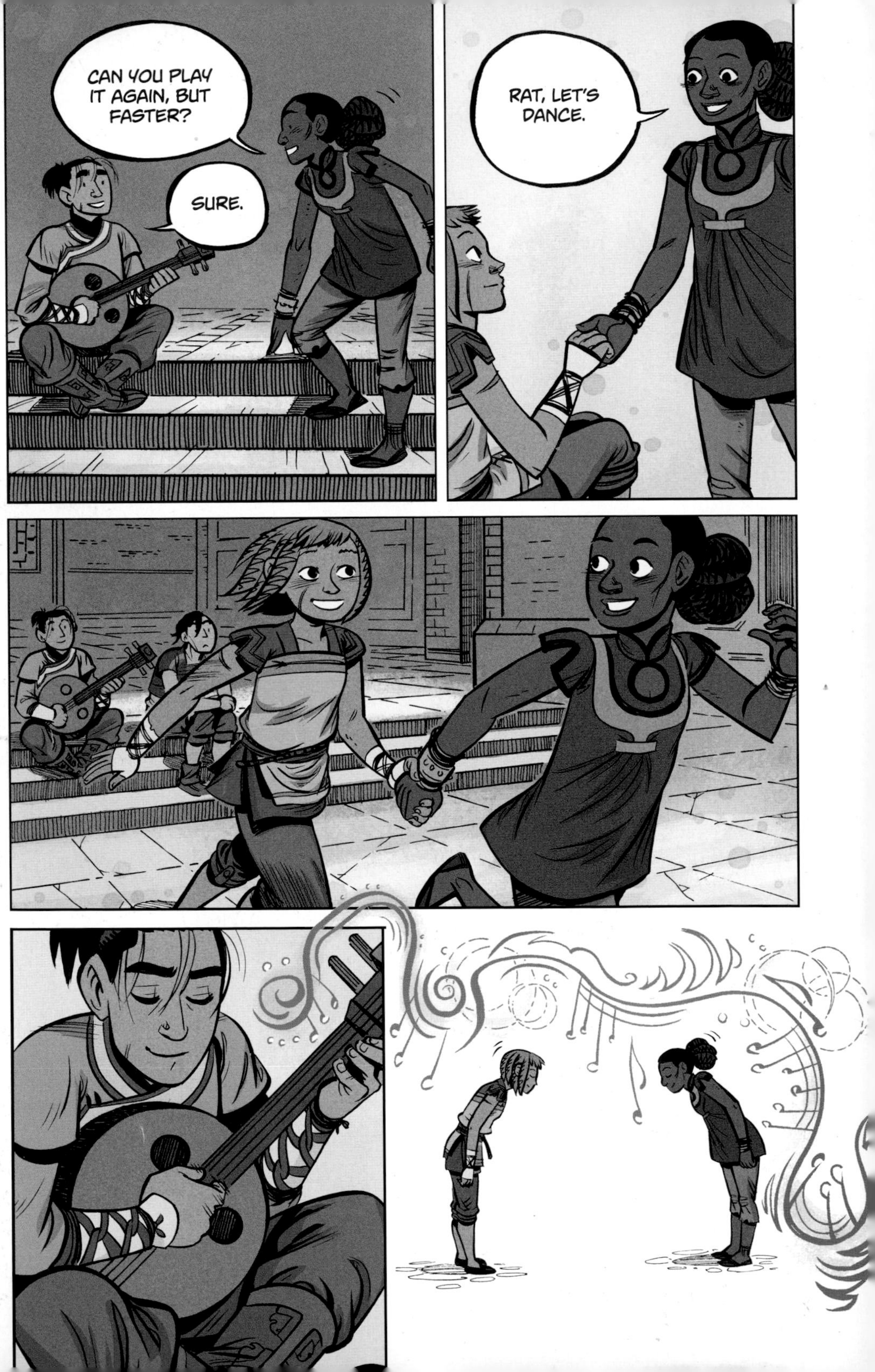
CAN YOU PLAY IT AGAIN, BUT FASTER?
SURE.
RAT, LET'S DANCE.

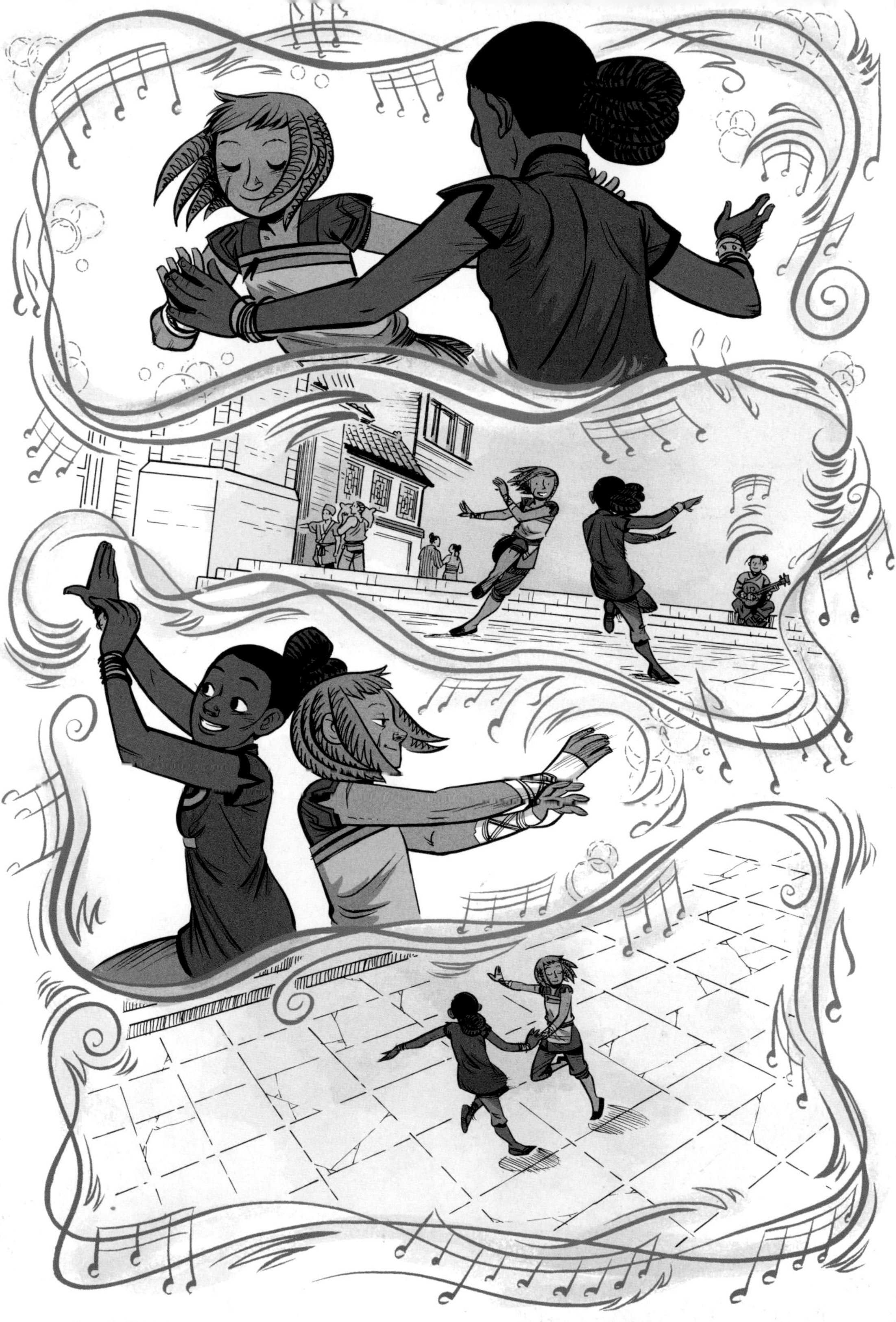

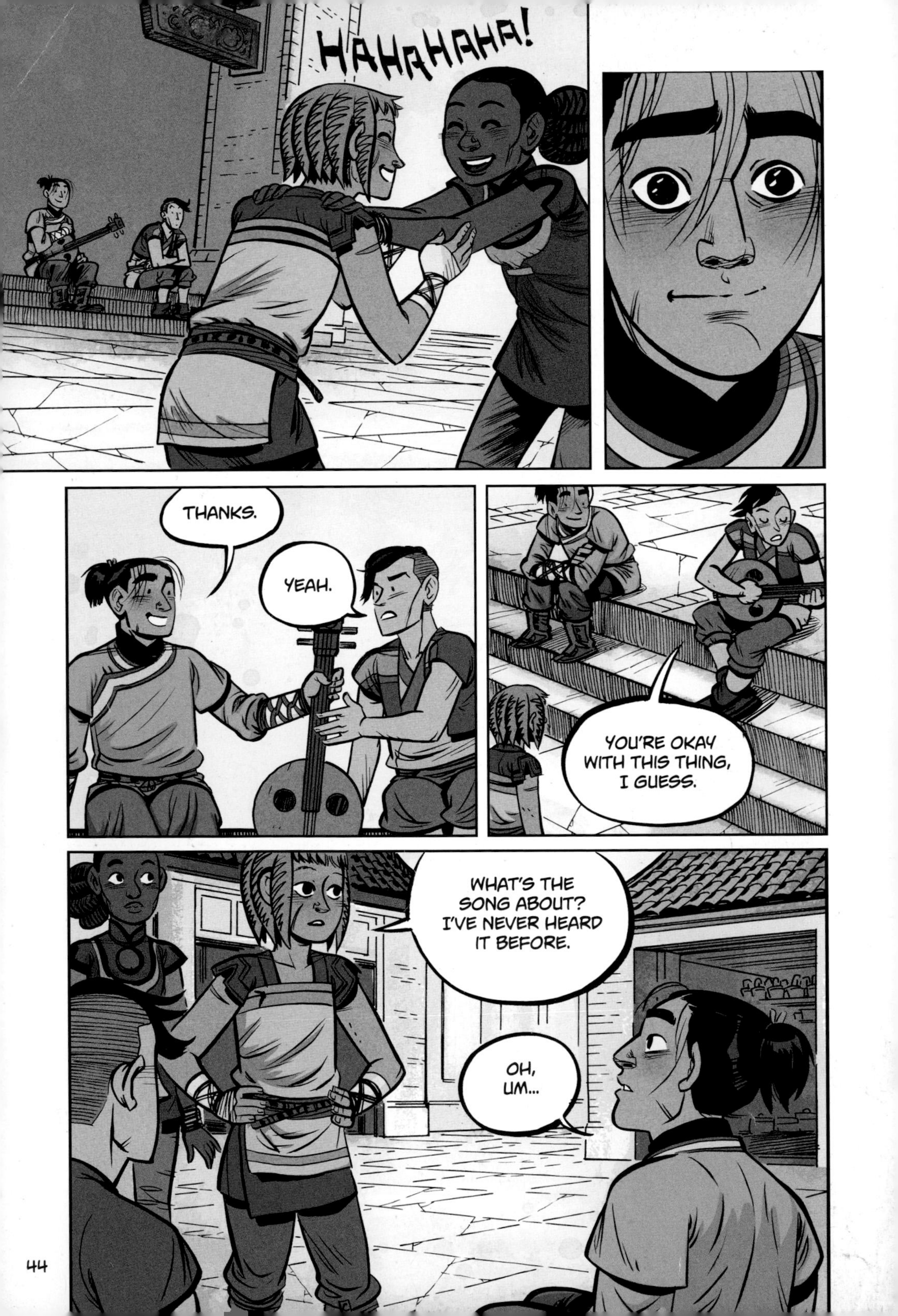
HAHAHAHA!
THANKS.
YEAH.
YOU'RE OKAY WITH THIS THING, I GUESS.
WHAT'S THE SONG ABOUT? I'VE NEVER HEARD IT BEFORE.
OH, UM...

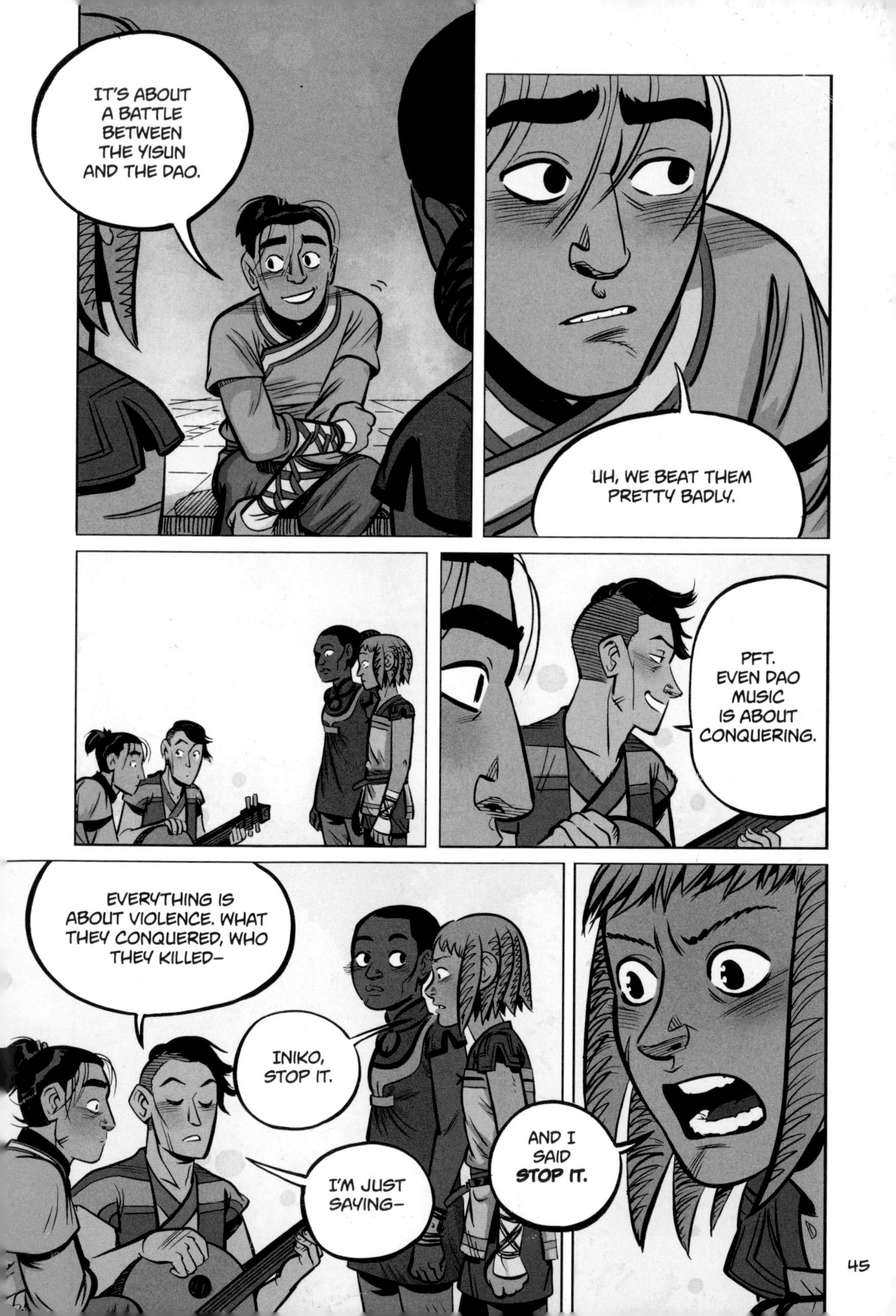
IT'S ABOUT A BATTLE BETWEEN THE YISUN AND THE DAO.
UH, WE BEAT THEM PRETTY BADLY.
PFT. EVEN DAO MUSIC IS ABOUT CONQUERING.
EVERYTHING IS ABOUT VIOLENCE. WHAT THEY CONQUERED, WHO THEY KILLED–
INIKO, STOP IT.
I'M JUST SAYING–
AND I SAID **STOP IT.**

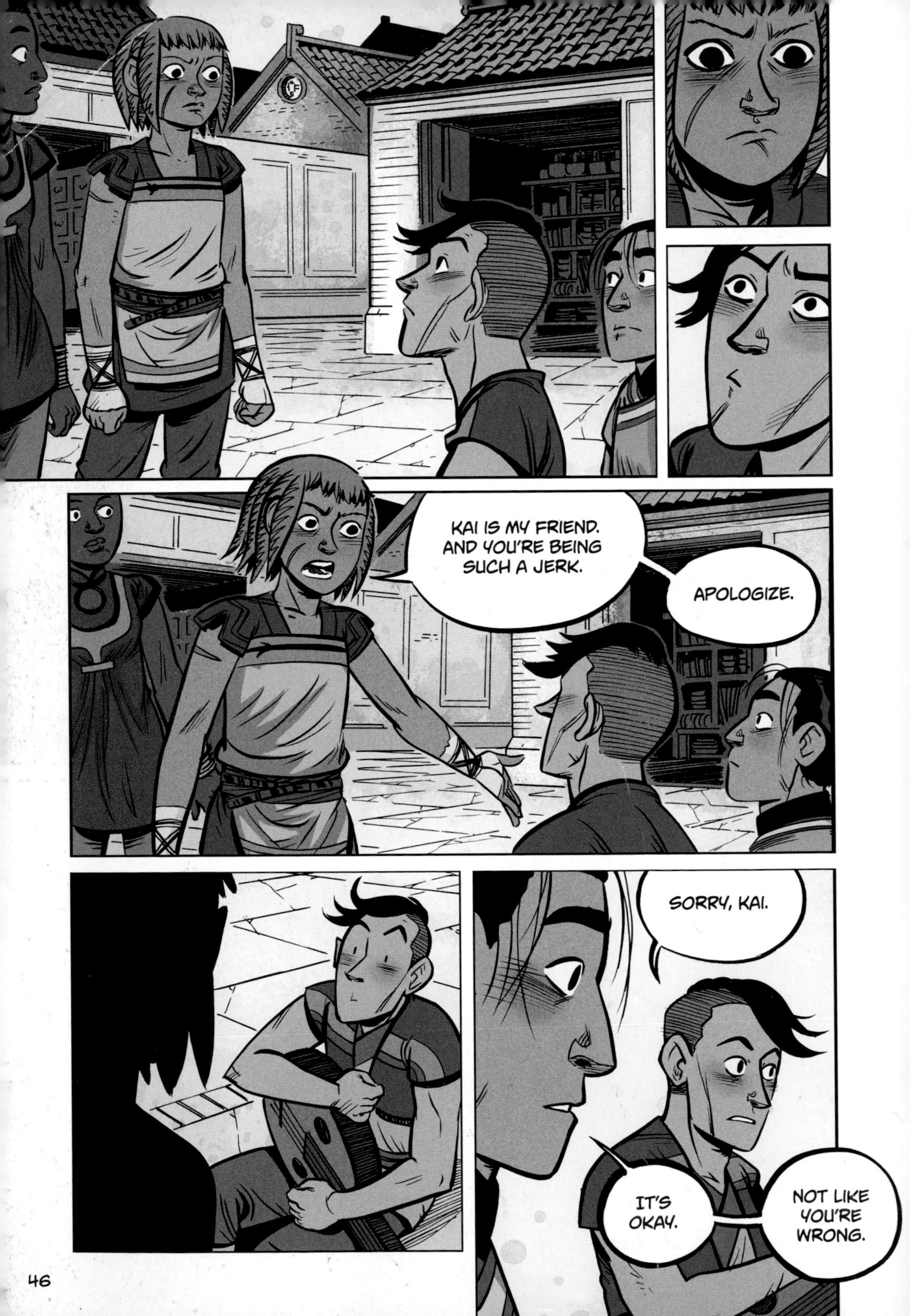
KAI IS MY FRIEND. AND YOU'RE BEING SUCH A JERK.
APOLOGIZE.
SORRY, KAI.
IT'S OKAY.
NOT LIKE YOU'RE WRONG.

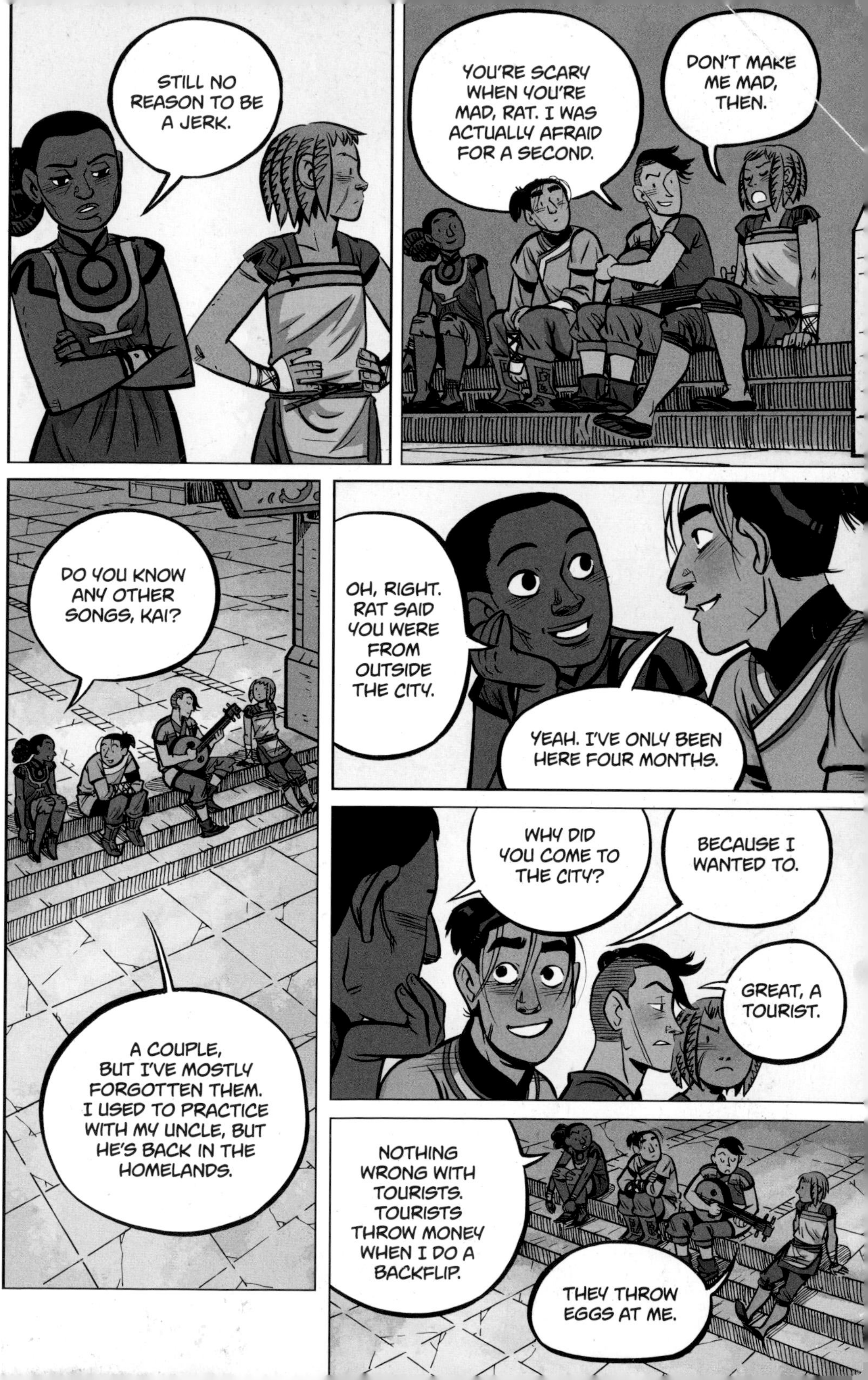
STILL NO REASON TO BE A JERK.
YOU'RE SCARY WHEN YOU'RE MAD, RAT. I WAS ACTUALLY AFRAID FOR A SECOND.
DON'T MAKE ME MAD, THEN.
DO YOU KNOW ANY OTHER SONGS, KAI?
A COUPLE, BUT I'VE MOSTLY FORGOTTEN THEM. I USED TO PRACTICE WITH MY UNCLE, BUT HE'S BACK IN THE HOMELANDS.
OH, RIGHT. RAT SAID YOU WERE FROM OUTSIDE THE CITY.
YEAH. I'VE ONLY BEEN HERE FOUR MONTHS.
WHY DID YOU COME TO THE CITY?
BECAUSE I WANTED TO.
GREAT, A TOURIST.
NOTHING WRONG WITH TOURISTS. TOURISTS THROW MONEY WHEN I DO A BACKFLIP.
THEY THROW EGGS AT ME.

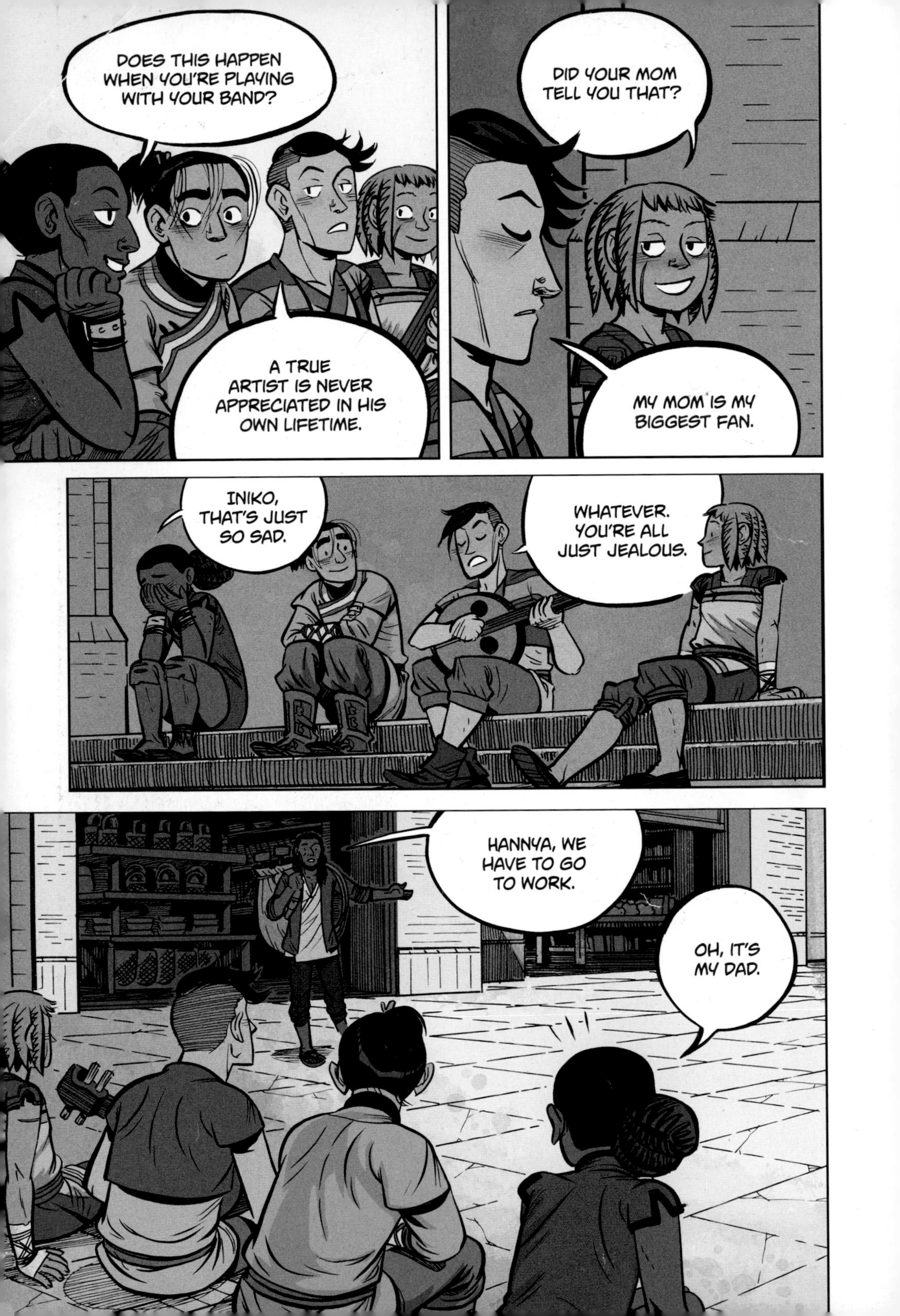
DOES THIS HAPPEN WHEN YOU'RE PLAYING WITH YOUR BAND?
A TRUE ARTIST IS NEVER APPRECIATED IN HIS OWN LIFETIME.
DID YOUR MOM TELL YOU THAT?
MY MOM IS MY BIGGEST FAN.
INIKO, THAT'S JUST SO SAD.
WHATEVER. YOU'RE ALL JUST JEALOUS.
HANNYA, WE HAVE TO GO TO WORK.
OH, IT'S MY DAD.

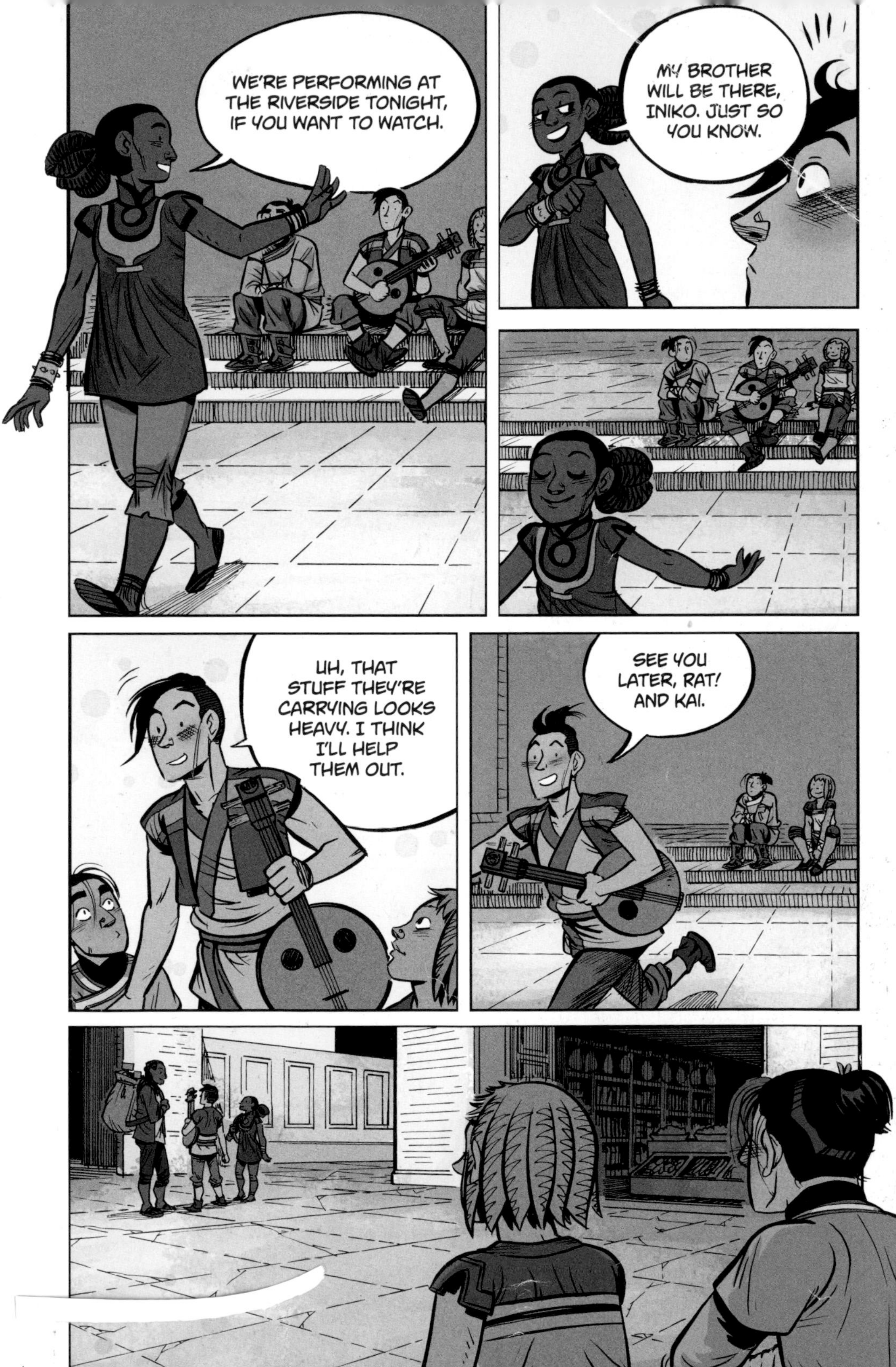
WE'RE PERFORMING AT THE RIVERSIDE TONIGHT, IF YOU WANT TO WATCH.
MY BROTHER WILL BE THERE, INIKO. JUST SO YOU KNOW.
UH, THAT STUFF THEY'RE CARRYING LOOKS HEAVY. I THINK I'LL HELP THEM OUT.
SEE YOU LATER, RAT! AND KAI.

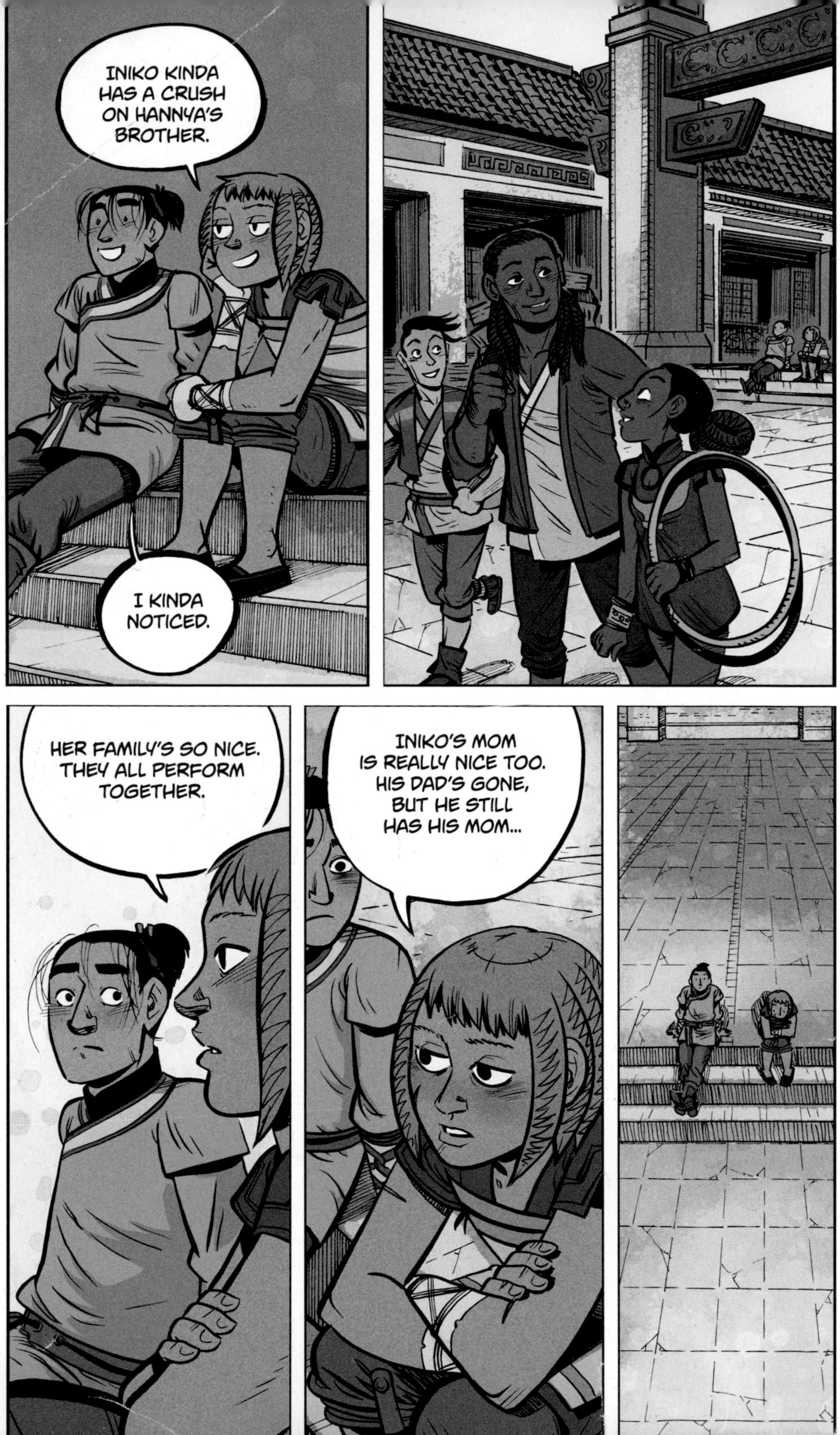
INIKO KINDA HAS A CRUSH ON HANNYA'S BROTHER.
I KINDA NOTICED.
HER FAMILY'S SO NICE. THEY ALL PERFORM TOGETHER.
INIKO'S MOM IS REALLY NICE TOO. HIS DAD'S GONE, BUT HE STILL HAS HIS MOM...

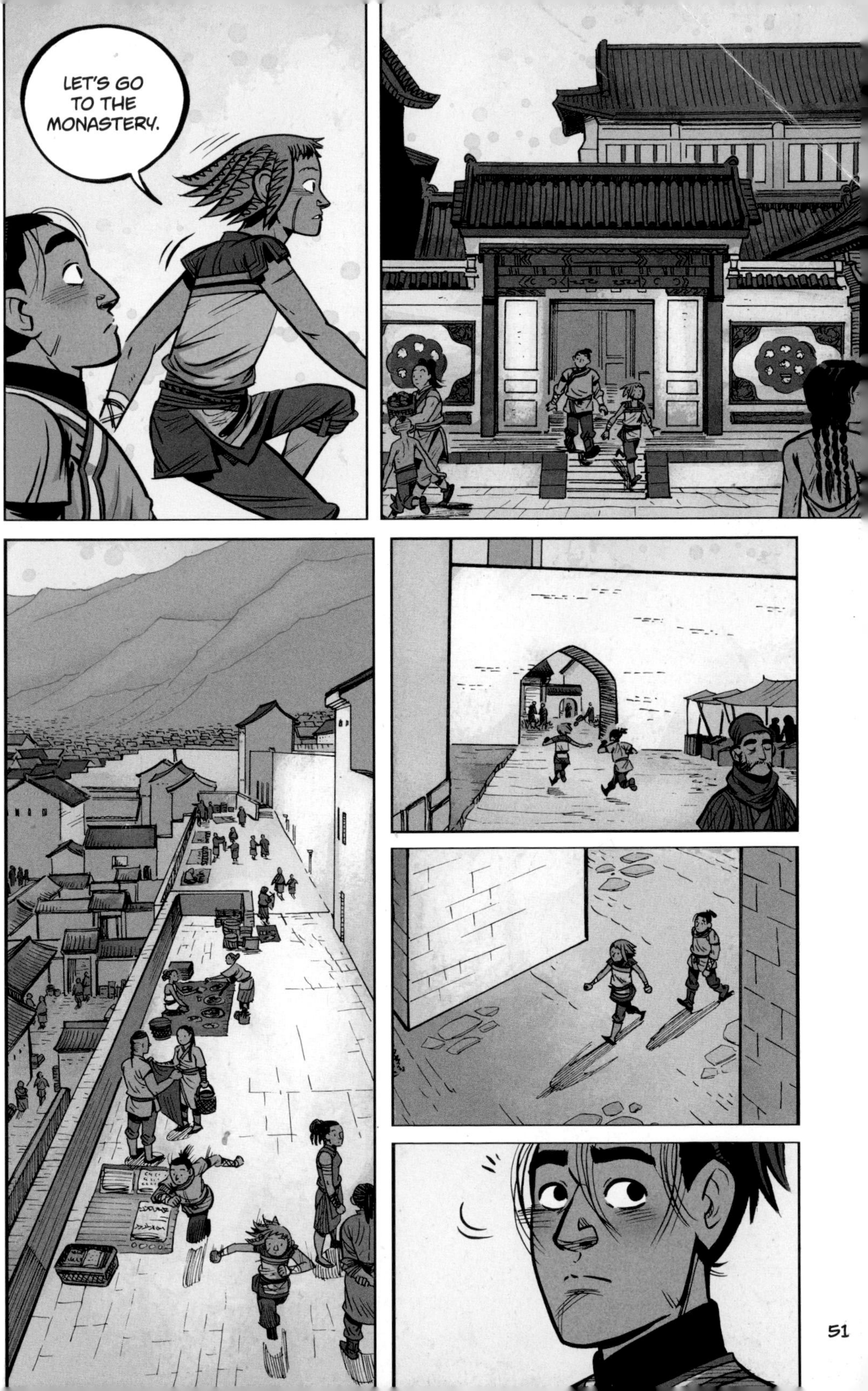
LET'S GO TO THE MONASTERY.

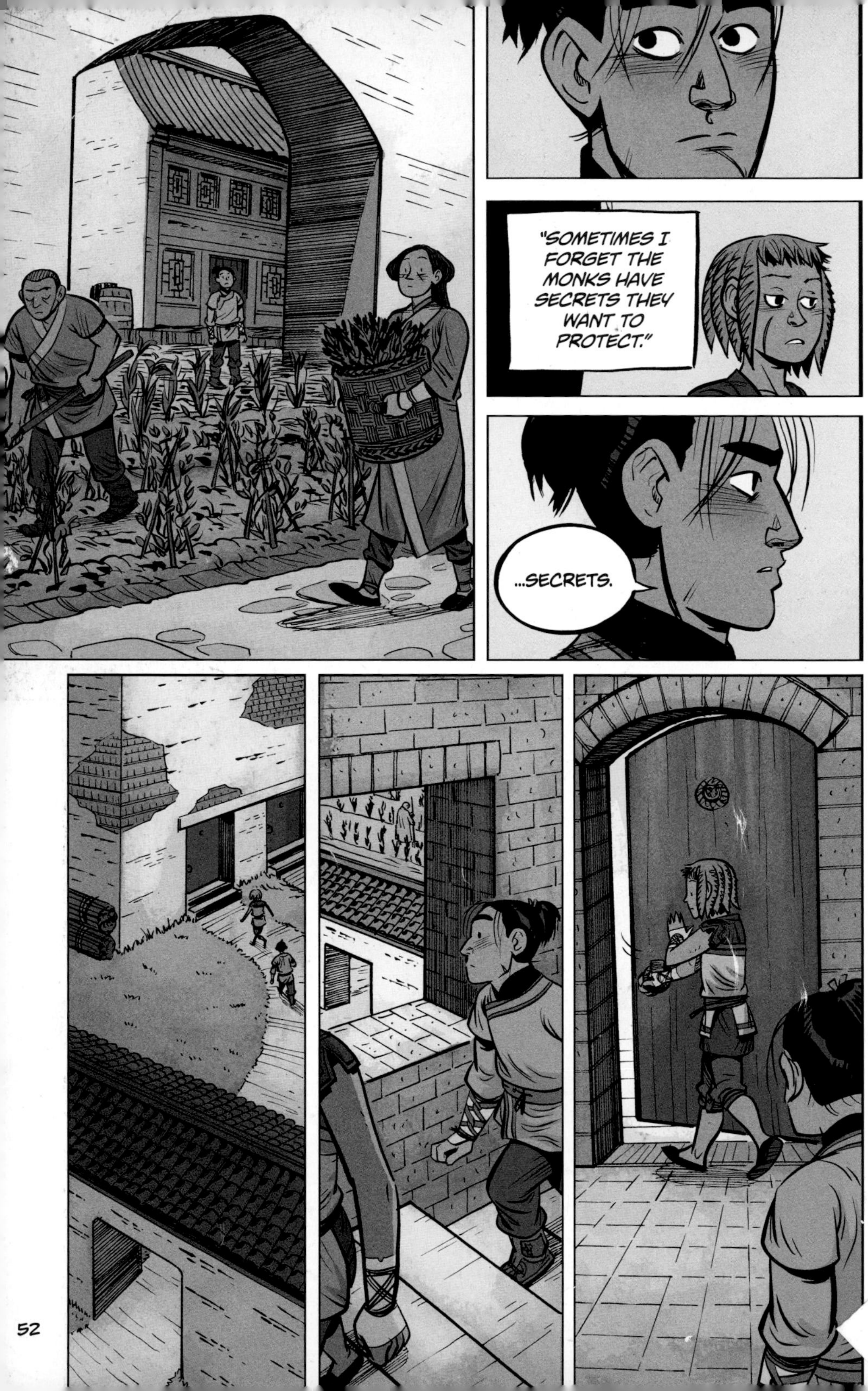
"SOMETIMES I FORGET THE MONKS HAVE SECRETS THEY WANT TO PROTECT."
...SECRETS.

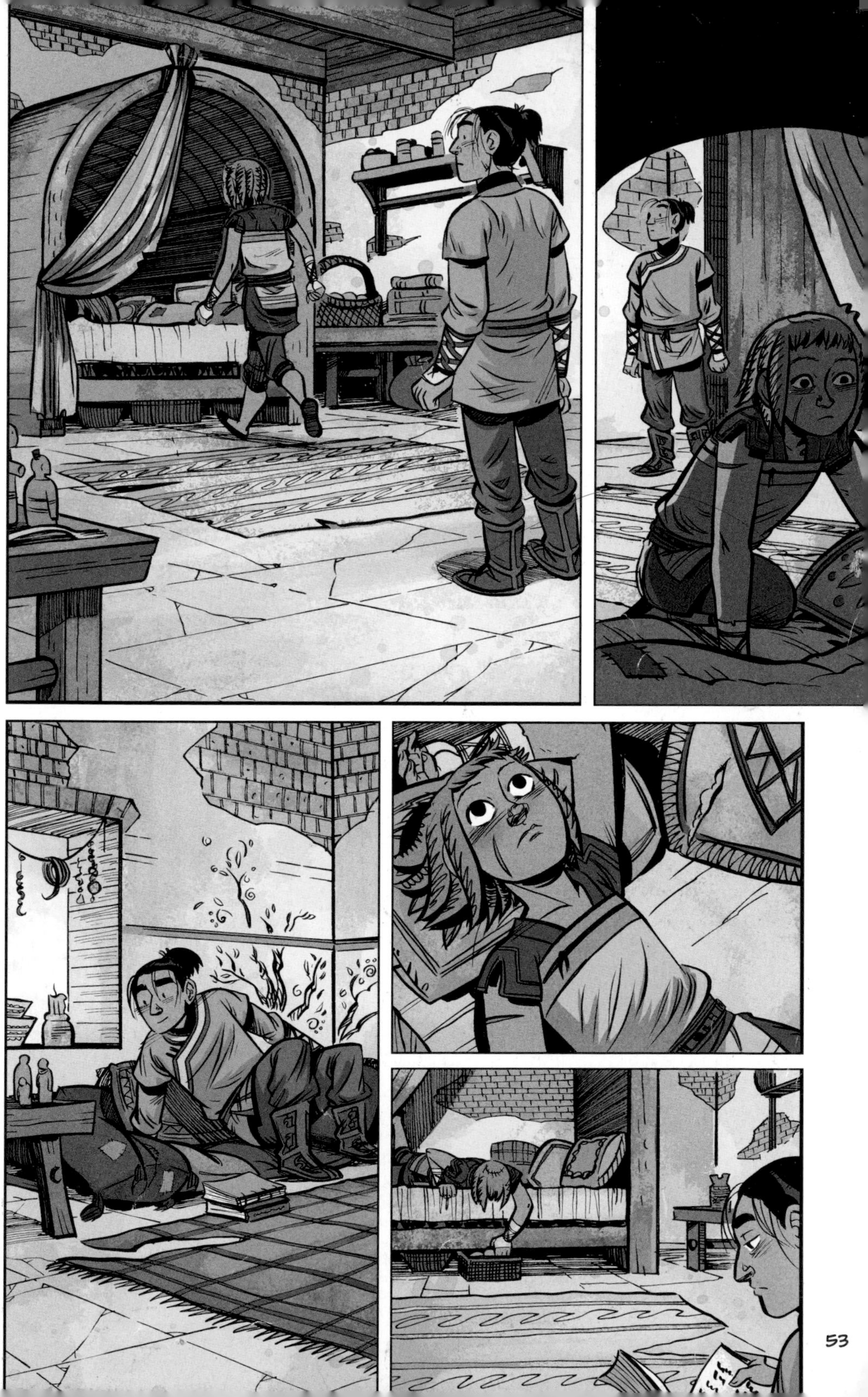

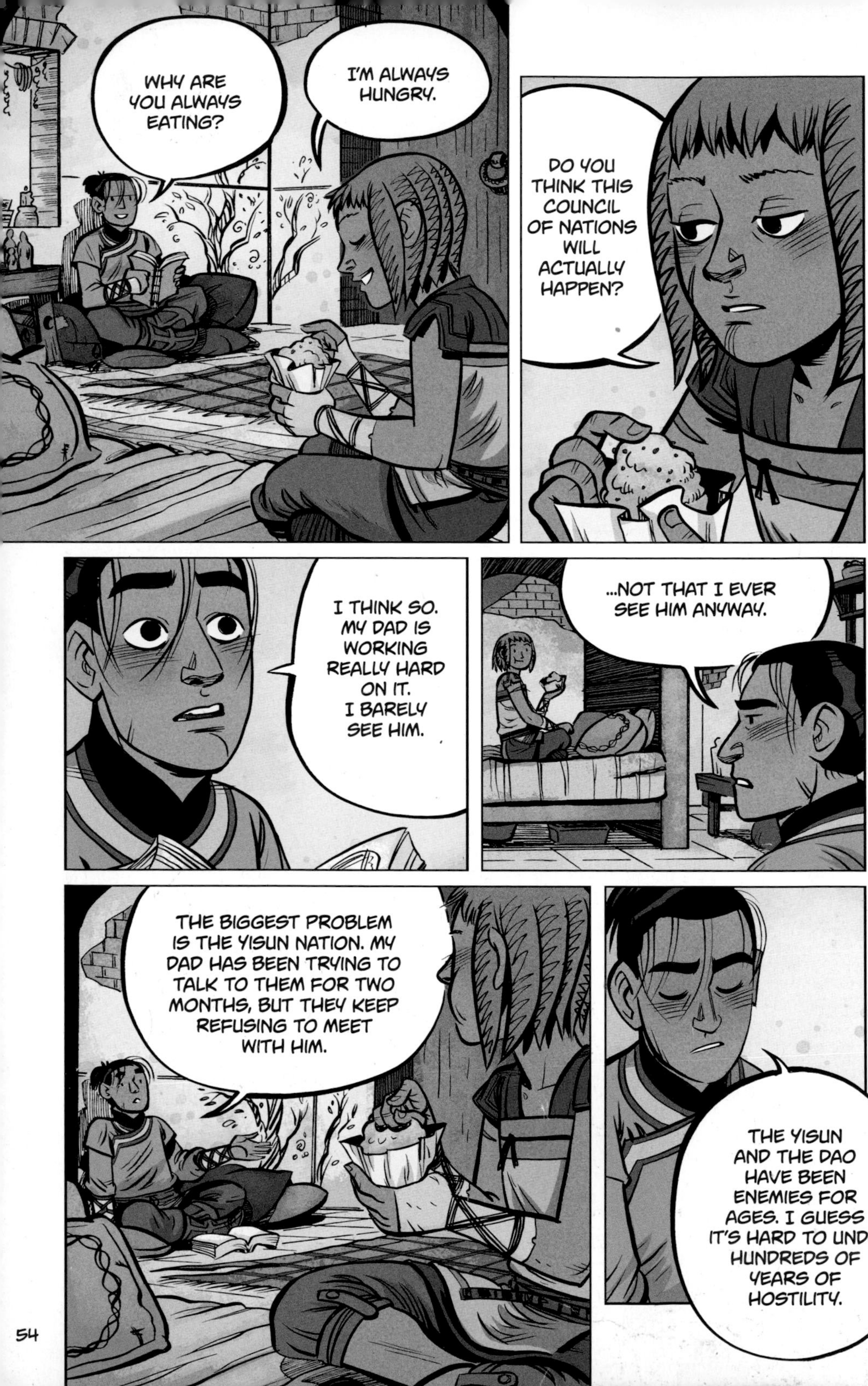
WHY ARE YOU ALWAYS EATING?
I'M ALWAYS HUNGRY.
DO YOU THINK THIS COUNCIL OF NATIONS WILL ACTUALLY HAPPEN?
I THINK SO. MY DAD IS WORKING REALLY HARD ON IT. I BARELY SEE HIM.
...NOT THAT I EVER SEE HIM ANYWAY.
THE BIGGEST PROBLEM IS THE YISUN NATION. MY DAD HAS BEEN TRYING TO TALK TO THEM FOR TWO MONTHS, BUT THEY KEEP REFUSING TO MEET WITH HIM.
THE YISUN AND THE DAO HAVE BEEN ENEMIES FOR AGES. I GUESS IT'S HARD TO UNDO HUNDREDS OF YEARS OF HOSTILITY.

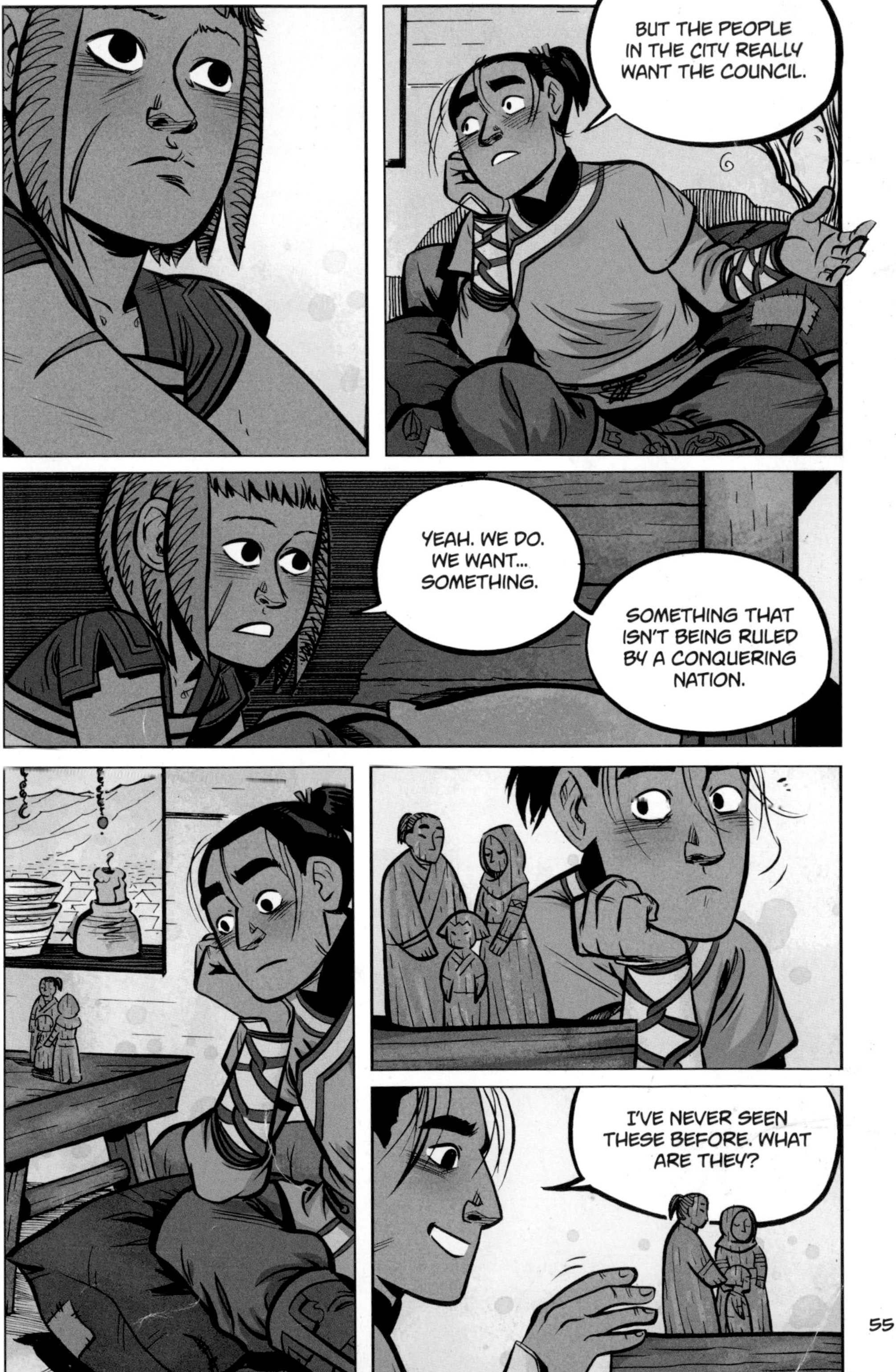
BUT THE PEOPLE IN THE CITY REALLY WANT THE COUNCIL.
YEAH. WE DO. WE WANT... SOMETHING.
SOMETHING THAT ISN'T BEING RULED BY A CONQUERING NATION.
I'VE NEVER SEEN THESE BEFORE. WHAT ARE THEY?

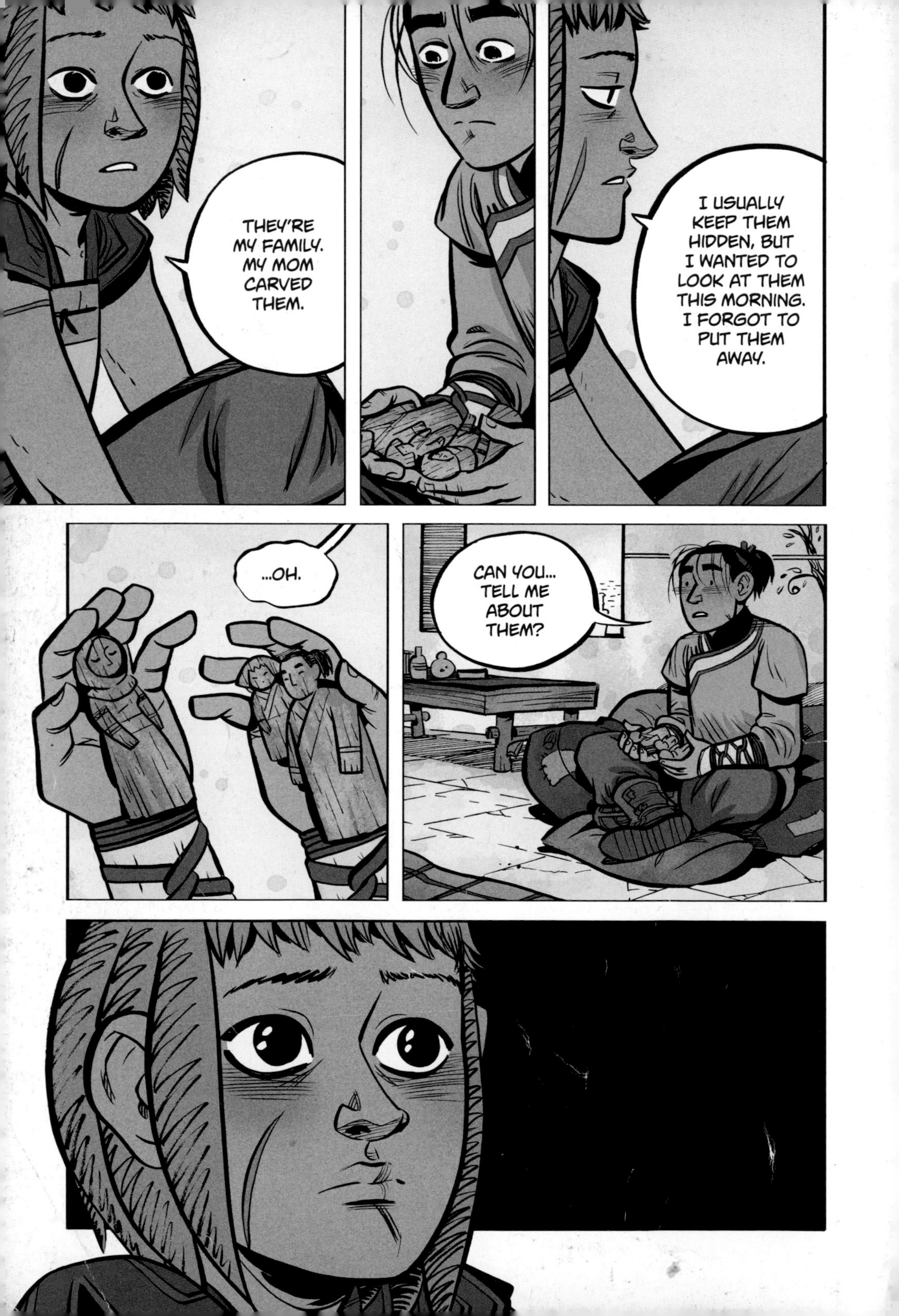
THEY'RE MY FAMILY. MY MOM CARVED THEM.
I USUALLY KEEP THEM HIDDEN, BUT I WANTED TO LOOK AT THEM THIS MORNING. I FORGOT TO PUT THEM AWAY.
...OH.
CAN YOU... TELL ME ABOUT THEM?

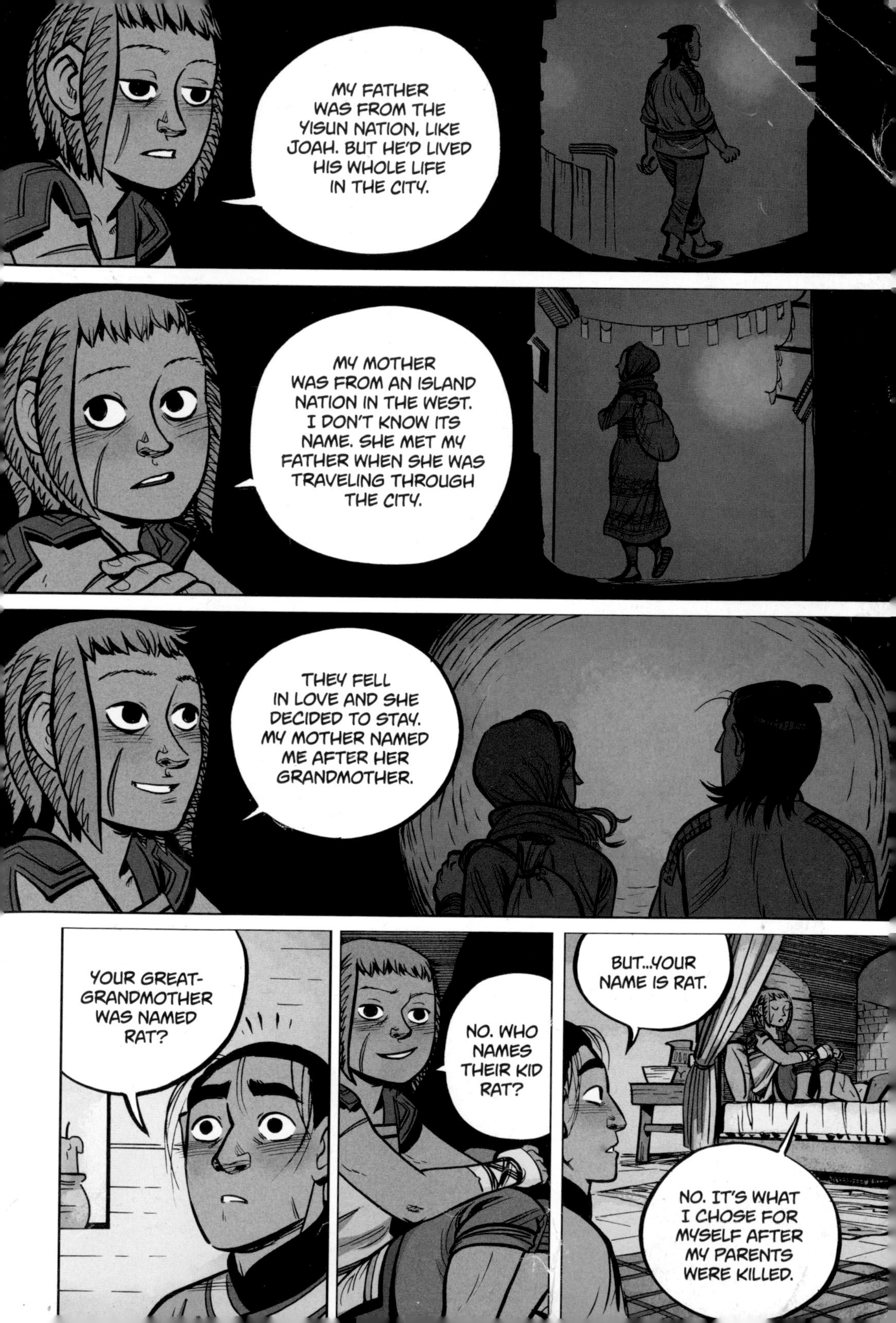
MY FATHER WAS FROM THE YISUN NATION, LIKE JOAH. BUT HE'D LIVED HIS WHOLE LIFE IN THE CITY.
MY MOTHER WAS FROM AN ISLAND NATION IN THE WEST. I DON'T KNOW ITS NAME. SHE MET MY FATHER WHEN SHE WAS TRAVELING THROUGH THE CITY.
THEY FELL IN LOVE AND SHE DECIDED TO STAY. MY MOTHER NAMED ME AFTER HER GRANDMOTHER.
YOUR GREAT-GRANDMOTHER WAS NAMED RAT?
NO. WHO NAMES THEIR KID RAT?
BUT...YOUR NAME IS RAT.
NO. IT'S WHAT I CHOSE FOR MYSELF AFTER MY PARENTS WERE KILLED.

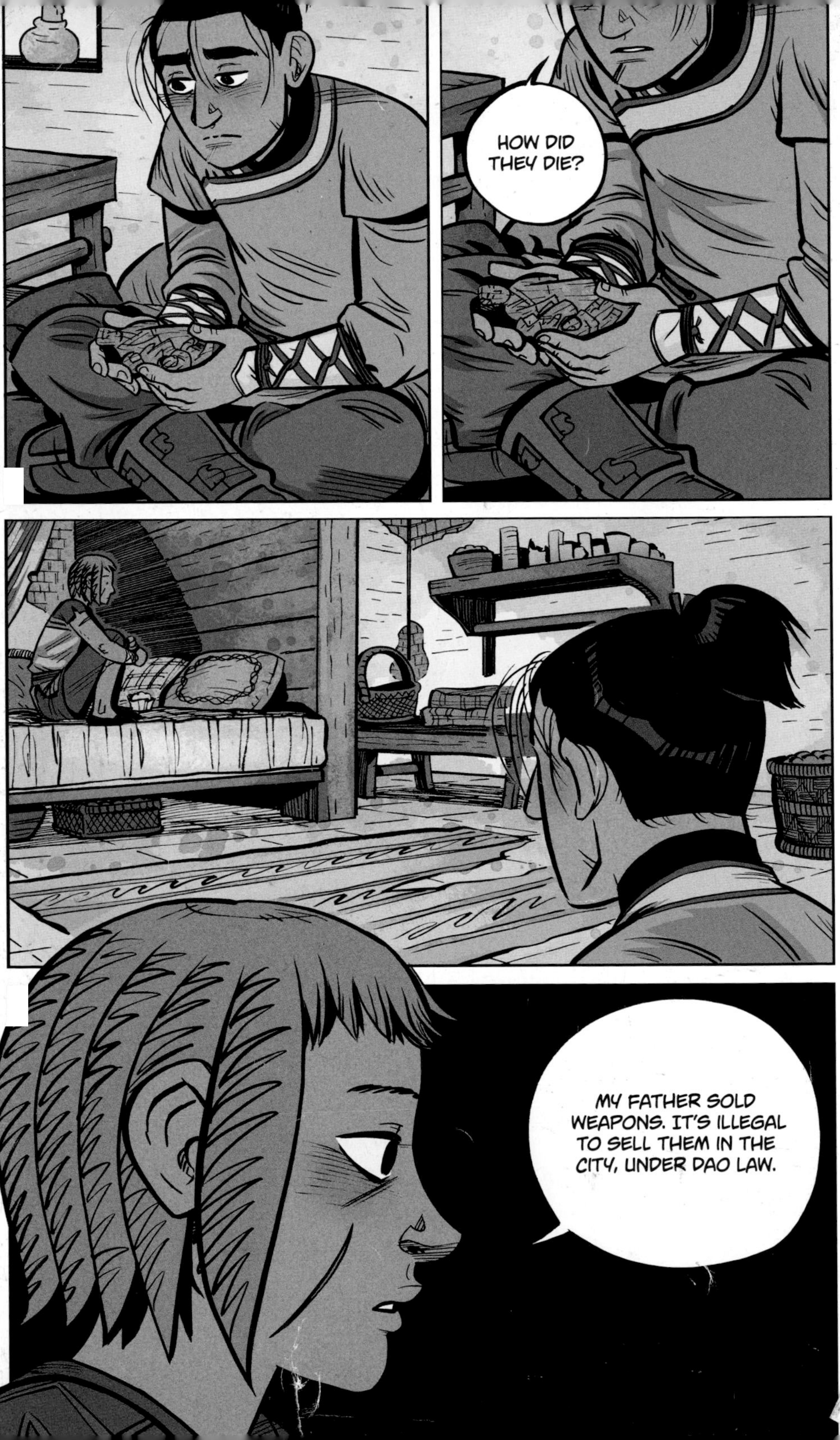
HOW DID THEY DIE?
MY FATHER SOLD WEAPONS. IT'S ILLEGAL TO SELL THEM IN THE CITY, UNDER DAO LAW.

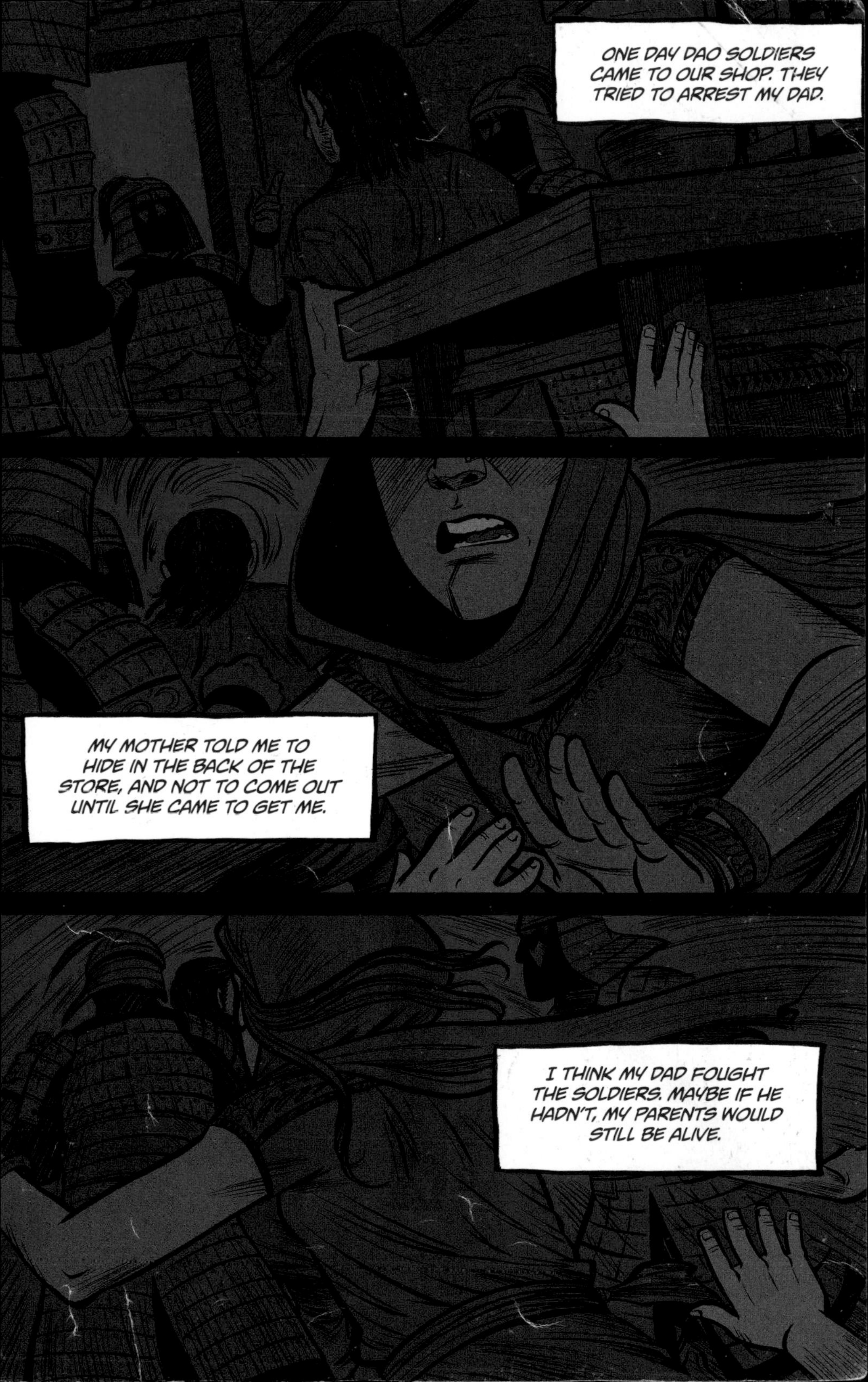
ONE DAY DAO SOLDIERS CAME TO OUR SHOP. THEY TRIED TO ARREST MY DAD.
MY MOTHER TOLD ME TO HIDE IN THE BACK OF THE STORE, AND NOT TO COME OUT UNTIL SHE CAME TO GET ME.
I THINK MY DAD FOUGHT THE SOLDIERS. MAYBE IF HE HADN'T, MY PARENTS WOULD STILL BE ALIVE.

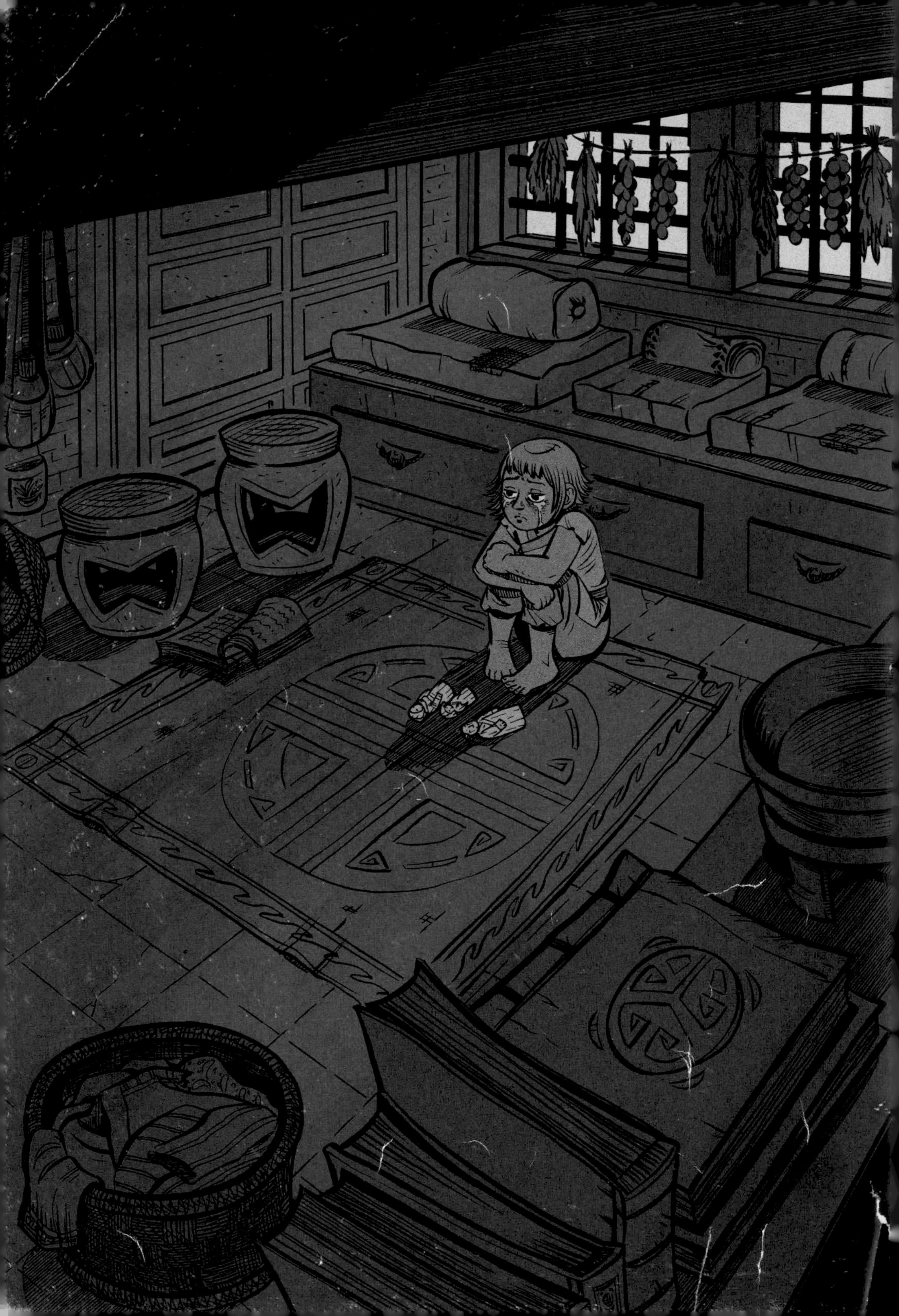

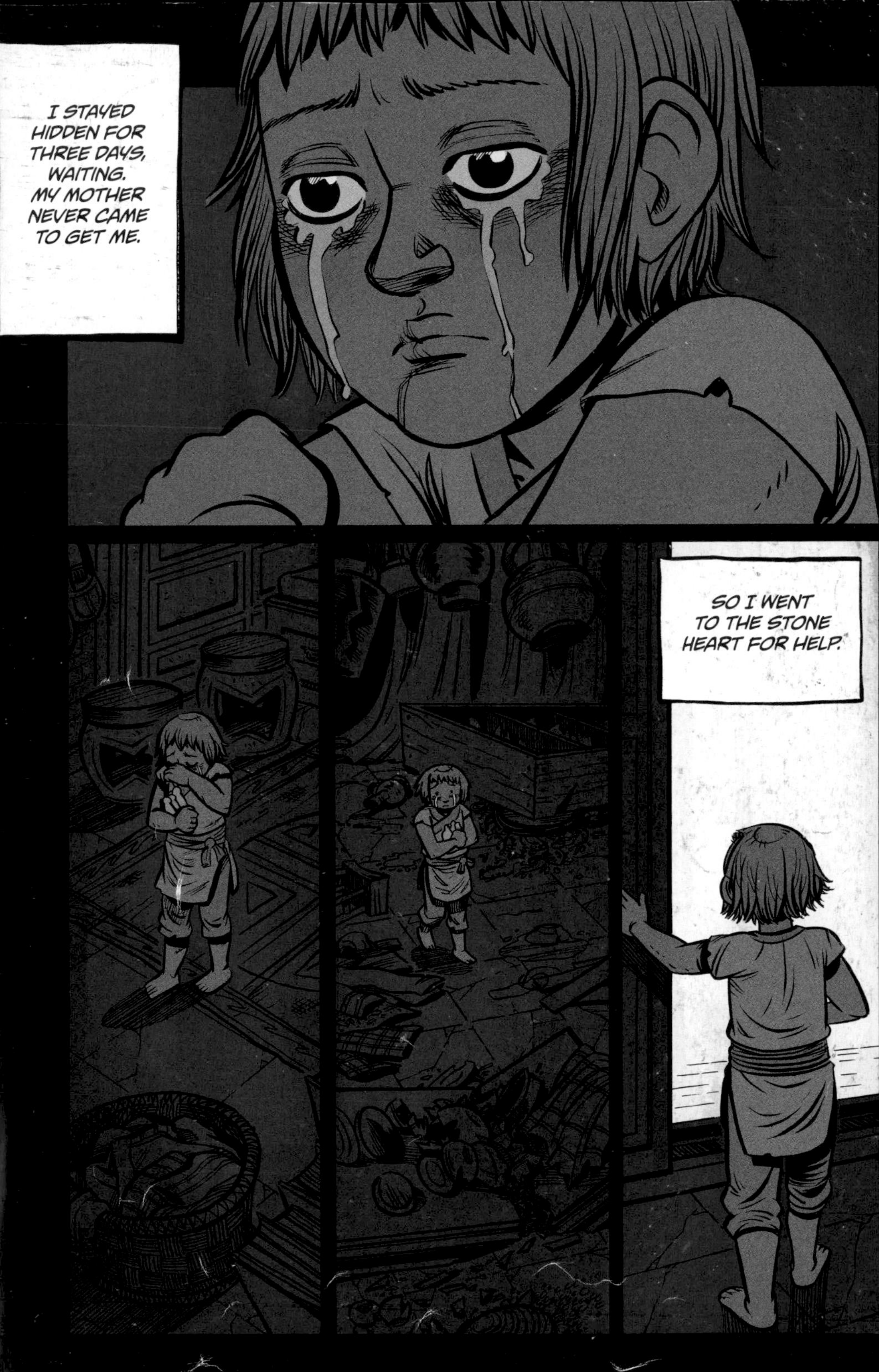
I STAYED HIDDEN FOR THREE DAYS, WAITING. MY MOTHER NEVER CAME TO GET ME.
SO I WENT TO THE STONE HEART FOR HELP.

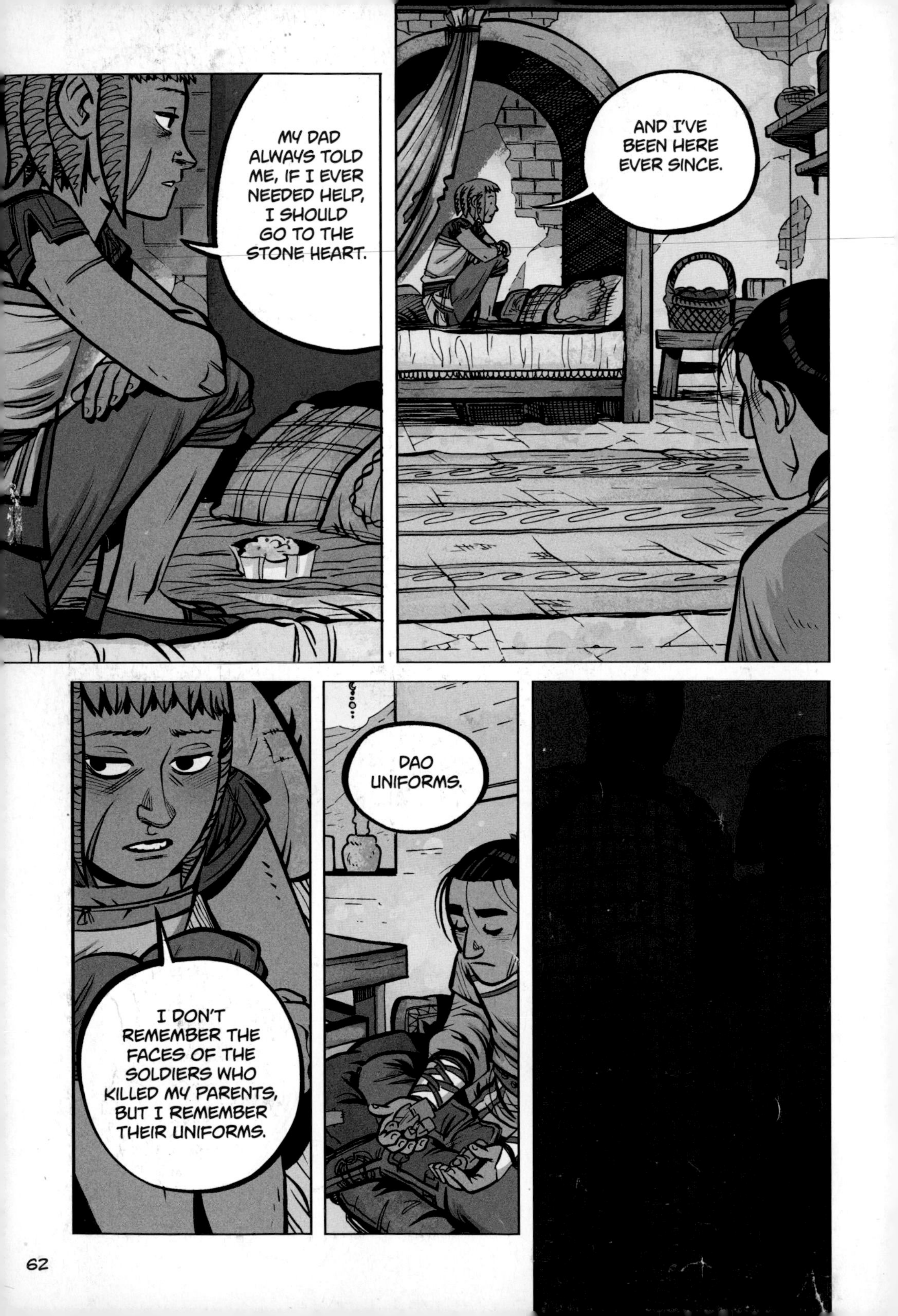
MY DAD ALWAYS TOLD ME, IF I EVER NEEDED HELP, I SHOULD GO TO THE STONE HEART.
AND I'VE BEEN HERE EVER SINCE.
I DON'T REMEMBER THE FACES OF THE SOLDIERS WHO KILLED MY PARENTS, BUT I REMEMBER THEIR UNIFORMS.
DAO UNIFORMS.

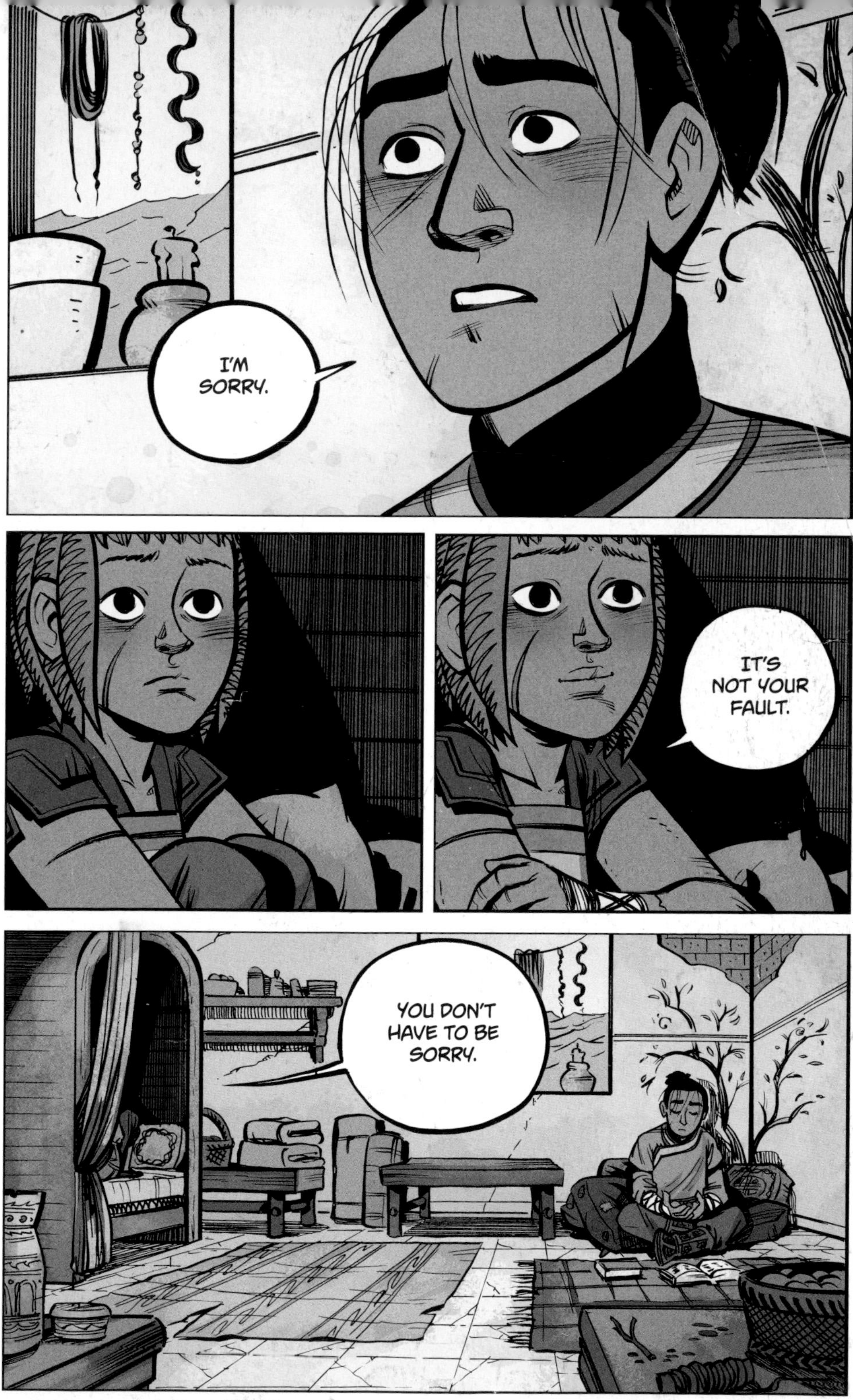
I'M SORRY.
IT'S NOT YOUR FAULT.
YOU DON'T HAVE TO BE SORRY.

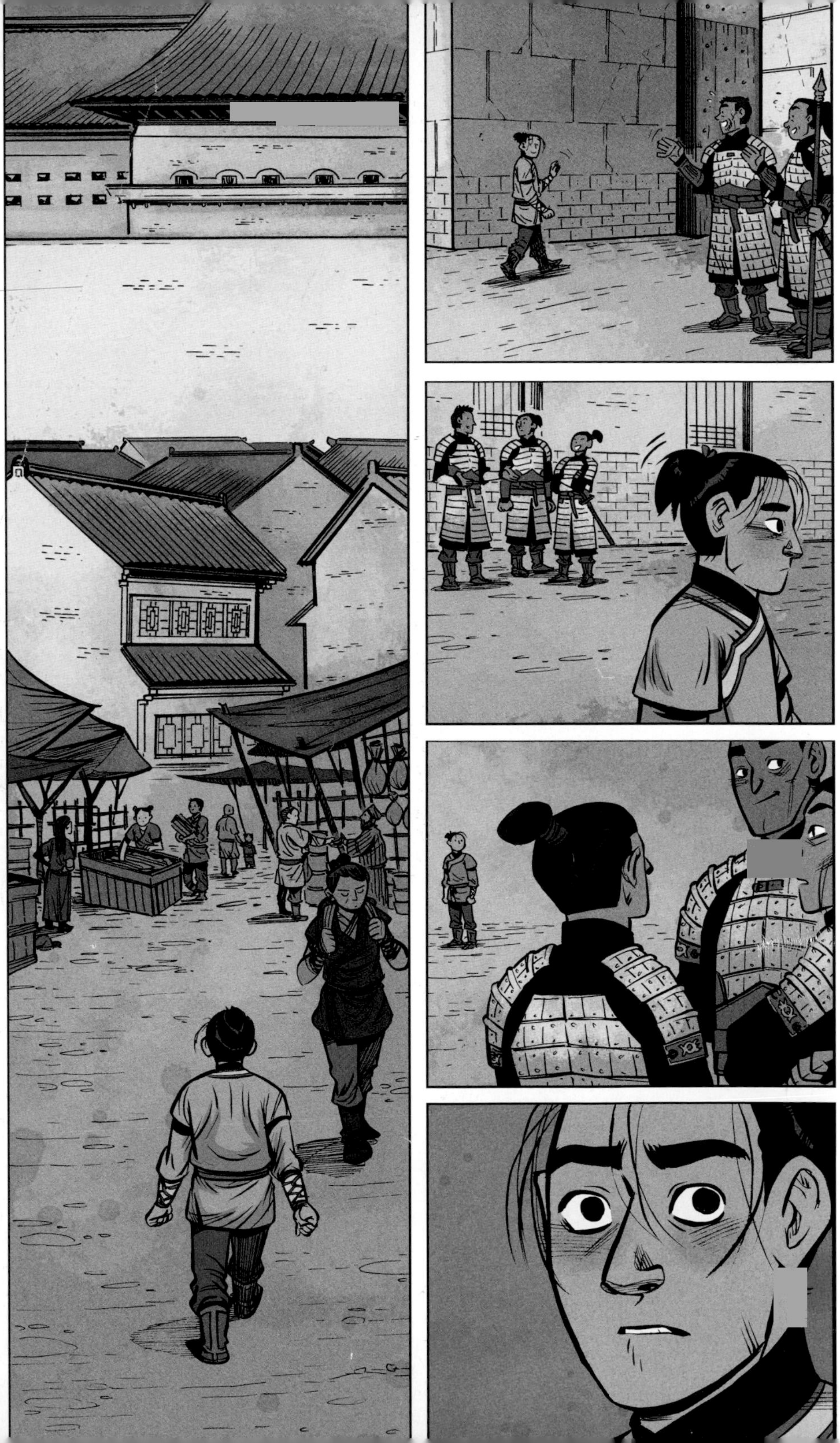

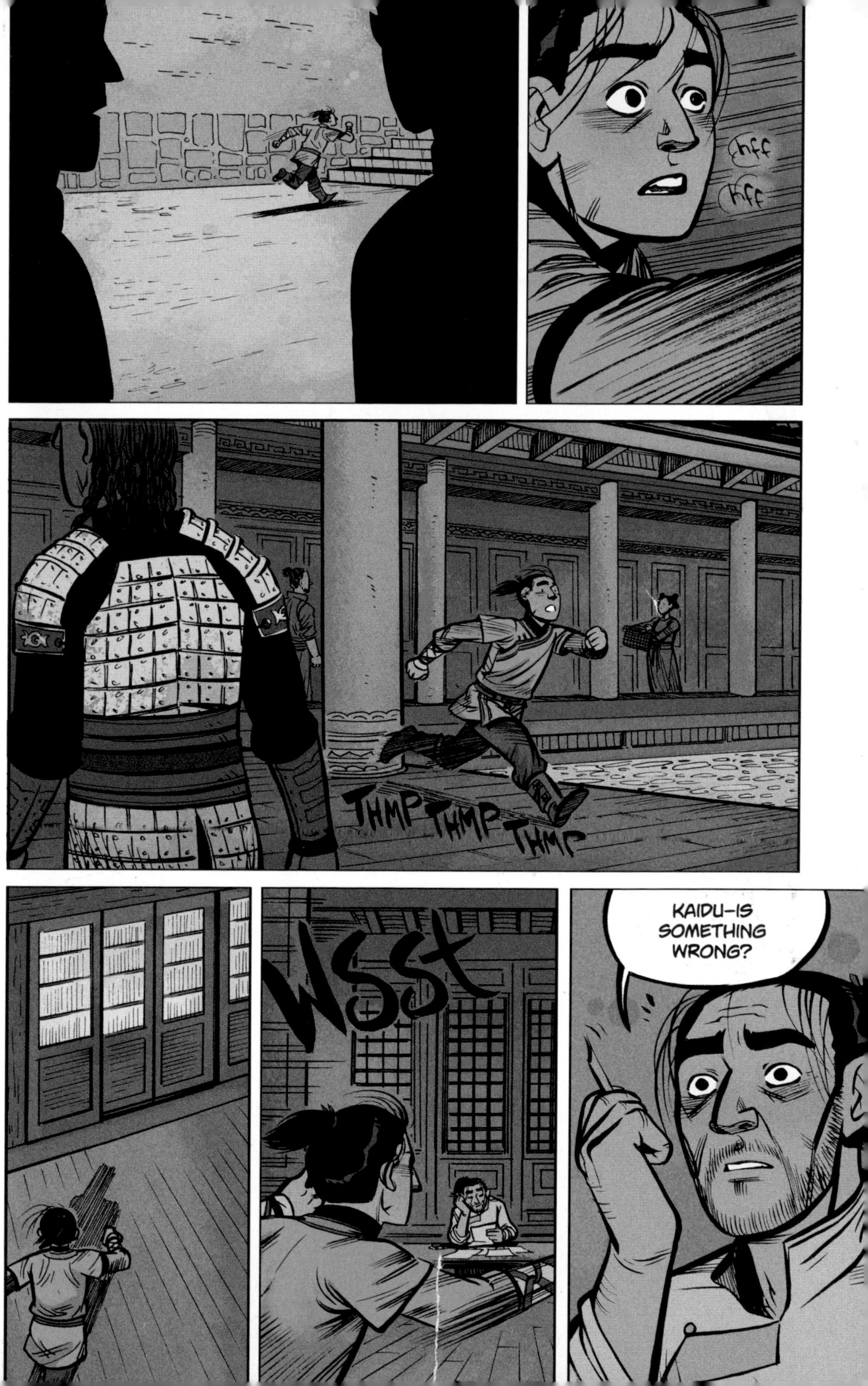
hff
hff
THMP THMP THMP
WSSt
KAIDU–IS SOMETHING WRONG?

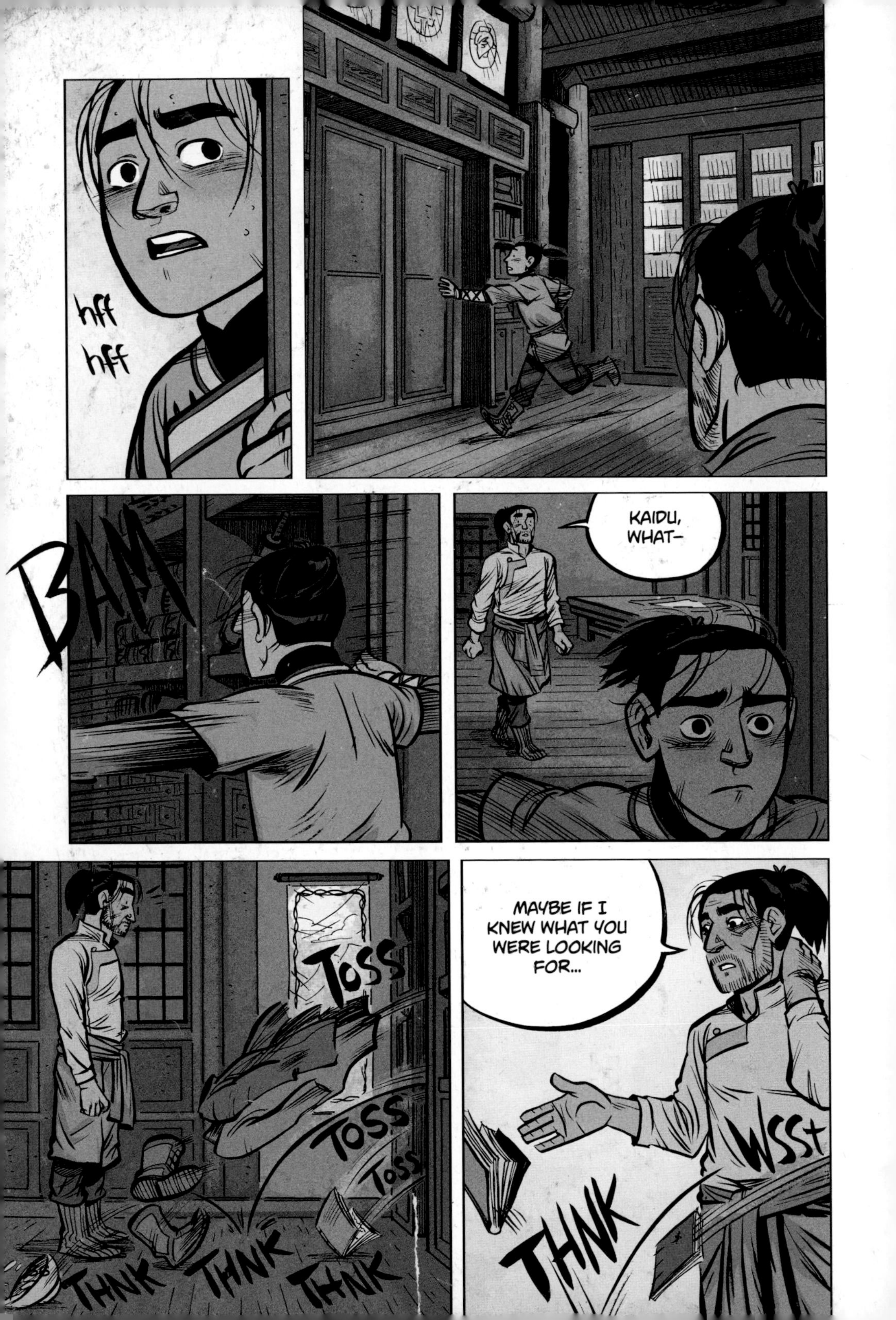
hff
hff
BAM
KAIDU, WHAT-
MAYBE IF I KNEW WHAT YOU WERE LOOKING FOR...
TOSS
TOSS
TOSS
THNK
THNK
THNK
WSSt
THNK

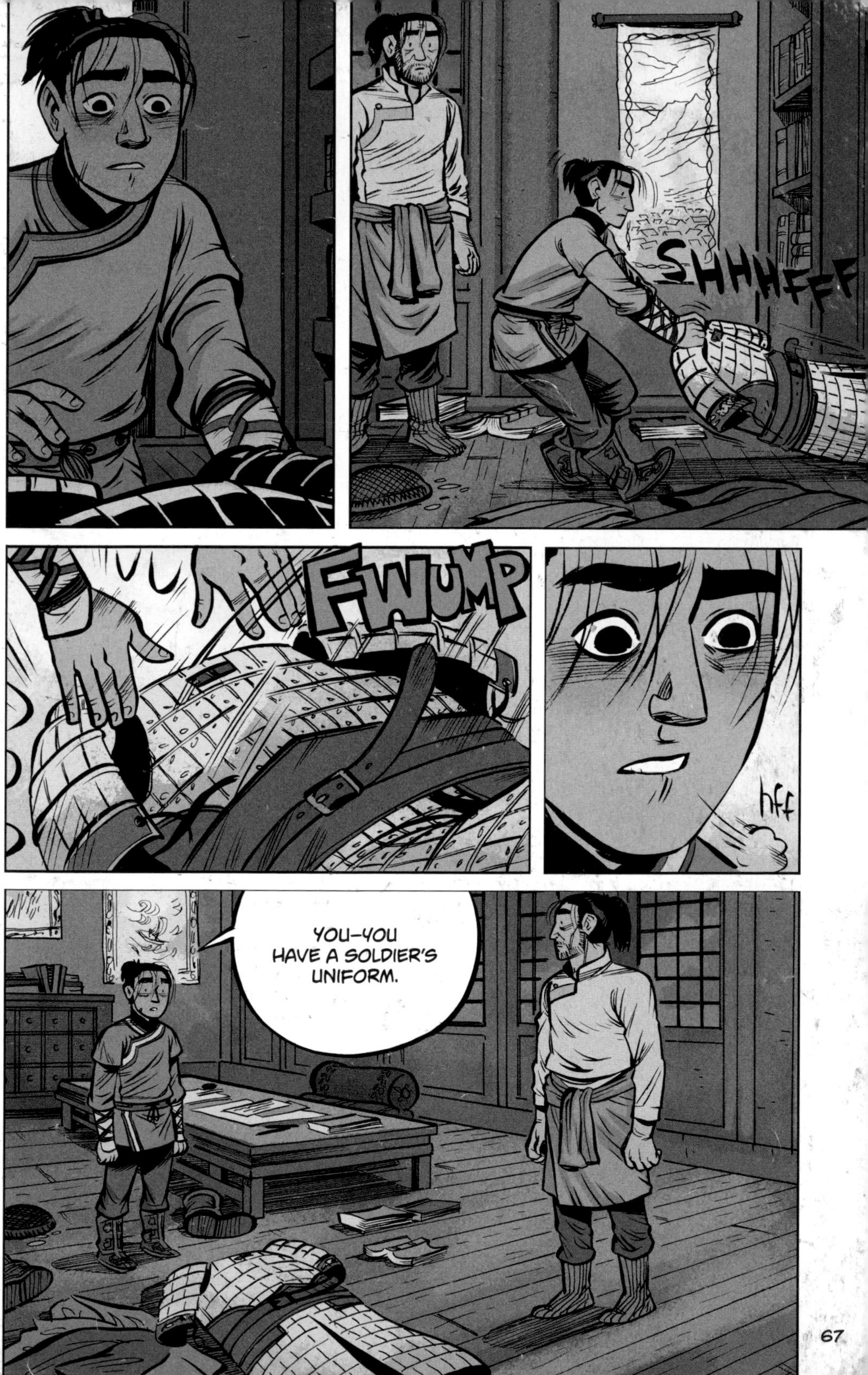
SHHHFFF
FWUMP
hff
YOU—YOU HAVE A SOLDIER'S UNIFORM.

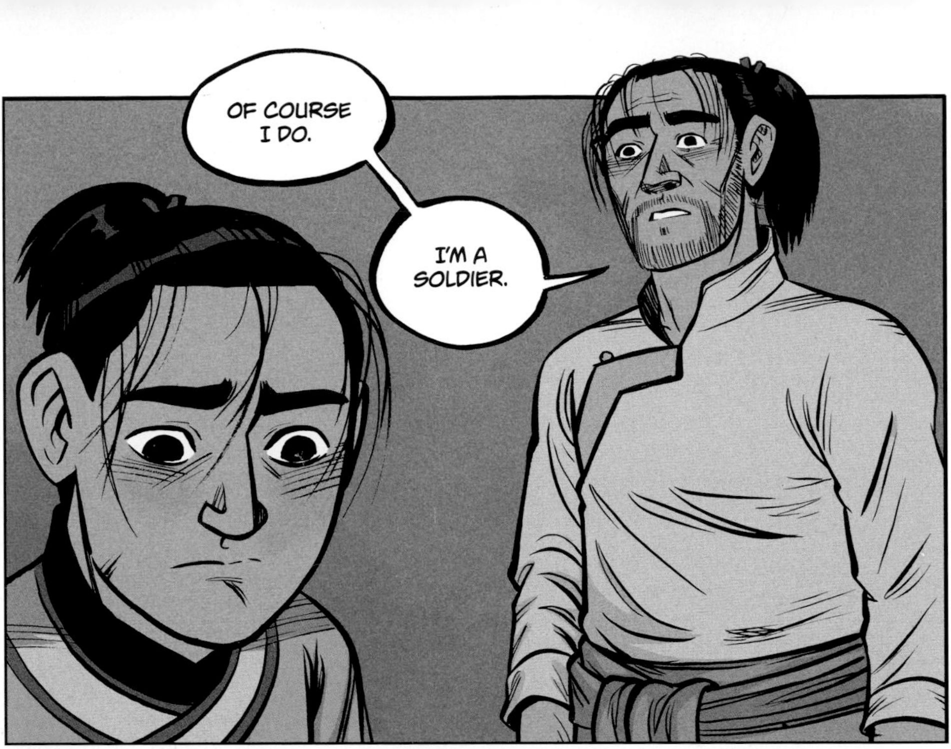
OF COURSE I DO.
I'M A SOLDIER.

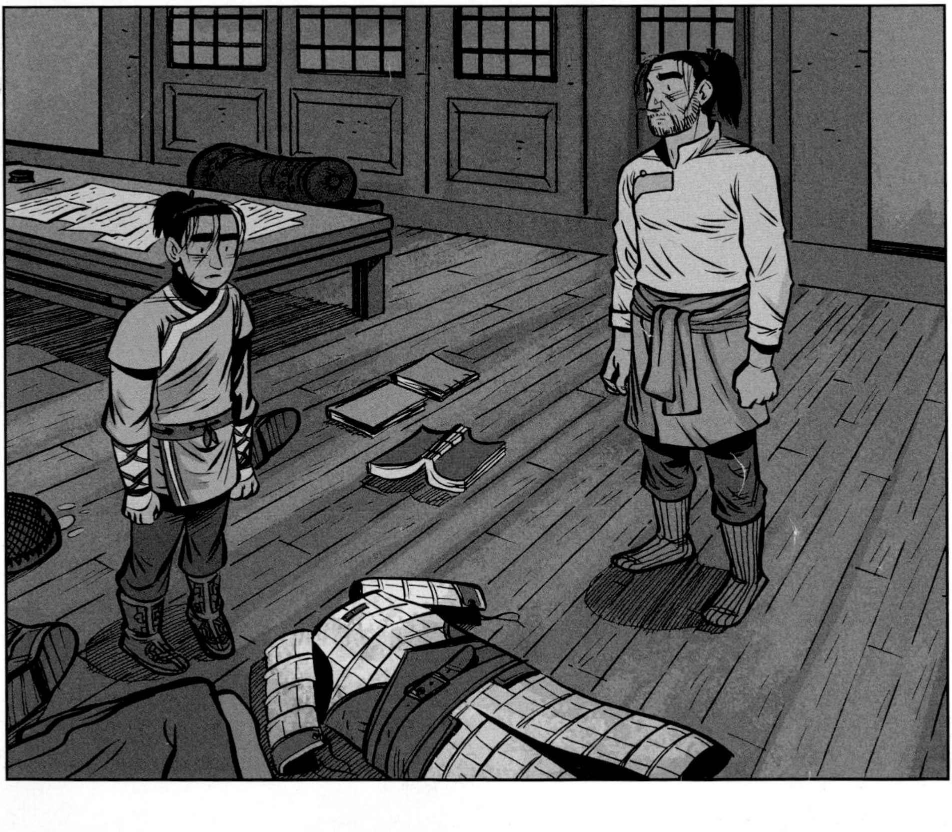

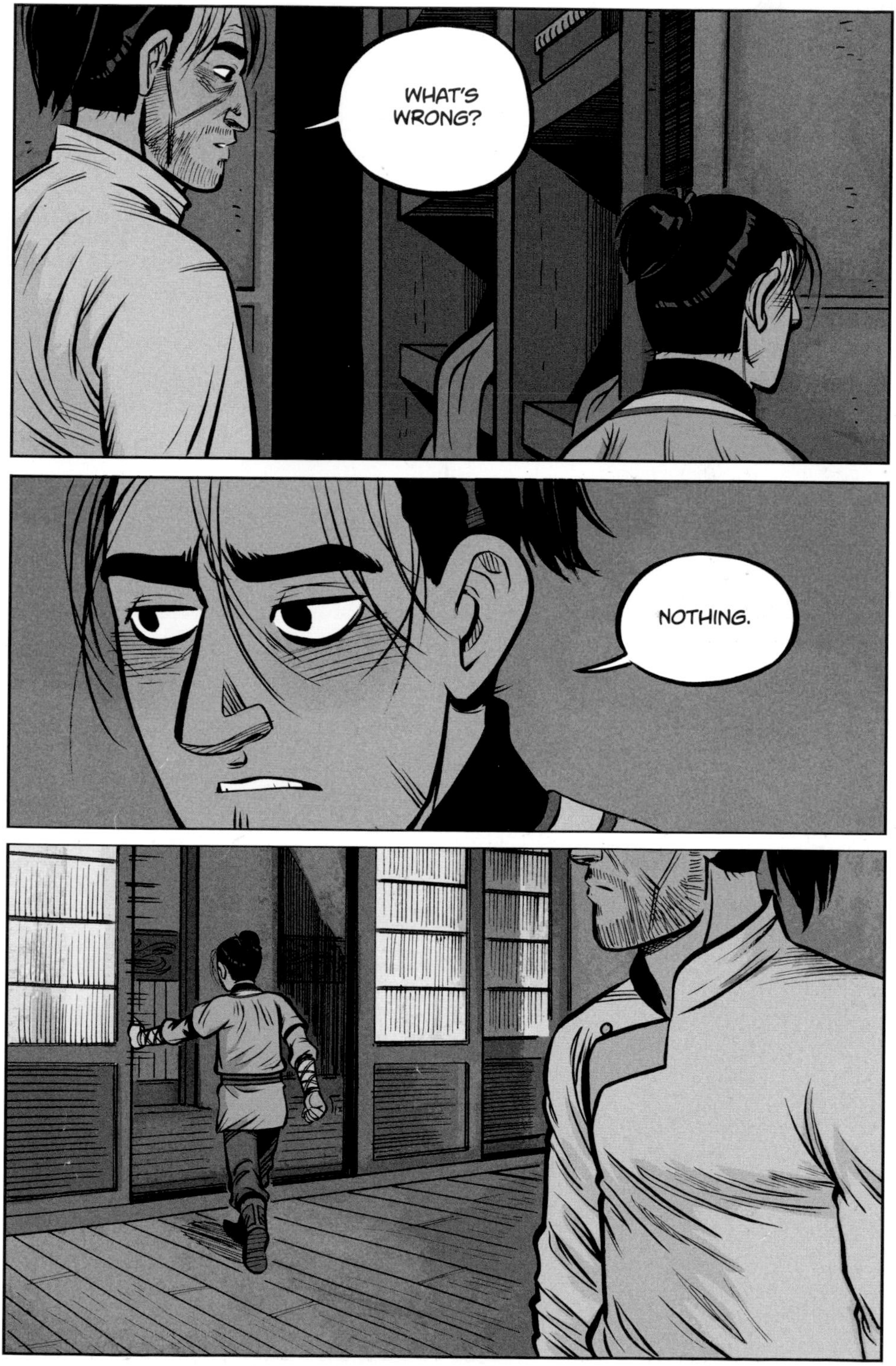
WHAT'S WRONG?
NOTHING.

SHHHHH

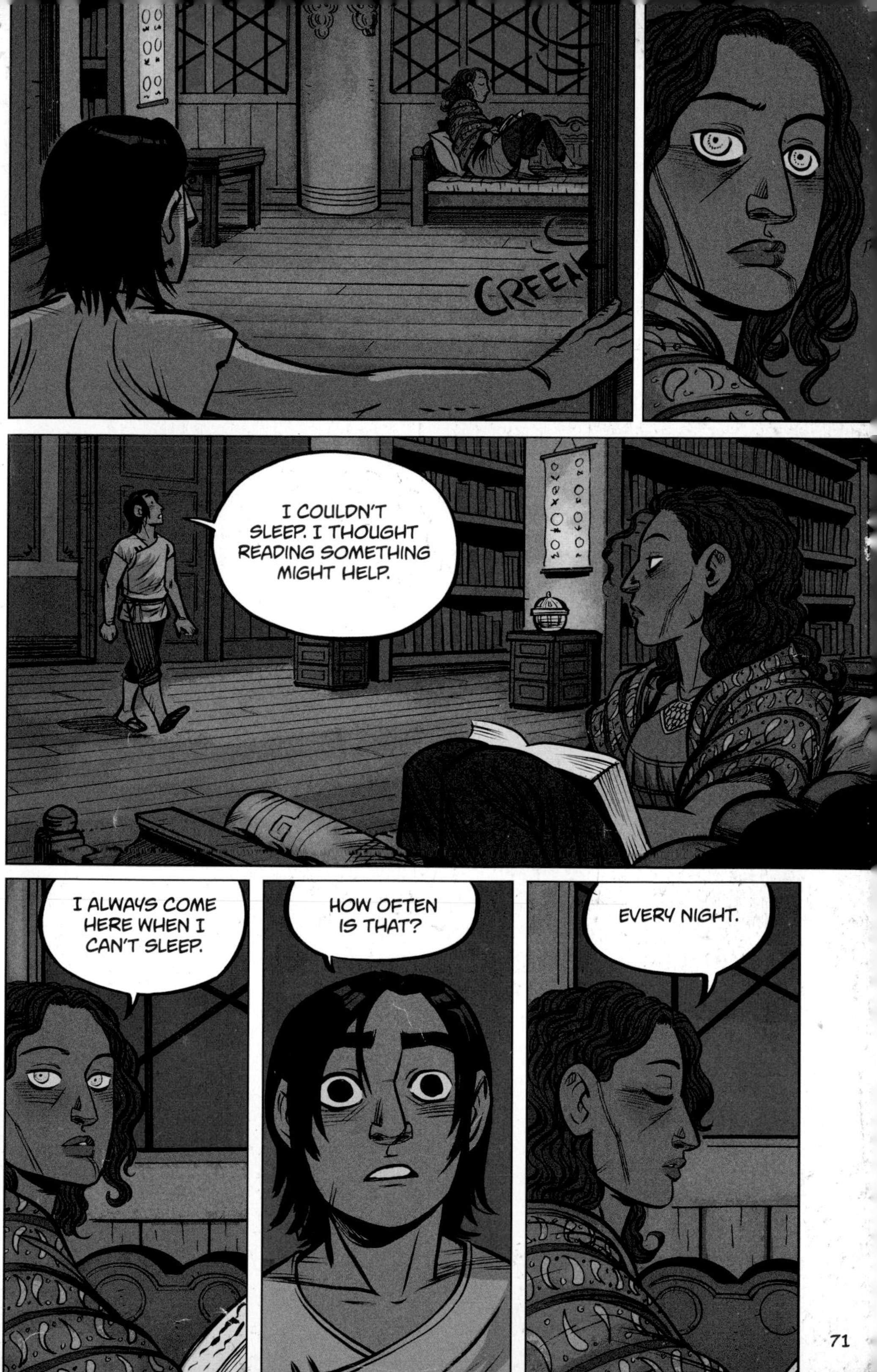
CREEAK
I COULDN'T SLEEP. I THOUGHT READING SOMETHING MIGHT HELP.
I ALWAYS COME HERE WHEN I CAN'T SLEEP.
HOW OFTEN IS THAT?
EVERY NIGHT.

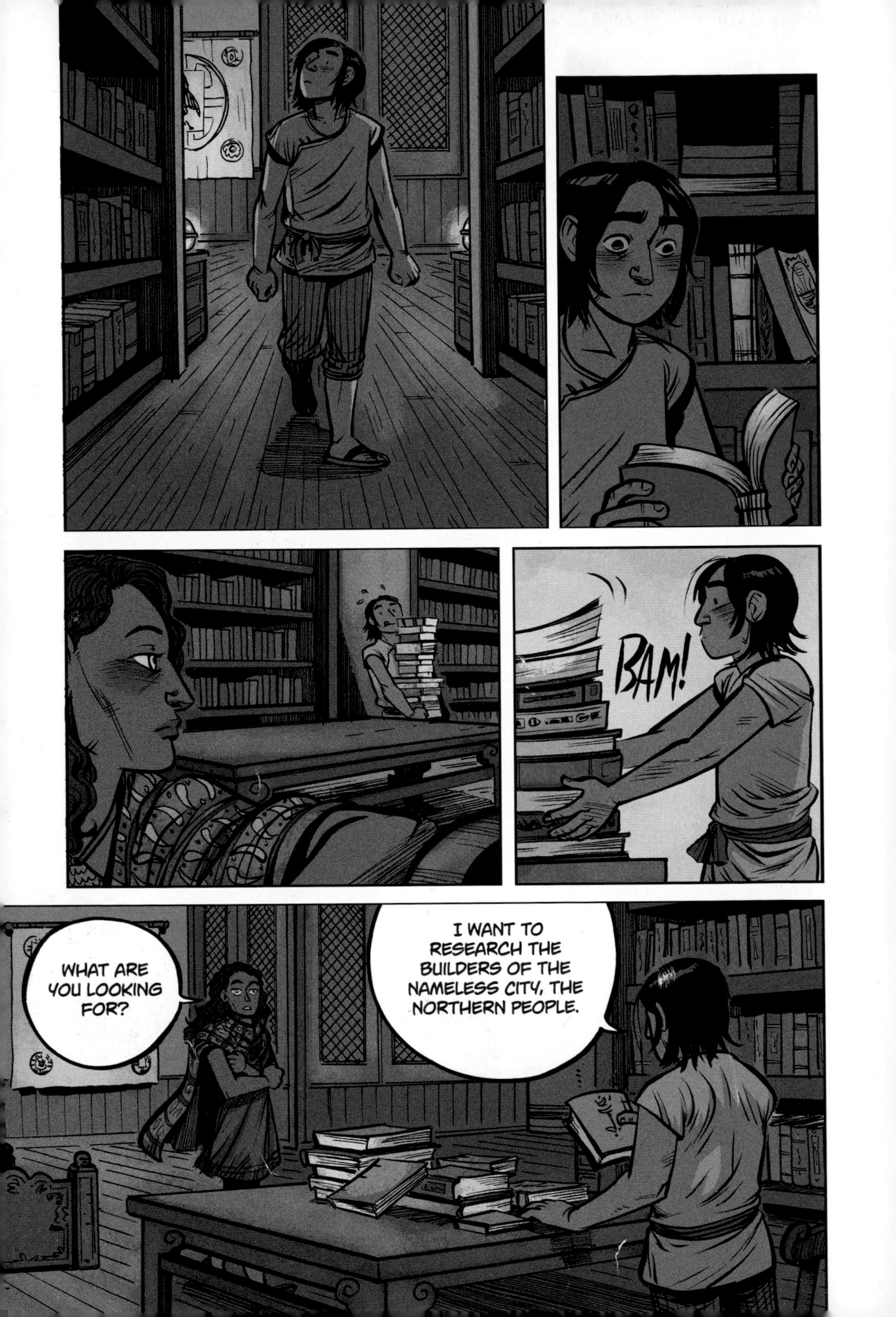
BAM!
WHAT ARE YOU LOOKING FOR?
I WANT TO RESEARCH THE BUILDERS OF THE NAMELESS CITY, THE NORTHERN PEOPLE.

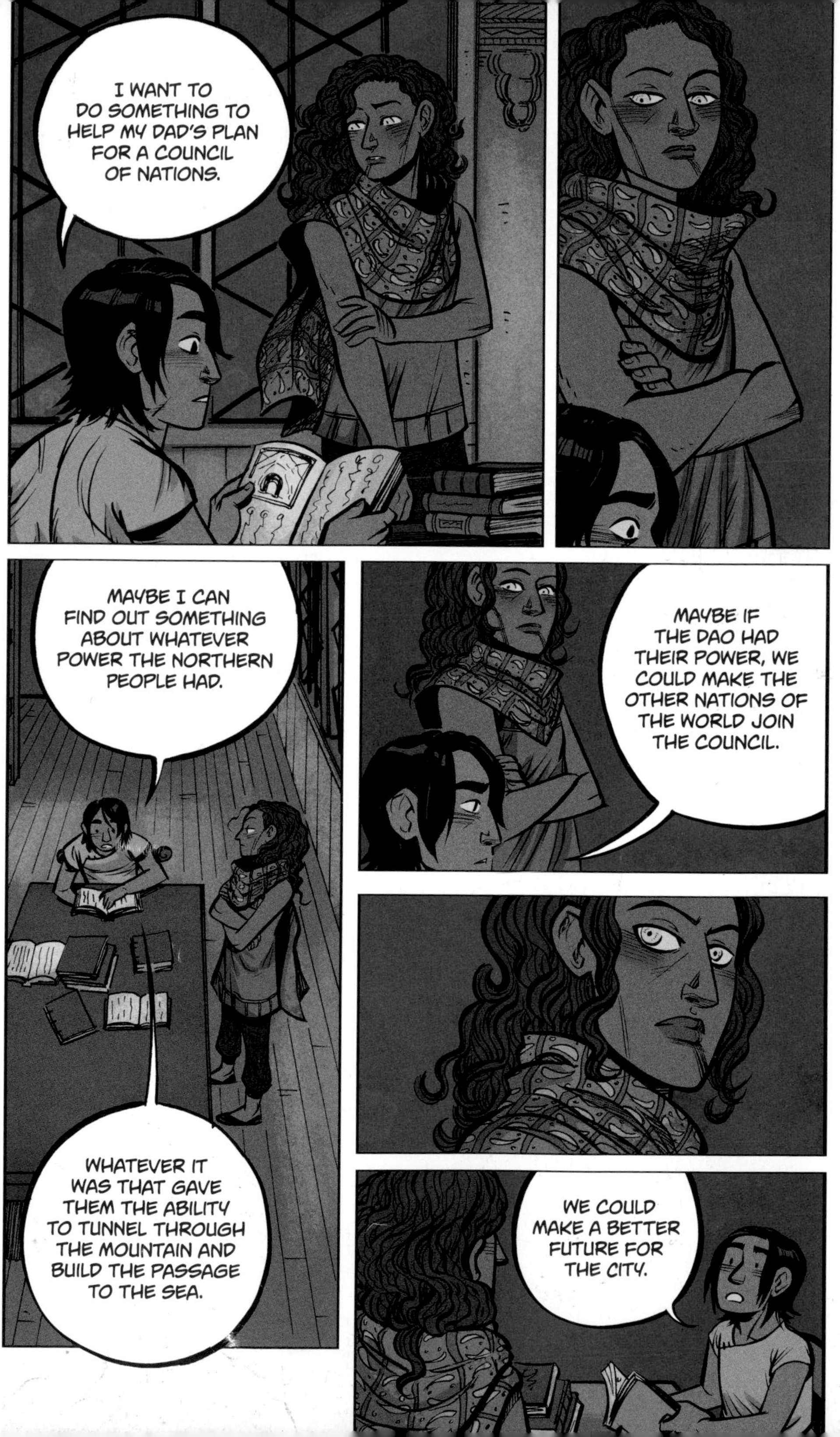
I WANT TO DO SOMETHING TO HELP MY DAD'S PLAN FOR A COUNCIL OF NATIONS.
MAYBE I CAN FIND OUT SOMETHING ABOUT WHATEVER POWER THE NORTHERN PEOPLE HAD.
WHATEVER IT WAS THAT GAVE THEM THE ABILITY TO TUNNEL THROUGH THE MOUNTAIN AND BUILD THE PASSAGE TO THE SEA.
MAYBE IF THE DAO HAD THEIR POWER, WE COULD MAKE THE OTHER NATIONS OF THE WORLD JOIN THE COUNCIL.
WE COULD MAKE A BETTER FUTURE FOR THE CITY.

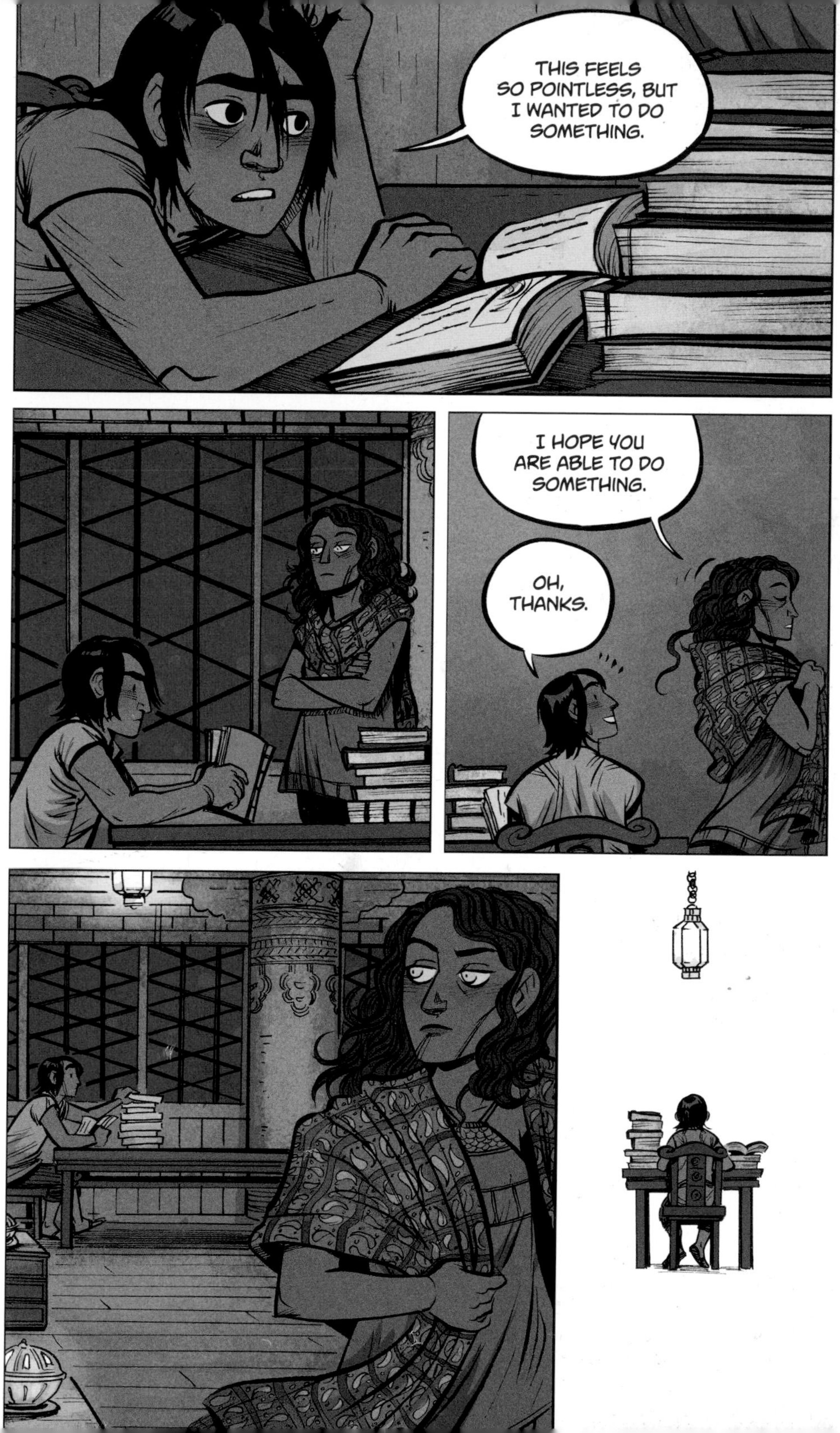
THIS FEELS SO POINTLESS, BUT I WANTED TO DO SOMETHING.
I HOPE YOU ARE ABLE TO DO SOMETHING.
OH, THANKS.

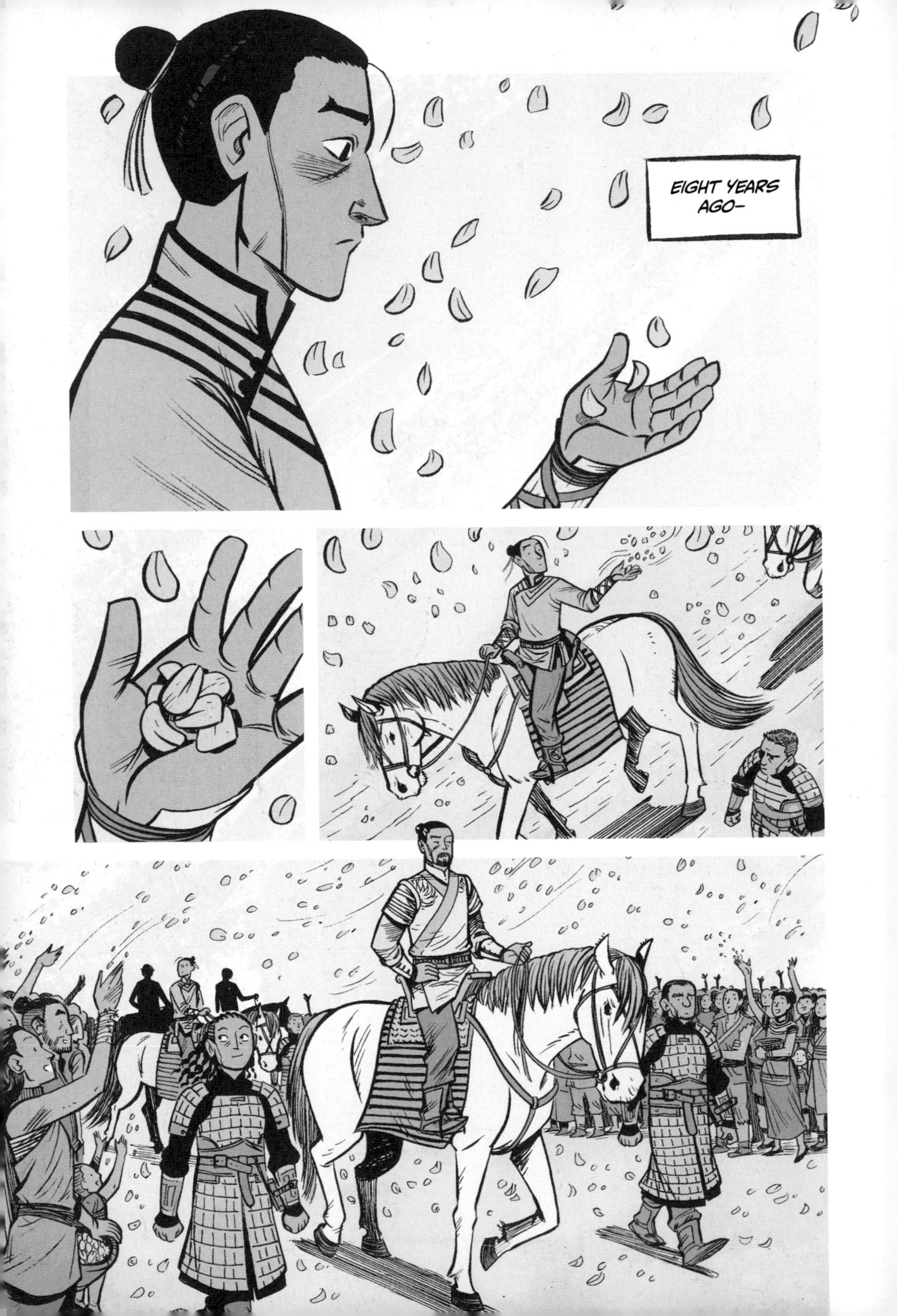
EIGHT YEARS AGO–

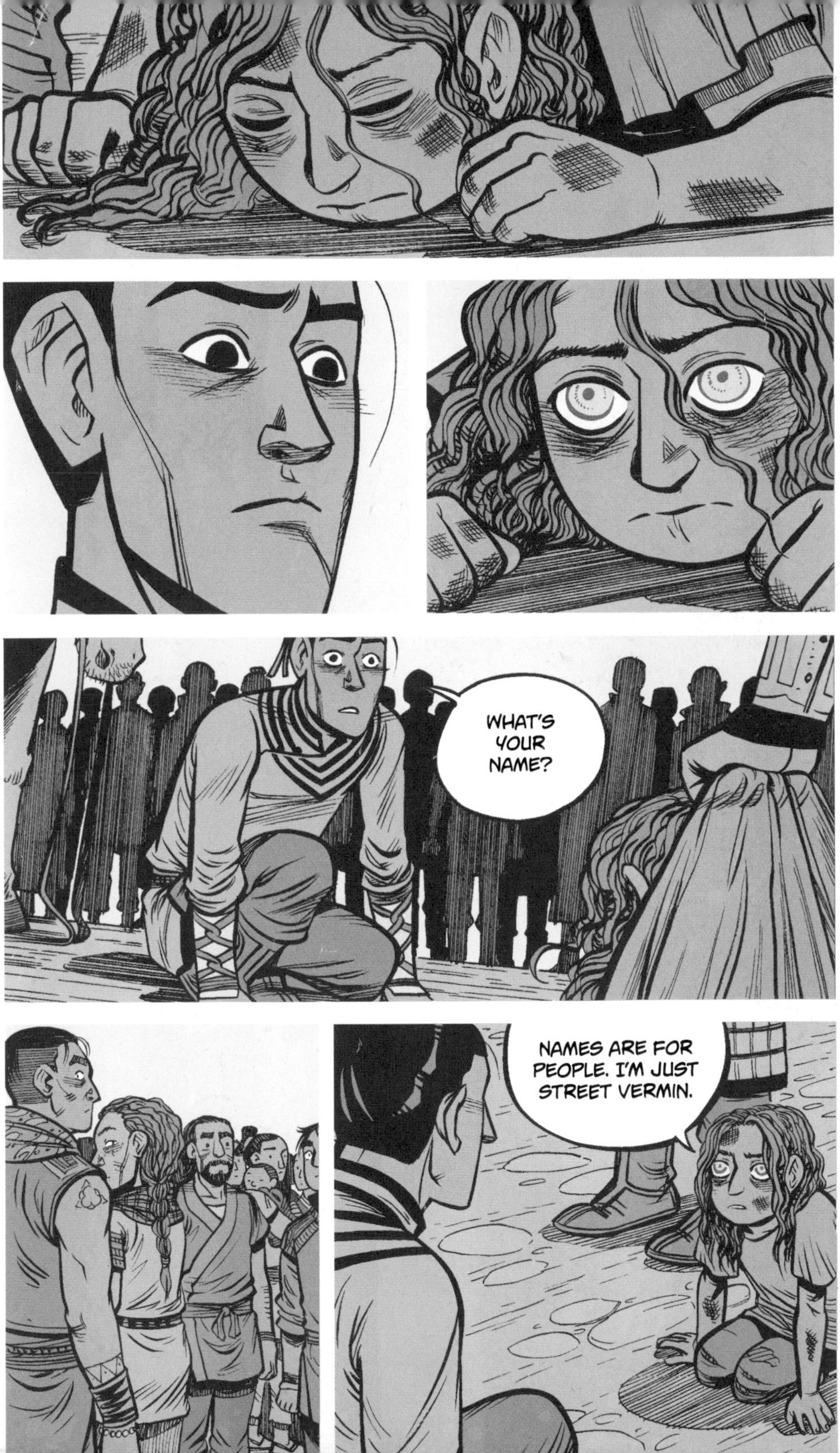
WHAT'S YOUR NAME?
NAMES ARE FOR PEOPLE. I'M JUST STREET VERMIN.

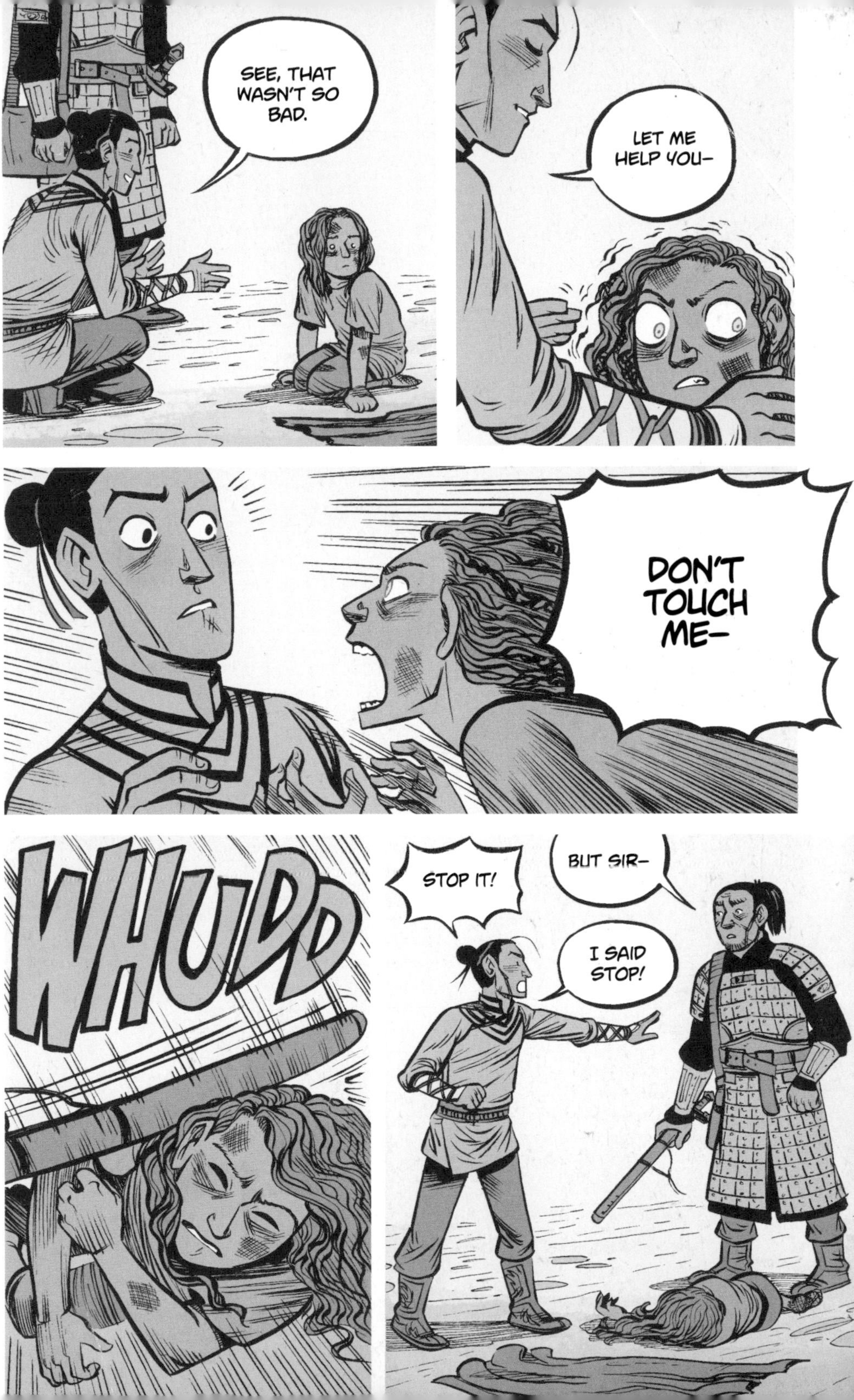
SEE, THAT WASN'T SO BAD.
LET ME HELP YOU–
DON'T TOUCH ME–
WHUDD
STOP IT!
BUT SIR–
I SAID STOP!

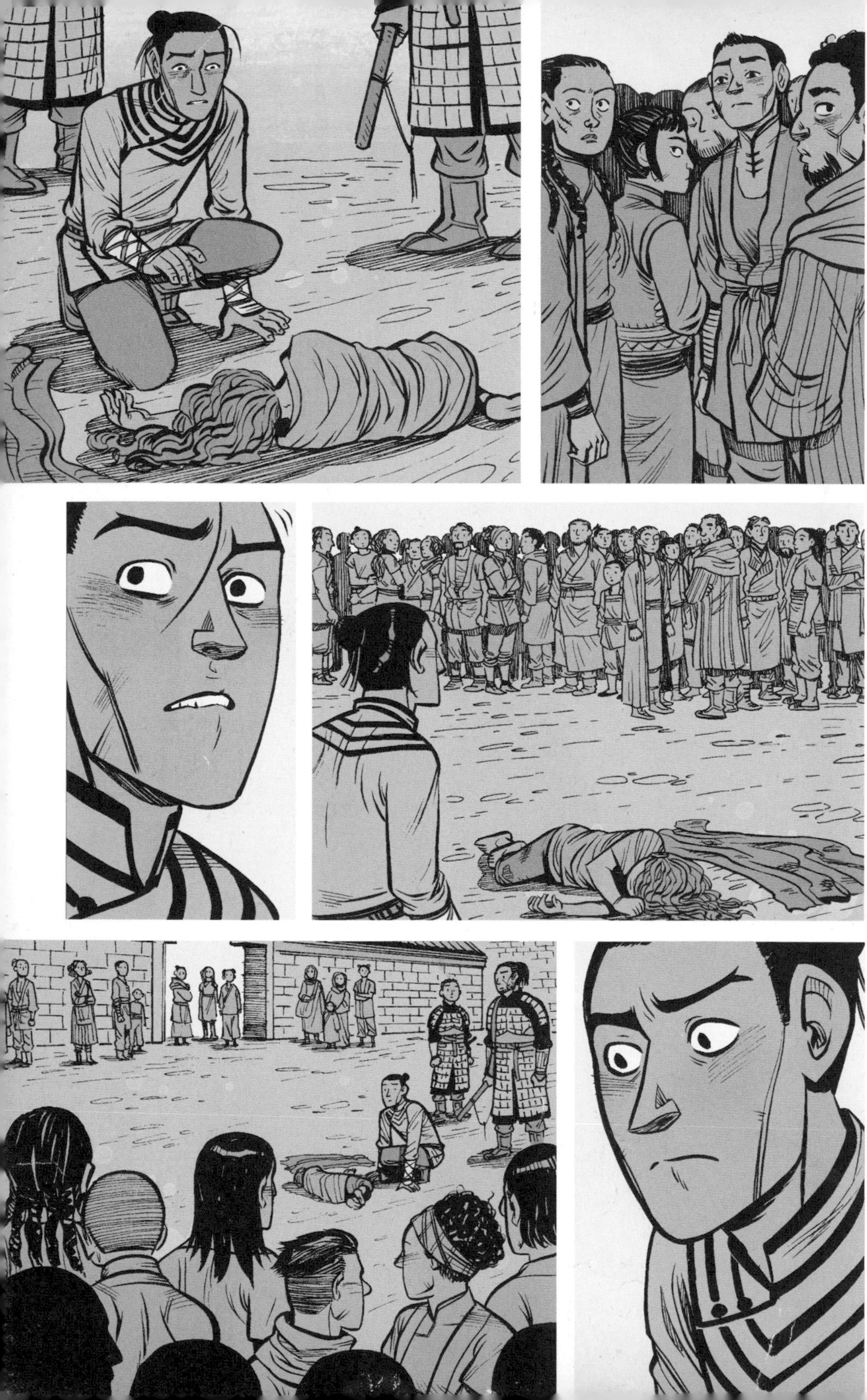

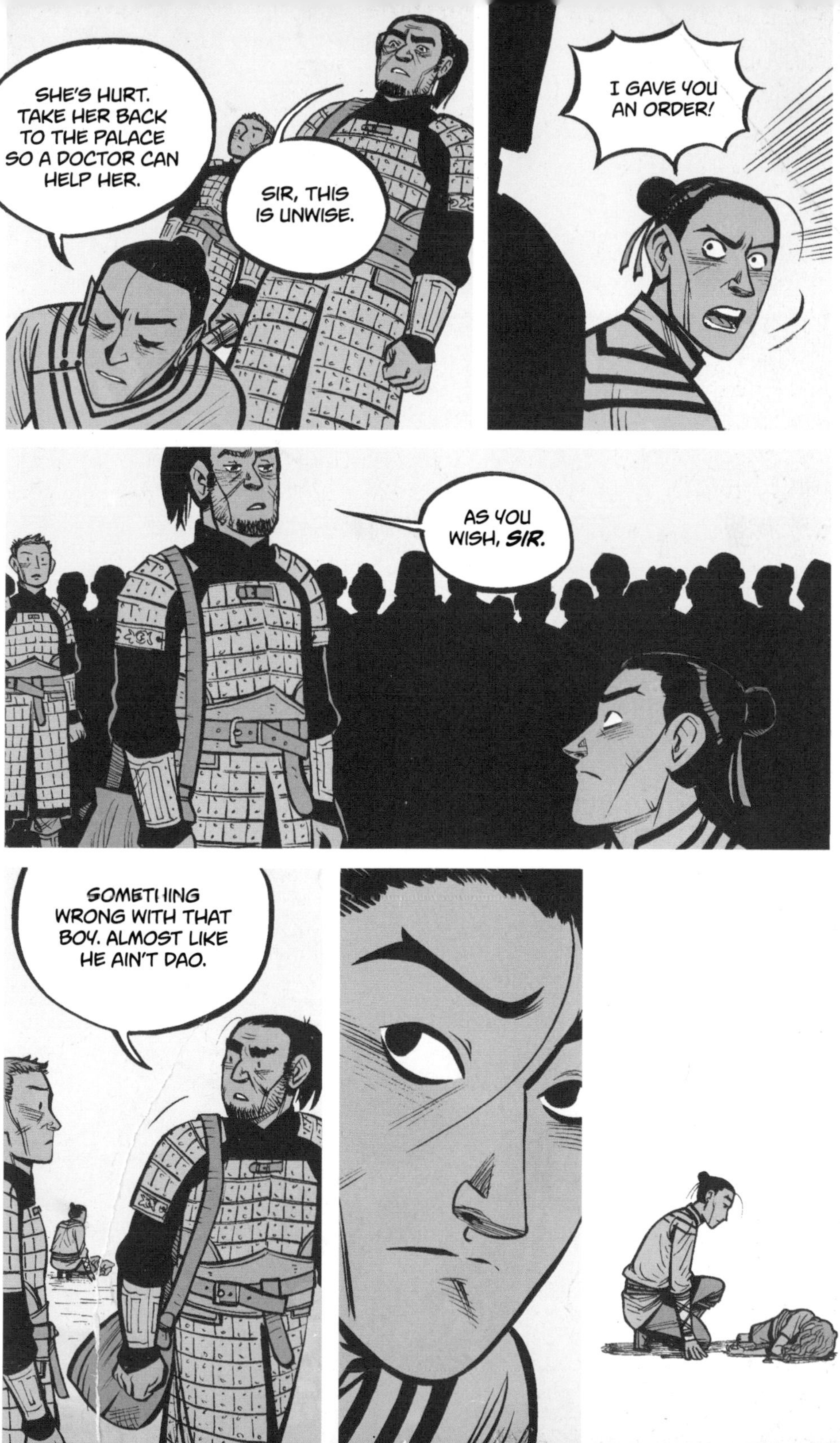
SHE'S HURT. TAKE HER BACK TO THE PALACE SO A DOCTOR CAN HELP HER.
SIR, THIS IS UNWISE.
I GAVE YOU AN ORDER!
AS YOU WISH, *SIR.*
SOMETHING WRONG WITH THAT BOY. ALMOST LIKE HE AIN'T DAO.

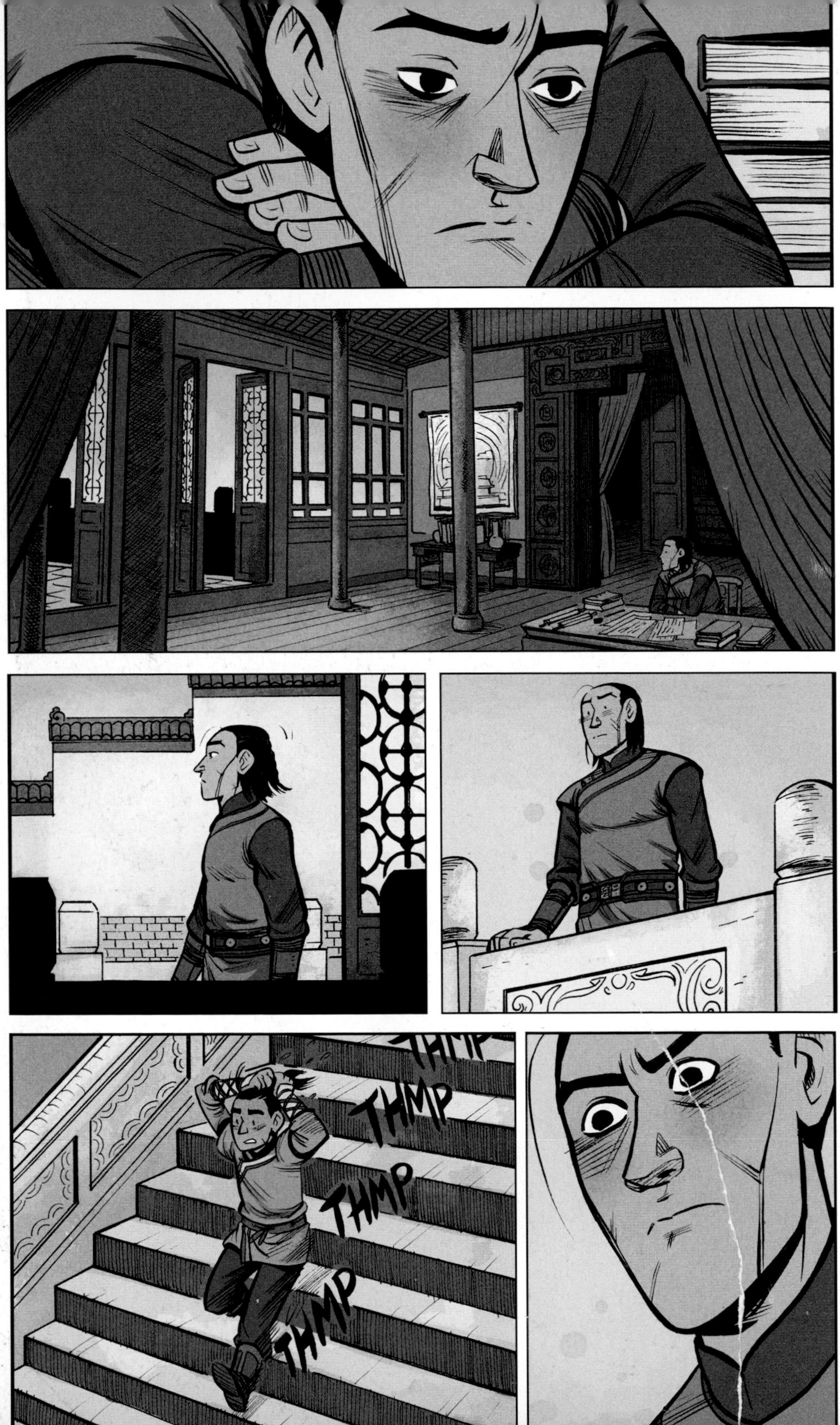
THMP
THMP
THMP
THMP
THMP

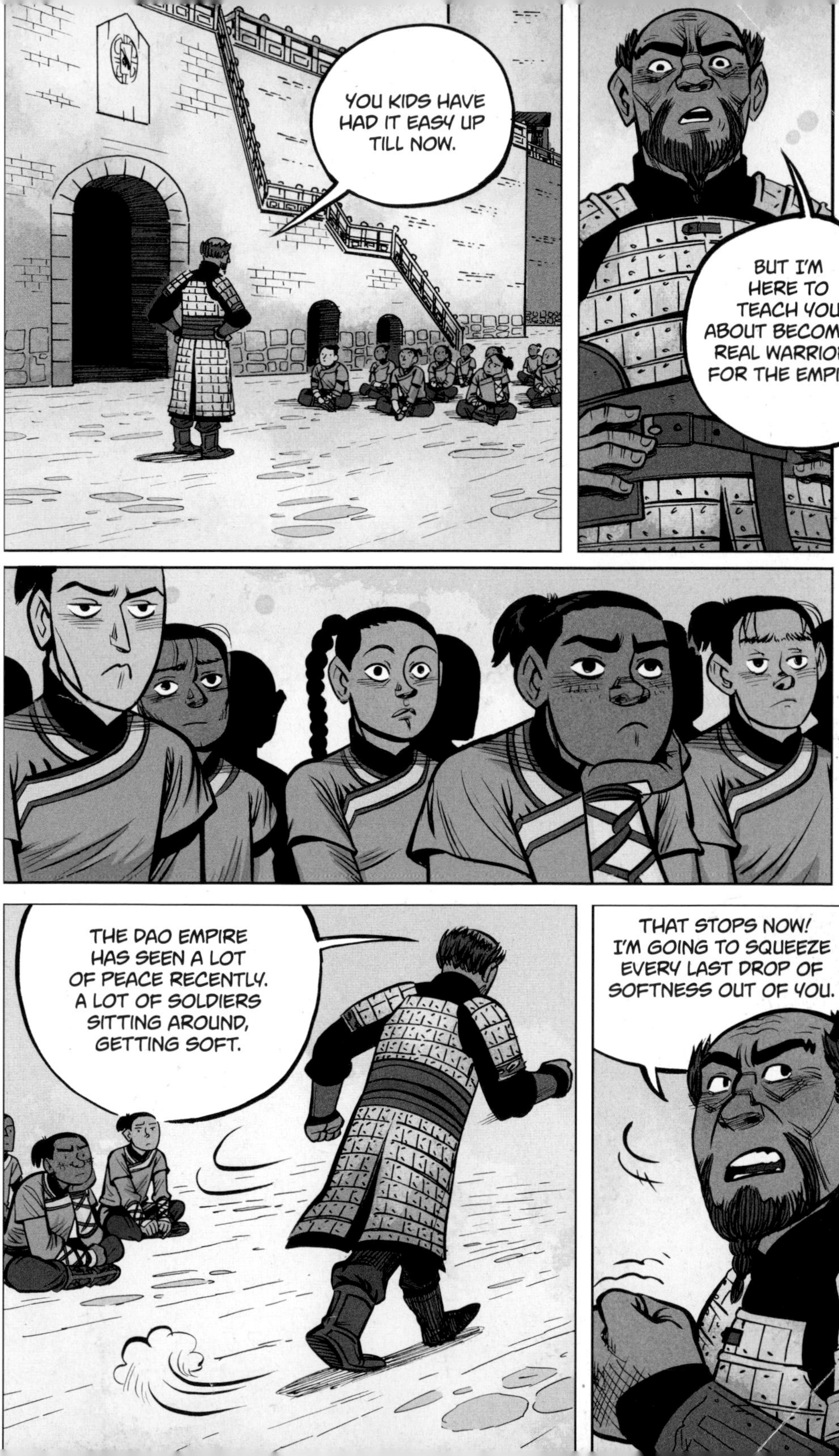
YOU KIDS HAVE HAD IT EASY UP TILL NOW.
BUT I'M HERE TO TEACH YOU ABOUT BECOMING REAL WARRIORS FOR THE EMPIRE.
THE DAO EMPIRE HAS SEEN A LOT OF PEACE RECENTLY. A LOT OF SOLDIERS SITTING AROUND, GETTING SOFT.
THAT STOPS NOW! I'M GOING TO SQUEEZE EVERY LAST DROP OF SOFTNESS OUT OF YOU.

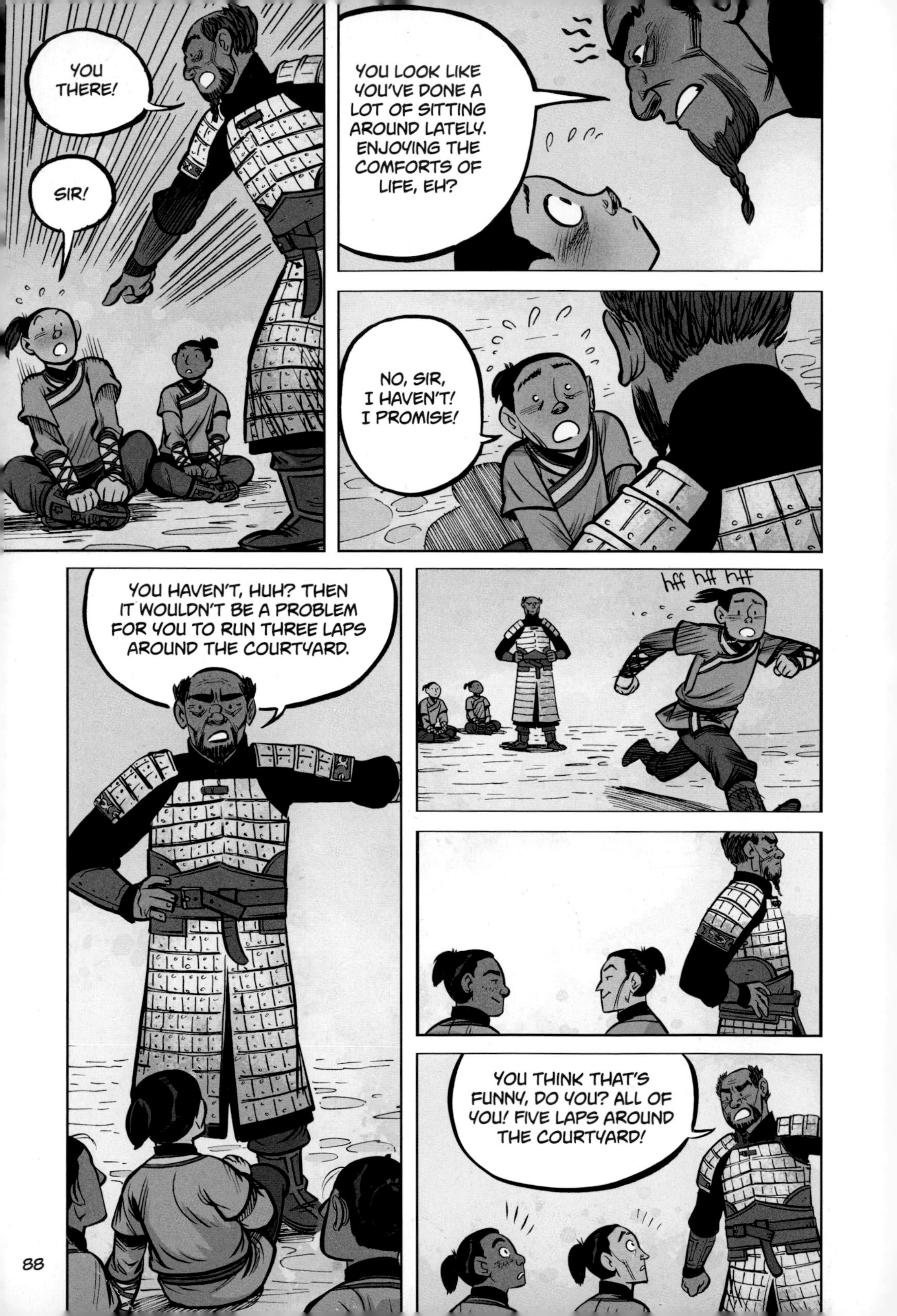
YOU THERE!
SIR!
YOU LOOK LIKE YOU'VE DONE A LOT OF SITTING AROUND LATELY. ENJOYING THE COMFORTS OF LIFE, EH?
NO, SIR, I HAVEN'T! I PROMISE!
YOU HAVEN'T, HUH? THEN IT WOULDN'T BE A PROBLEM FOR YOU TO RUN THREE LAPS AROUND THE COURTYARD.
hff hff hff
YOU THINK THAT'S FUNNY, DO YOU? ALL OF YOU! FIVE LAPS AROUND THE COURTYARD!

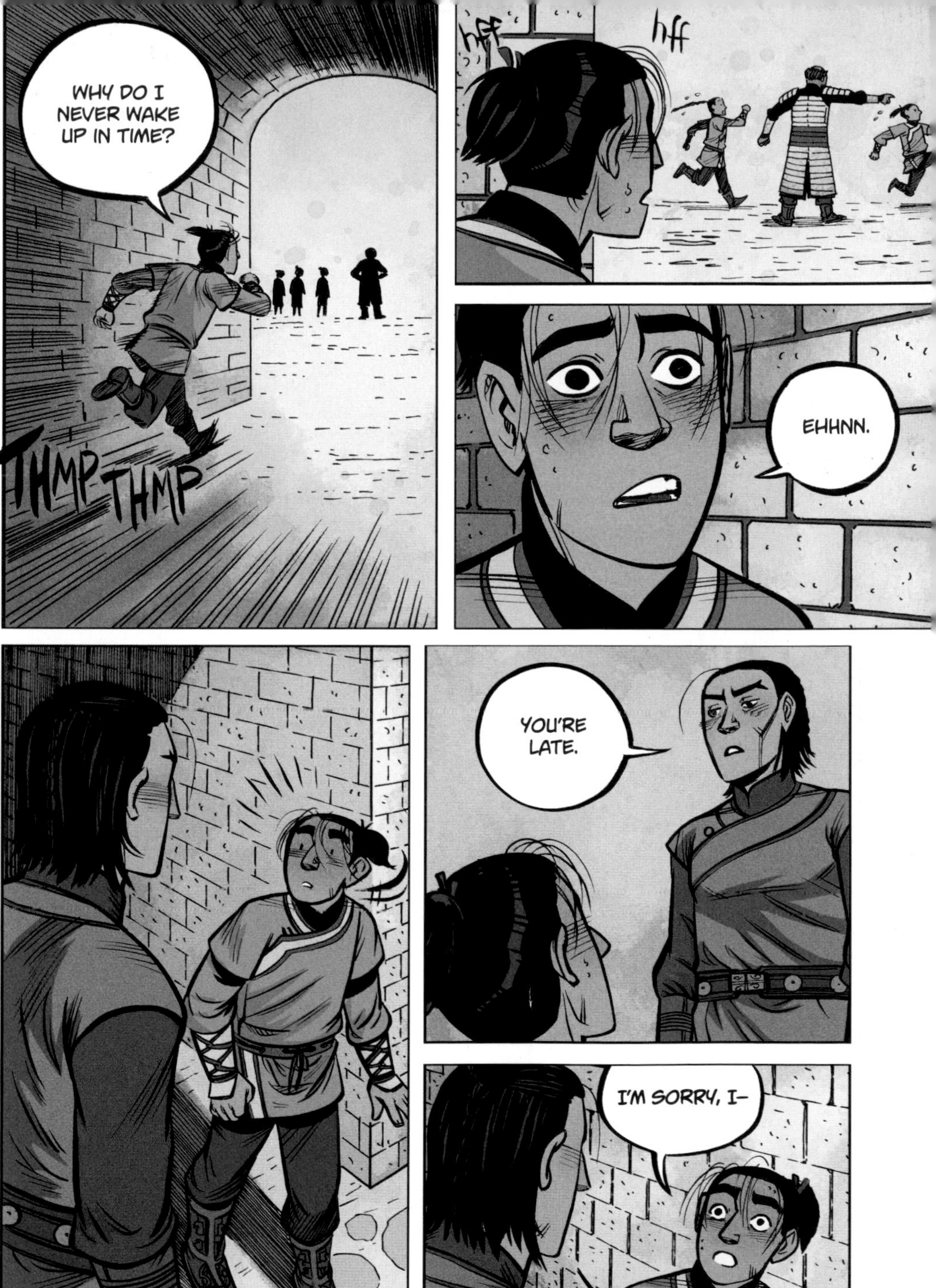
WHY DO I NEVER WAKE UP IN TIME?
THMP THMP
hff
hff
EHHNN.
YOU'RE LATE.
I'M SORRY, I—
BE QUIET.

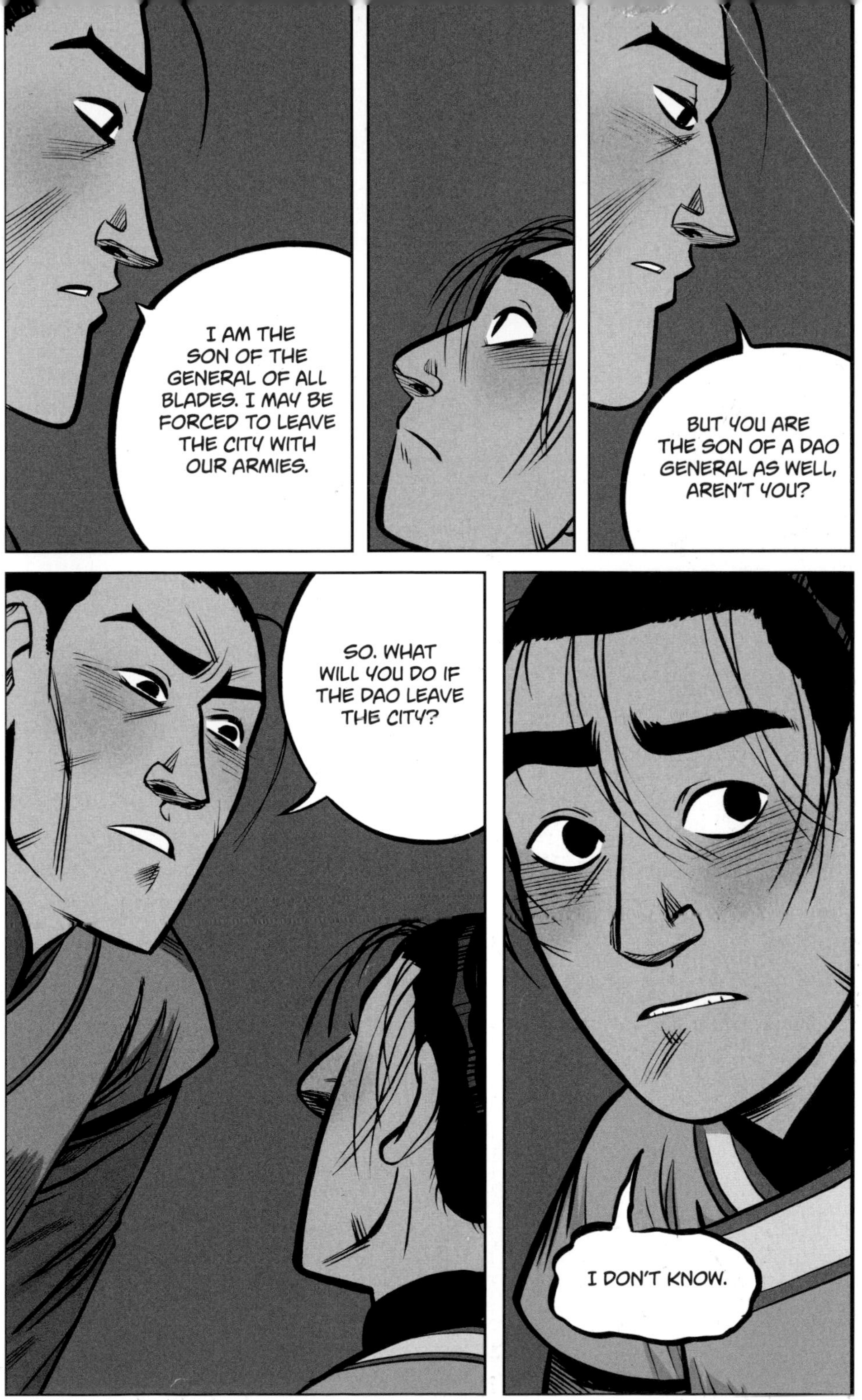
I AM THE SON OF THE GENERAL OF ALL BLADES. I MAY BE FORCED TO LEAVE THE CITY WITH OUR ARMIES.
BUT YOU ARE THE SON OF A DAO GENERAL AS WELL, AREN'T YOU?
SO. WHAT WILL YOU DO IF THE DAO LEAVE THE CITY?
I DON'T KNOW.

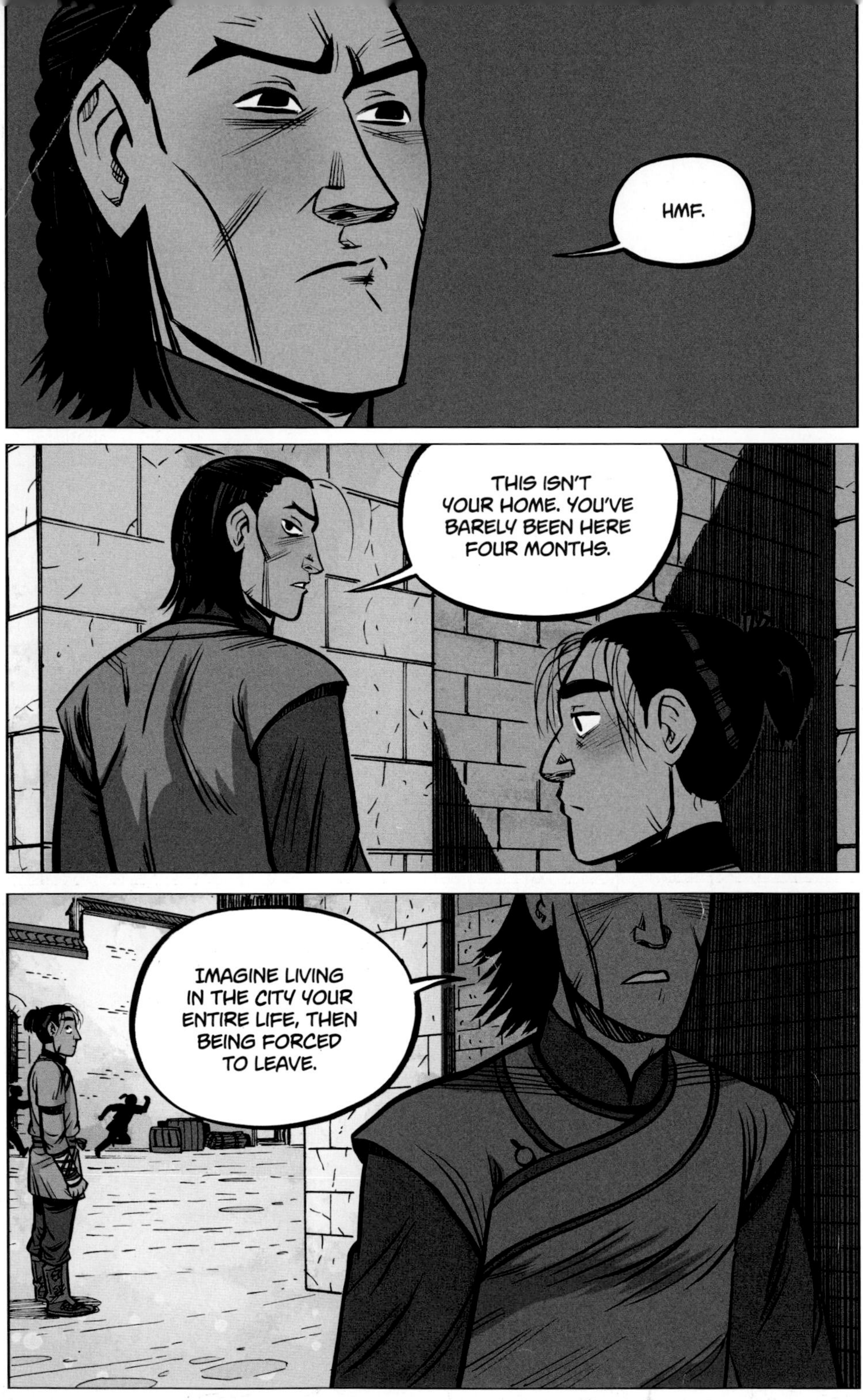
HMF.
THIS ISN'T YOUR HOME. YOU'VE BARELY BEEN HERE FOUR MONTHS.
IMAGINE LIVING IN THE CITY YOUR ENTIRE LIFE, THEN BEING FORCED TO LEAVE.

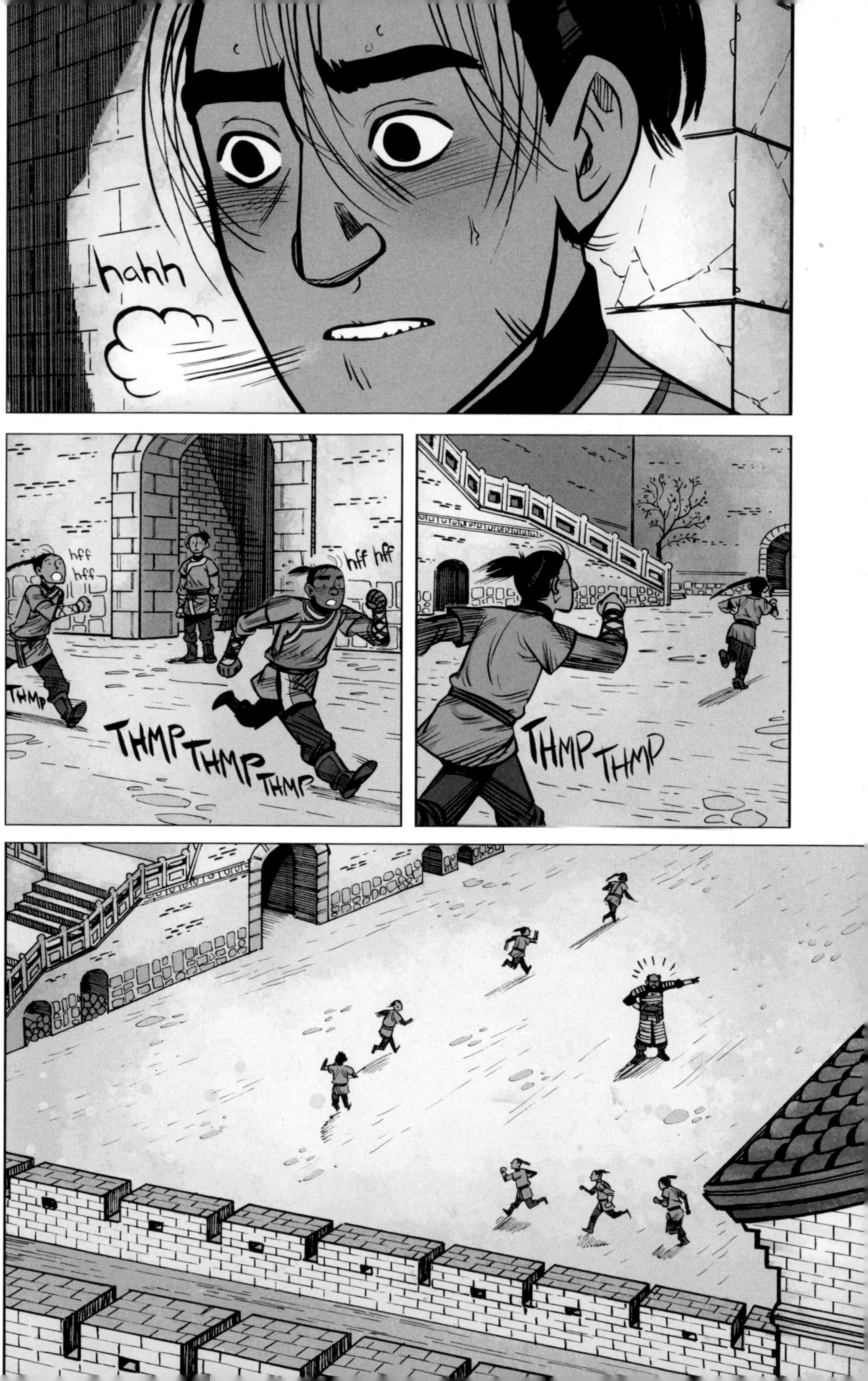
hahh
hff hff
hff hff
THMP
THMP THMP THMP
THMP THMP

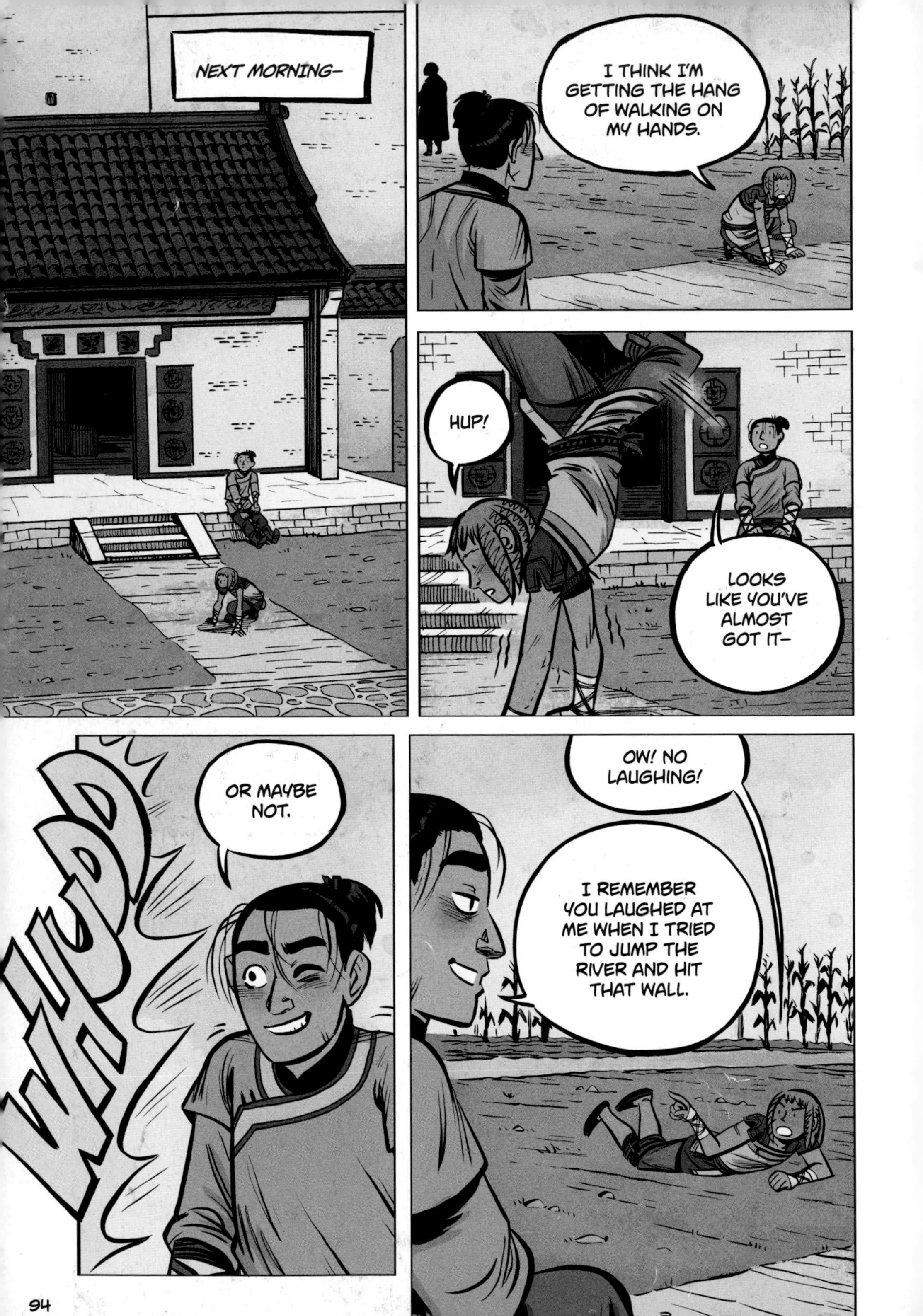
NEXT MORNING–
I THINK I'M GETTING THE HANG OF WALKING ON MY HANDS.
HUP!
LOOKS LIKE YOU'VE ALMOST GOT IT–
WHUD
OR MAYBE NOT.
OW! NO LAUGHING!
I REMEMBER YOU LAUGHED AT ME WHEN I TRIED TO JUMP THE RIVER AND HIT THAT WALL.

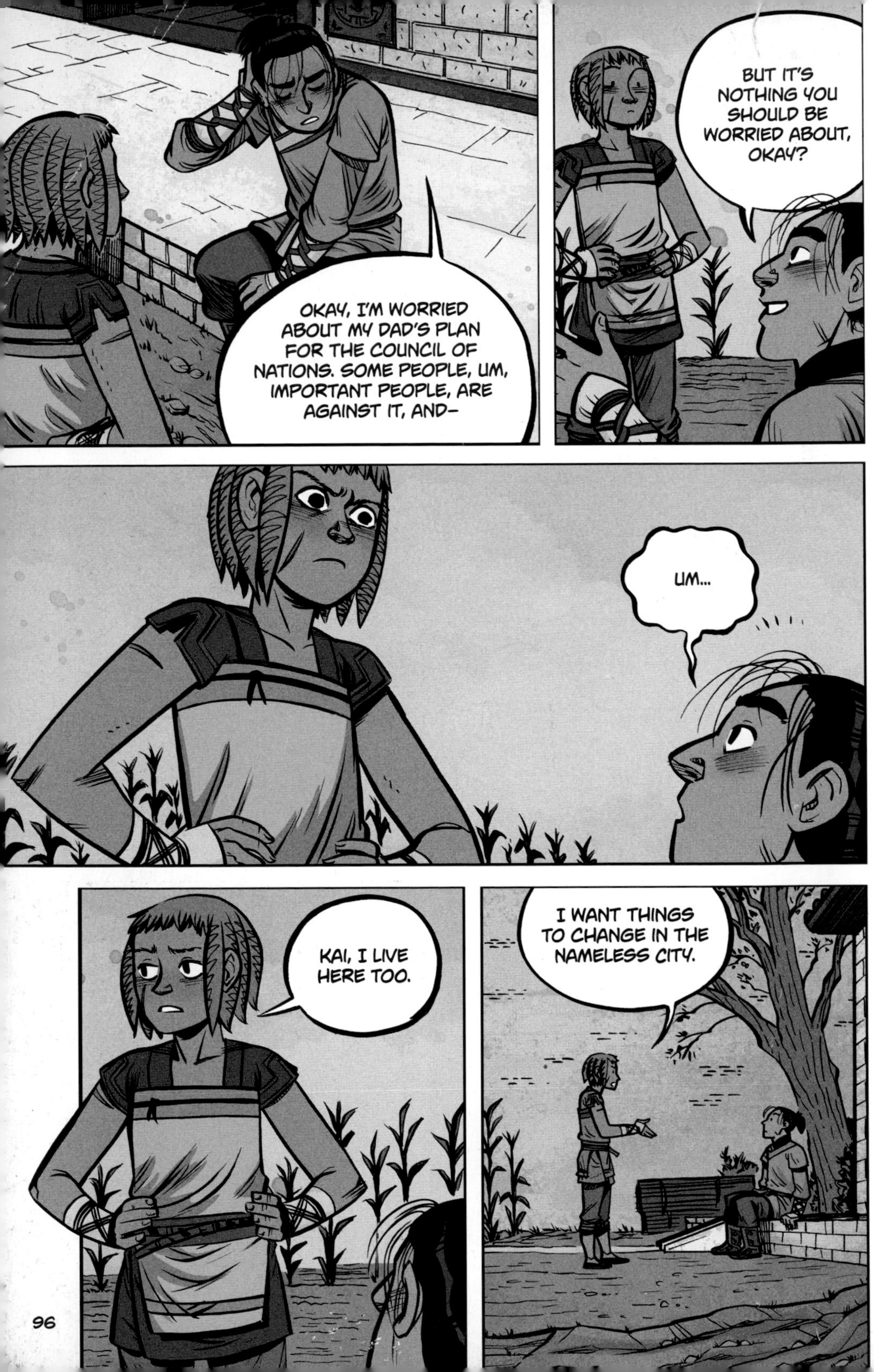
OKAY, I'M WORRIED ABOUT MY DAD'S PLAN FOR THE COUNCIL OF NATIONS. SOME PEOPLE, UM, IMPORTANT PEOPLE, ARE AGAINST IT, AND–
BUT IT'S NOTHING YOU SHOULD BE WORRIED ABOUT, OKAY?
UM...
KAI, I LIVE HERE TOO.
I WANT THINGS TO CHANGE IN THE NAMELESS CITY.

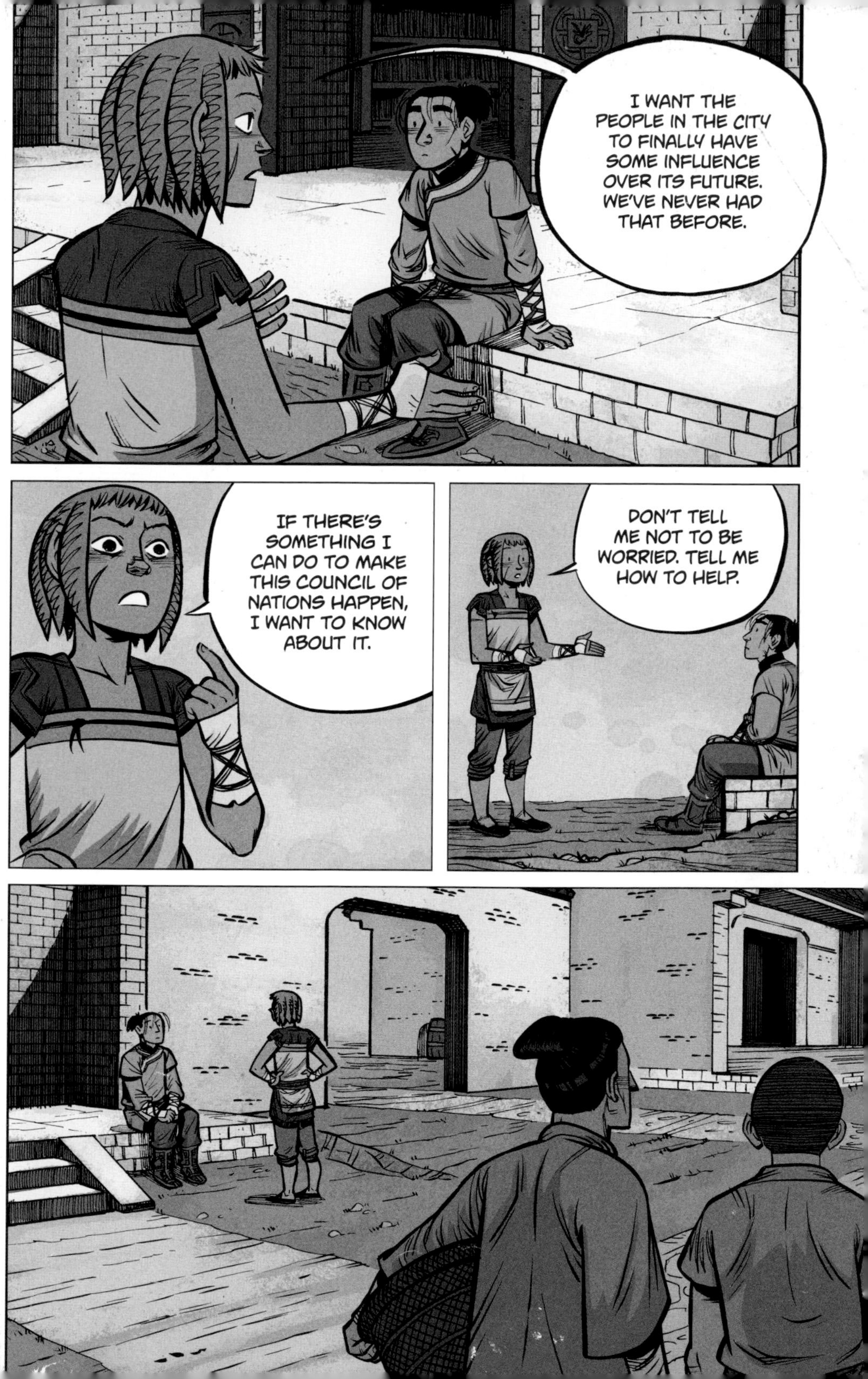
I WANT THE PEOPLE IN THE CITY TO FINALLY HAVE SOME INFLUENCE OVER ITS FUTURE. WE'VE NEVER HAD THAT BEFORE.
IF THERE'S SOMETHING I CAN DO TO MAKE THIS COUNCIL OF NATIONS HAPPEN, I WANT TO KNOW ABOUT IT.
DON'T TELL ME NOT TO BE WORRIED. TELL ME HOW TO HELP.

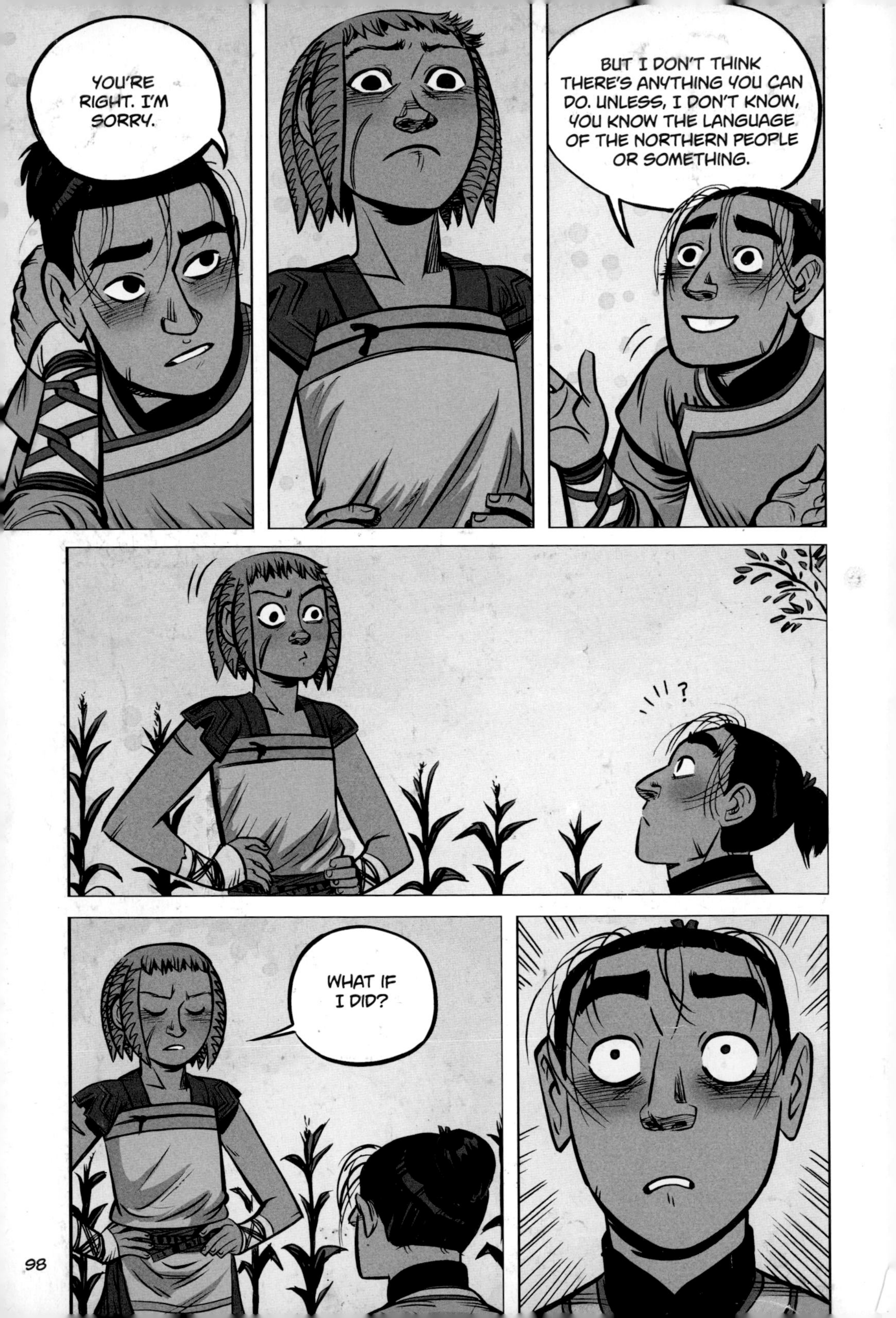
YOU'RE RIGHT. I'M SORRY.
BUT I DON'T THINK THERE'S ANYTHING YOU CAN DO. UNLESS, I DON'T KNOW, YOU KNOW THE LANGUAGE OF THE NORTHERN PEOPLE OR SOMETHING.
?
WHAT IF I DID?

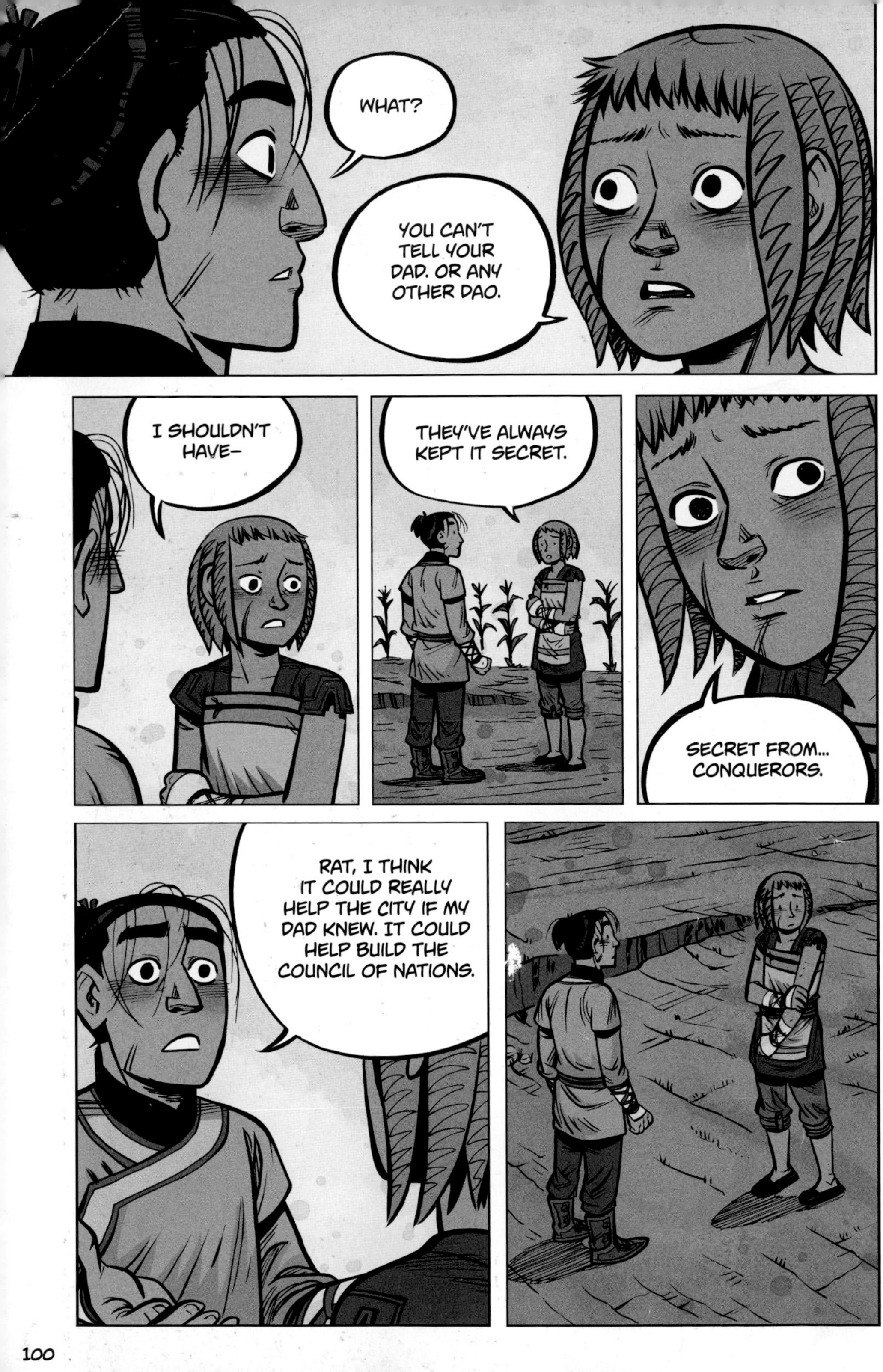
WHAT?
YOU CAN'T TELL YOUR DAD. OR ANY OTHER DAO.
I SHOULDN'T HAVE—
THEY'VE ALWAYS KEPT IT SECRET.
SECRET FROM... CONQUERORS.
RAT, I THINK IT COULD REALLY HELP THE CITY IF MY DAD KNEW. IT COULD HELP BUILD THE COUNCIL OF NATIONS.

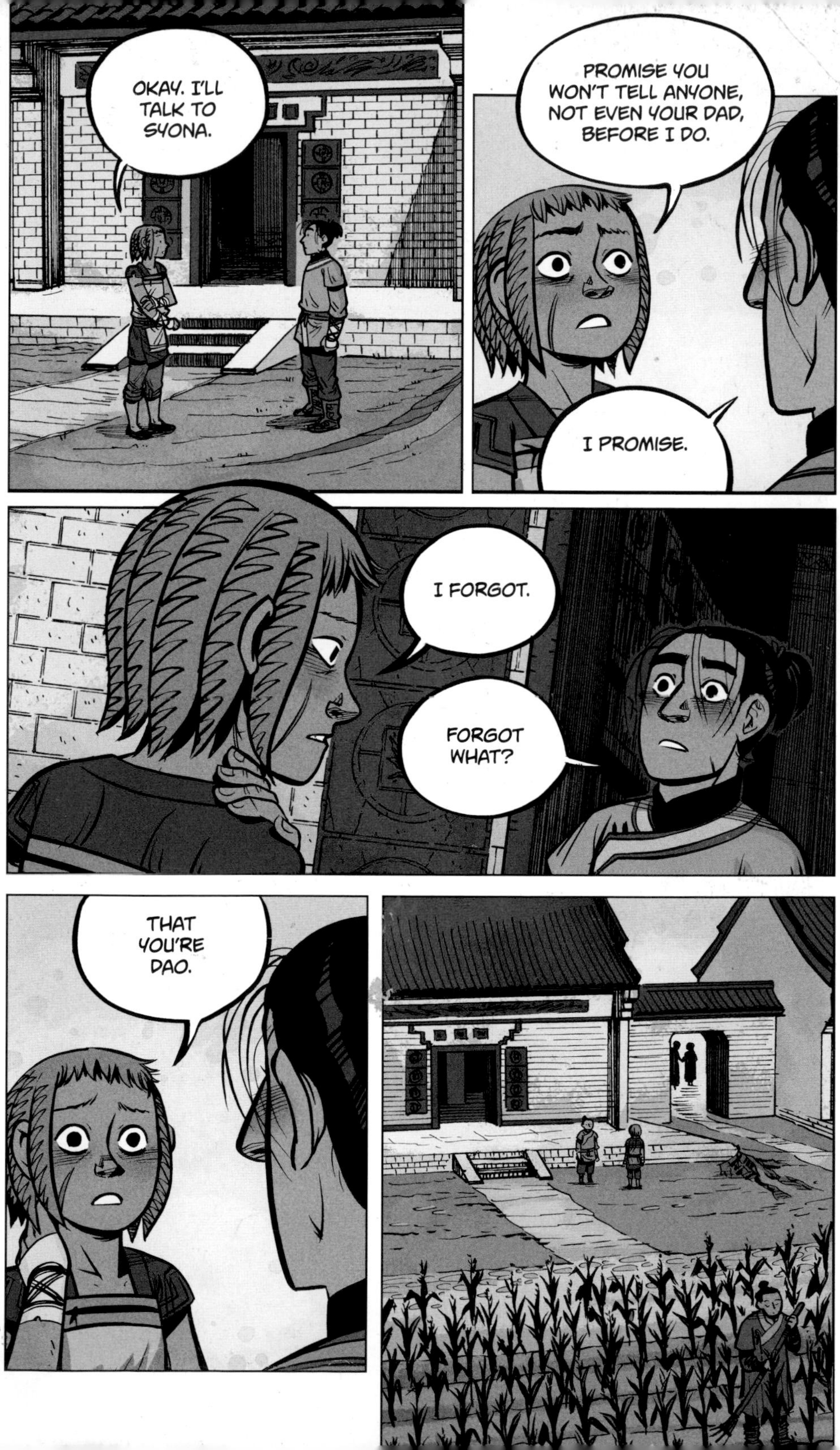
OKAY. I'LL TALK TO SYONA.
PROMISE YOU WON'T TELL ANYONE, NOT EVEN YOUR DAD, BEFORE I DO.
I PROMISE.
I FORGOT.
FORGOT WHAT?
THAT YOU'RE DAO.

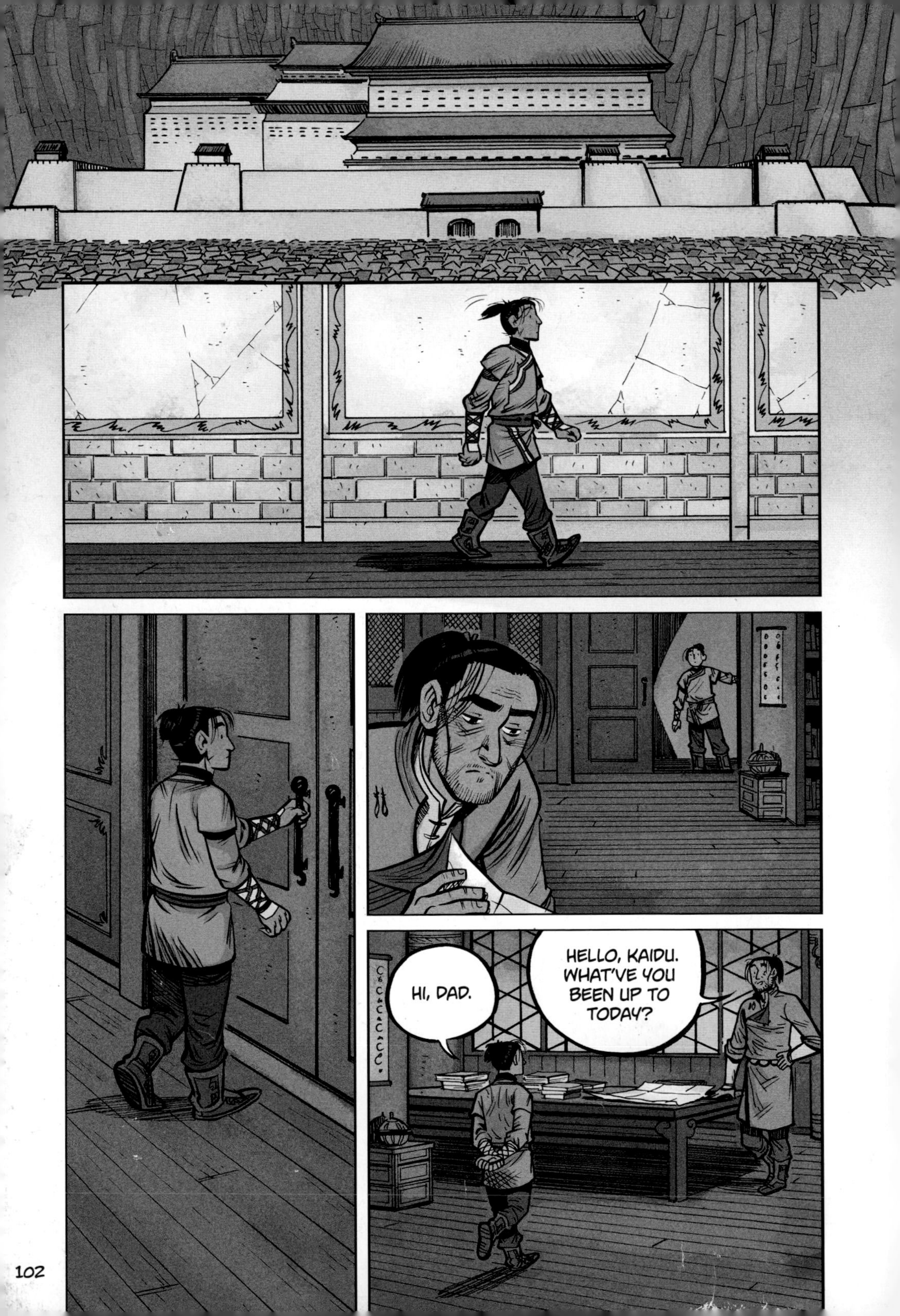
HI, DAD.
HELLO, KAIDU. WHAT'VE YOU BEEN UP TO TODAY?

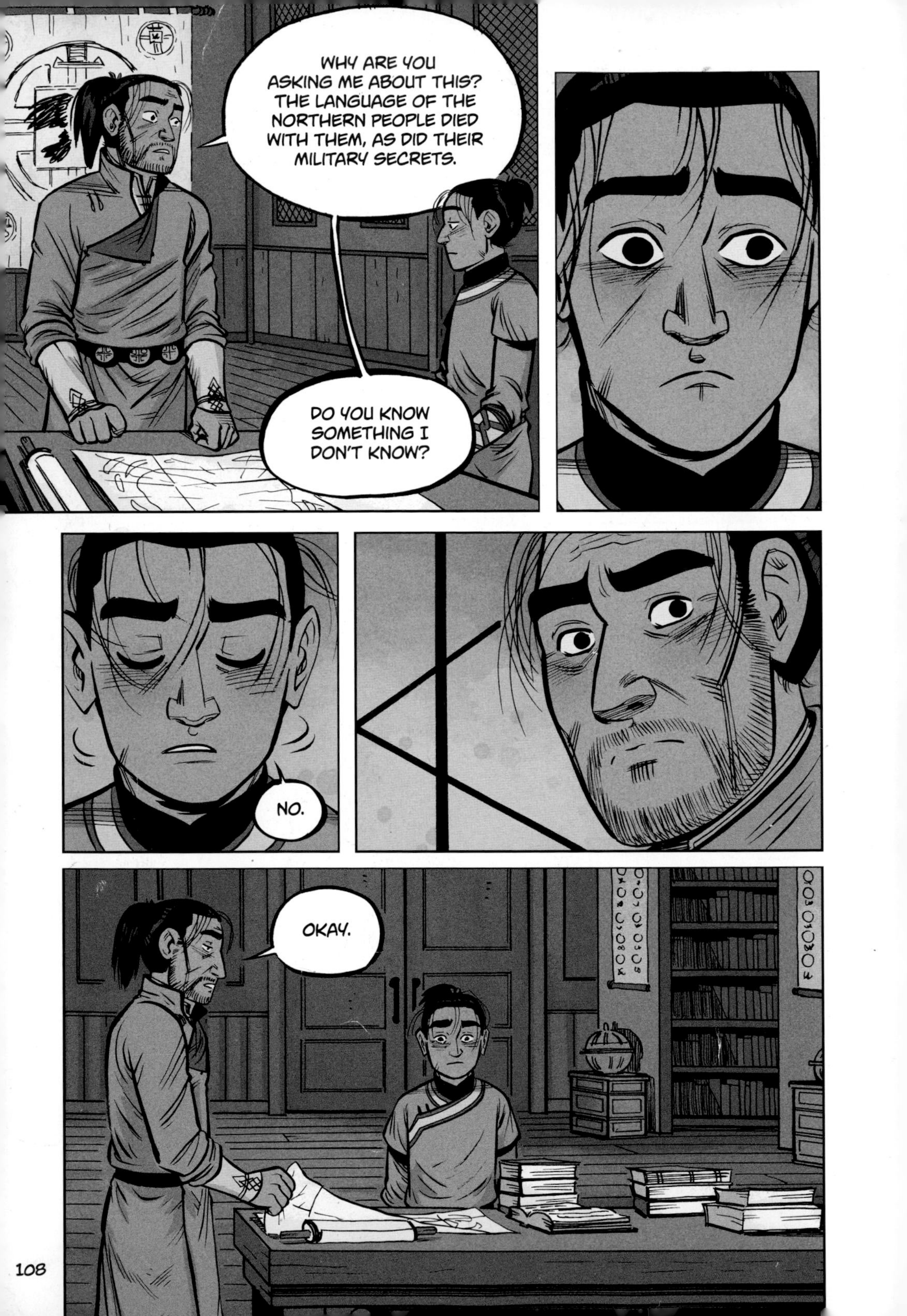
WHY ARE YOU ASKING ME ABOUT THIS? THE LANGUAGE OF THE NORTHERN PEOPLE DIED WITH THEM, AS DID THEIR MILITARY SECRETS.
DO YOU KNOW SOMETHING I DON'T KNOW?
NO.
OKAY.

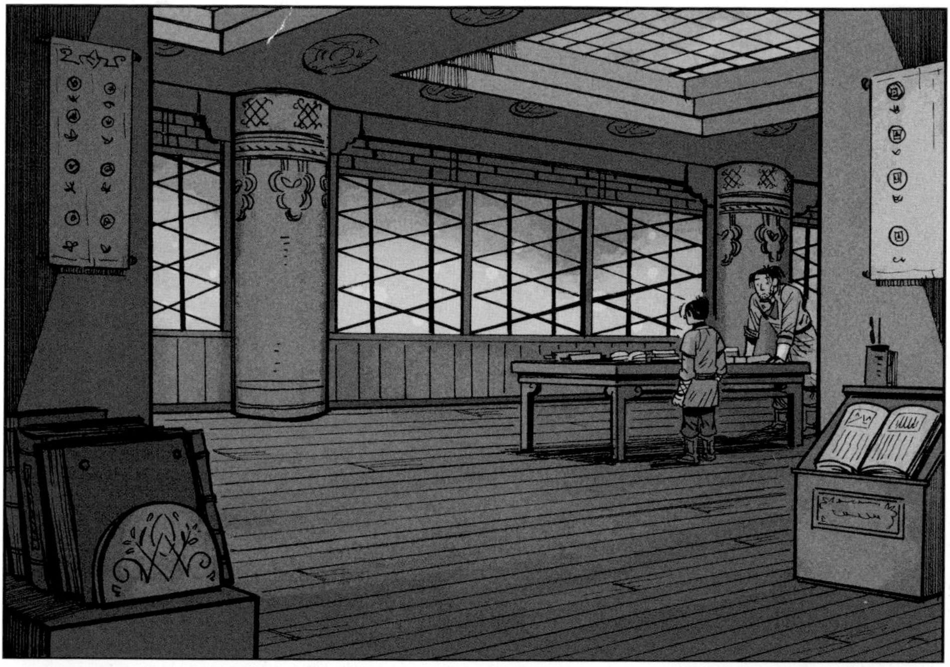
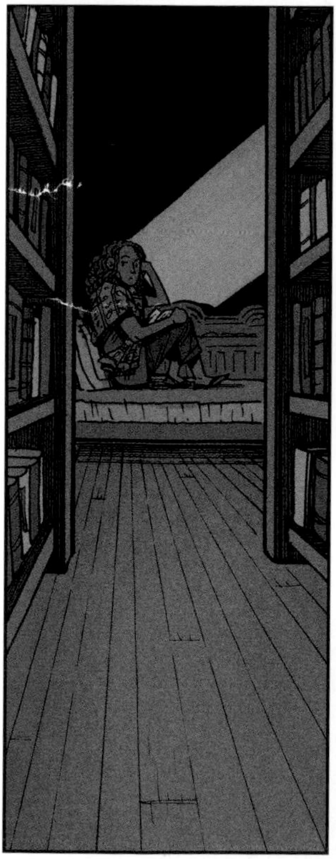
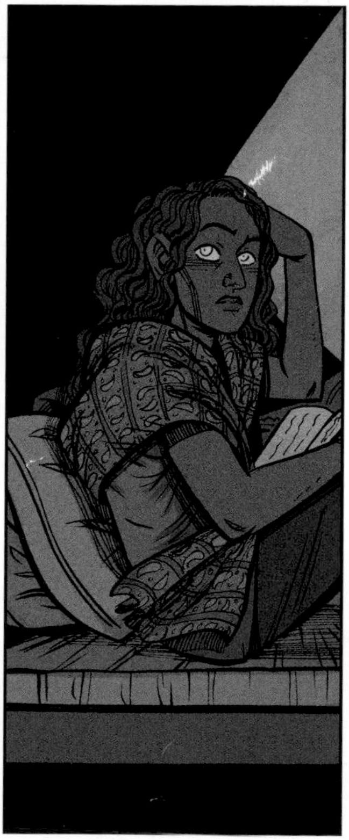
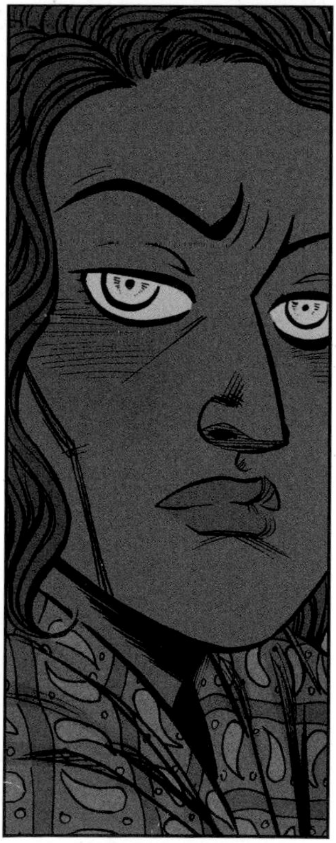

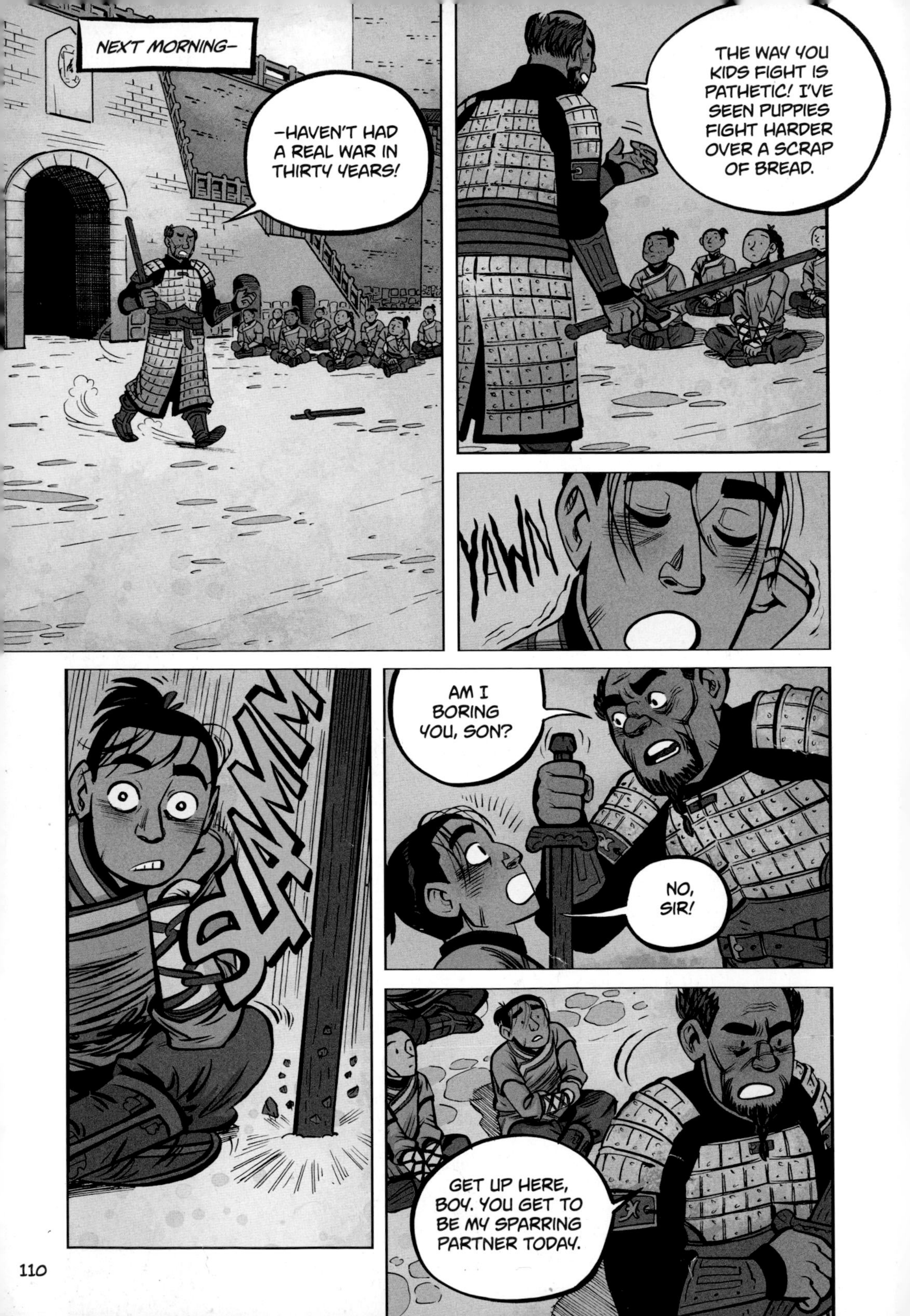
NEXT MORNING–
–HAVEN'T HAD A REAL WAR IN THIRTY YEARS!
THE WAY YOU KIDS FIGHT IS PATHETIC! I'VE SEEN PUPPIES FIGHT HARDER OVER A SCRAP OF BREAD.
YAWN
SLAMM
AM I BORING YOU, SON?
NO, SIR!
GET UP HERE, BOY. YOU GET TO BE MY SPARRING PARTNER TODAY.

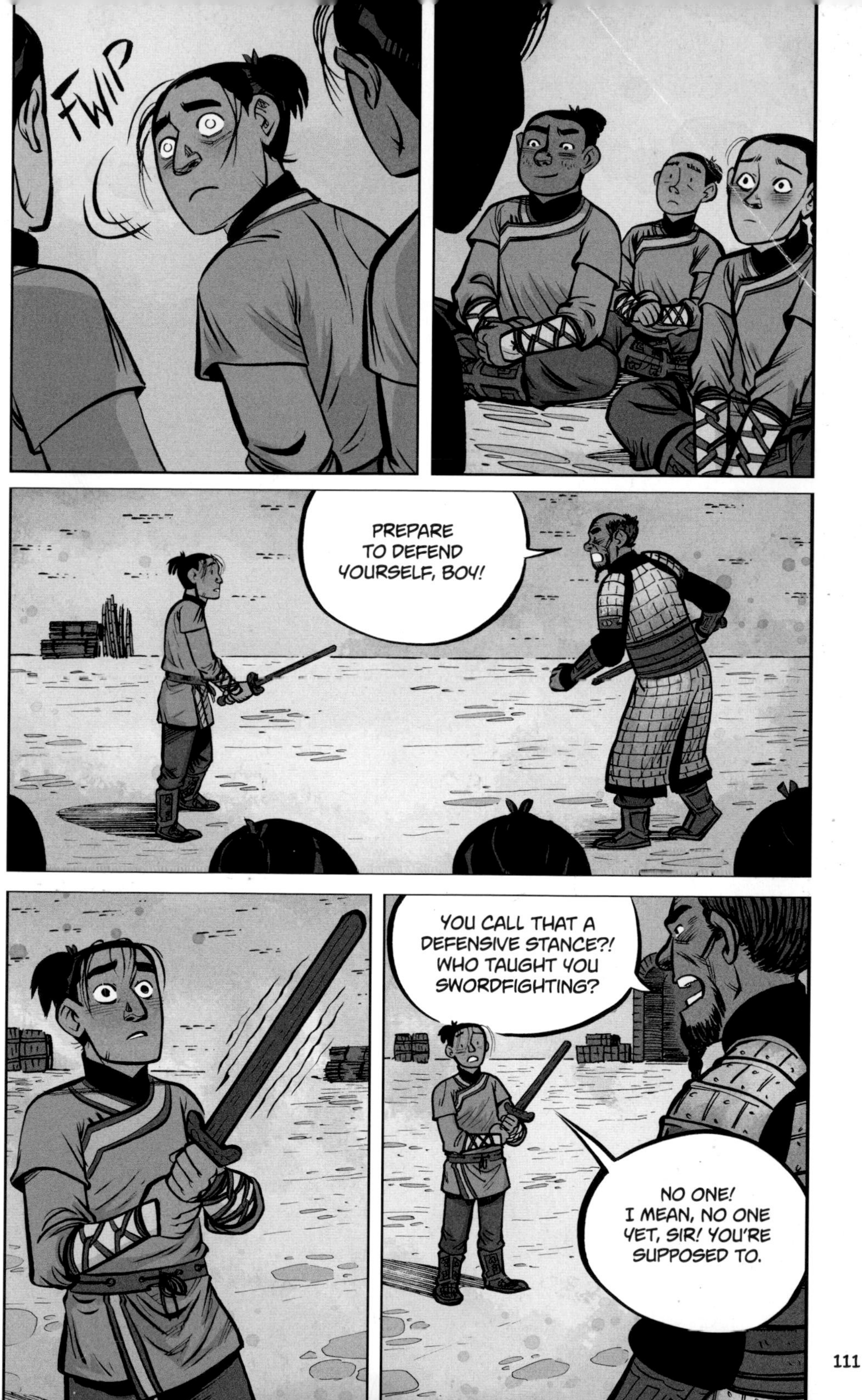
FWIP
PREPARE TO DEFEND YOURSELF, BOY!
YOU CALL THAT A DEFENSIVE STANCE?! WHO TAUGHT YOU SWORDFIGHTING?
NO ONE! I MEAN, NO ONE YET, SIR! YOU'RE SUPPOSED TO.

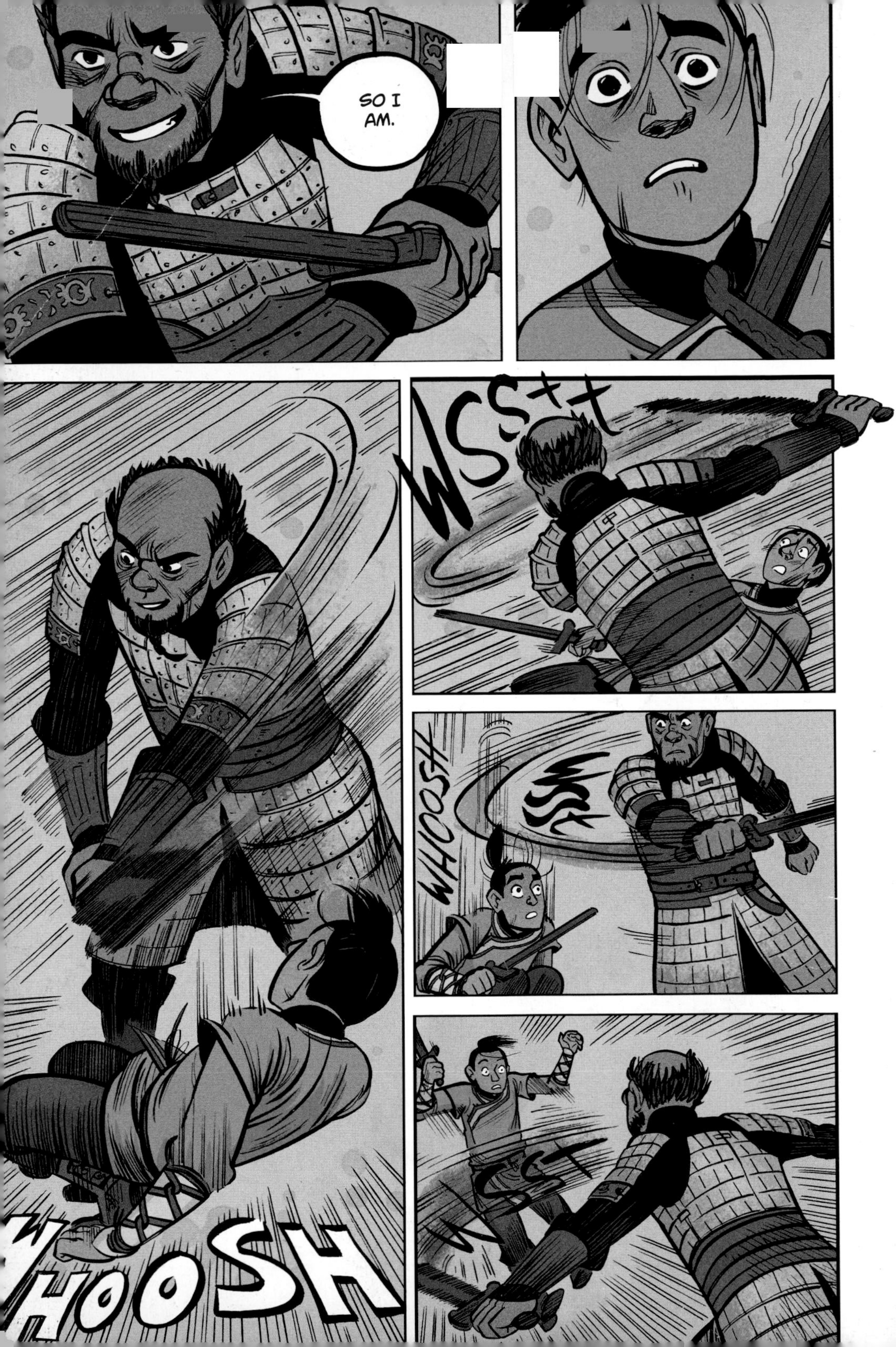
SO I AM.
WHOOSH
WHOOSH

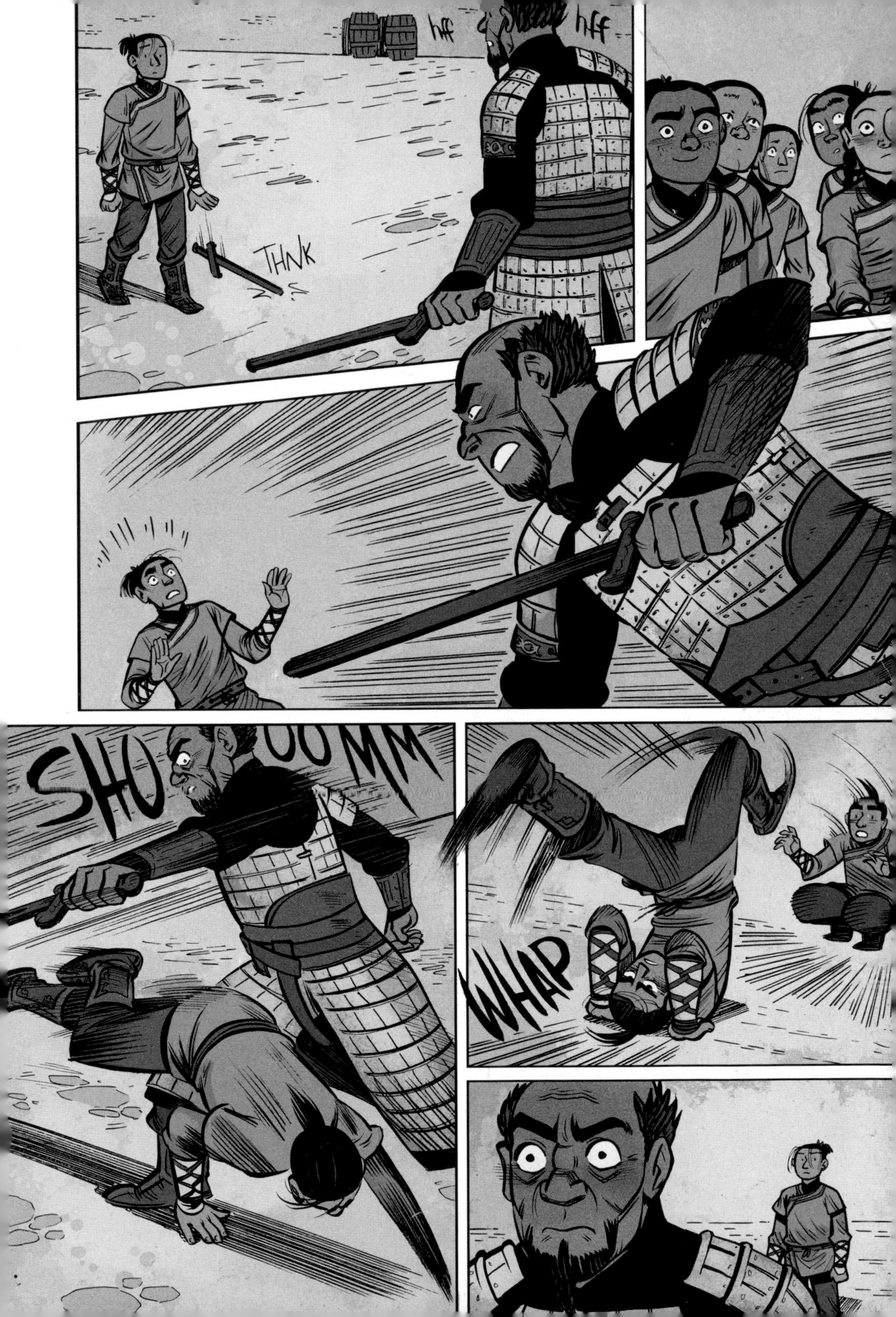
hff
hff
THNK
SHOOOMM
WHAP

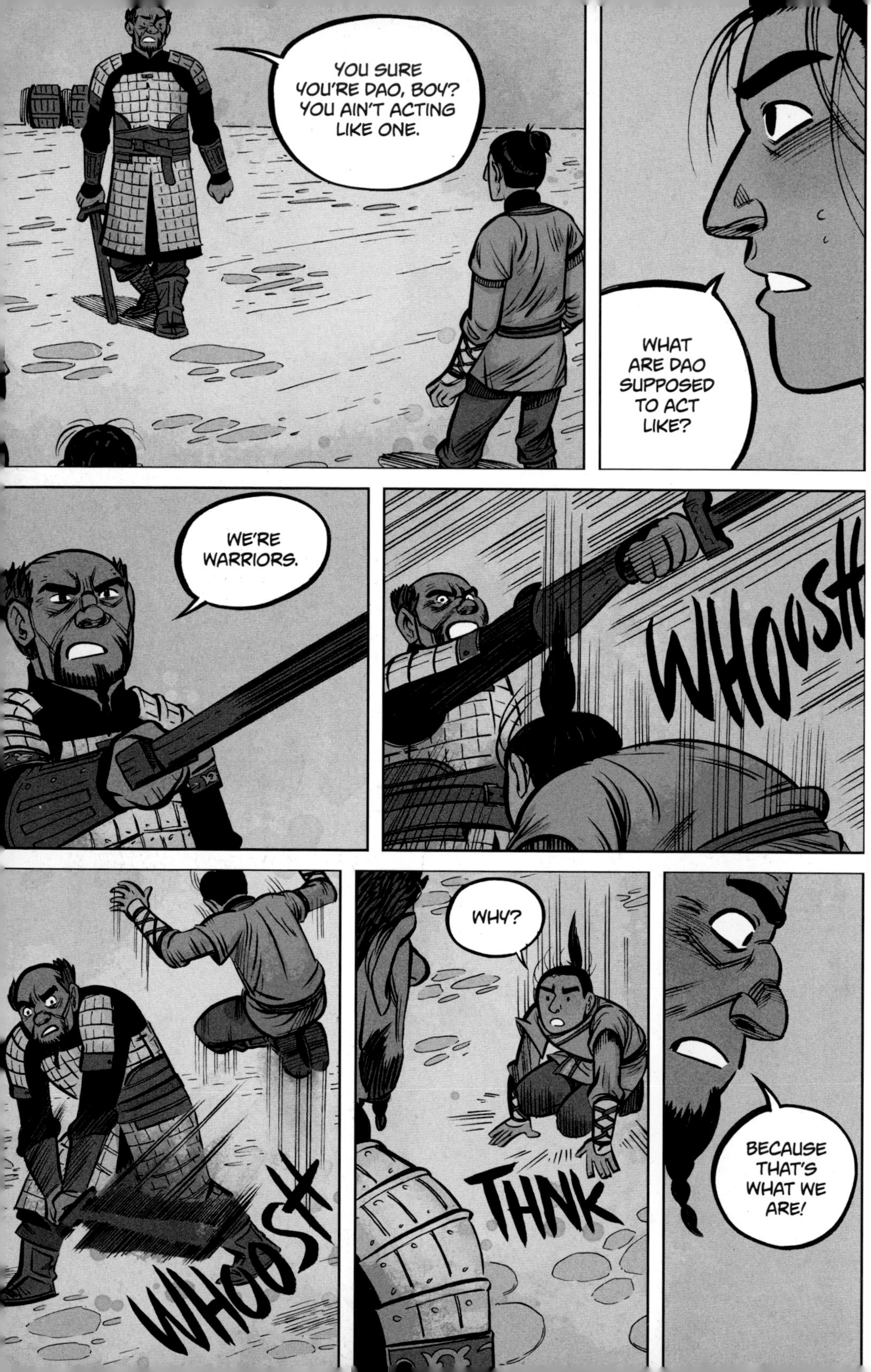
YOU SURE YOU'RE DAO, BOY? YOU AIN'T ACTING LIKE ONE.
WHAT ARE DAO SUPPOSED TO ACT LIKE?
WE'RE WARRIORS.
WHOOSH
WHOOSH
WHY?
THNK
BECAUSE THAT'S WHAT WE ARE!

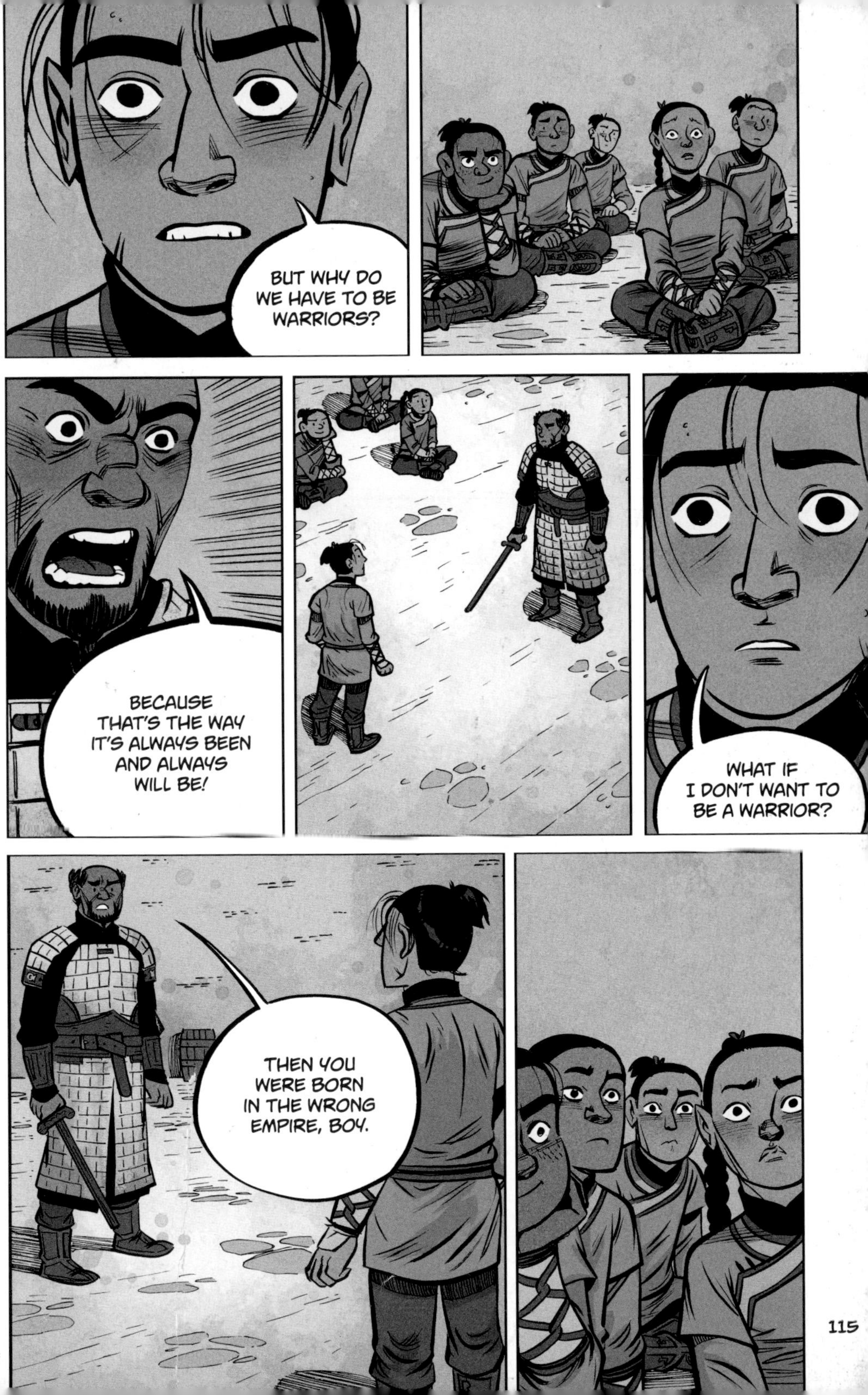
BUT WHY DO WE HAVE TO BE WARRIORS?
BECAUSE THAT'S THE WAY IT'S ALWAYS BEEN AND ALWAYS WILL BE!
WHAT IF I DON'T WANT TO BE A WARRIOR?
THEN YOU WERE BORN IN THE WRONG EMPIRE, BOY.

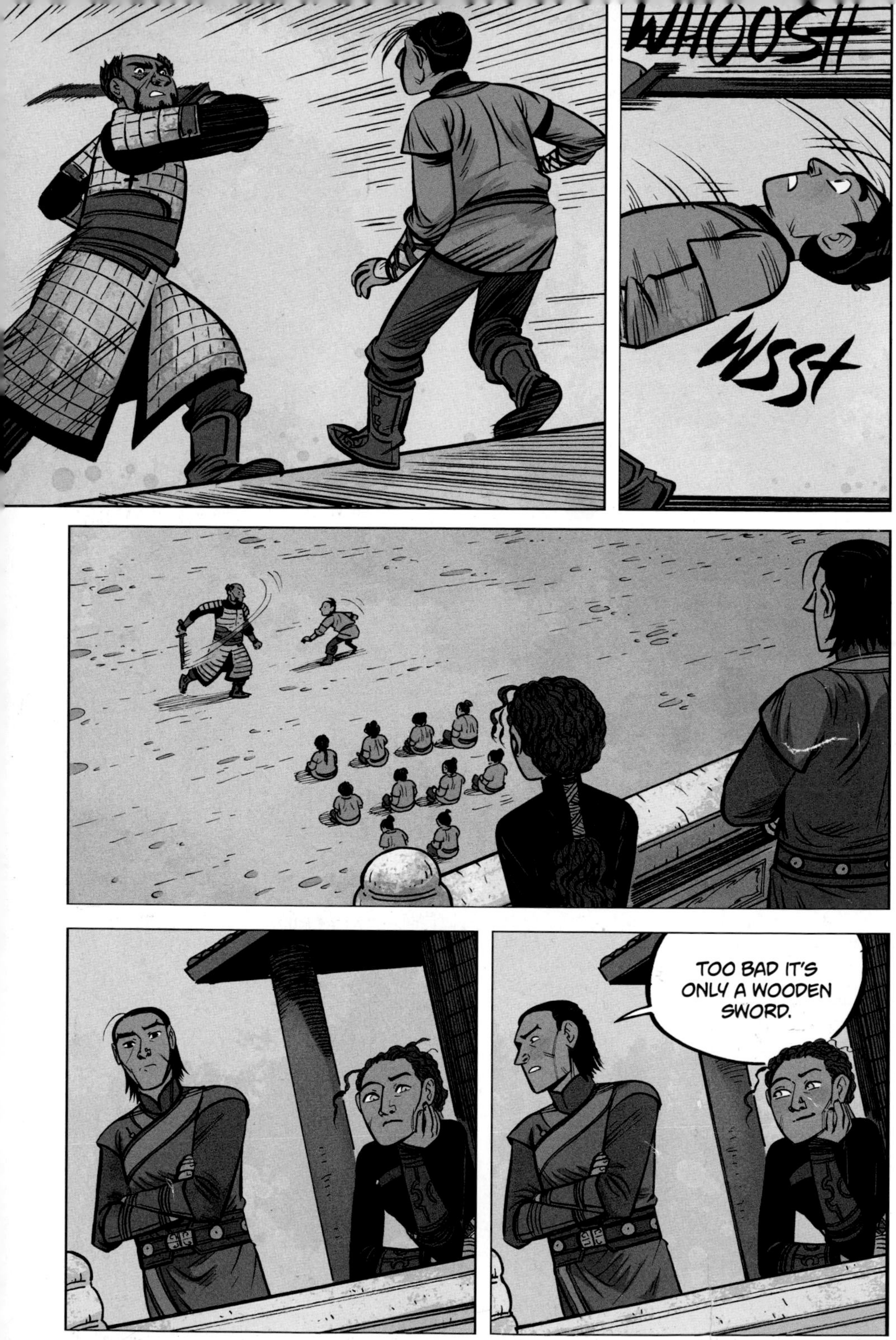
WHOOSH
WSST
TOO BAD IT'S ONLY A WOODEN SWORD.

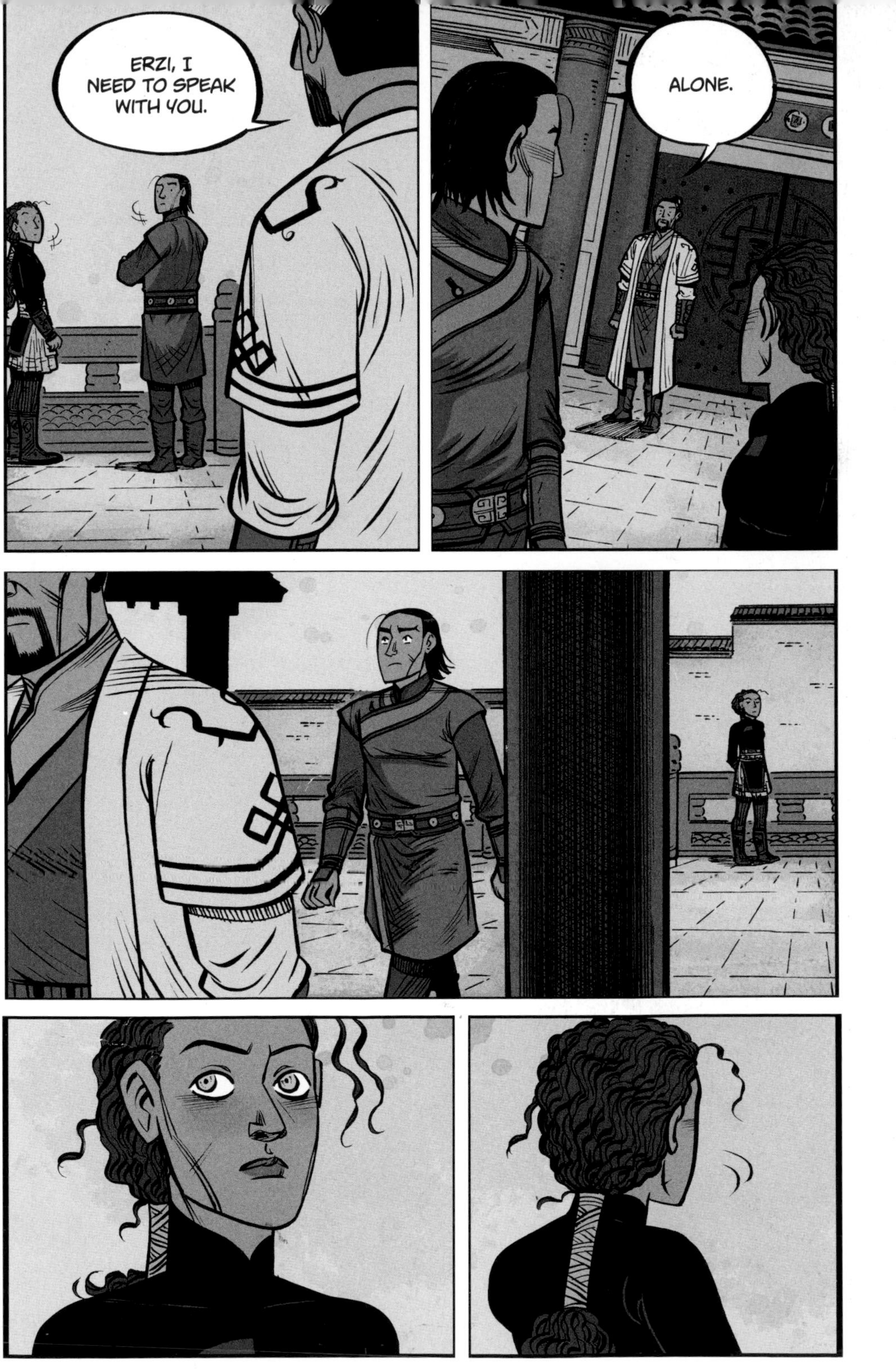
ERZI, I NEED TO SPEAK WITH YOU.
ALONE.

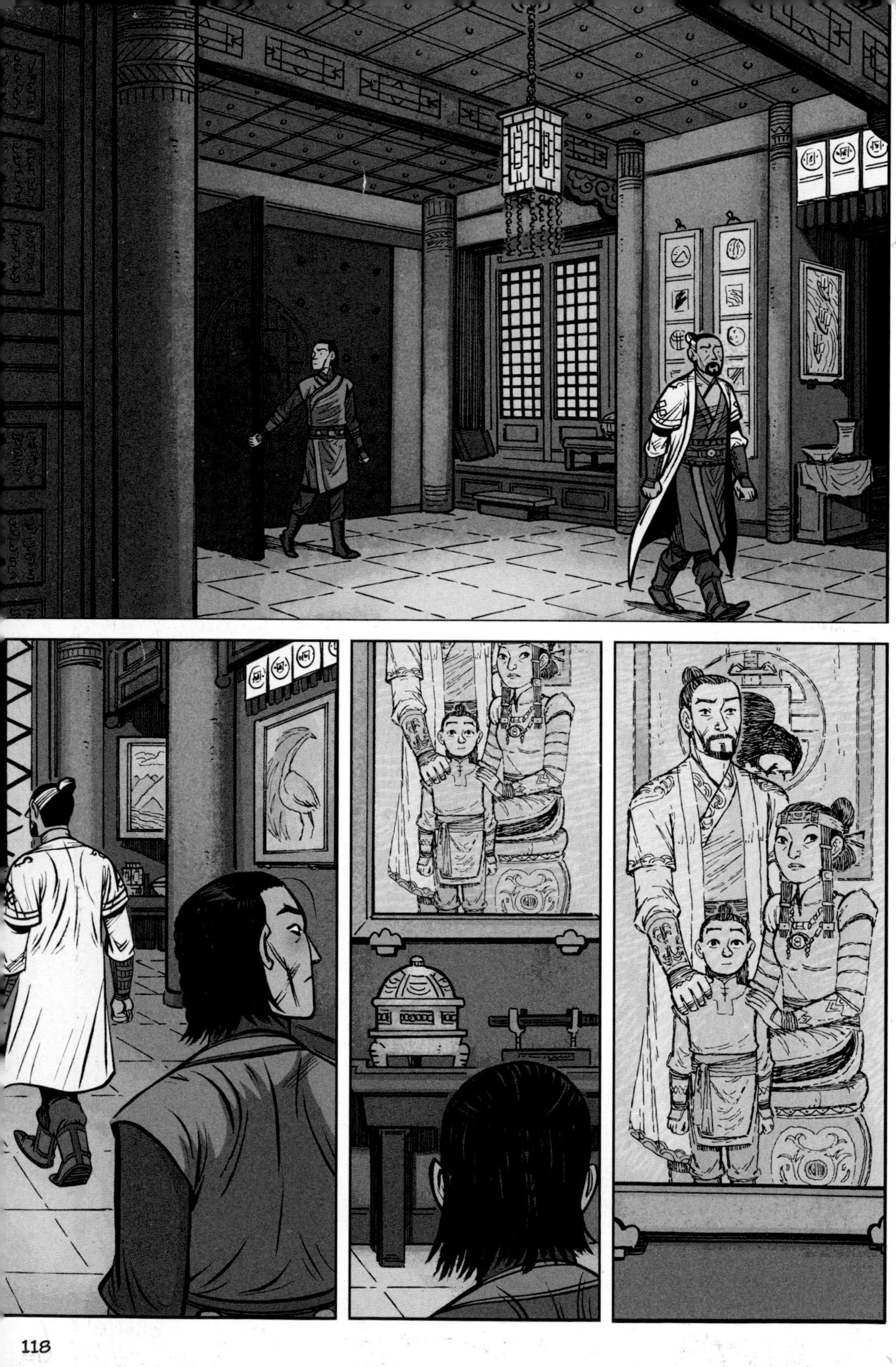

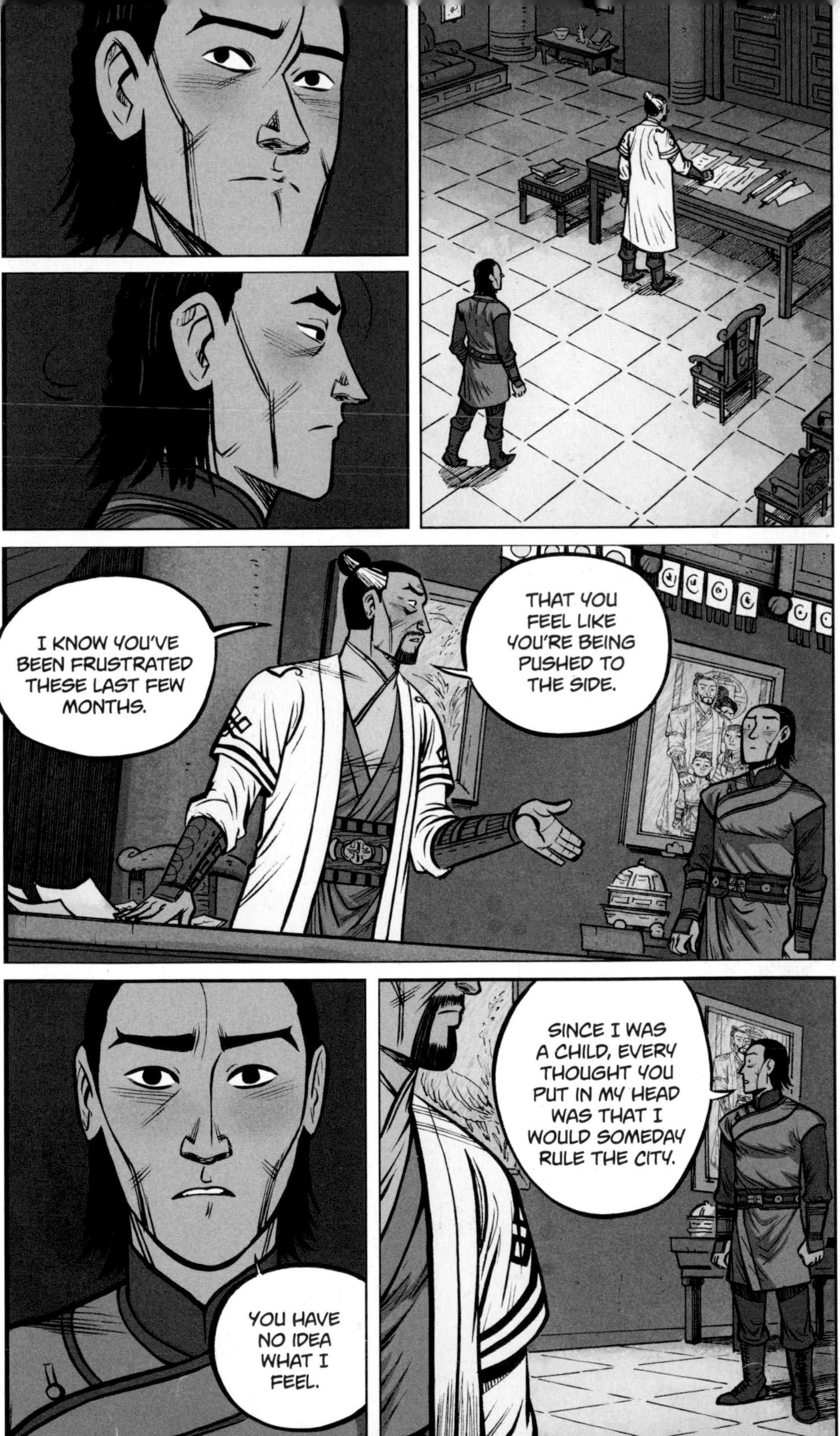
I KNOW YOU'VE BEEN FRUSTRATED THESE LAST FEW MONTHS.
THAT YOU FEEL LIKE YOU'RE BEING PUSHED TO THE SIDE.
YOU HAVE NO IDEA WHAT I FEEL.
SINCE I WAS A CHILD, EVERY THOUGHT YOU PUT IN MY HEAD WAS THAT I WOULD SOMEDAY RULE THE CITY.

122

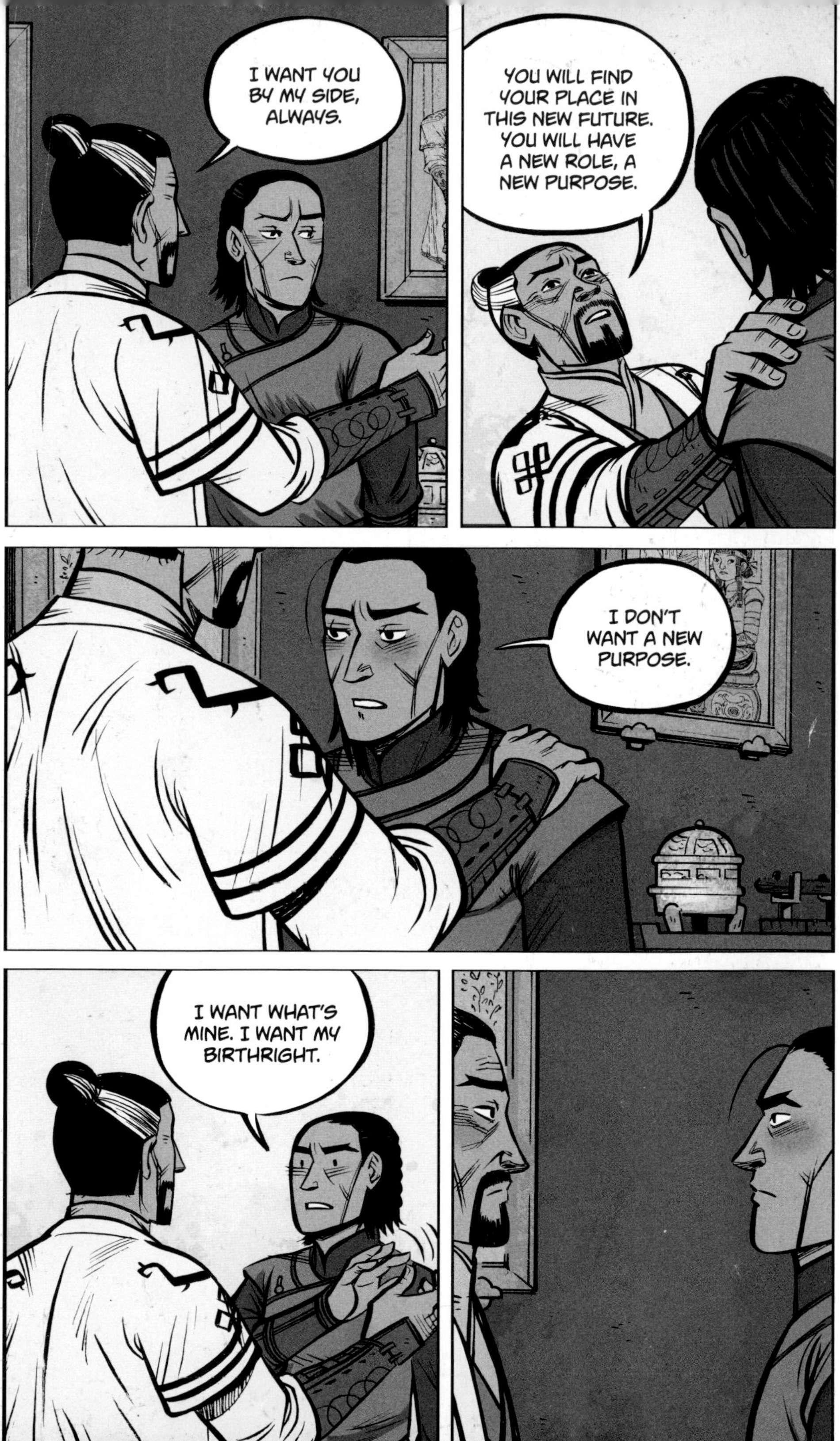
I WANT YOU BY MY SIDE, ALWAYS.
YOU WILL FIND YOUR PLACE IN THIS NEW FUTURE. YOU WILL HAVE A NEW ROLE, A NEW PURPOSE.
I DON'T WANT A NEW PURPOSE.
I WANT WHAT'S MINE. I WANT MY BIRTHRIGHT.

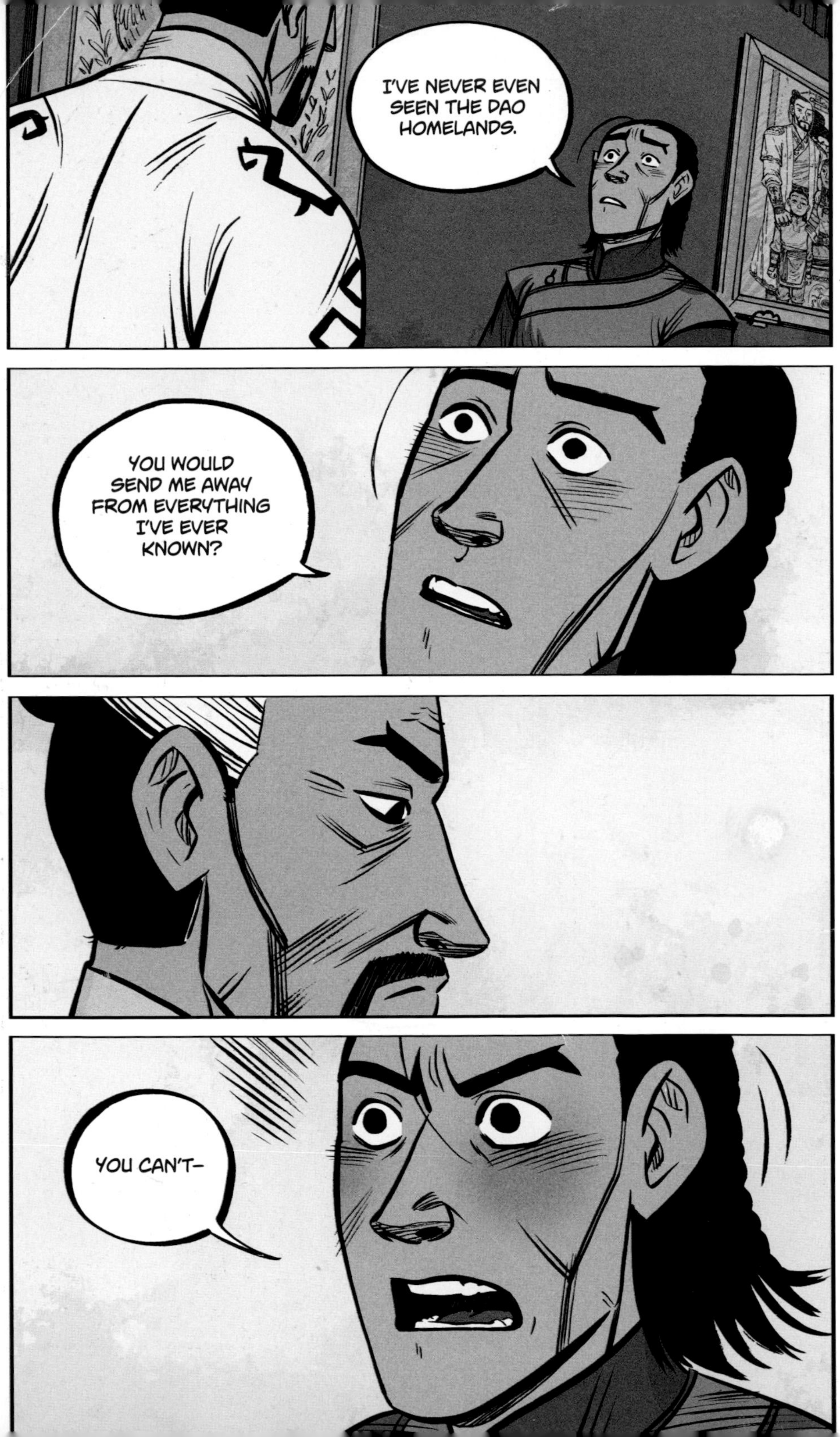
I'VE NEVER EVEN SEEN THE DAO HOMELANDS.
YOU WOULD SEND ME AWAY FROM EVERYTHING I'VE EVER KNOWN?
YOU CAN'T-

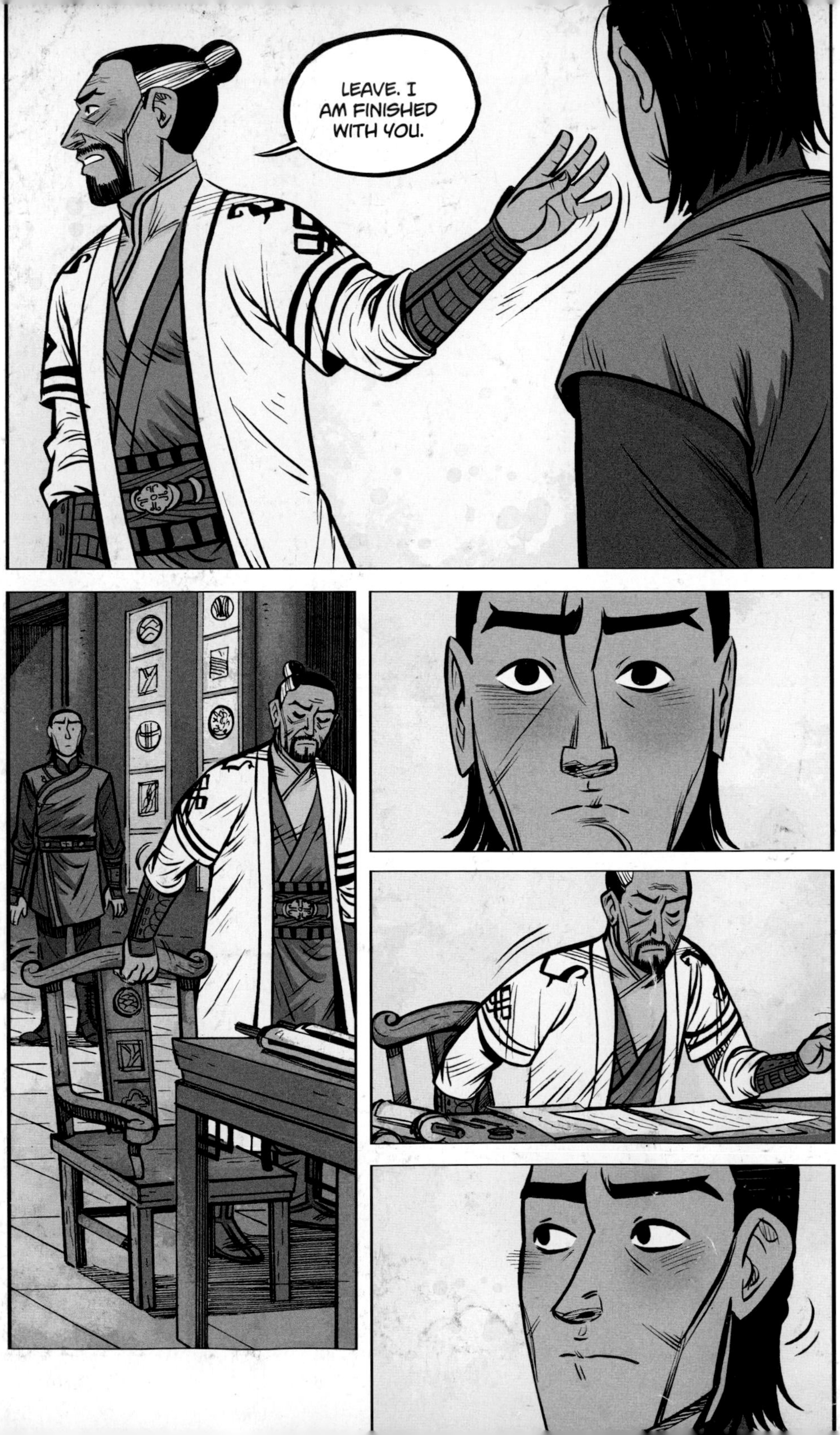
LEAVE. I AM FINISHED WITH YOU.

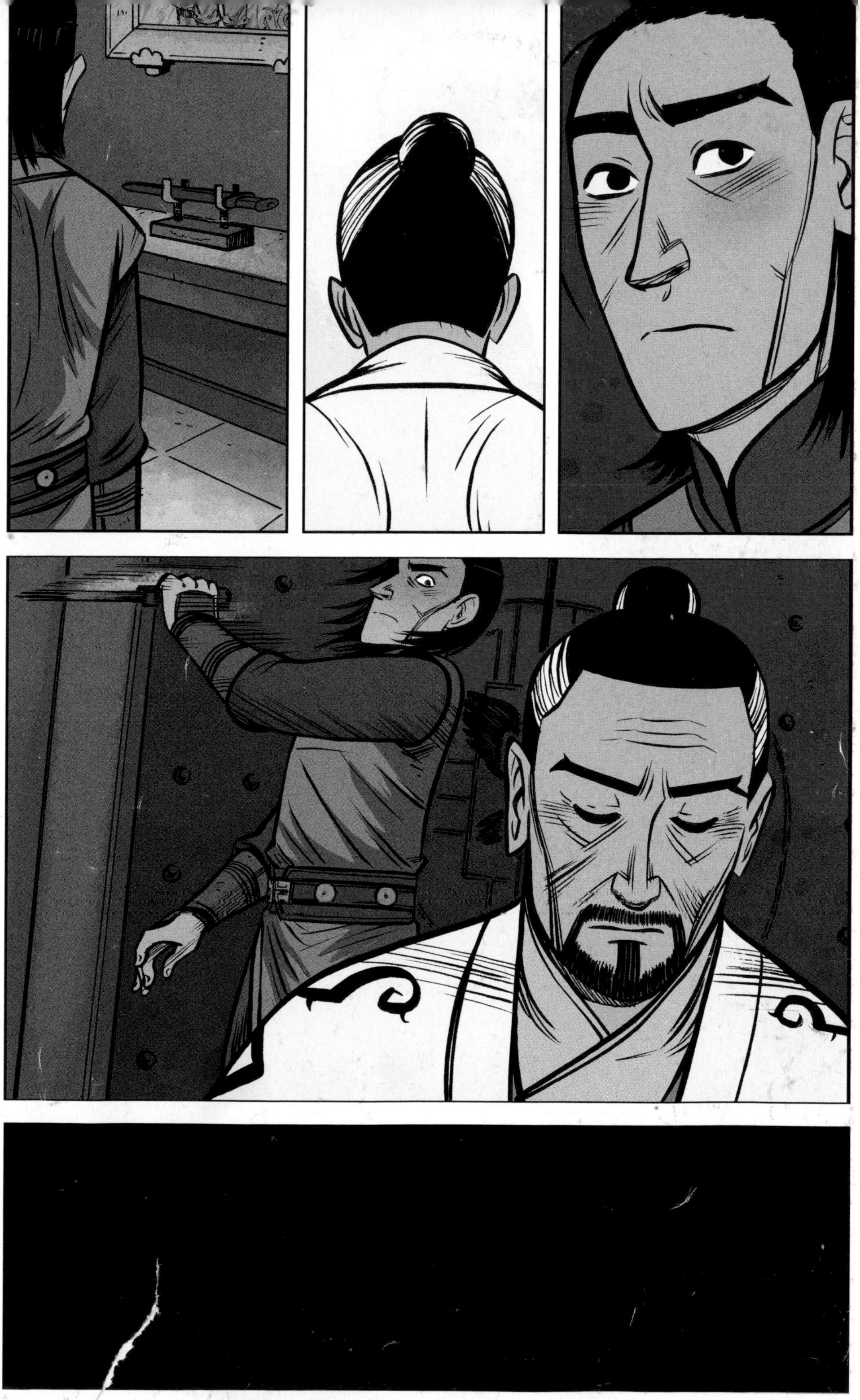

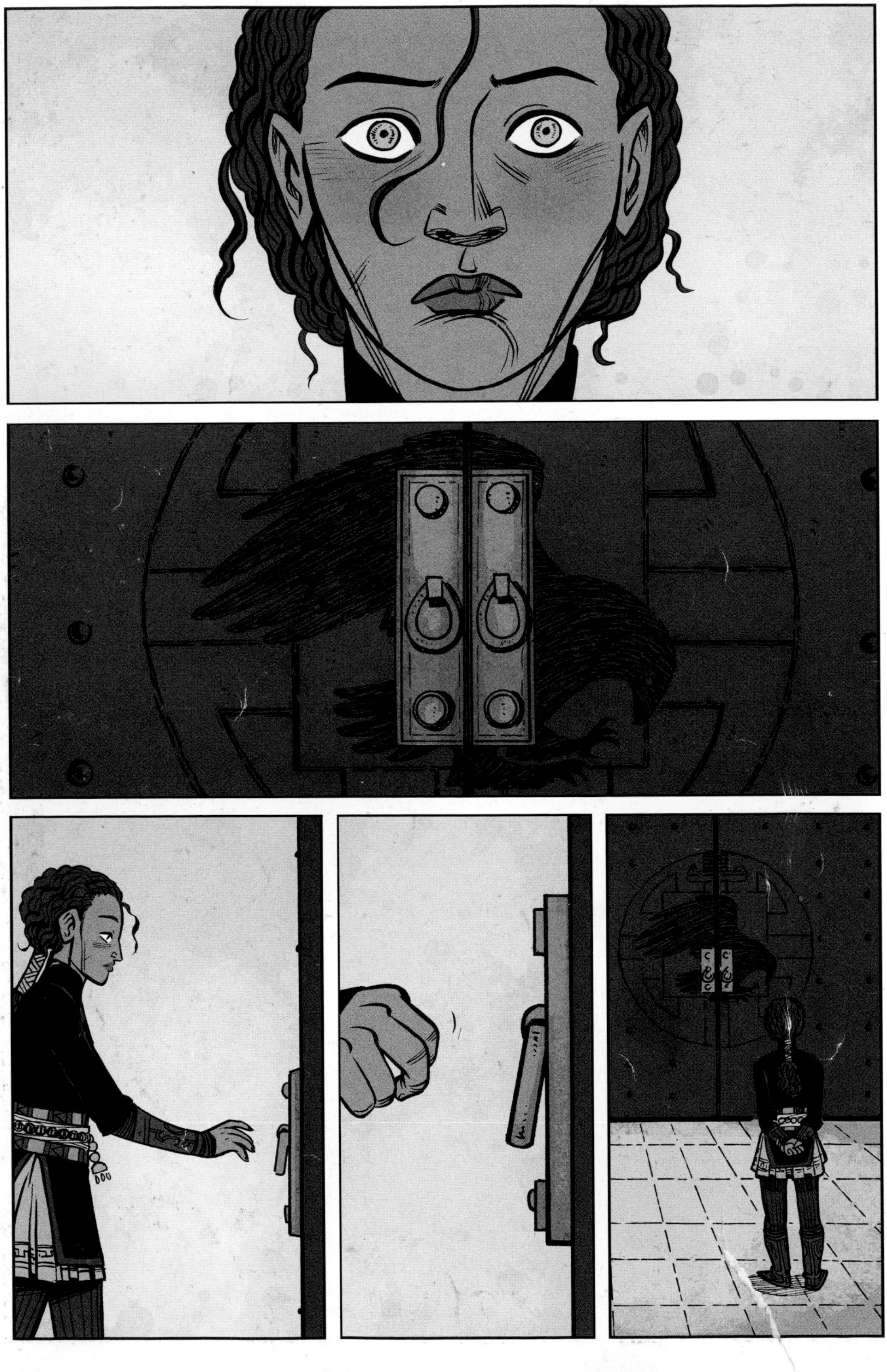

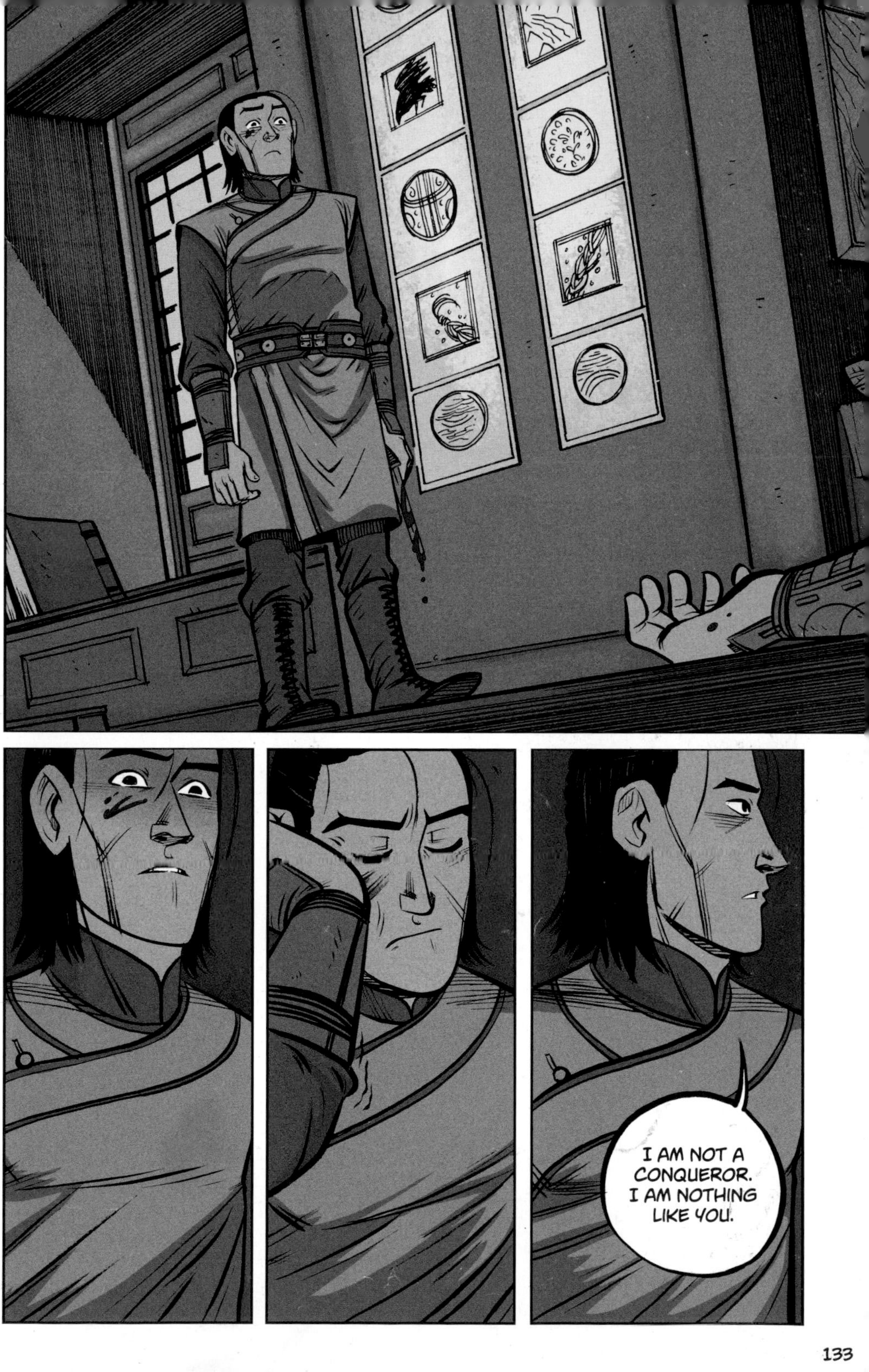
I AM NOT A CONQUEROR. I AM NOTHING LIKE YOU.

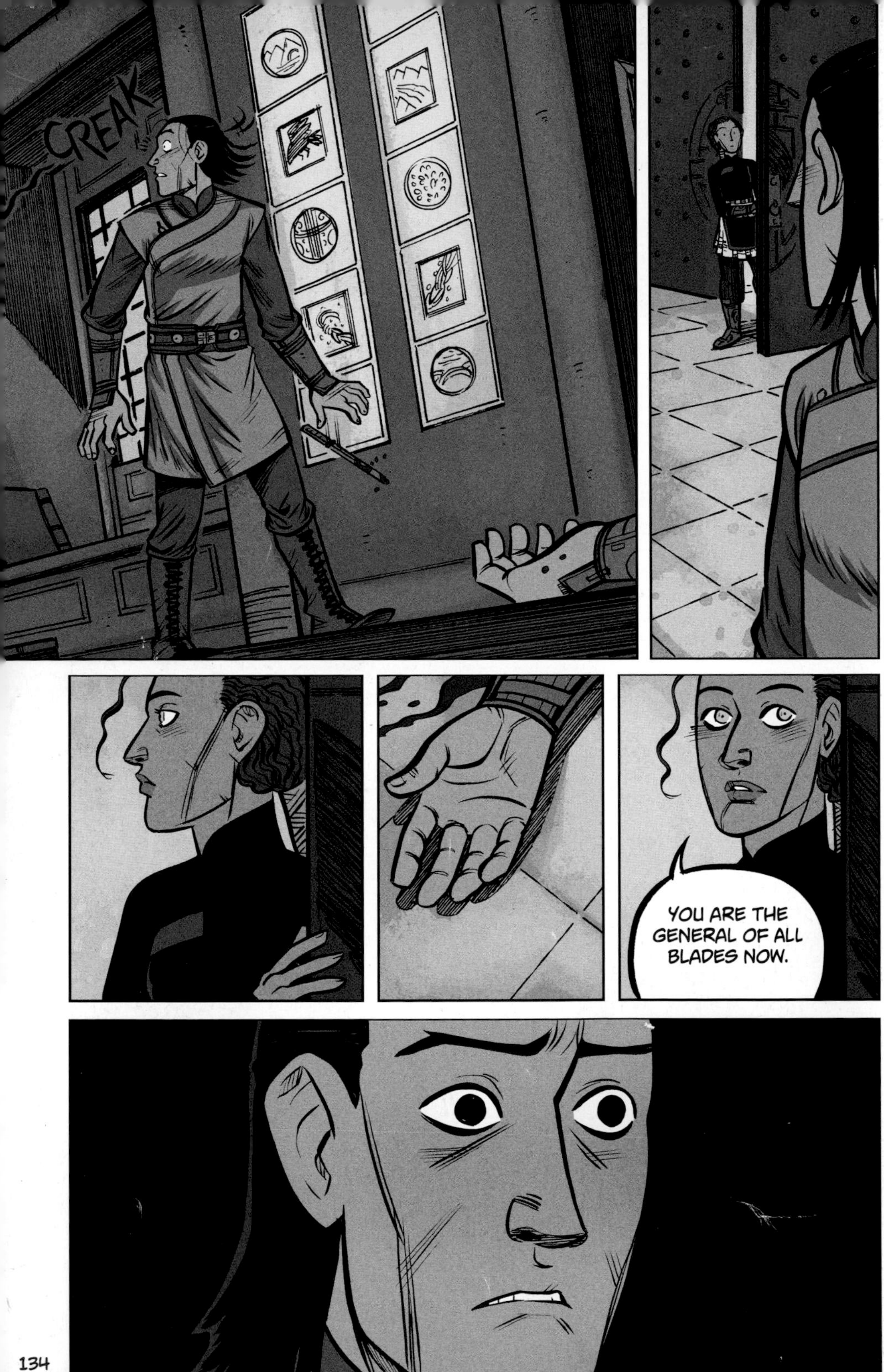
CREAK
YOU ARE THE GENERAL OF ALL BLADES NOW.

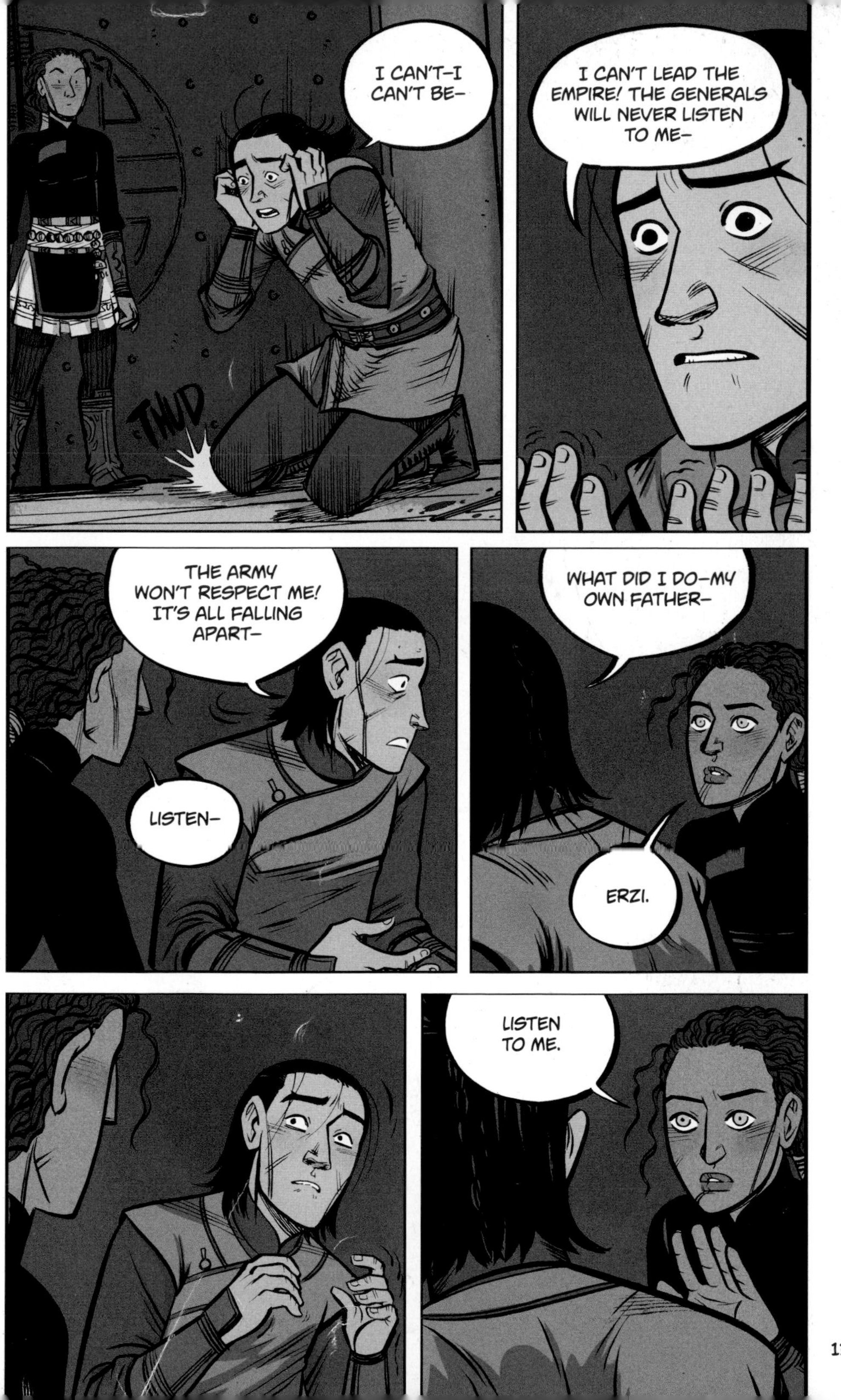
I CAN'T–I CAN'T BE–
THUD
I CAN'T LEAD THE EMPIRE! THE GENERALS WILL NEVER LISTEN TO ME–
THE ARMY WON'T RESPECT ME! IT'S ALL FALLING APART–
LISTEN–
WHAT DID I DO–MY OWN FATHER–
ERZI.
LISTEN TO ME.

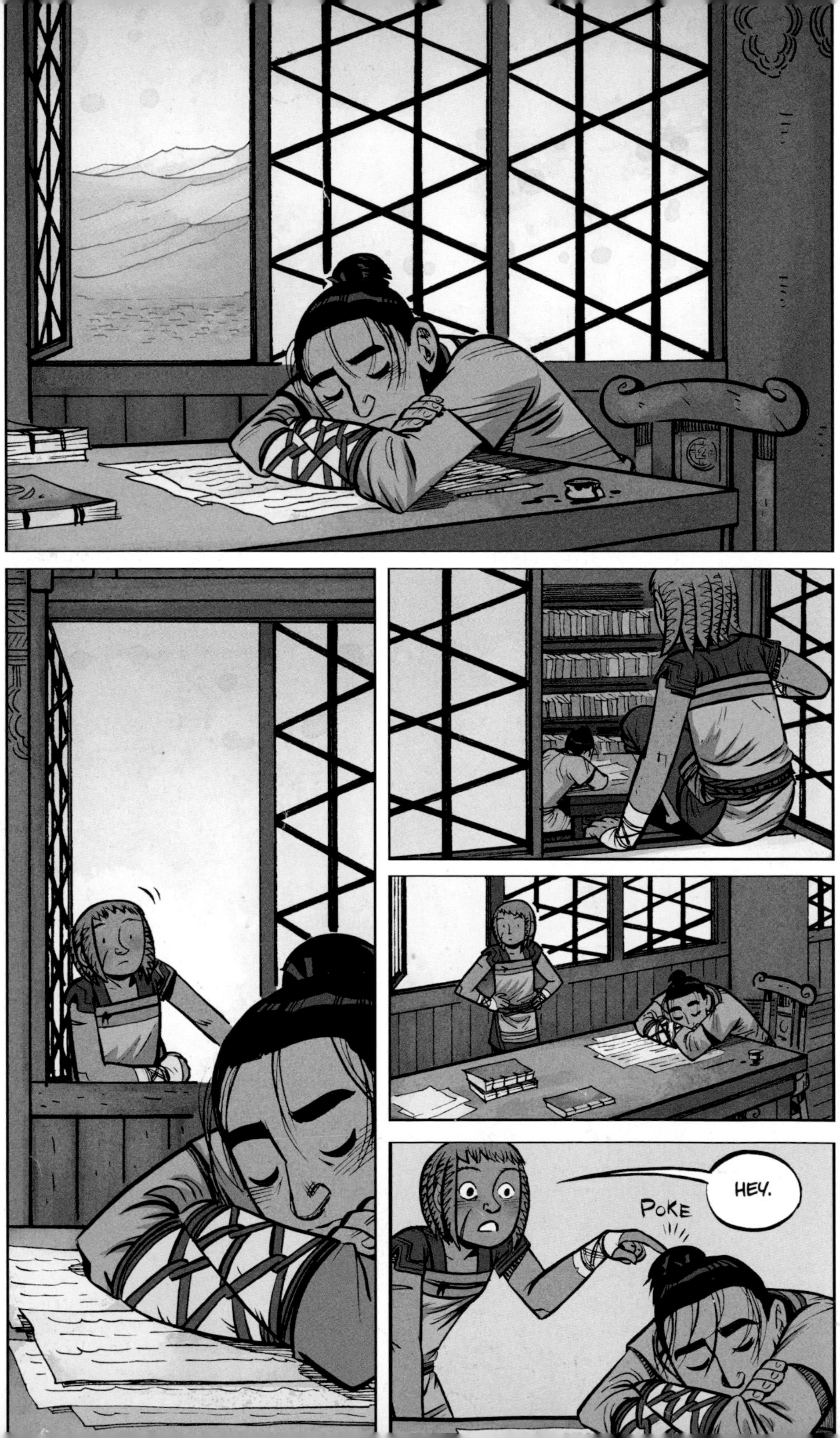
HEY.
POKE

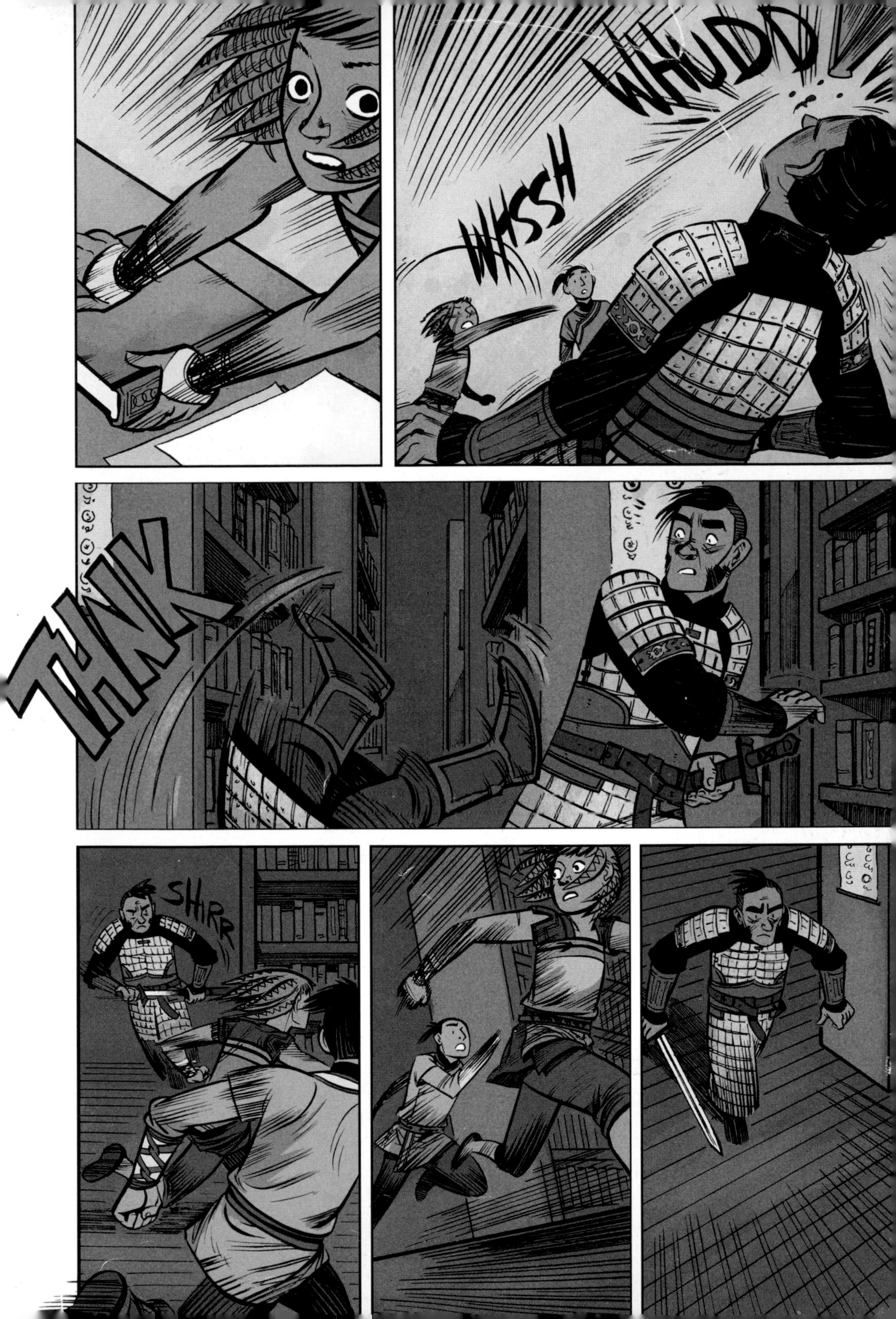
WHUDD!
WHSSH
THNK
SHIRR

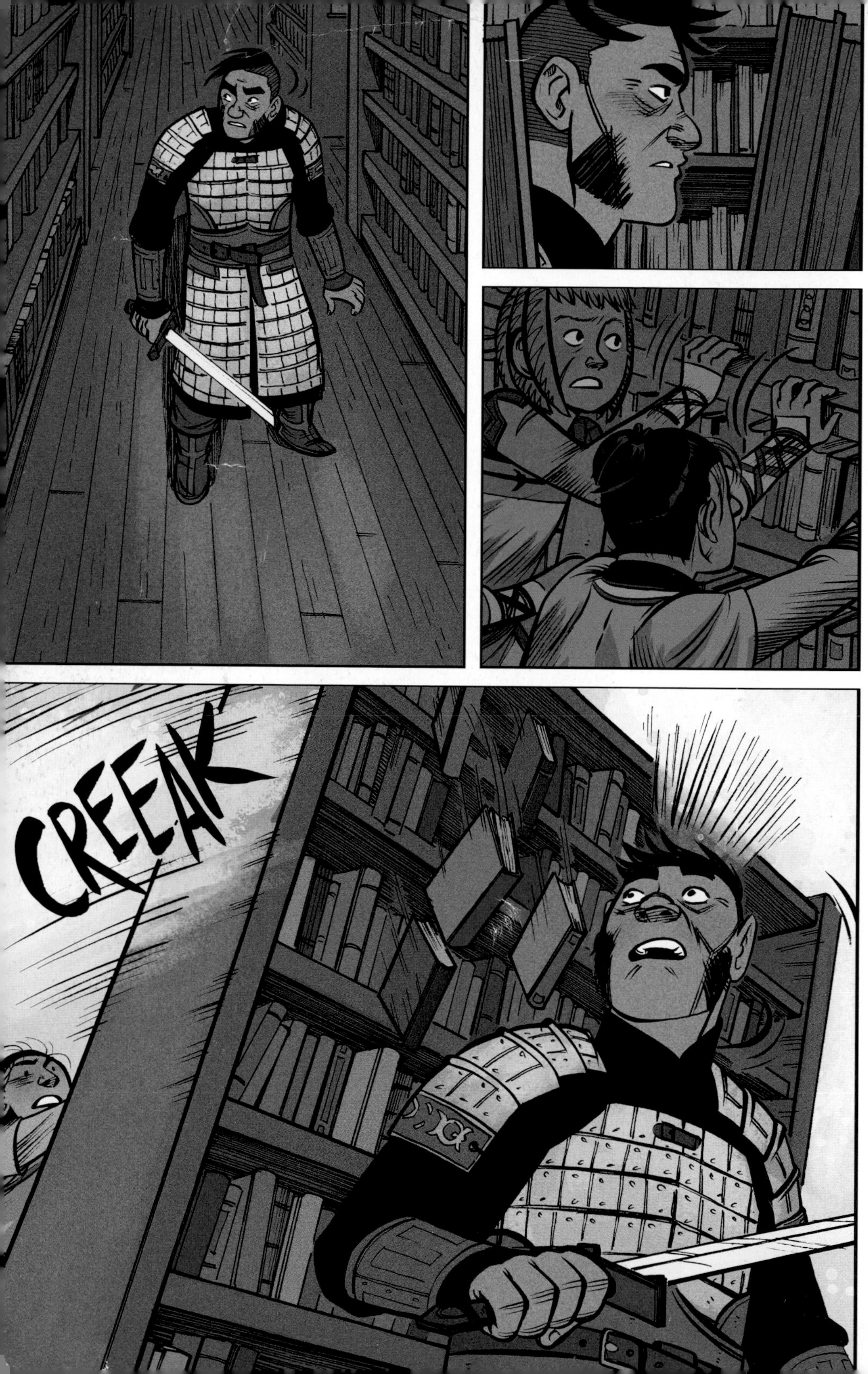
CREEAK

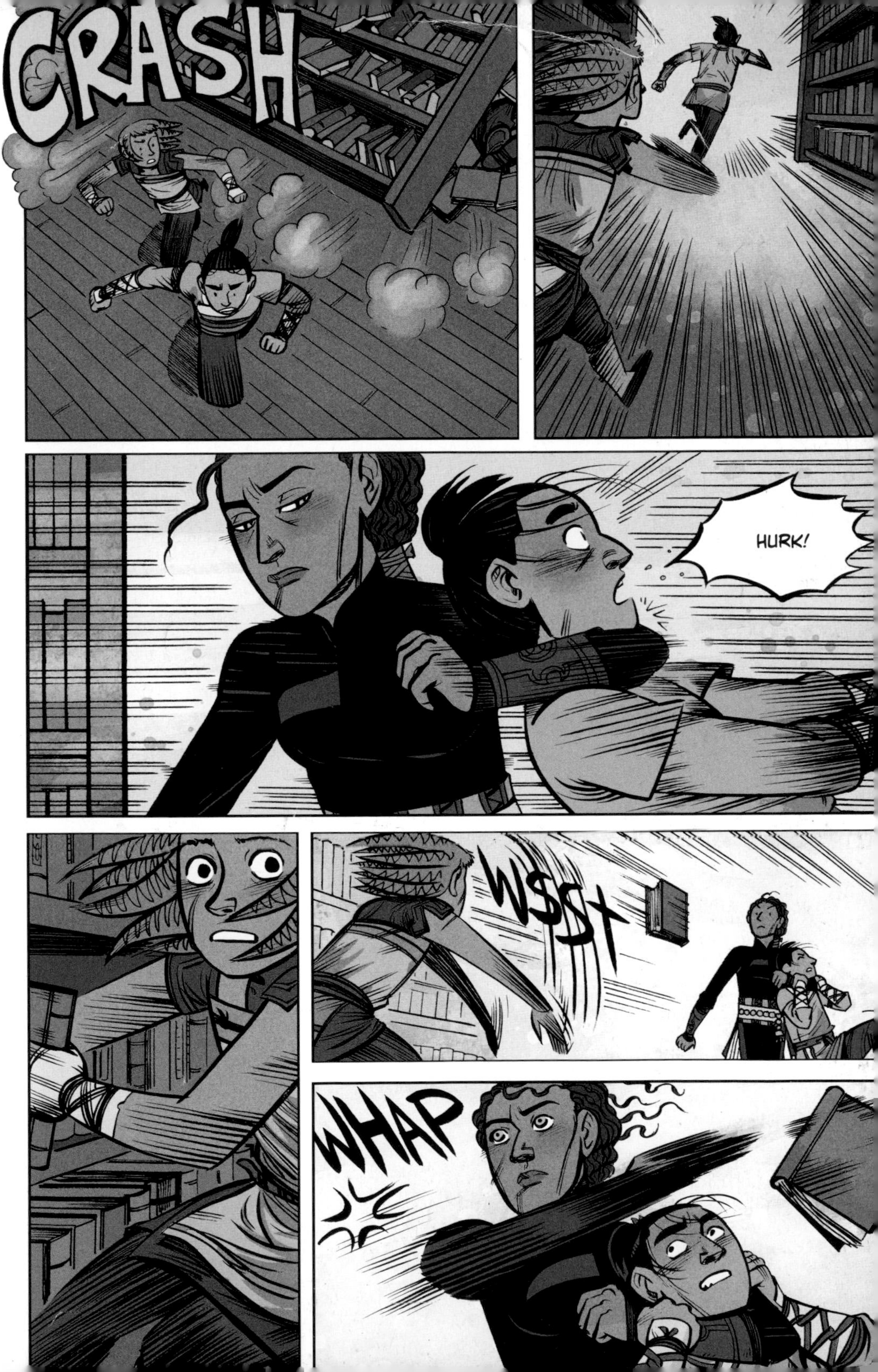
CRASH
HURK!
WSSSH
WHAP

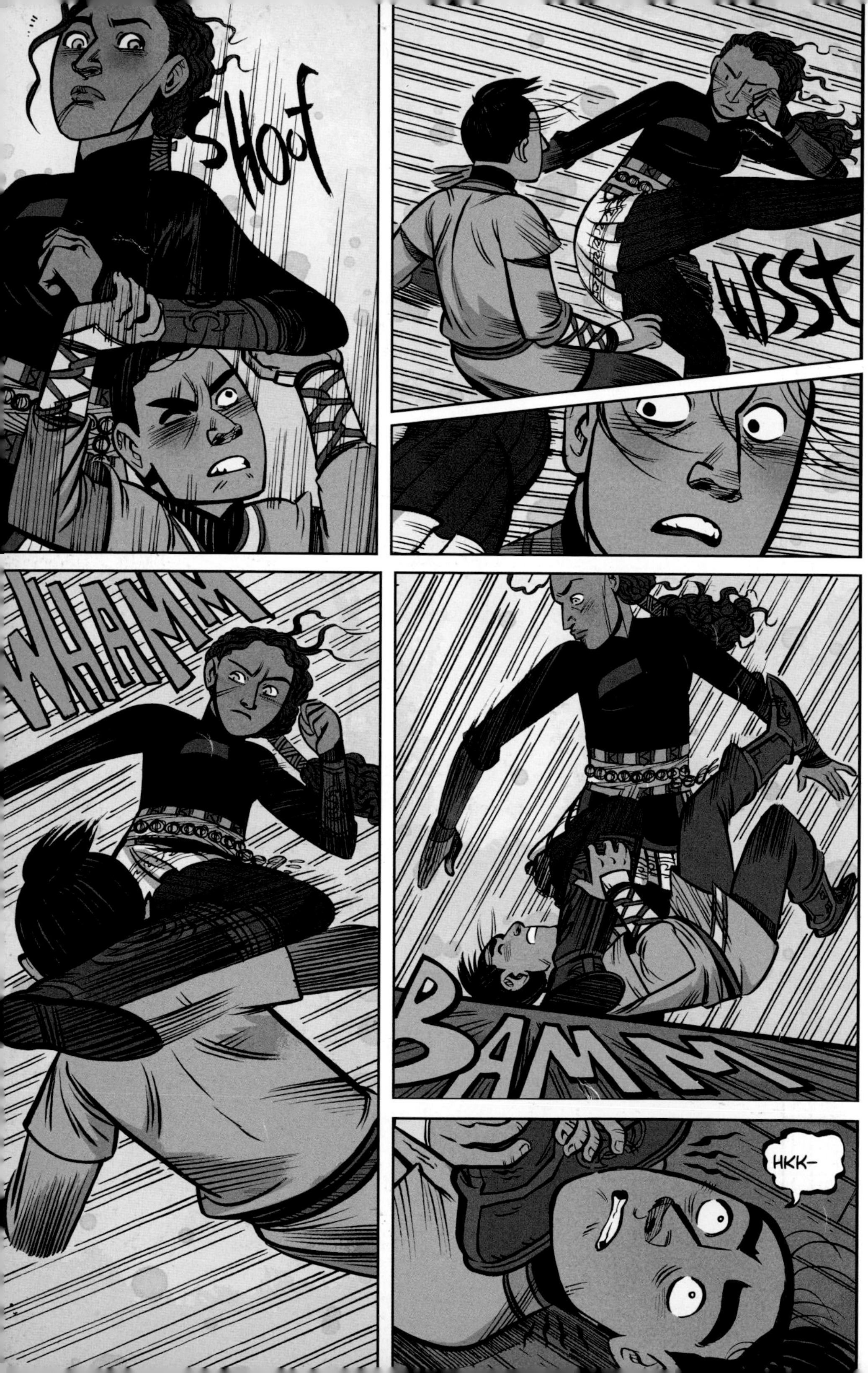
SHOOF
WSST
WHAMM
BAMM
HKK-

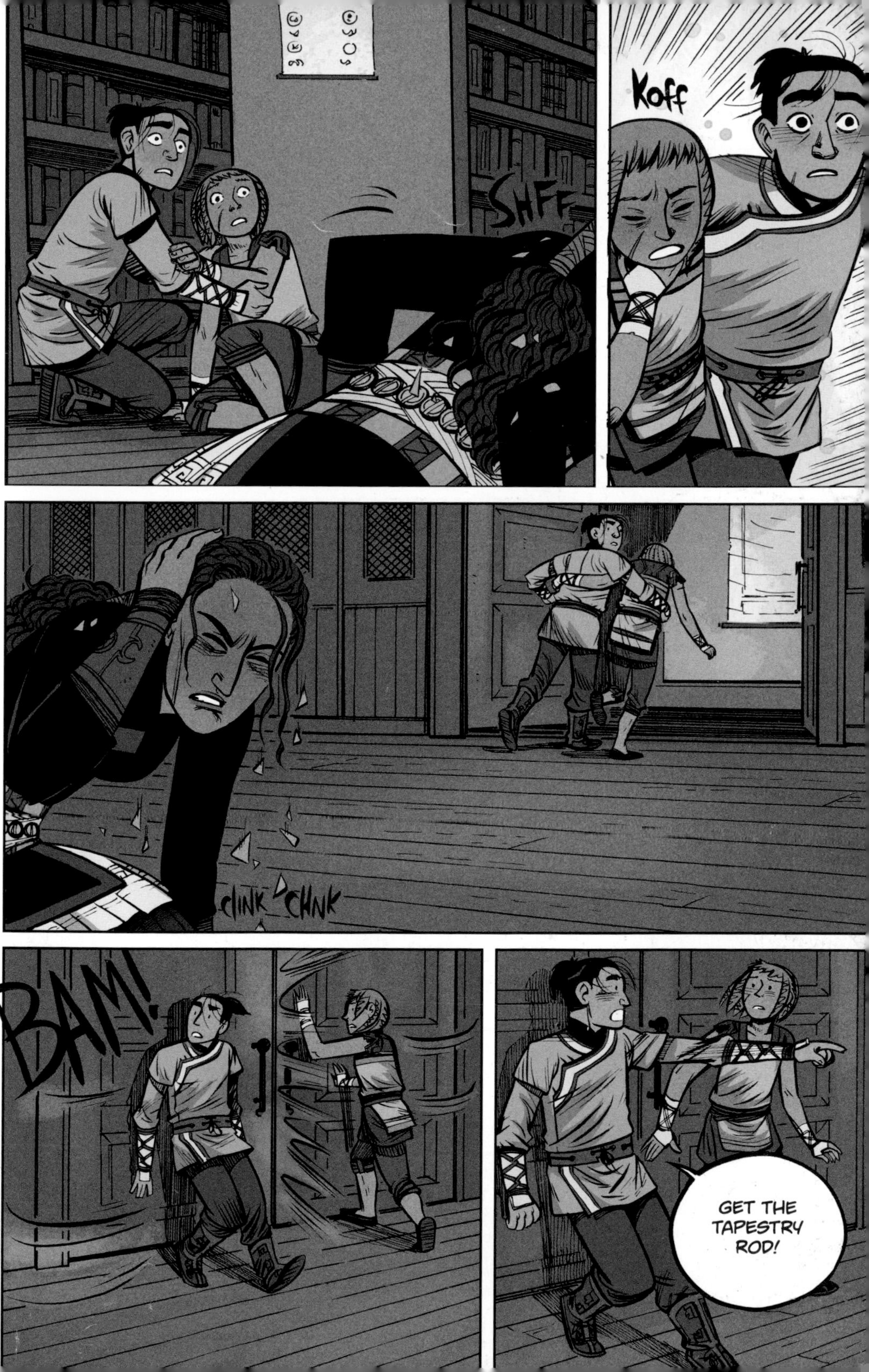
SHFF
Koff
CLINK CHNK
BAM!
GET THE TAPESTRY ROD!

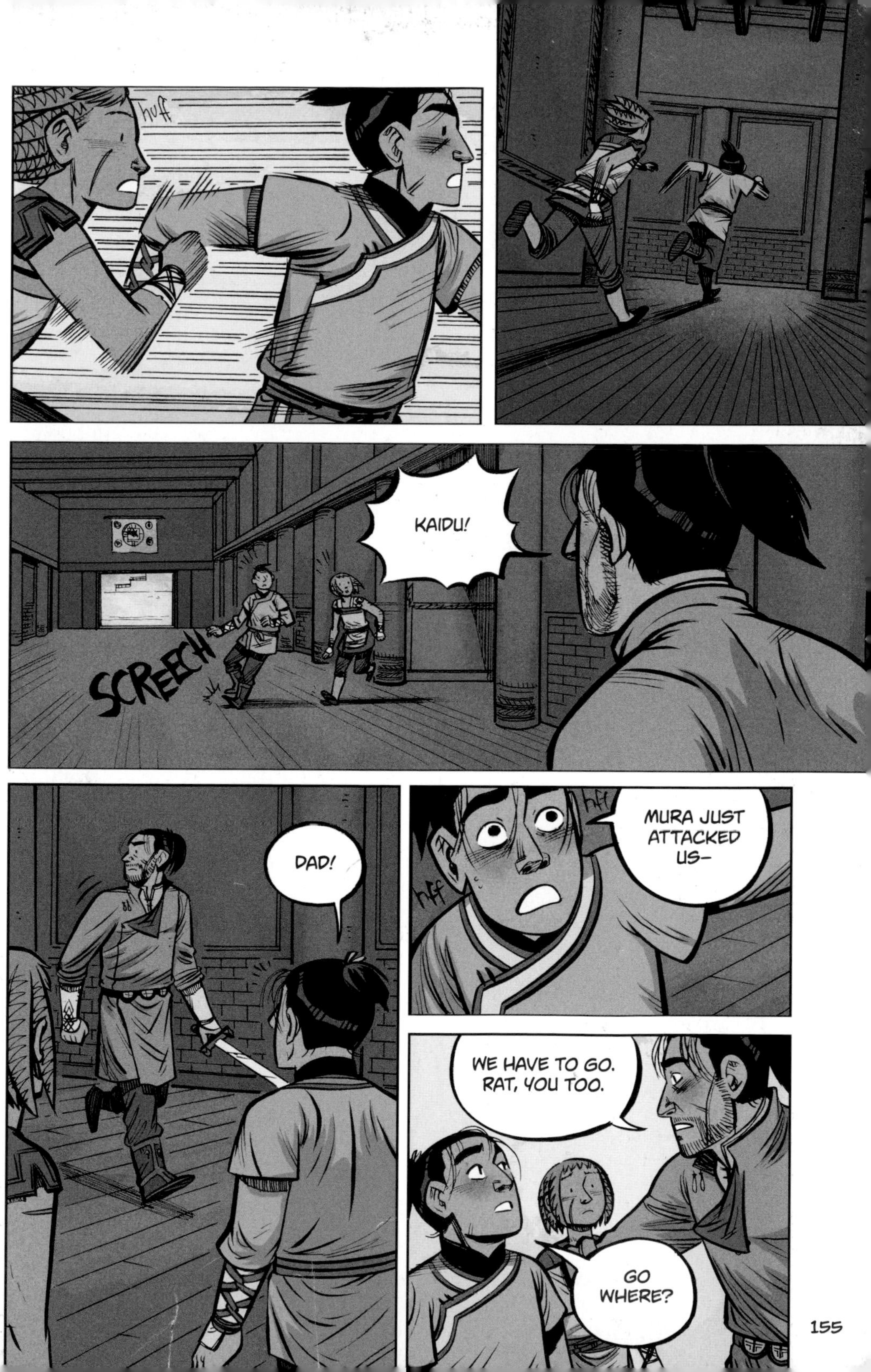
huff
KAIDU!
SCREECH
DAD!
hff
MURA JUST ATTACKED US–
hff
WE HAVE TO GO. RAT, YOU TOO.
GO WHERE?

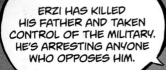

ERZI HAS KILLED HIS FATHER AND TAKEN CONTROL OF THE MILITARY. HE'S ARRESTING ANYONE WHO OPPOSES HIM.

I NEVER LIKED THAT BOY. APPARENTLY THE FEELING IS MUTUAL.

THE GENERAL OF ALL BLADES ...IS DEAD?

YES. AND NOW WE MUST LEAVE THE CITY.

DAD...THERE'S BLOOD ON YOUR COAT.

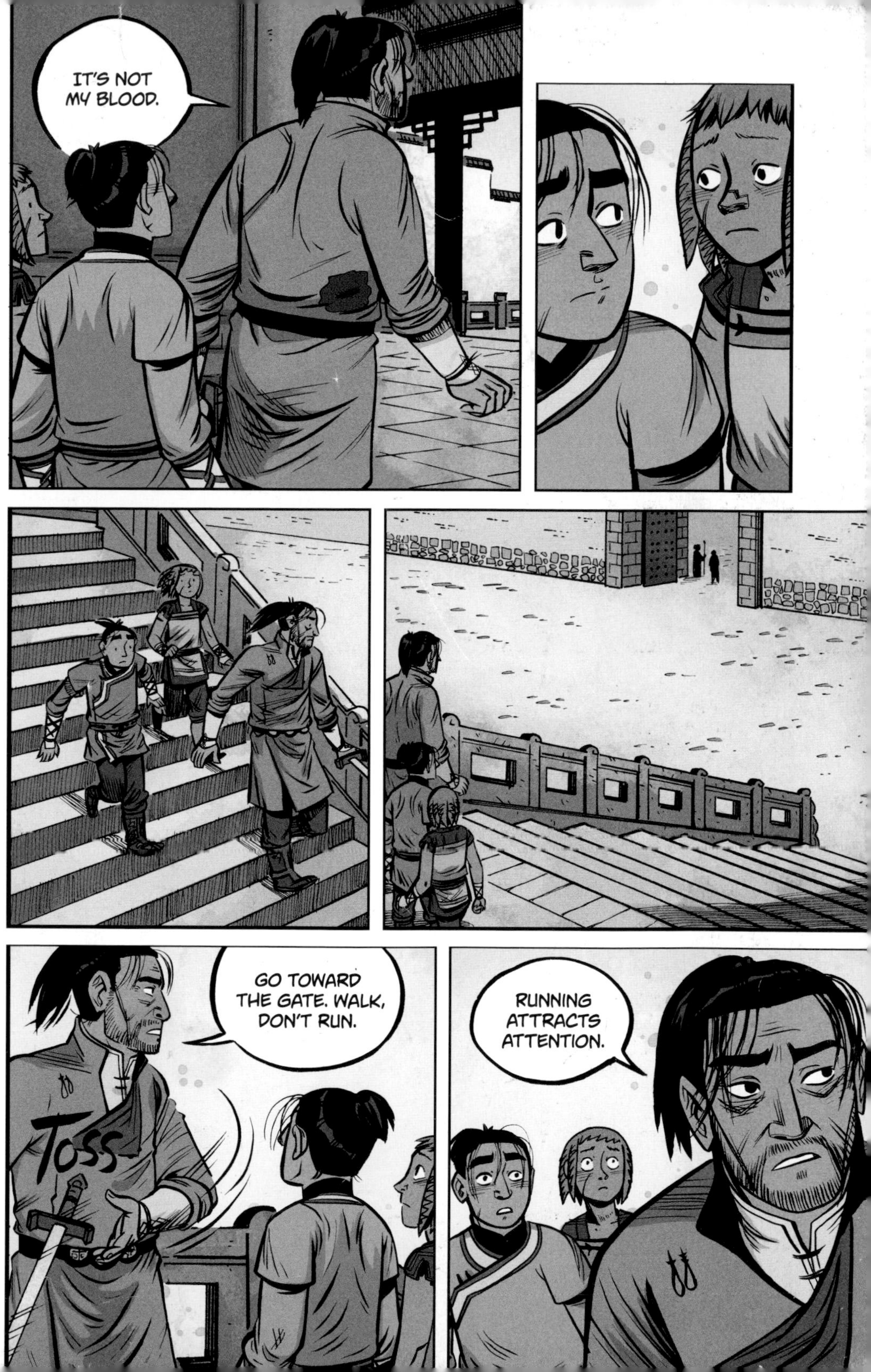
IT'S NOT MY BLOOD.
GO TOWARD THE GATE. WALK, DON'T RUN.
TOSS
RUNNING ATTRACTS ATTENTION.

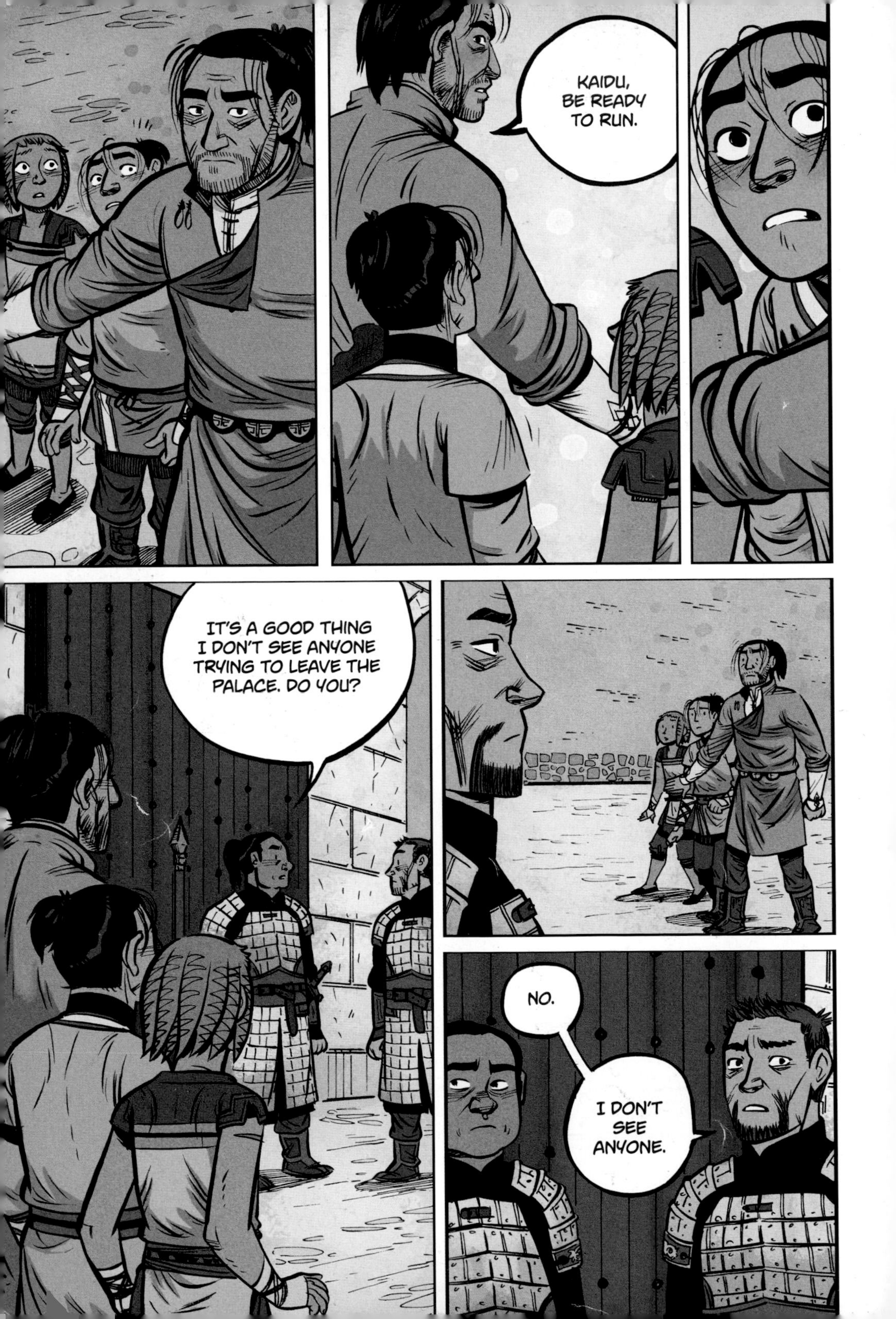
KAIDU, BE READY TO RUN.
IT'S A GOOD THING I DON'T SEE ANYONE TRYING TO LEAVE THE PALACE. DO YOU?
NO.
I DON'T SEE ANYONE.

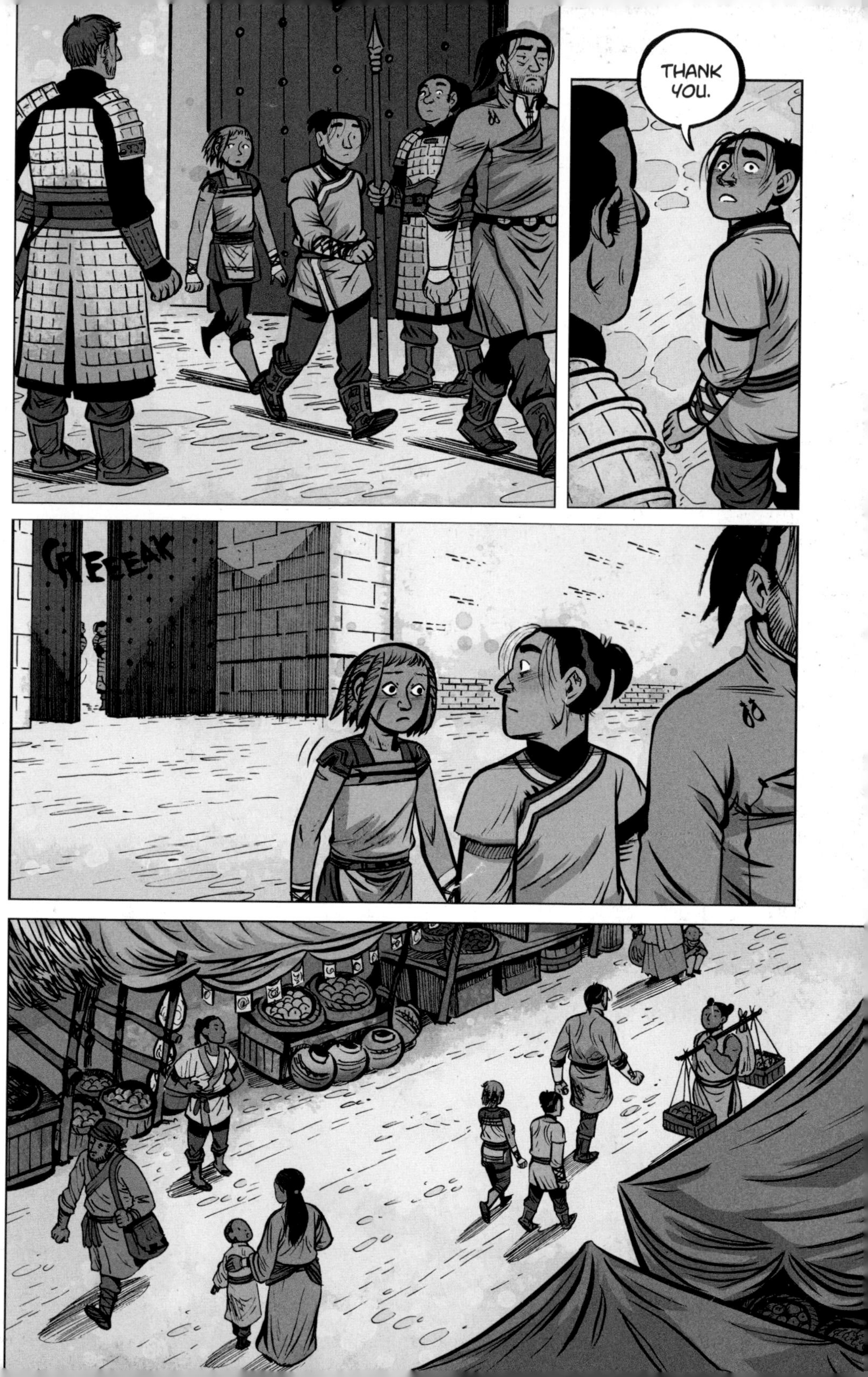
THANK YOU.
CREEEAK

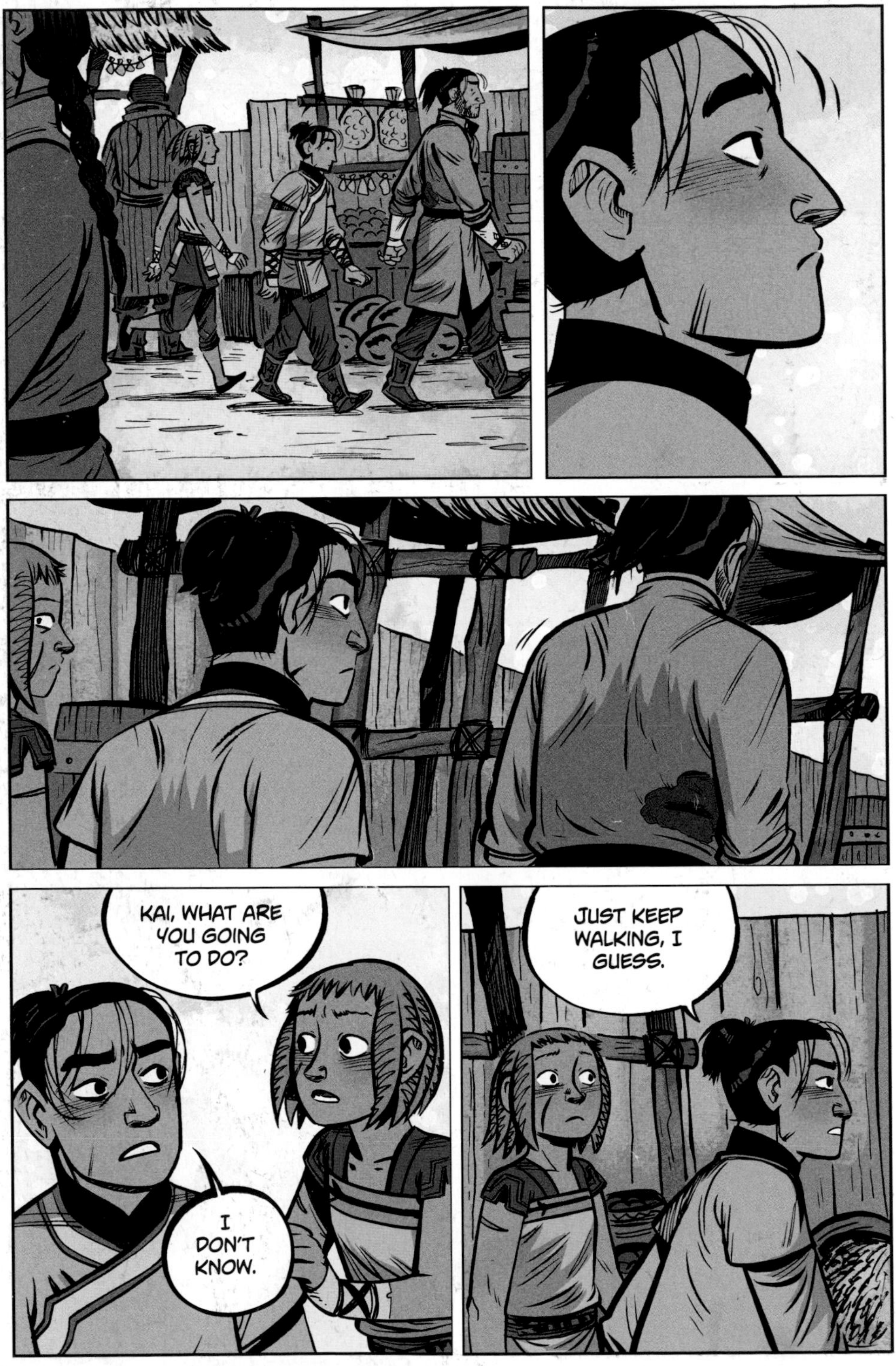
KAI, WHAT ARE YOU GOING TO DO?
I DON'T KNOW.
JUST KEEP WALKING, I GUESS.

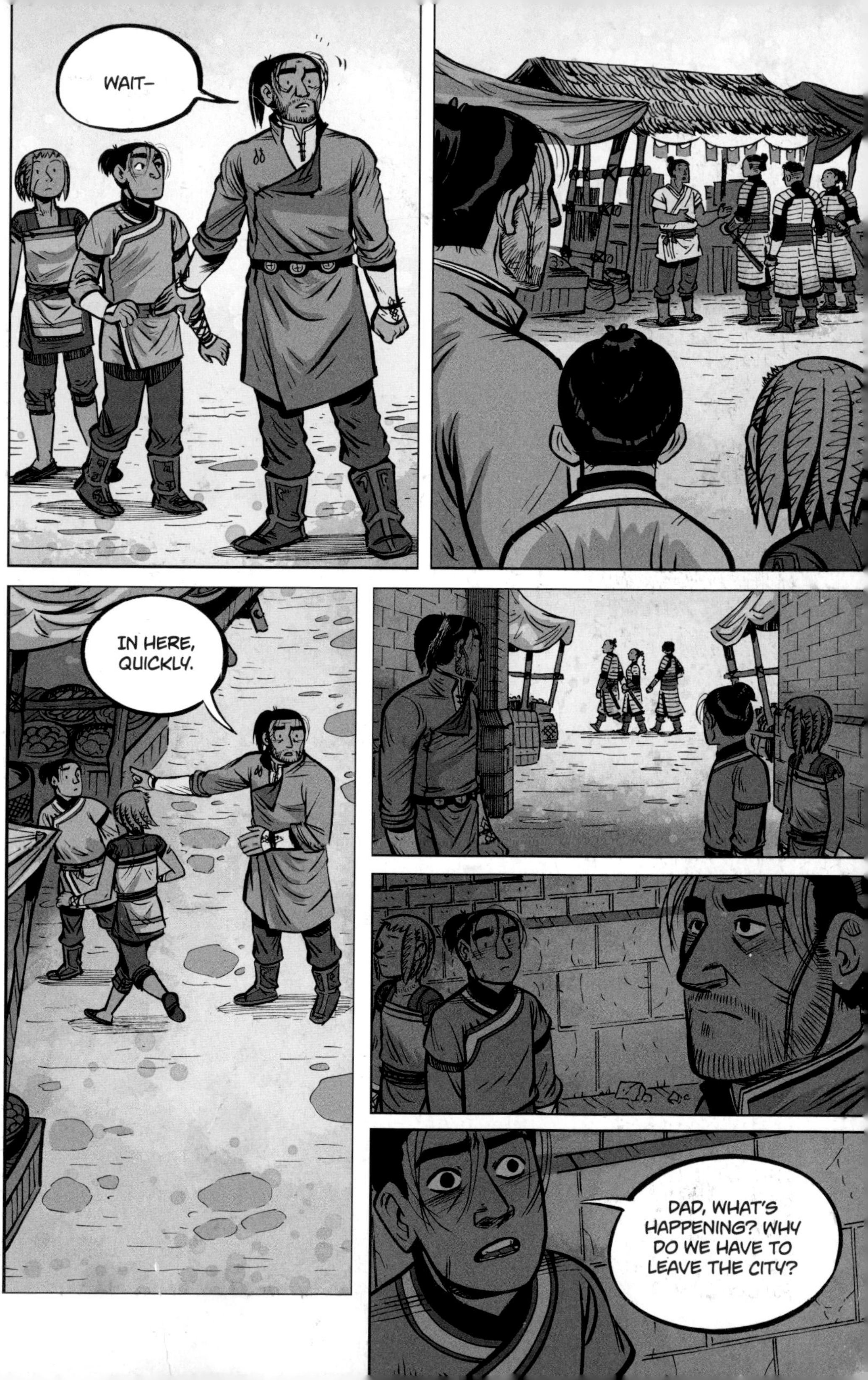
WAIT-
IN HERE, QUICKLY.
DAD, WHAT'S HAPPENING? WHY DO WE HAVE TO LEAVE THE CITY?

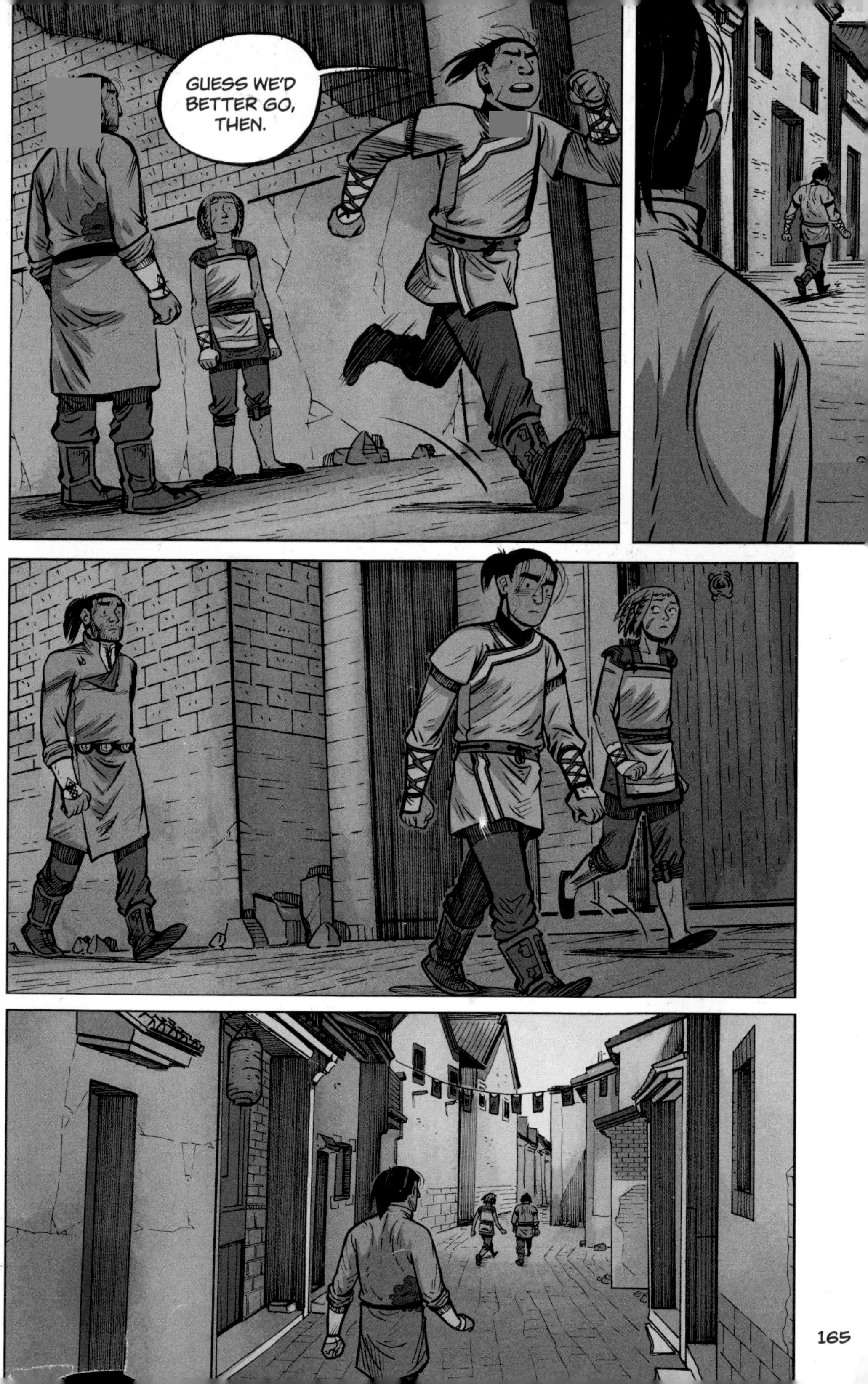
GUESS WE'D BETTER GO, THEN.

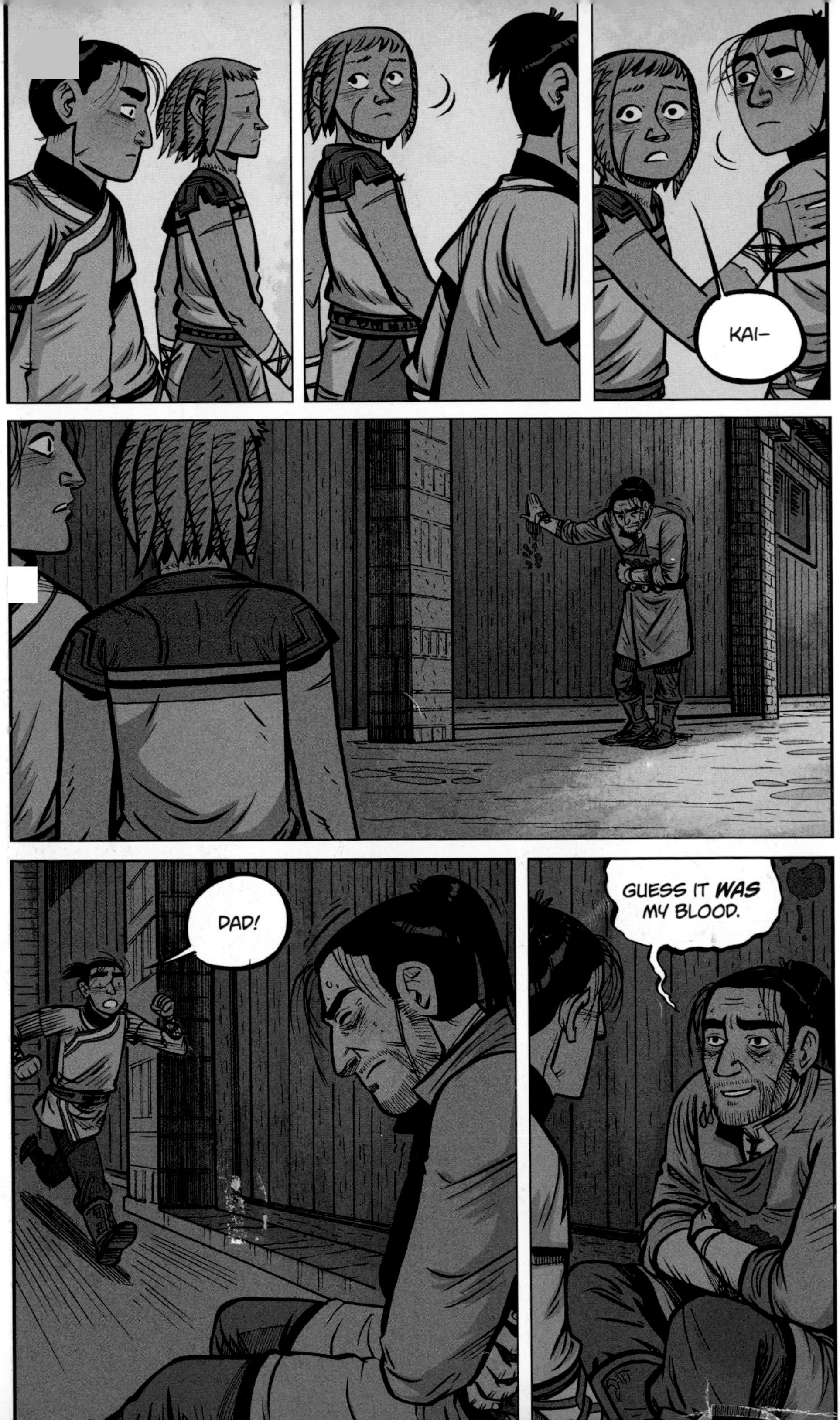
KAI–
DAD!
GUESS IT WAS MY BLOOD.

167

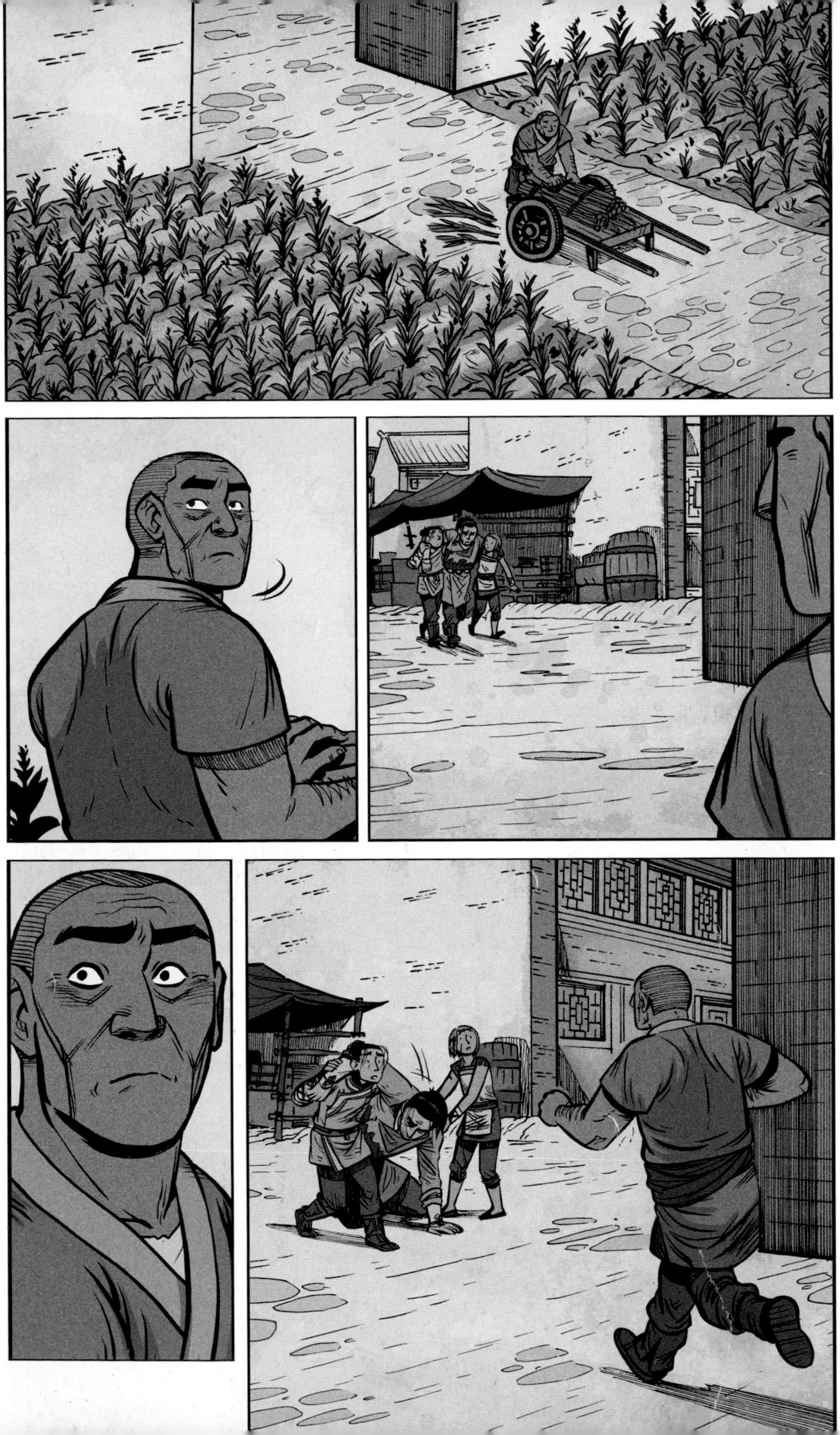

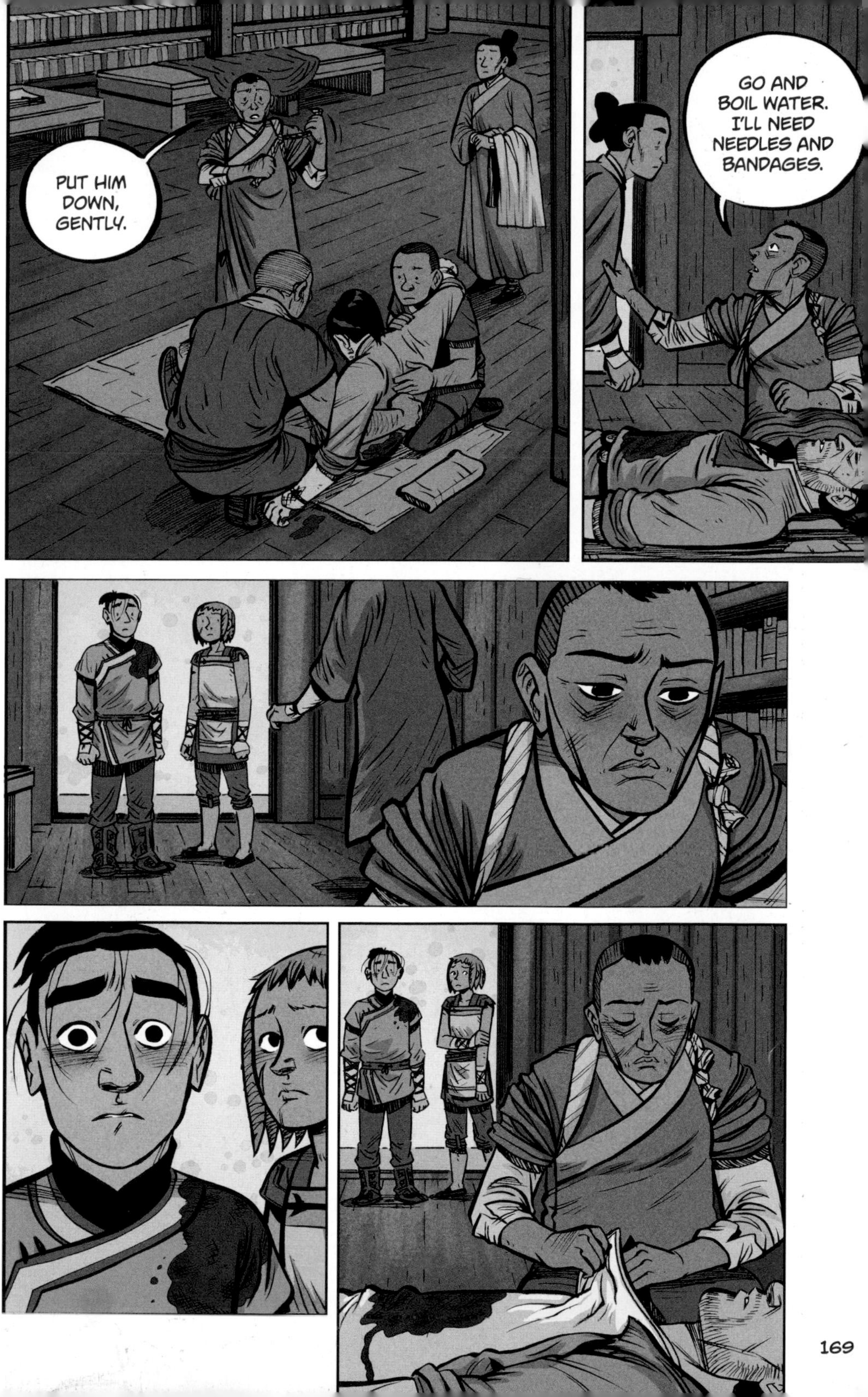
PUT HIM DOWN, GENTLY.
GO AND BOIL WATER. I'LL NEED NEEDLES AND BANDAGES.

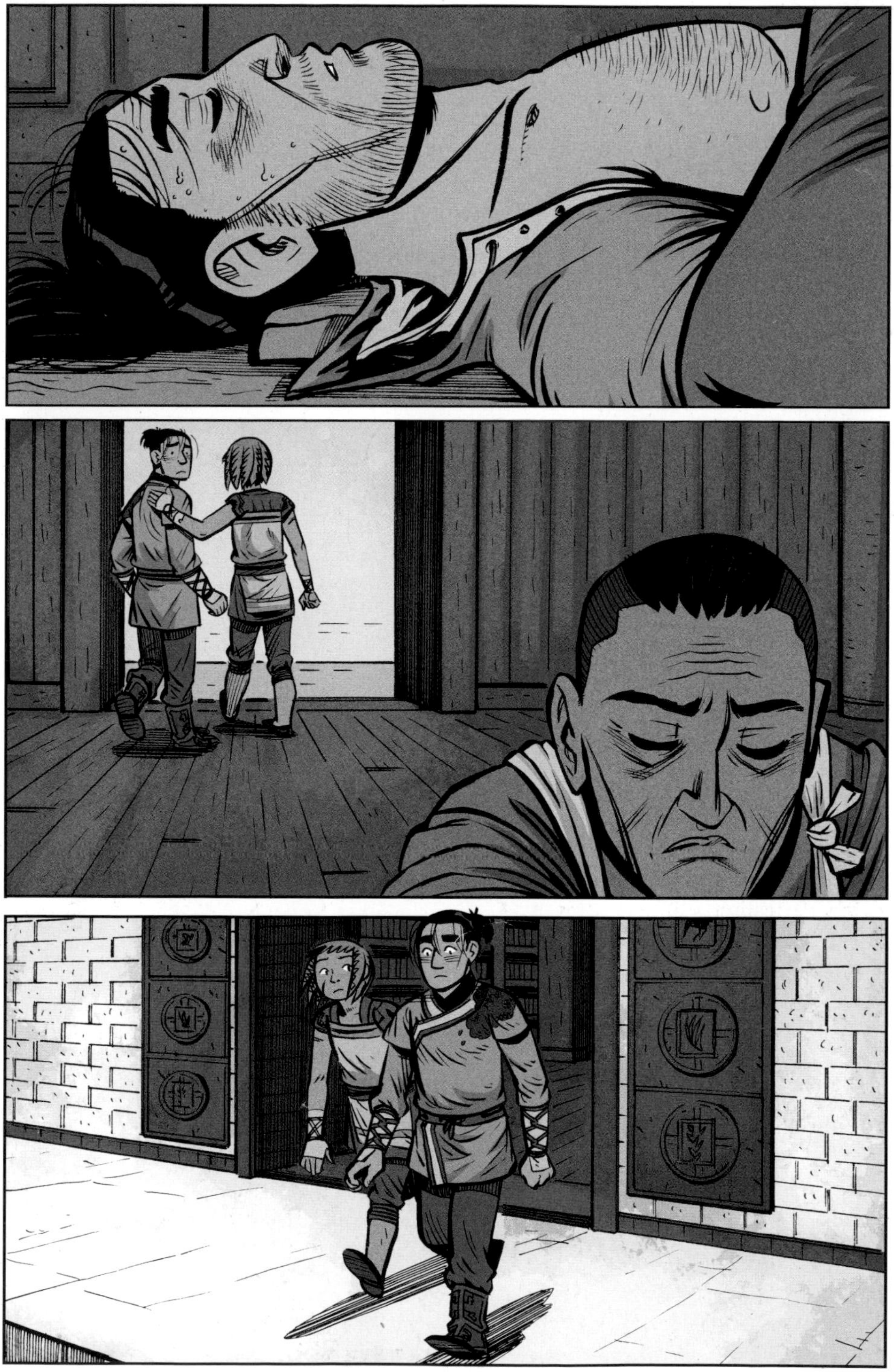

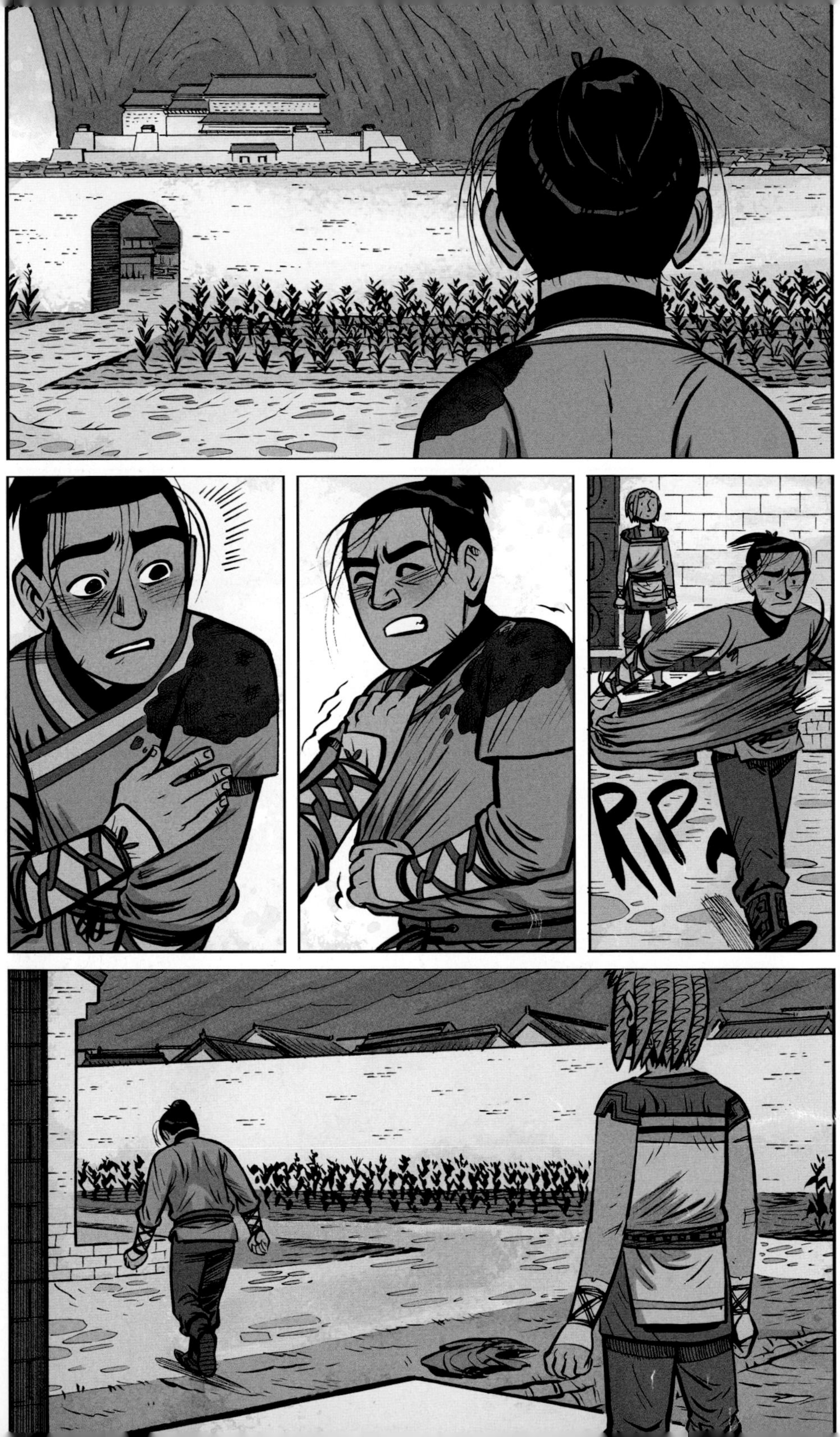
RIP

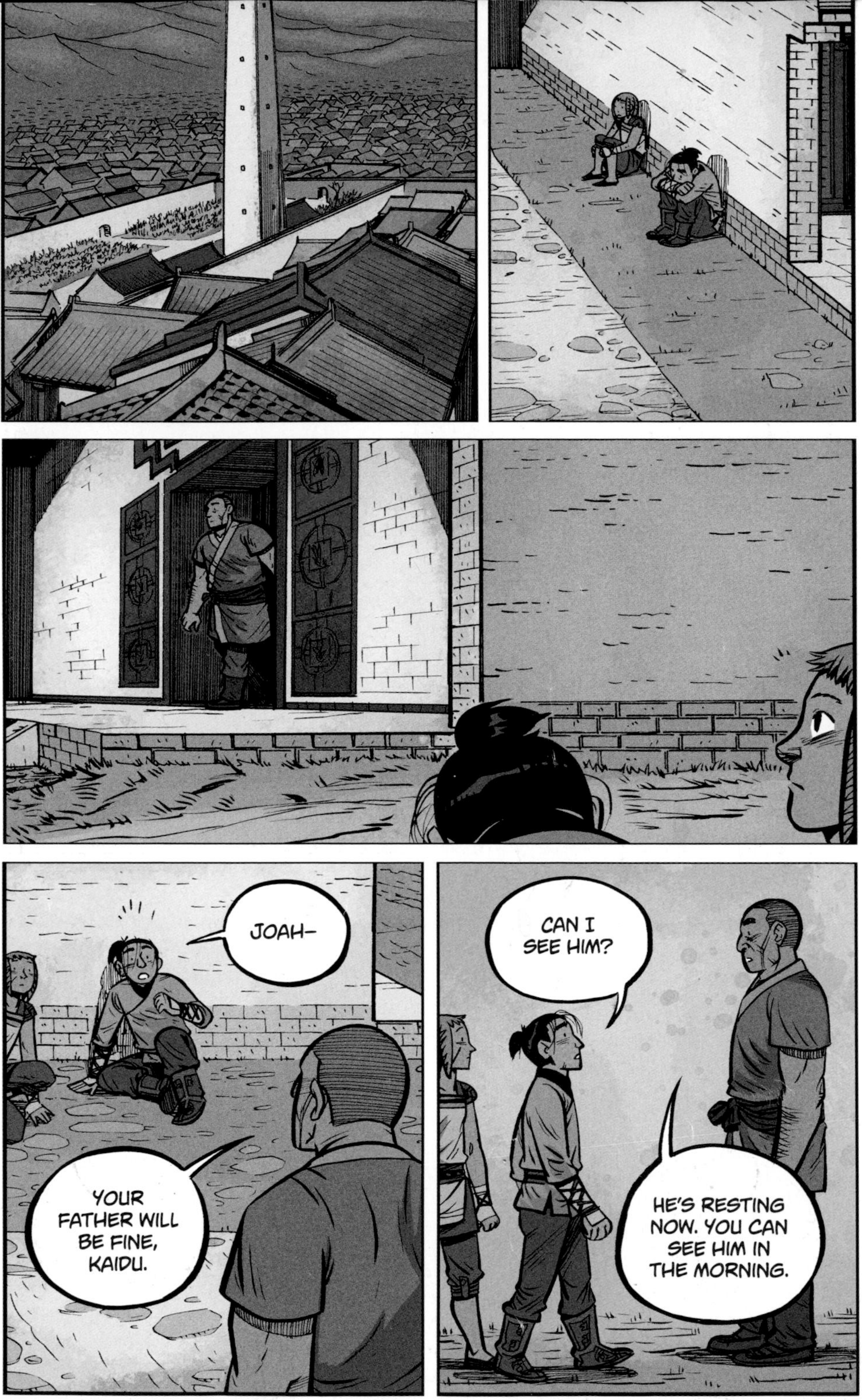
JOAH–
YOUR FATHER WILL BE FINE, KAIDU.
CAN I SEE HIM?
HE'S RESTING NOW. YOU CAN SEE HIM IN THE MORNING.

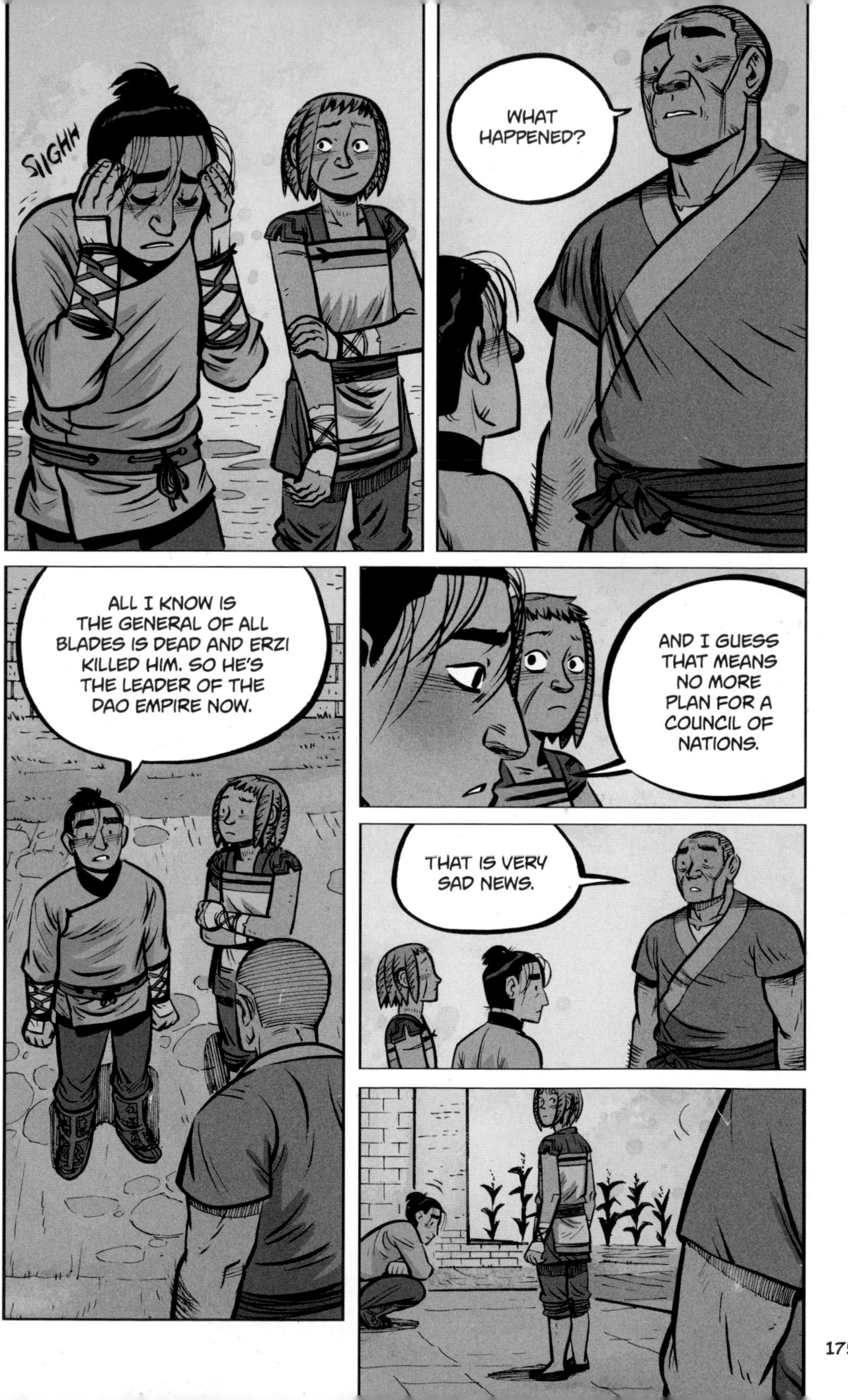
SIIGHH
WHAT HAPPENED?
ALL I KNOW IS THE GENERAL OF ALL BLADES IS DEAD AND ERZI KILLED HIM. SO HE'S THE LEADER OF THE DAO EMPIRE NOW.
AND I GUESS THAT MEANS NO MORE PLAN FOR A COUNCIL OF NATIONS.
THAT IS VERY SAD NEWS.

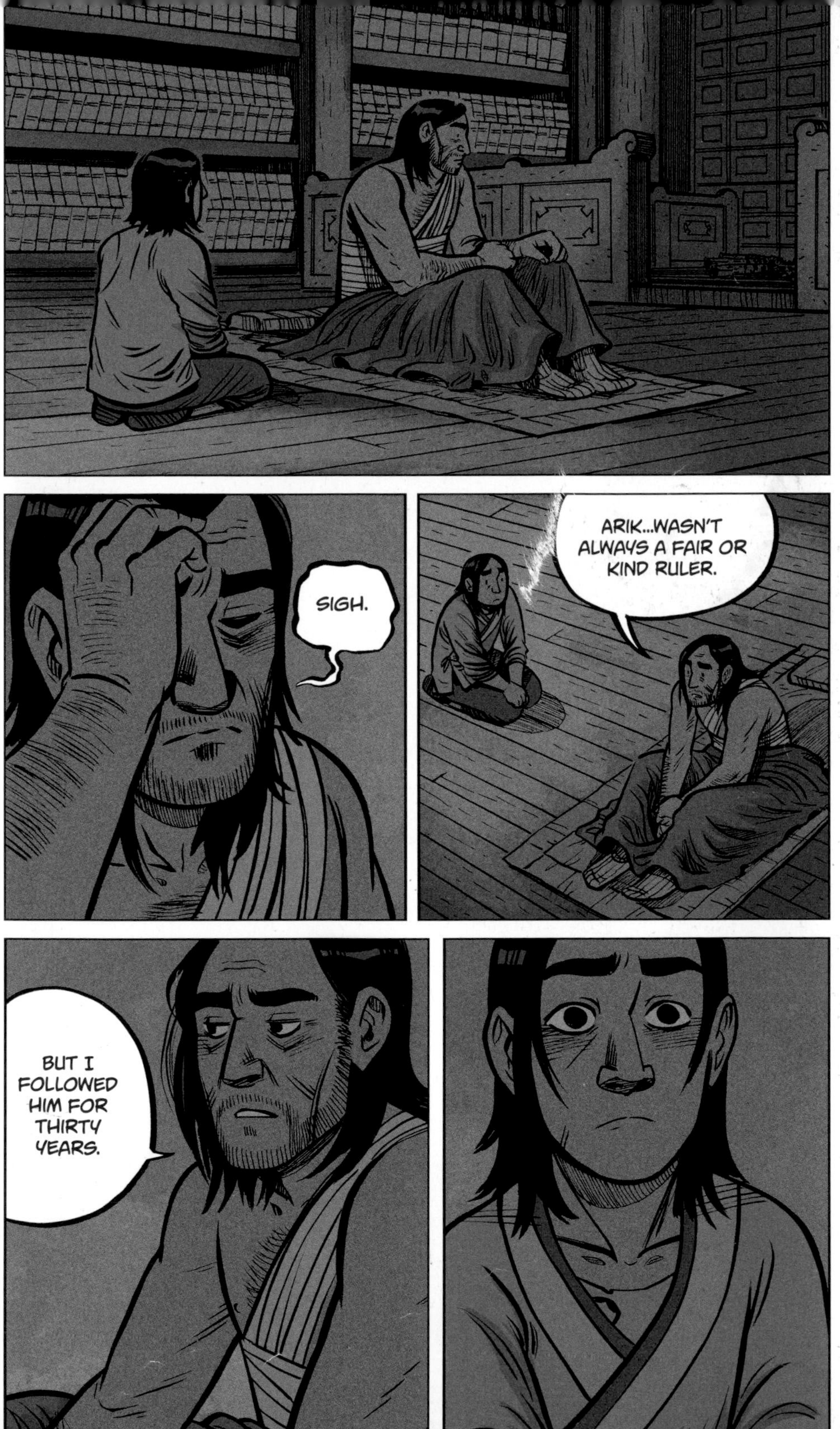
SIGH.
ARIK...WASN'T ALWAYS A FAIR OR KIND RULER.
BUT I FOLLOWED HIM FOR THIRTY YEARS.

187

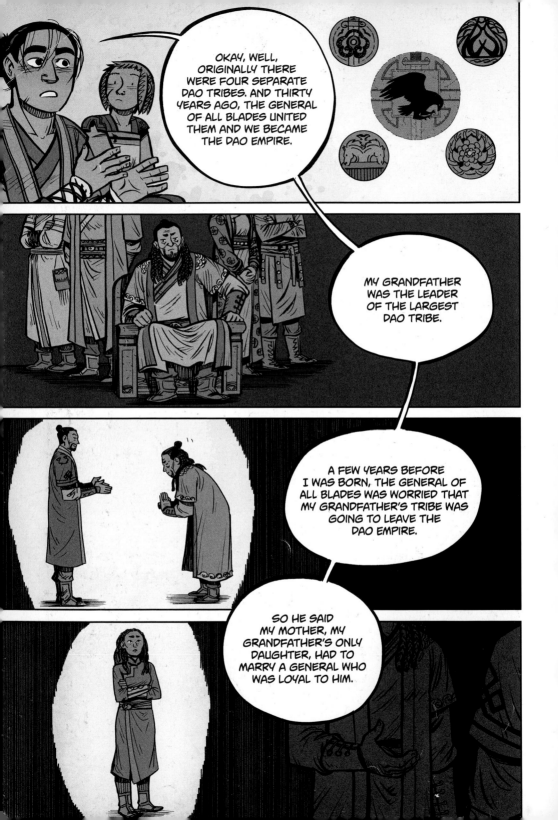

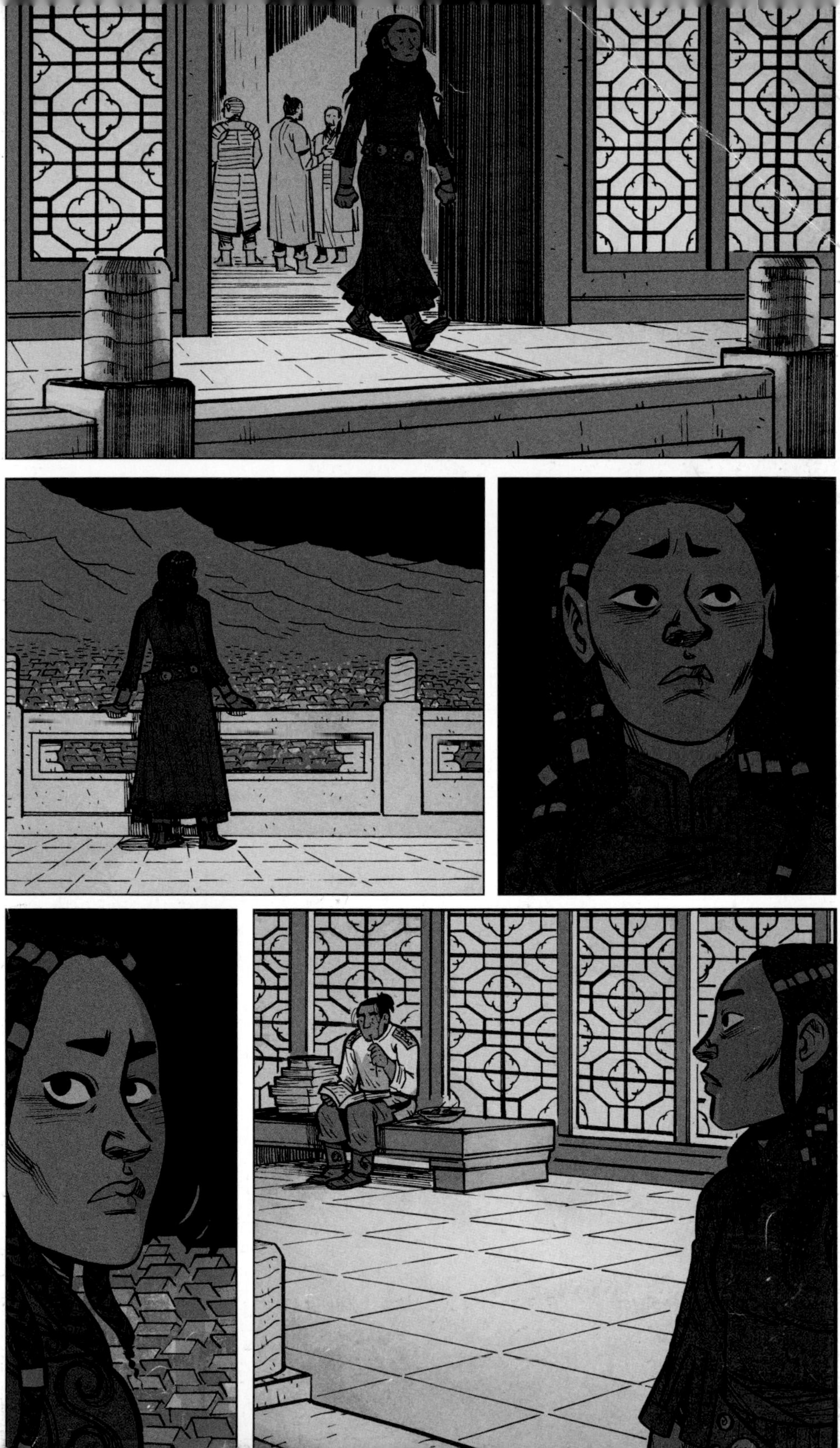

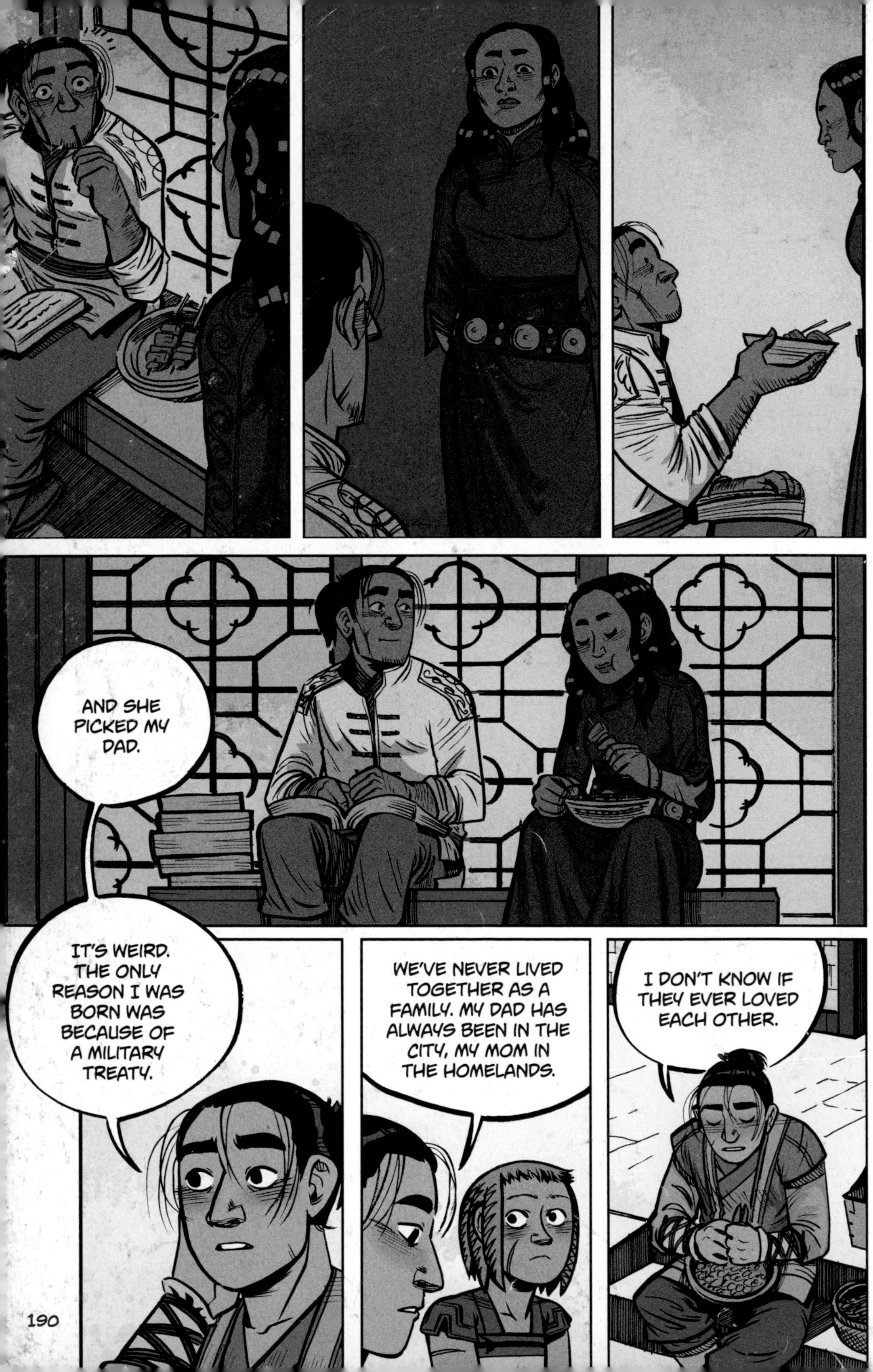
AND SHE PICKED MY DAD.
IT'S WEIRD. THE ONLY REASON I WAS BORN WAS BECAUSE OF A MILITARY TREATY.
WE'VE NEVER LIVED TOGETHER AS A FAMILY. MY DAD HAS ALWAYS BEEN IN THE CITY, MY MOM IN THE HOMELANDS.
I DON'T KNOW IF THEY EVER LOVED EACH OTHER.

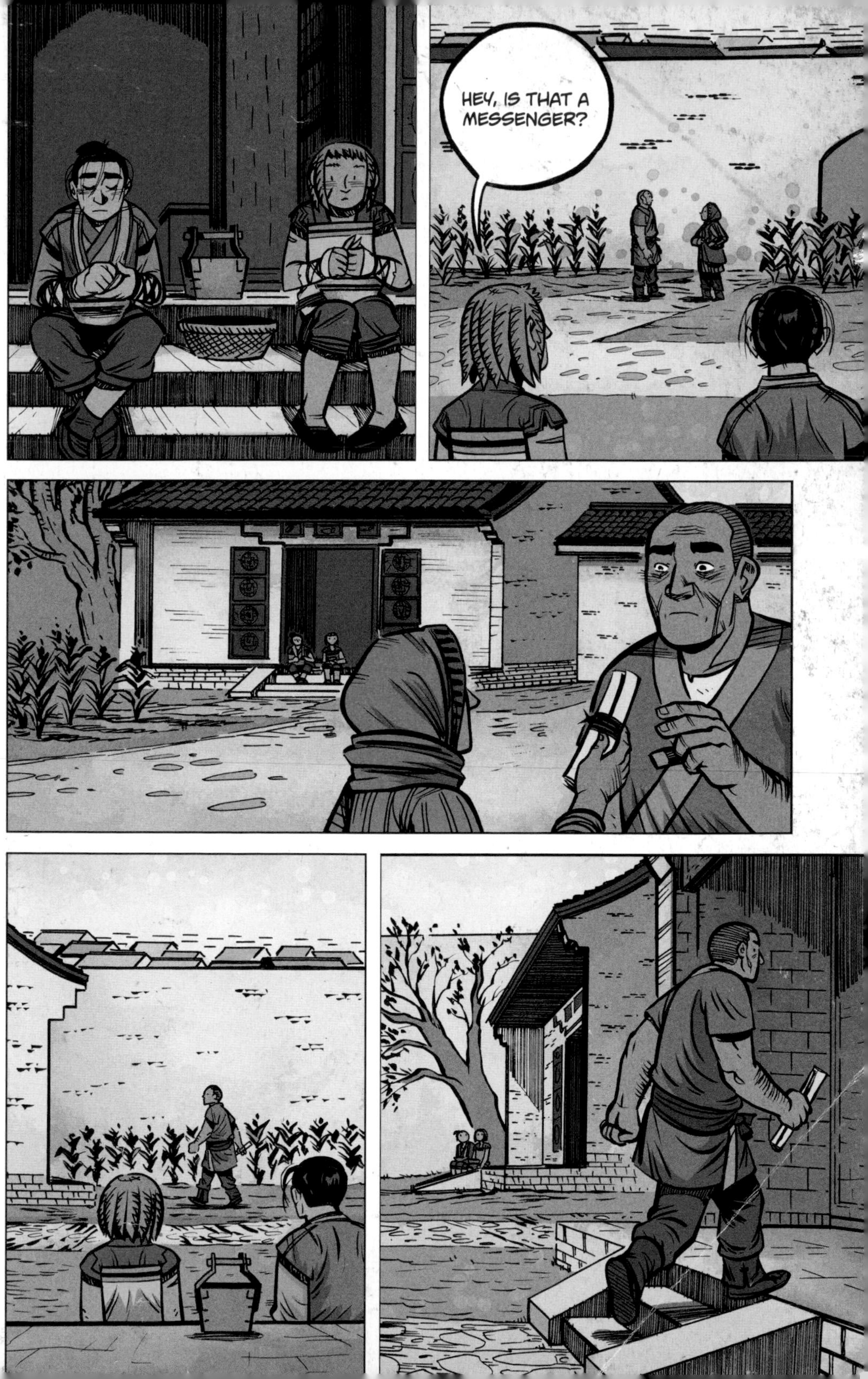
HEY, IS THAT A MESSENGER?

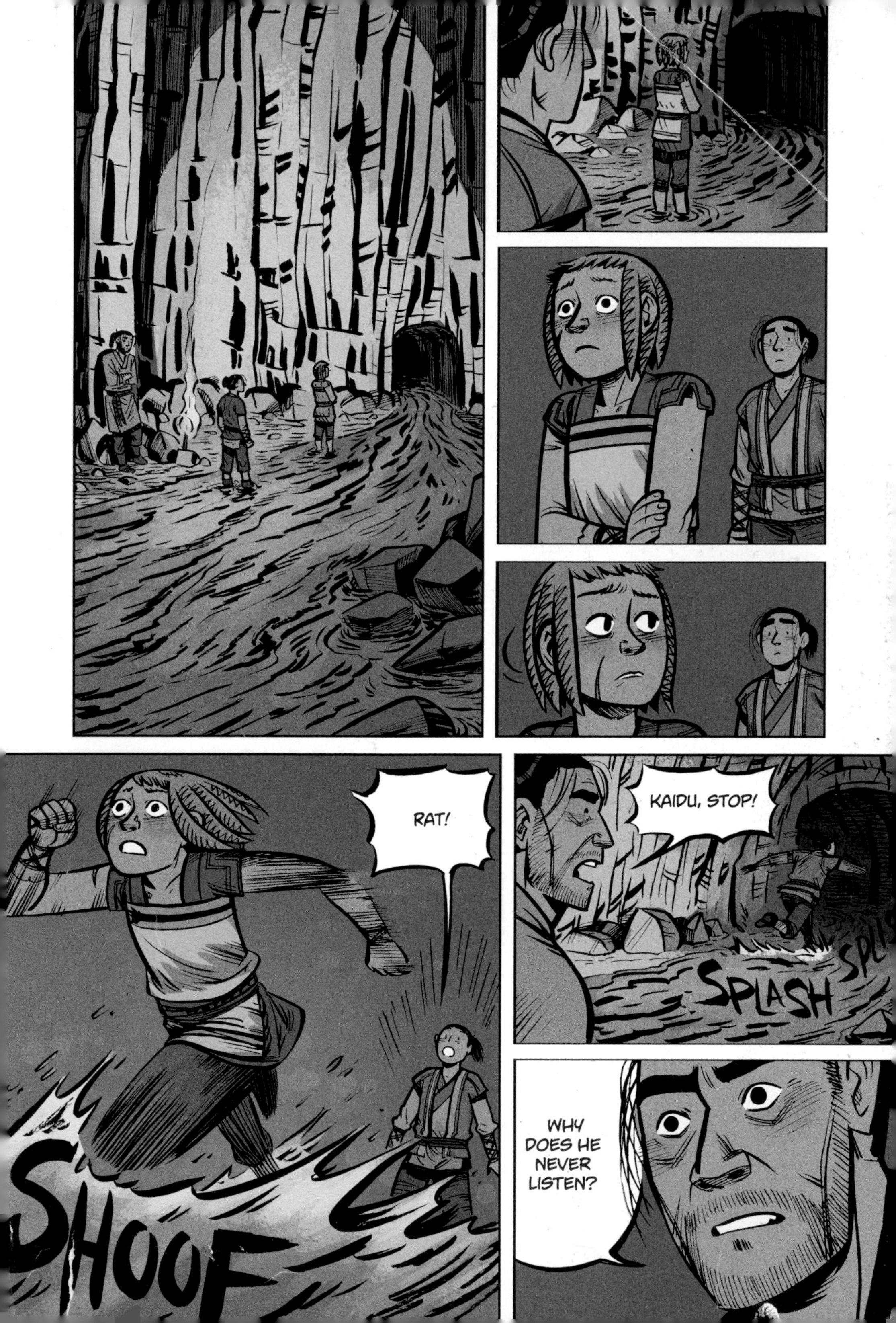
RAT!
SHOOF
KAIDU, STOP!
SPLASH
SPLASH
WHY DOES HE NEVER LISTEN?

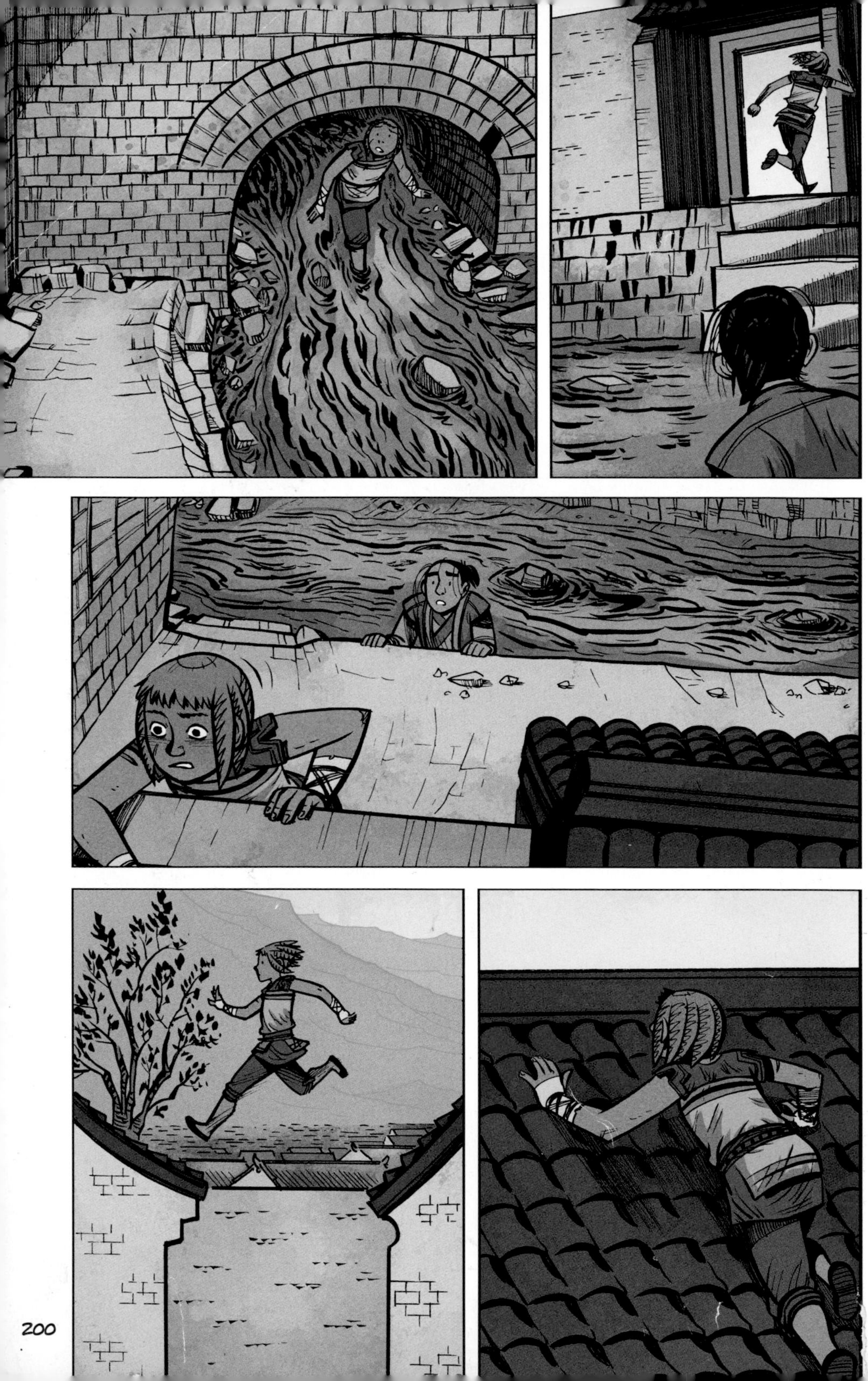

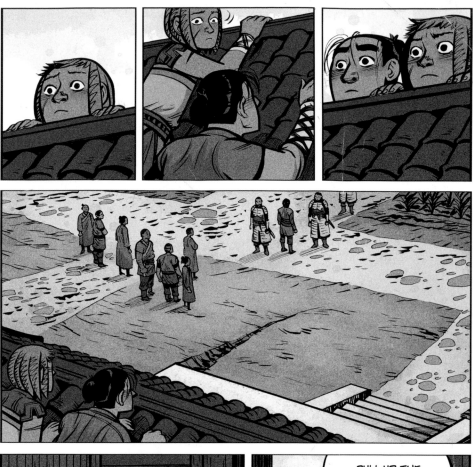

PULL UP THE FLOORBOARDS. IT'S HIDDEN UNDERNEATH.

FWAP

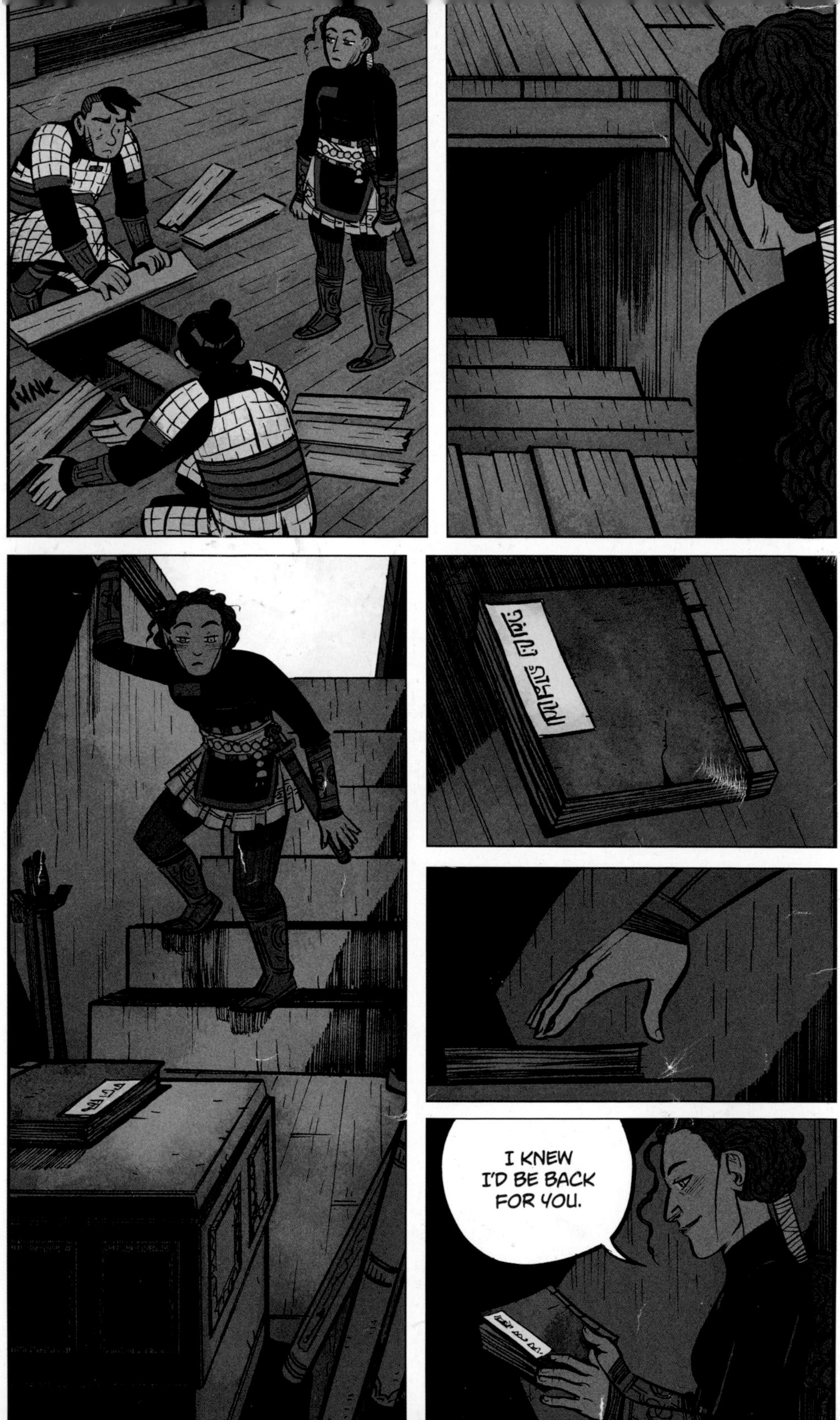
THNK
I KNEW I'D BE BACK FOR YOU.

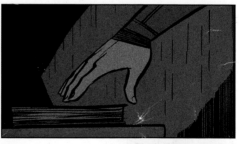

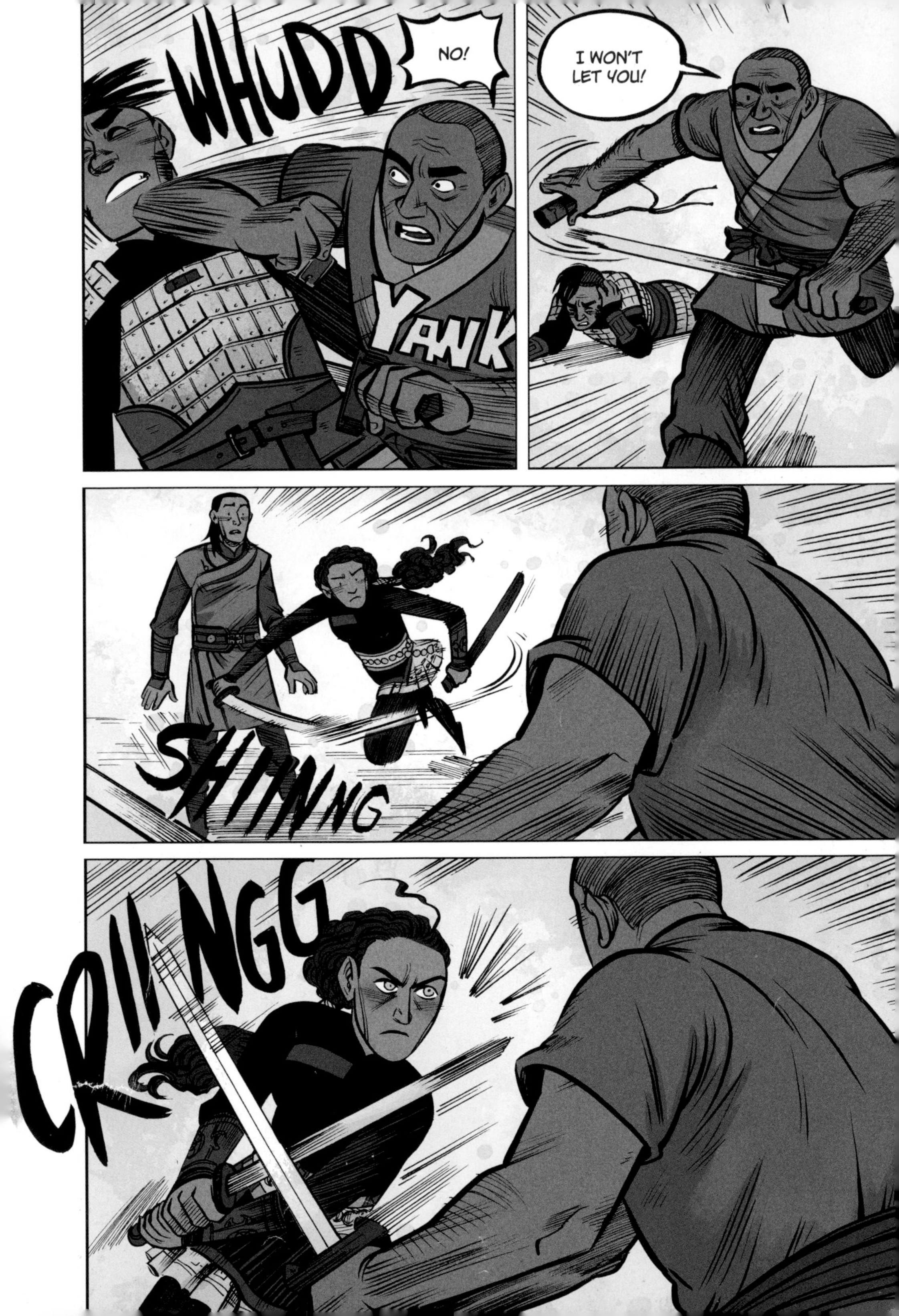
WHUDD
NO!
YANK
I WON'T LET YOU!
SHIIINNG
CRIINGG

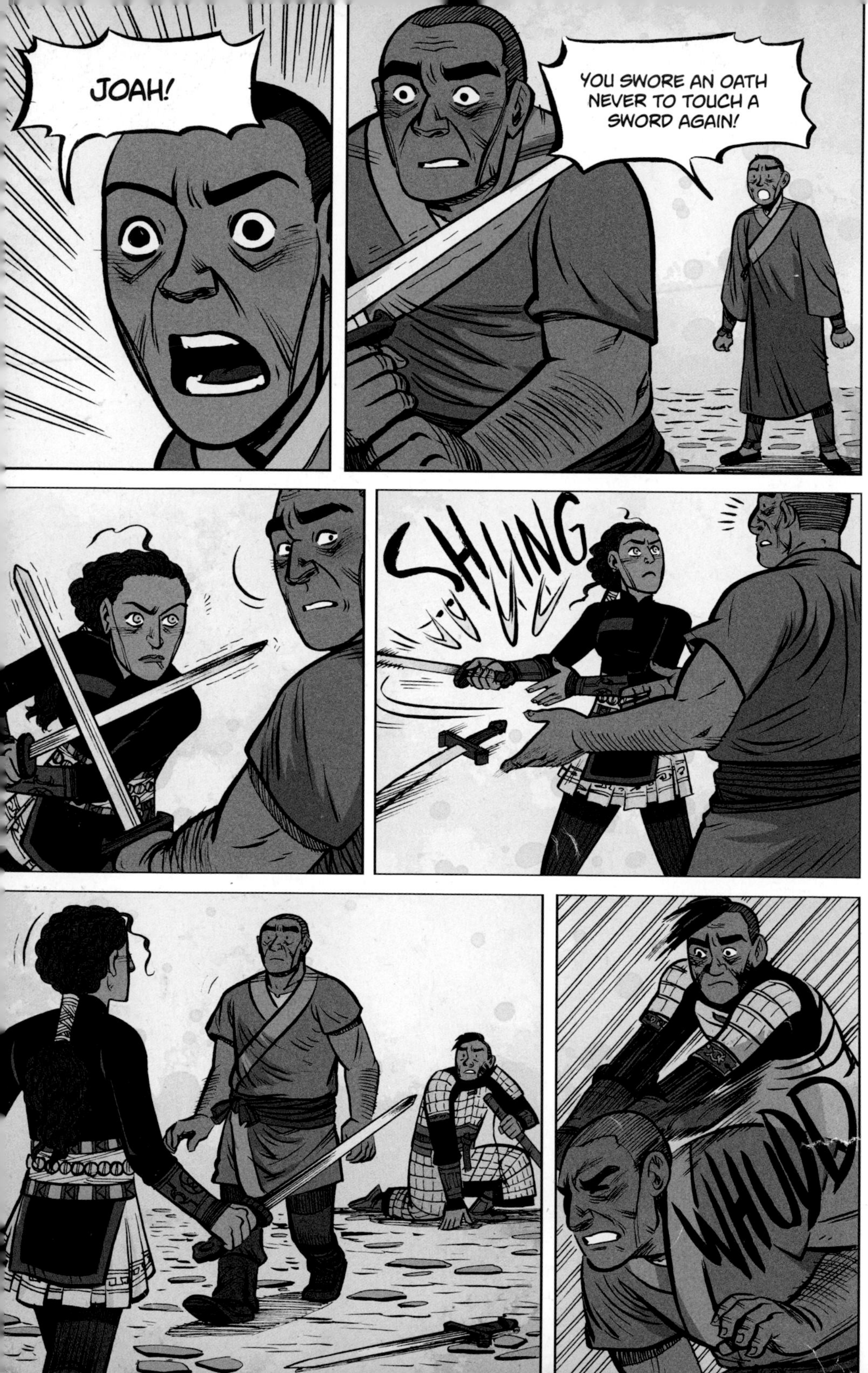
JOAH!
YOU SWORE AN OATH NEVER TO TOUCH A SWORD AGAIN!
SHING
WHUD

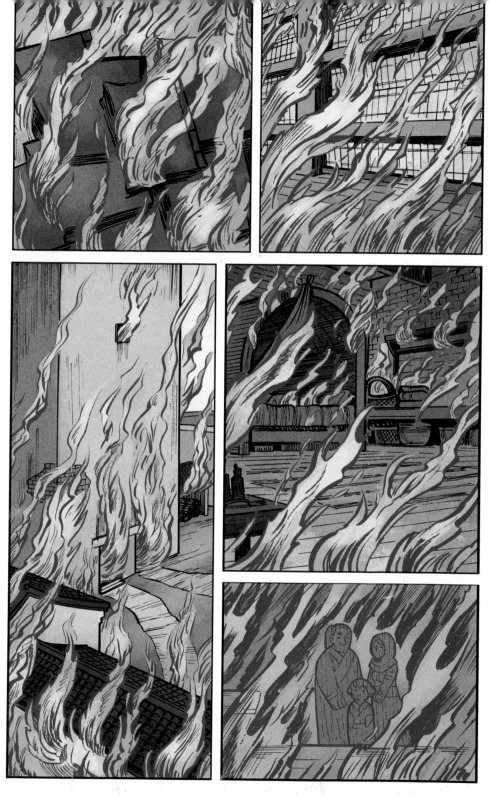

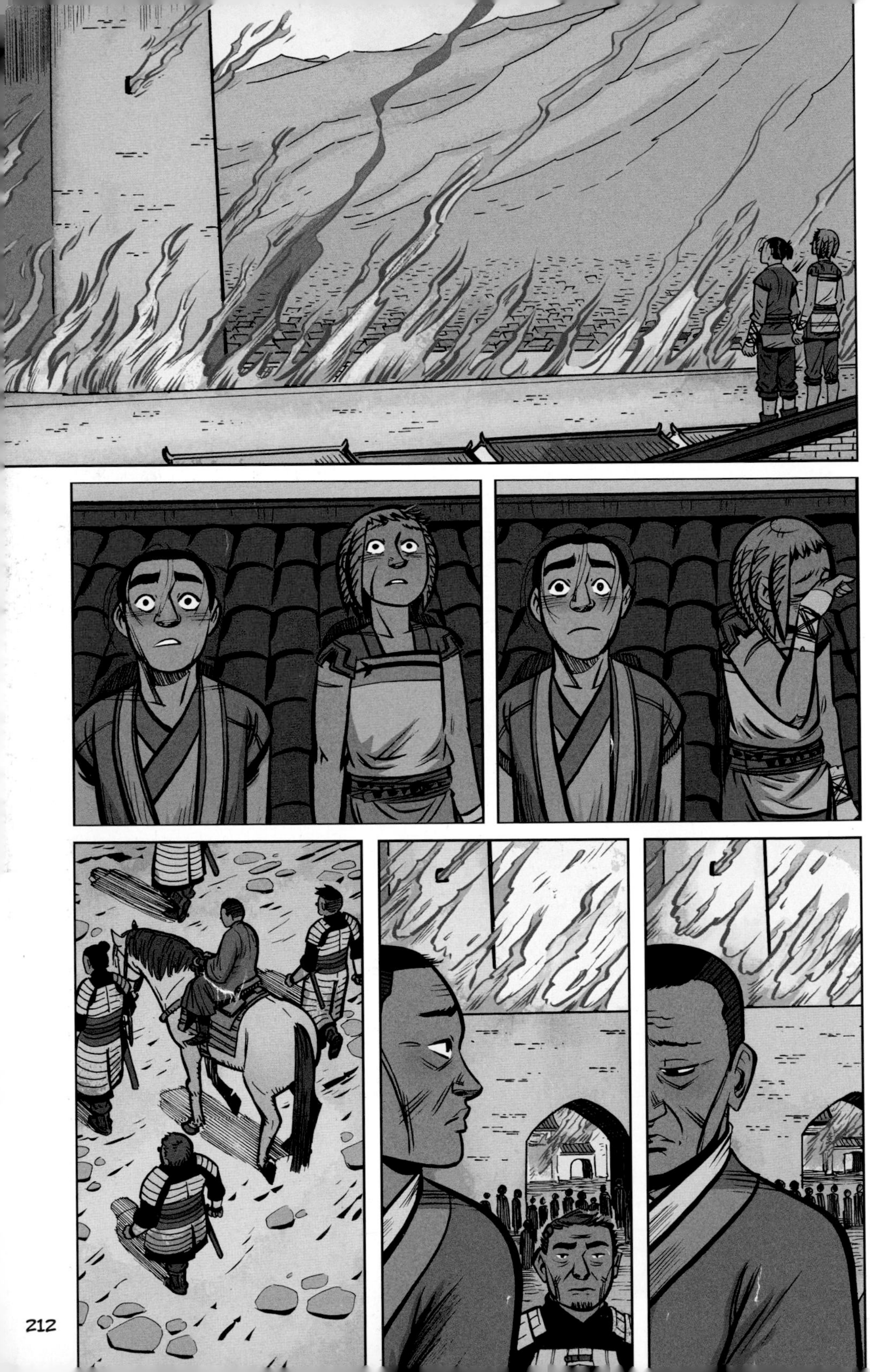

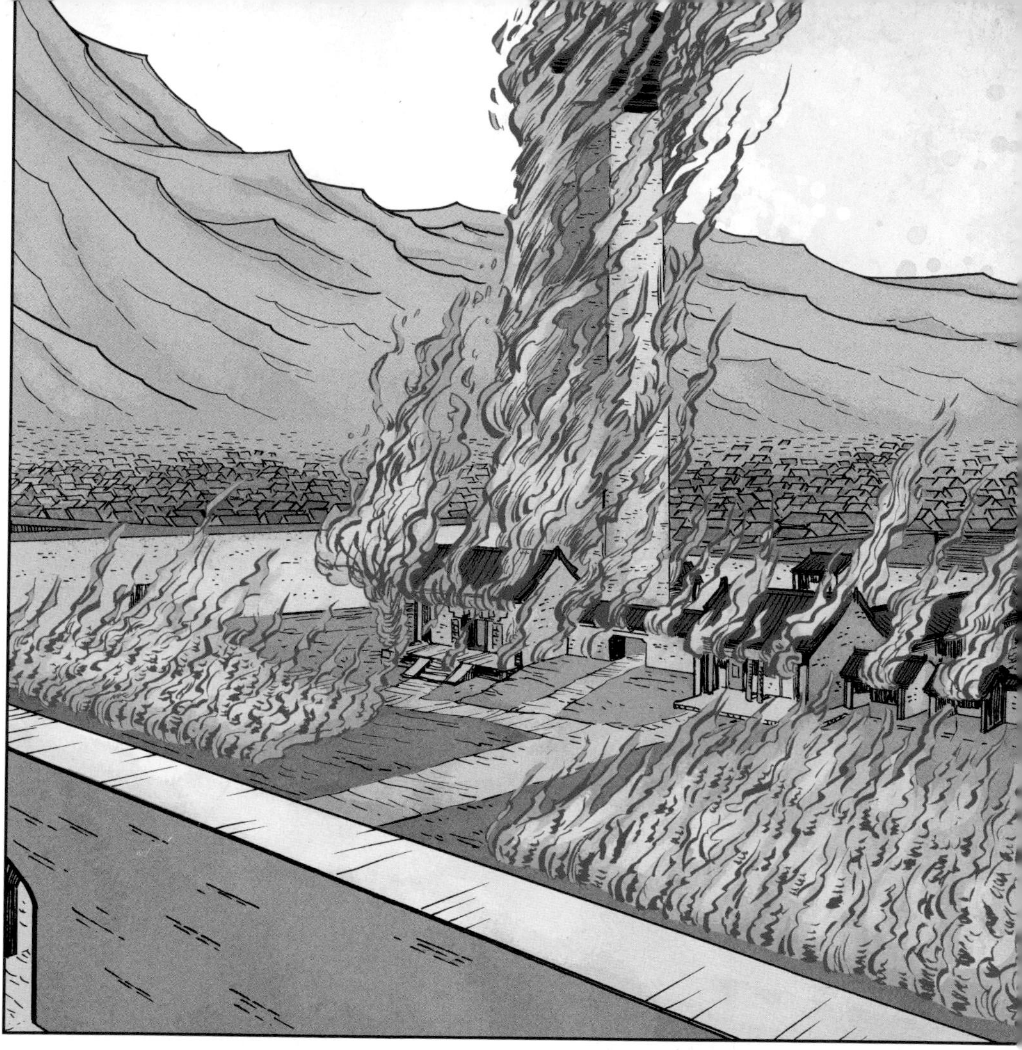
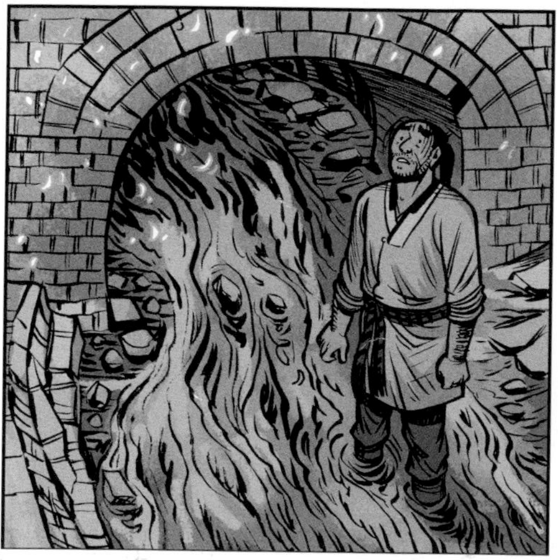
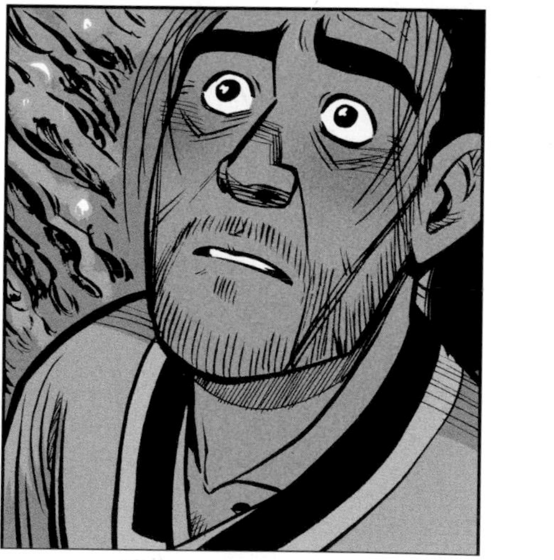

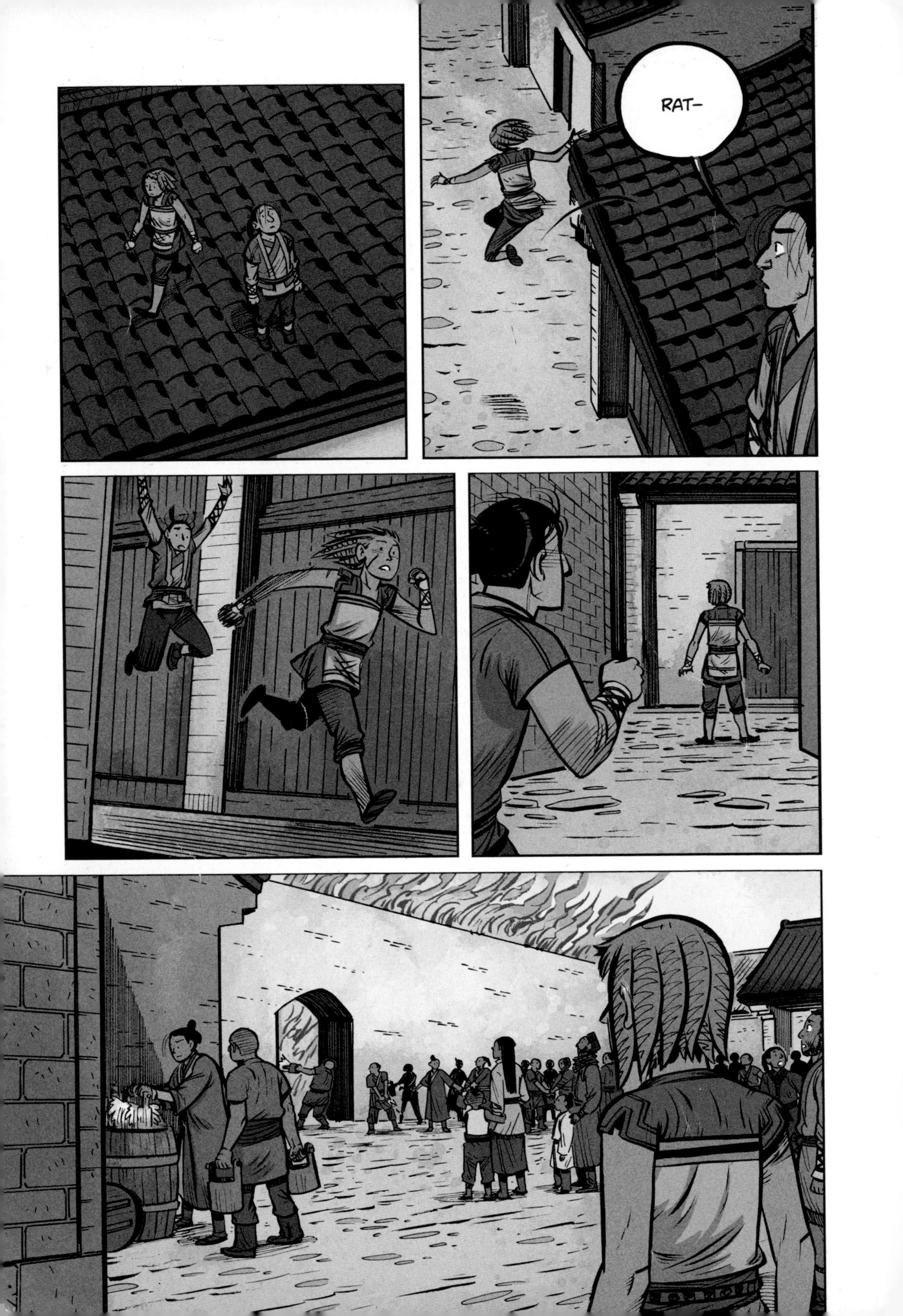
RAT-

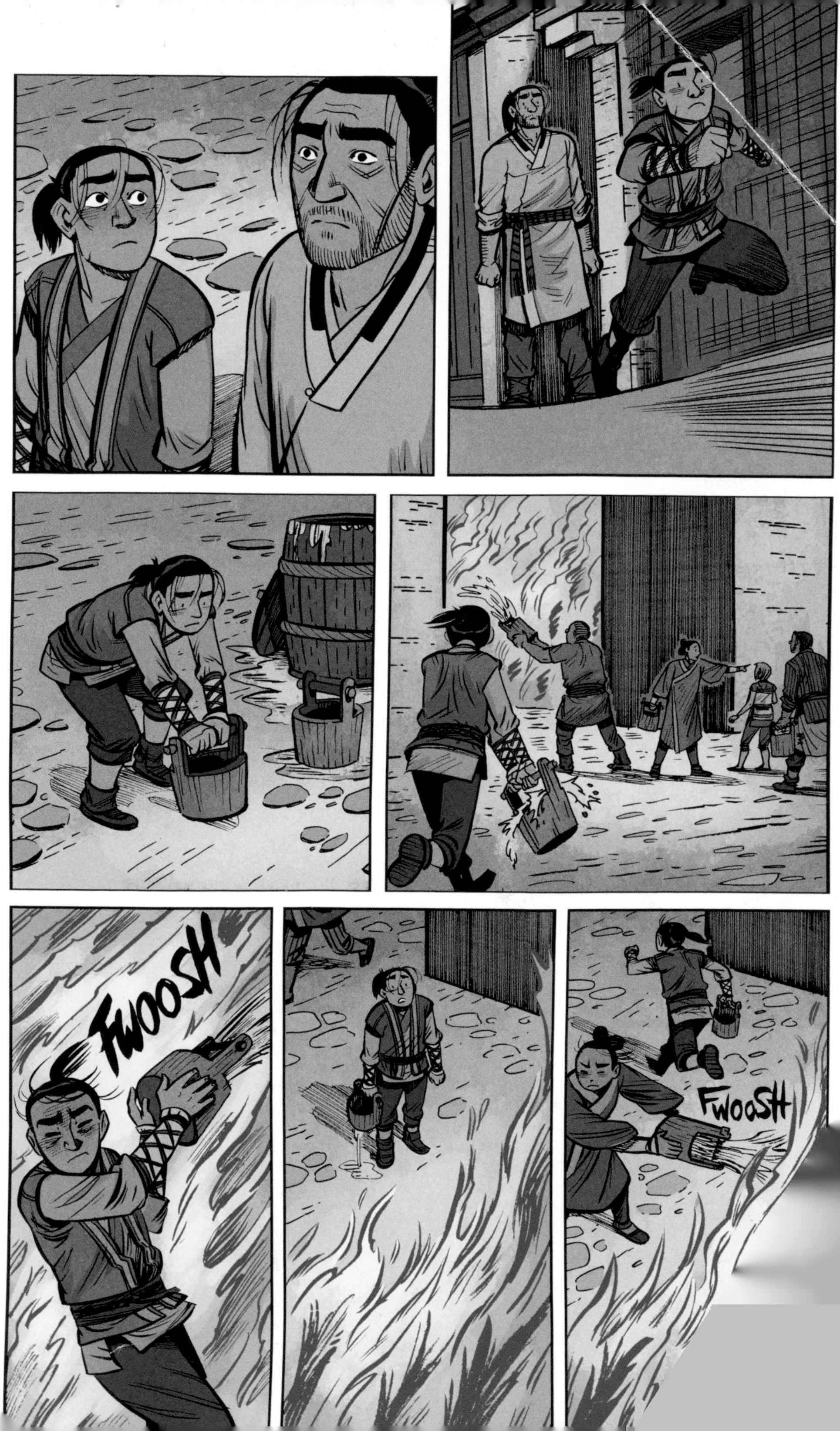
FWOOSH
FWOOSH

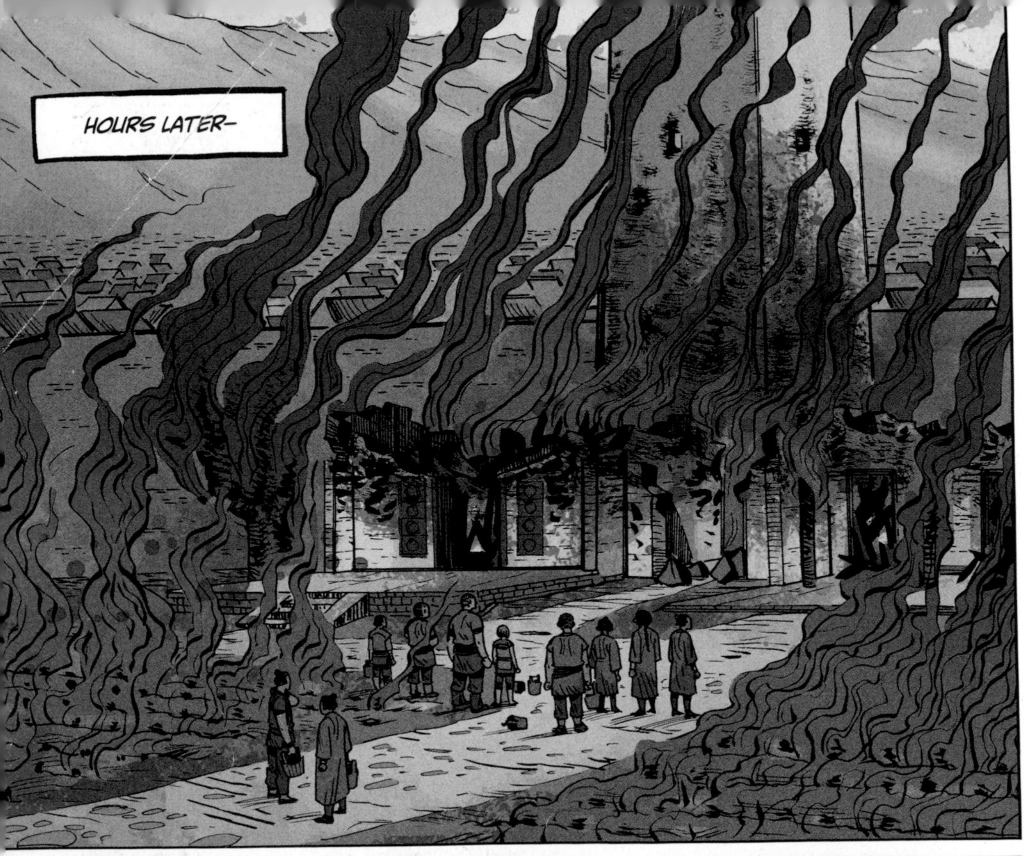
HOURS LATER-

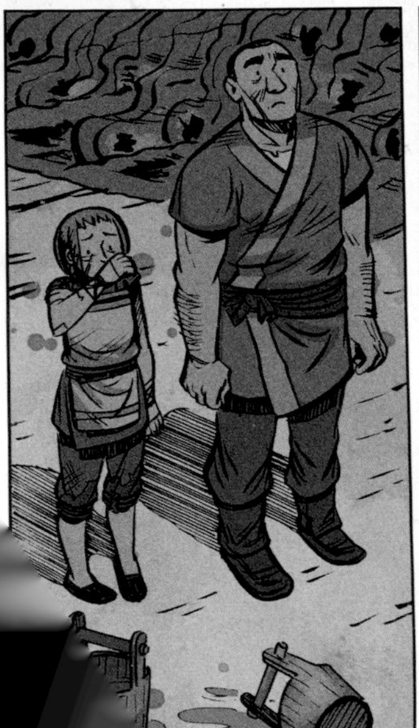

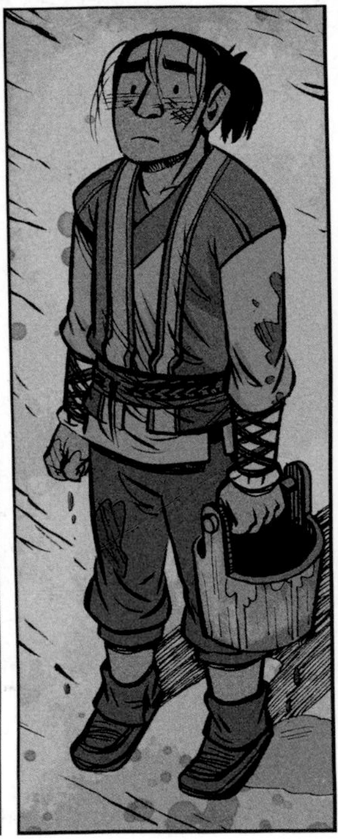

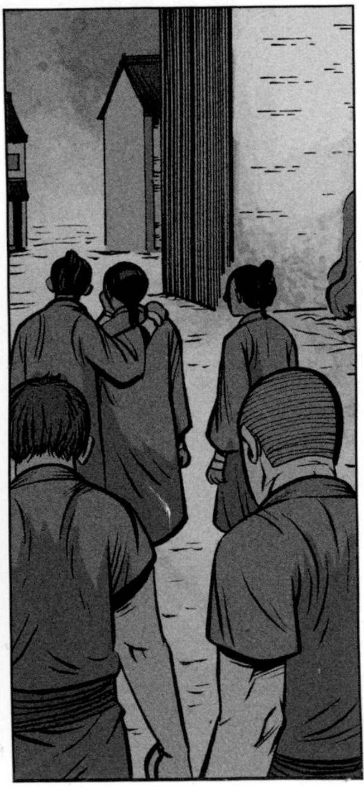

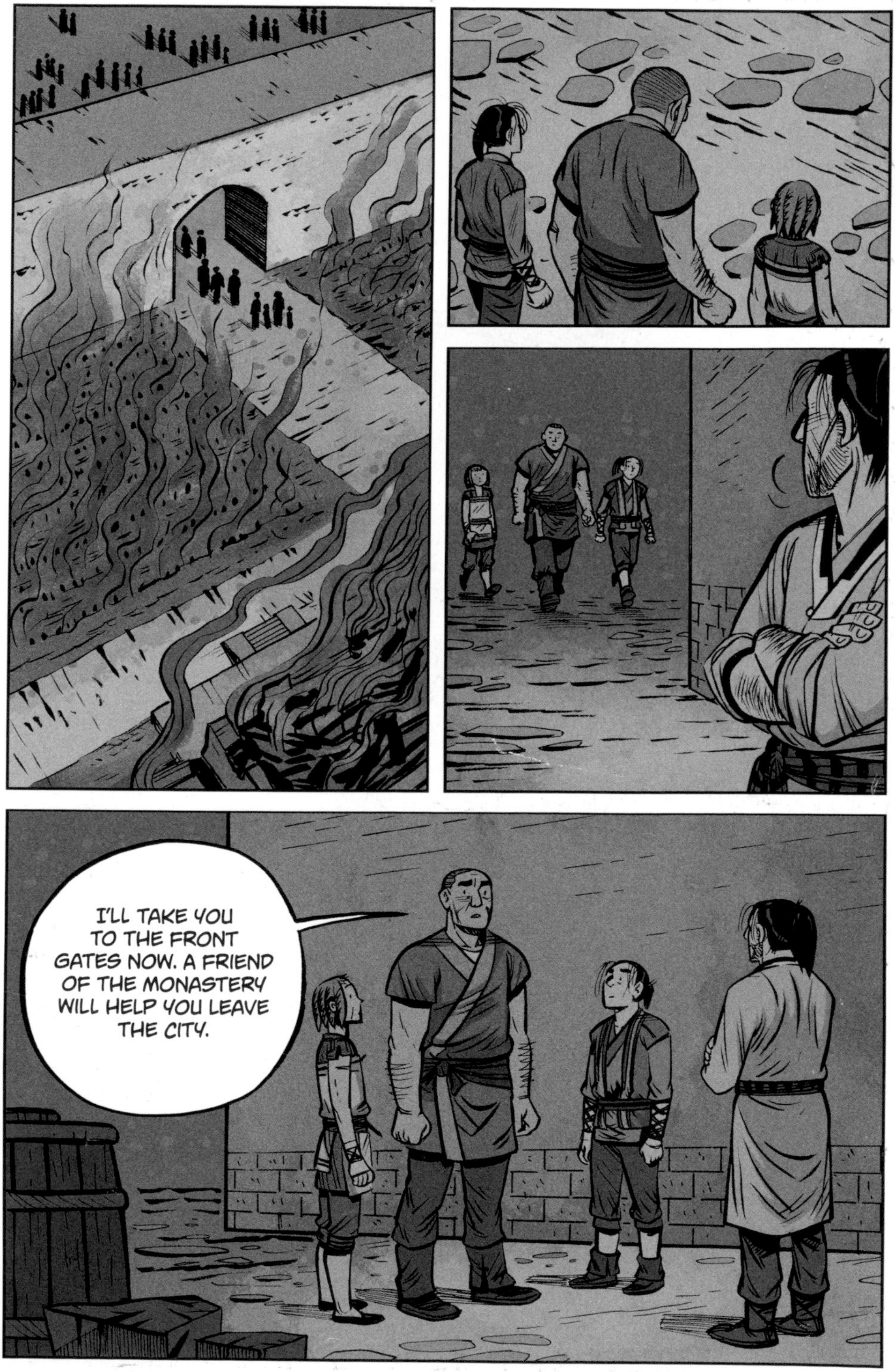
I'LL TAKE YOU TO THE FRONT GATES NOW. A FRIEND OF THE MONASTERY WILL HELP YOU LEAVE THE CITY.

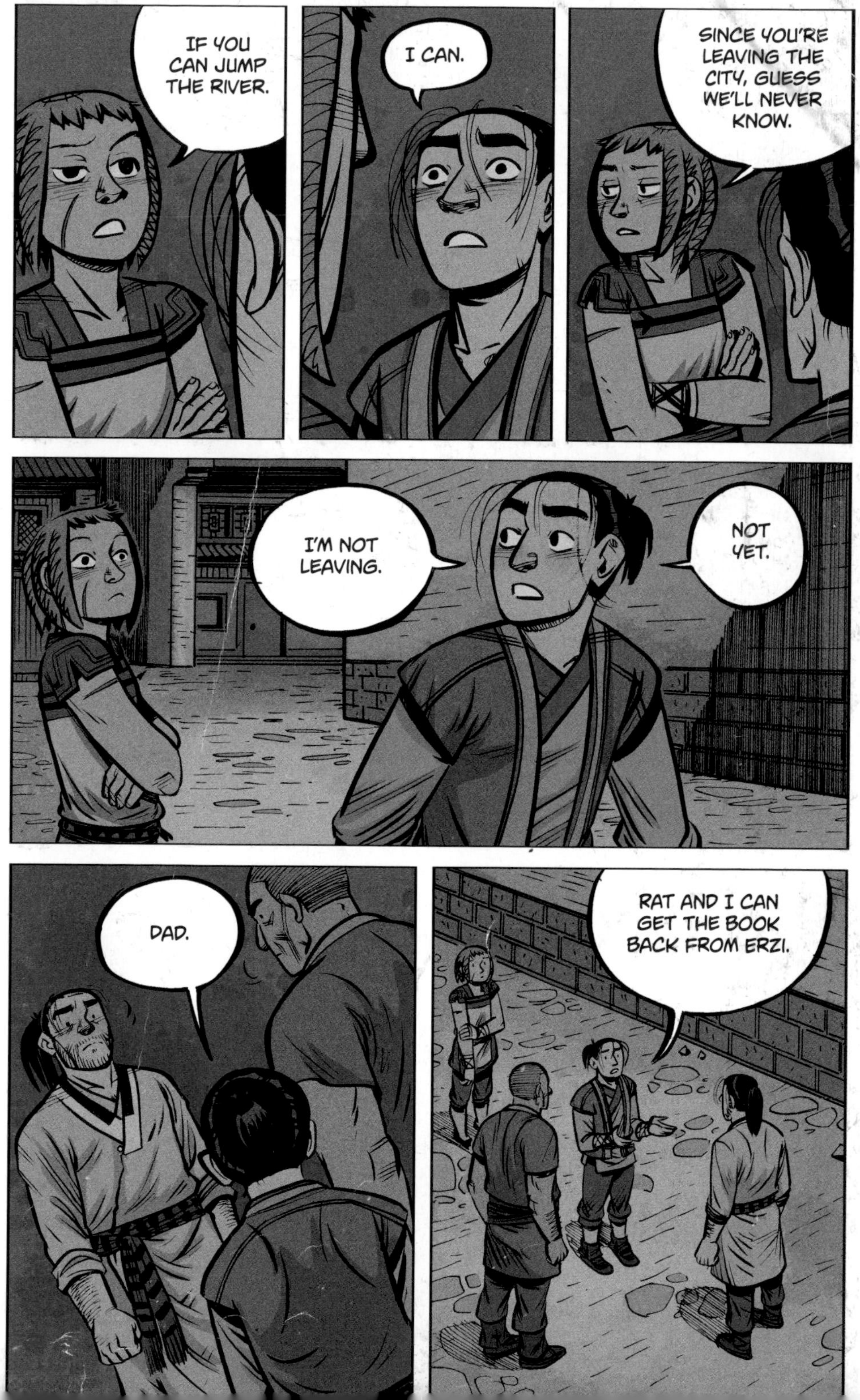
IF YOU CAN JUMP THE RIVER.
I CAN.
SINCE YOU'RE LEAVING THE CITY, GUESS WE'LL NEVER KNOW.
I'M NOT LEAVING.
NOT YET.
DAD.
RAT AND I CAN GET THE BOOK BACK FROM ERZI.

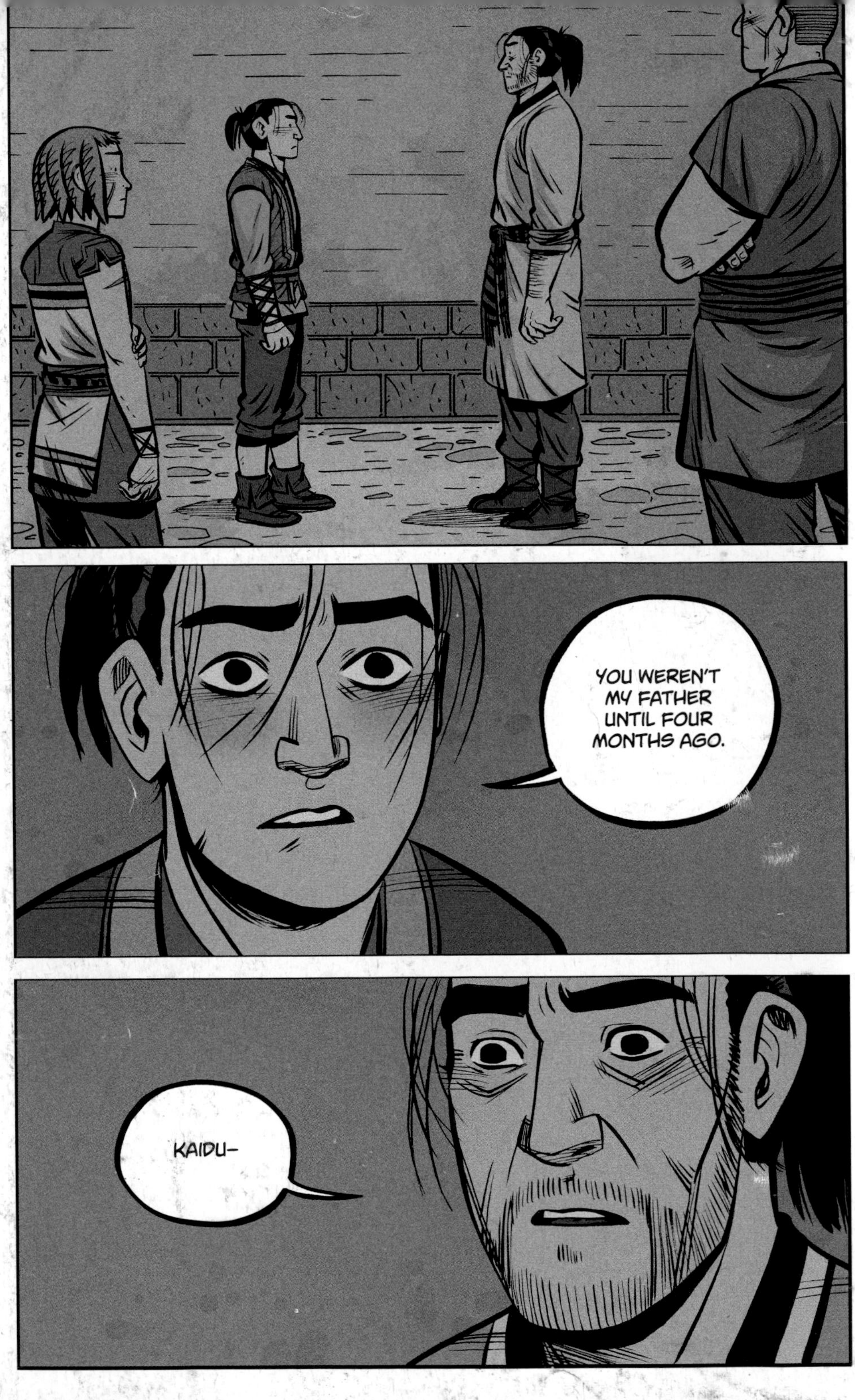
YOU WEREN'T MY FATHER UNTIL FOUR MONTHS AGO.
KAIDU-

232

233

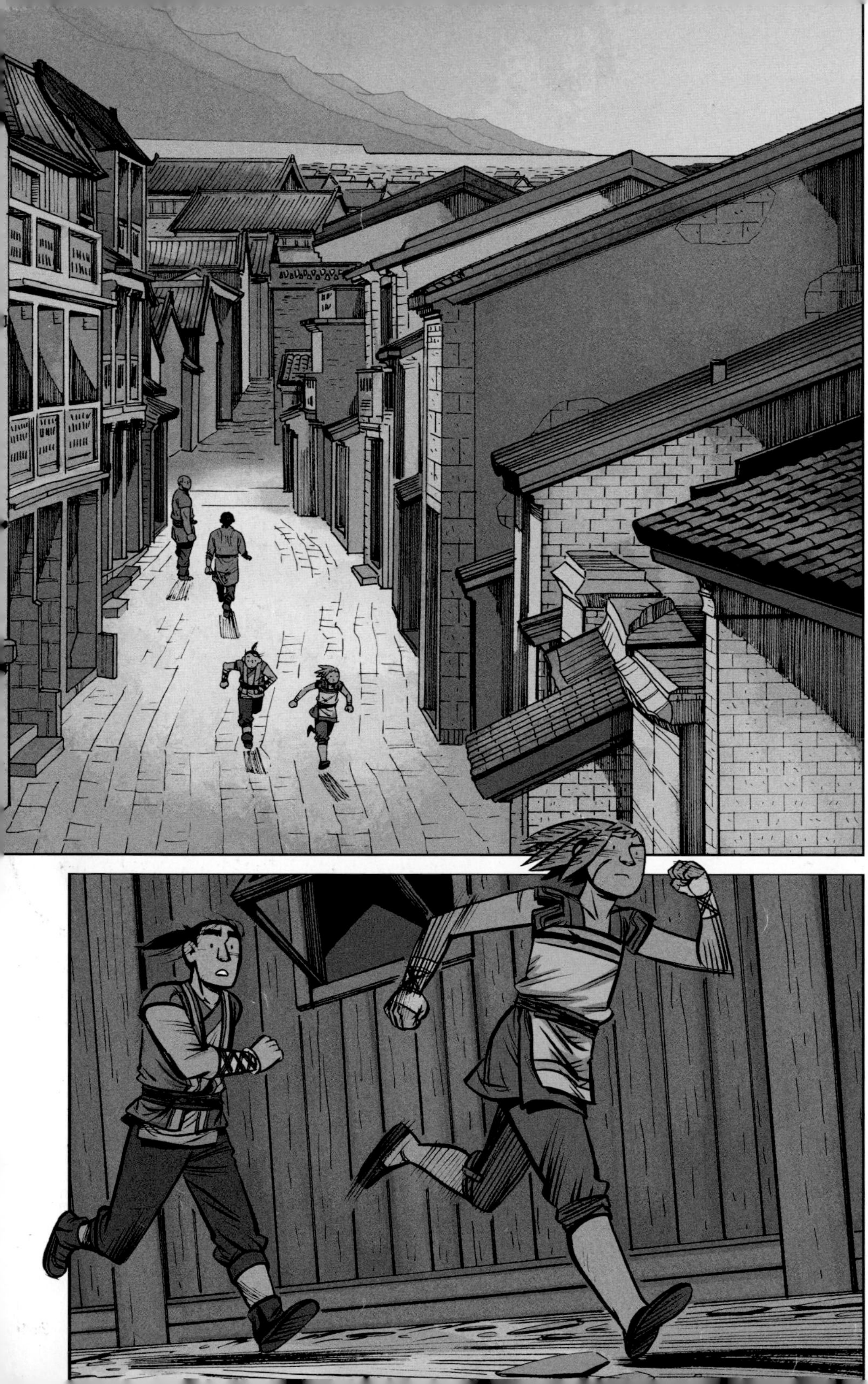

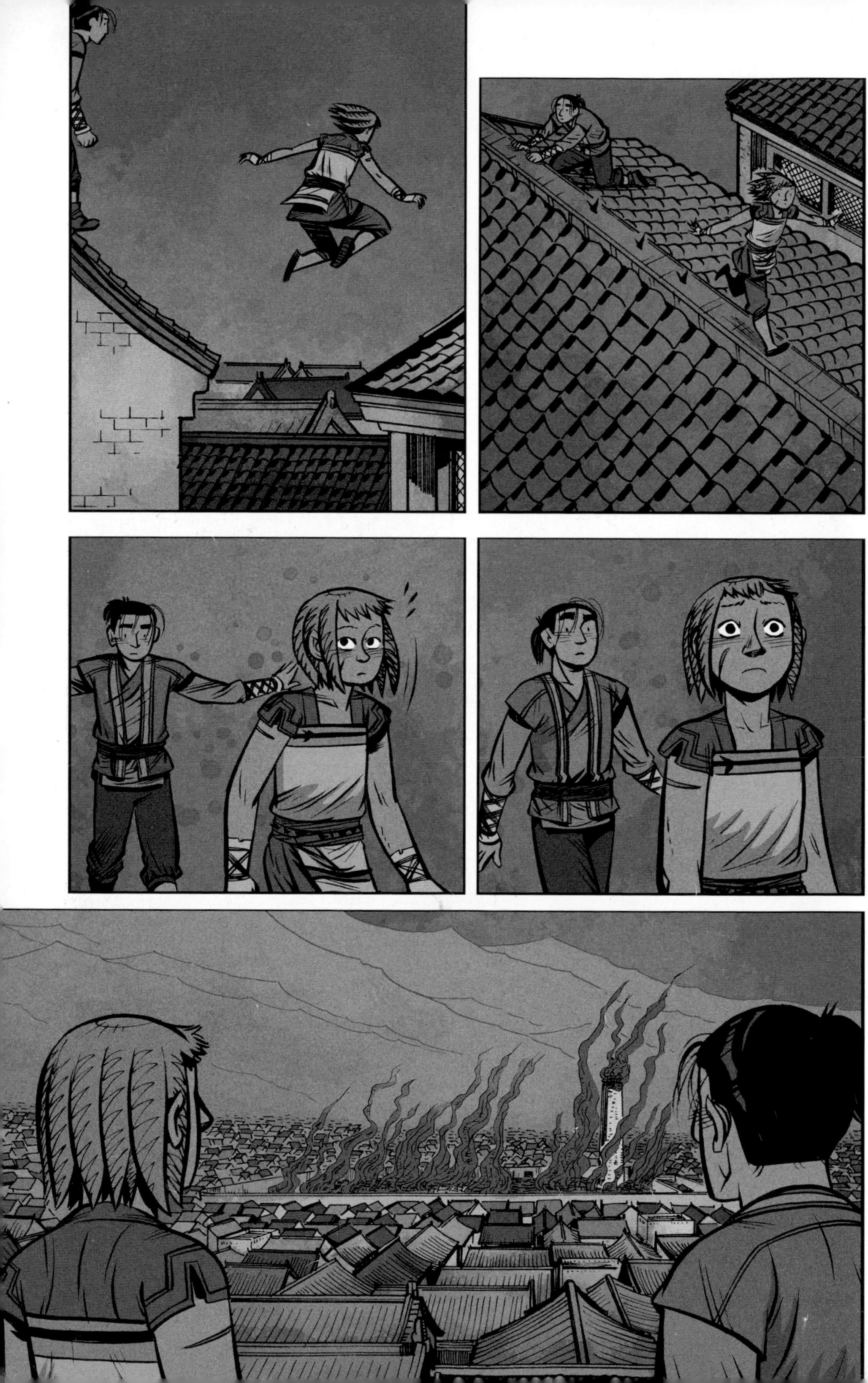

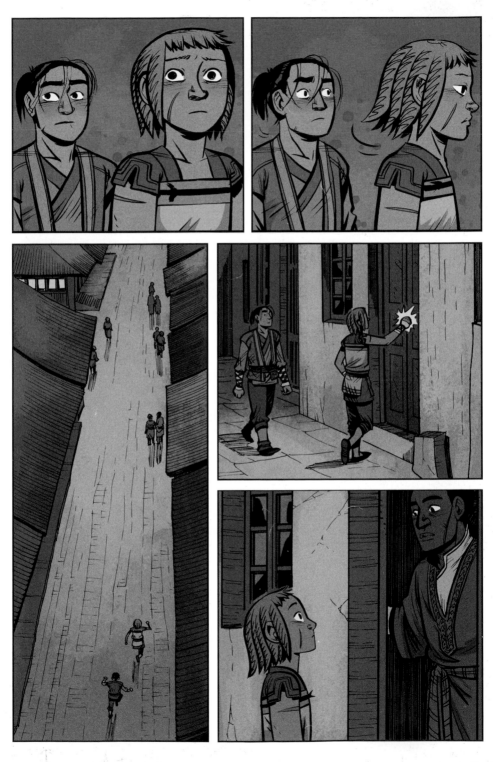

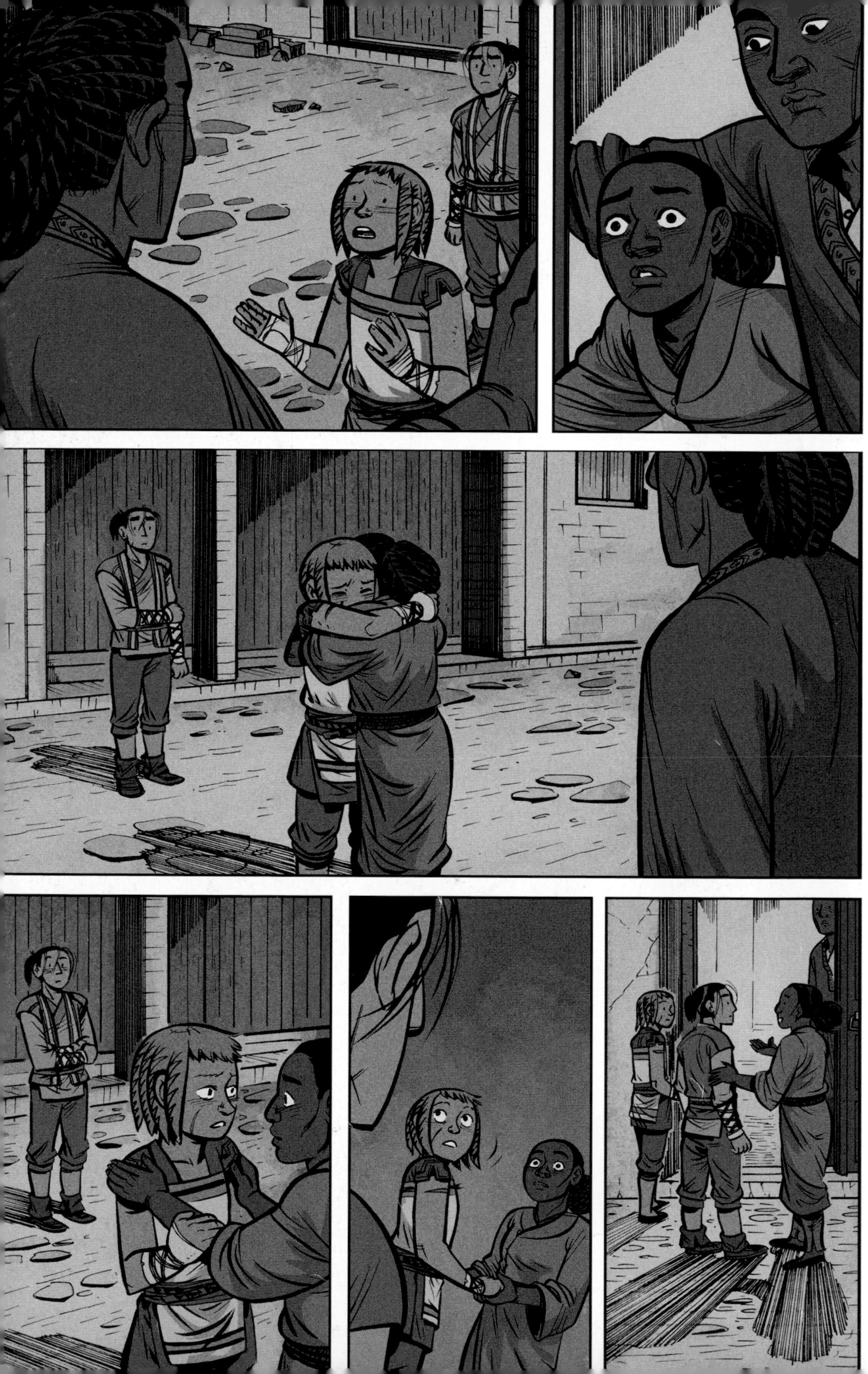

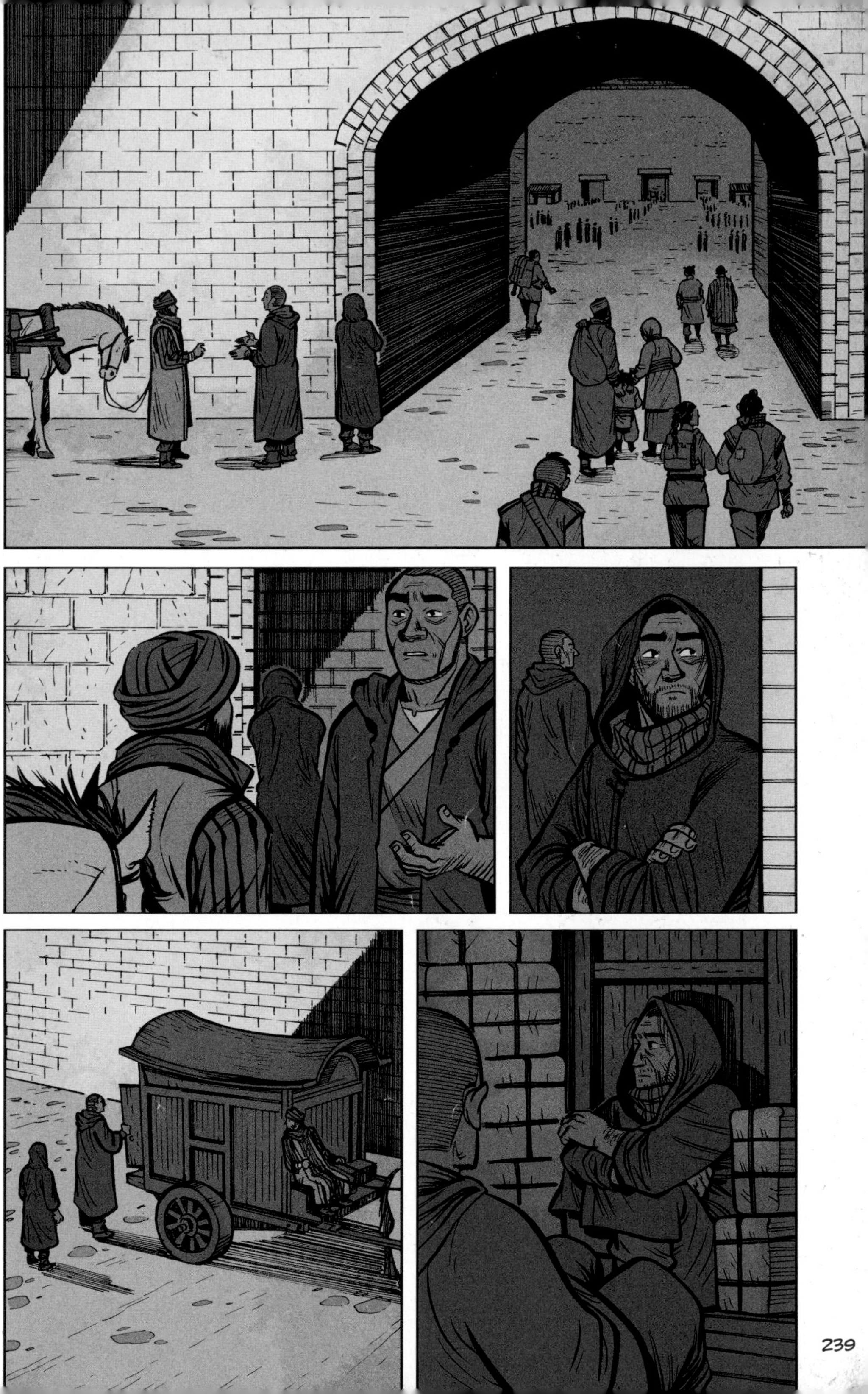

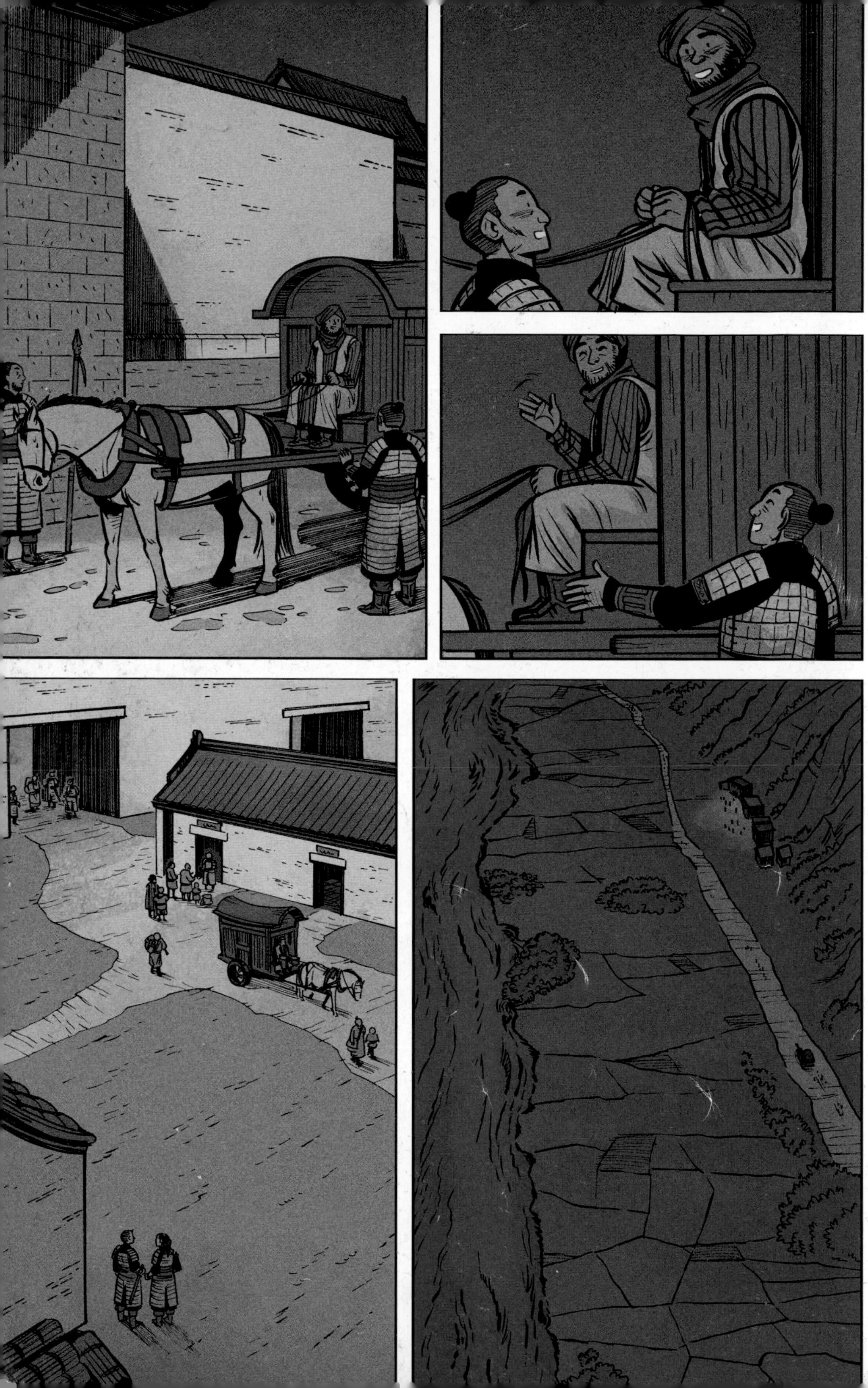

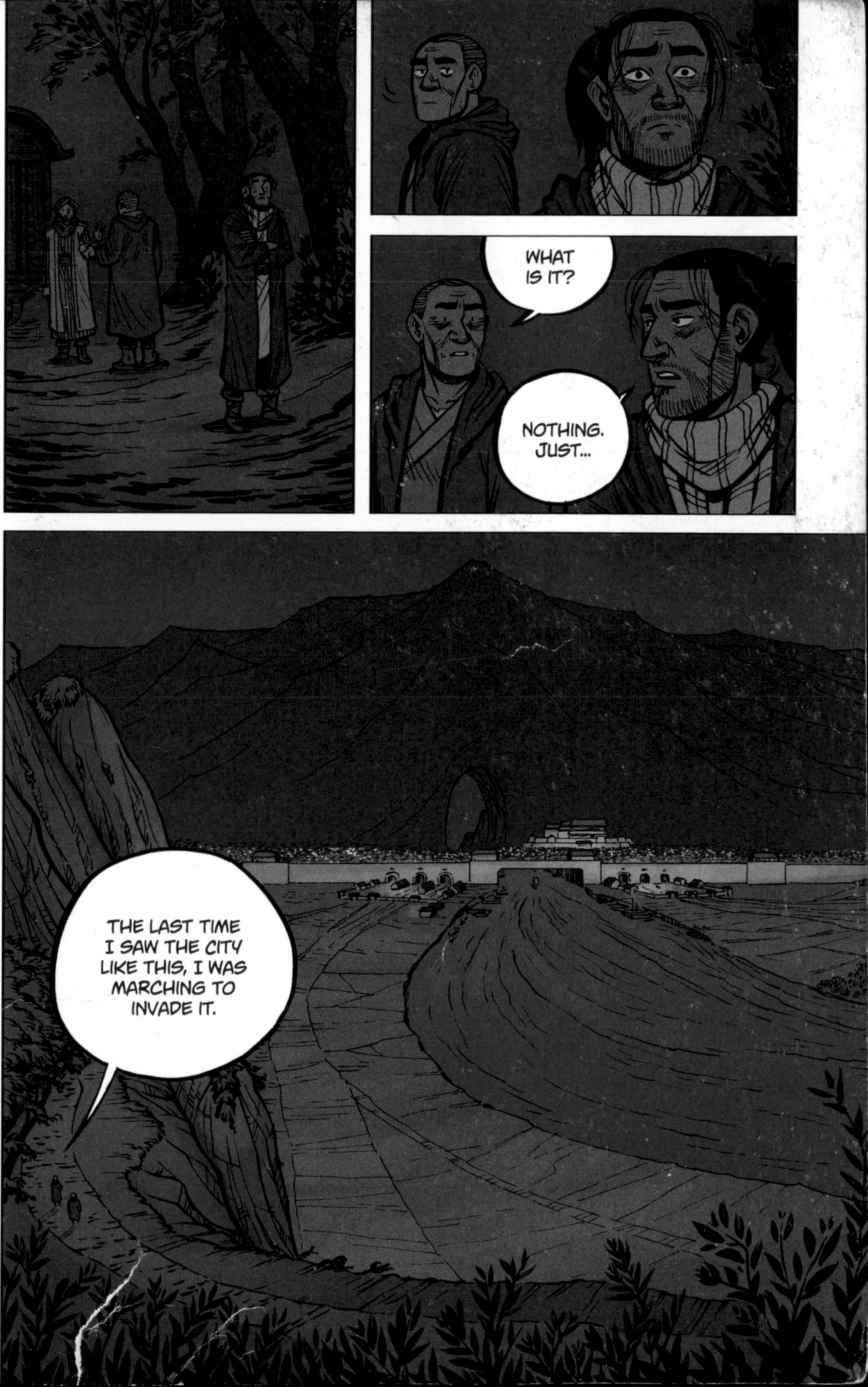
WHAT IS IT?
NOTHING. JUST...
THE LAST TIME I SAW THE CITY LIKE THIS, I WAS MARCHING TO INVADE IT.

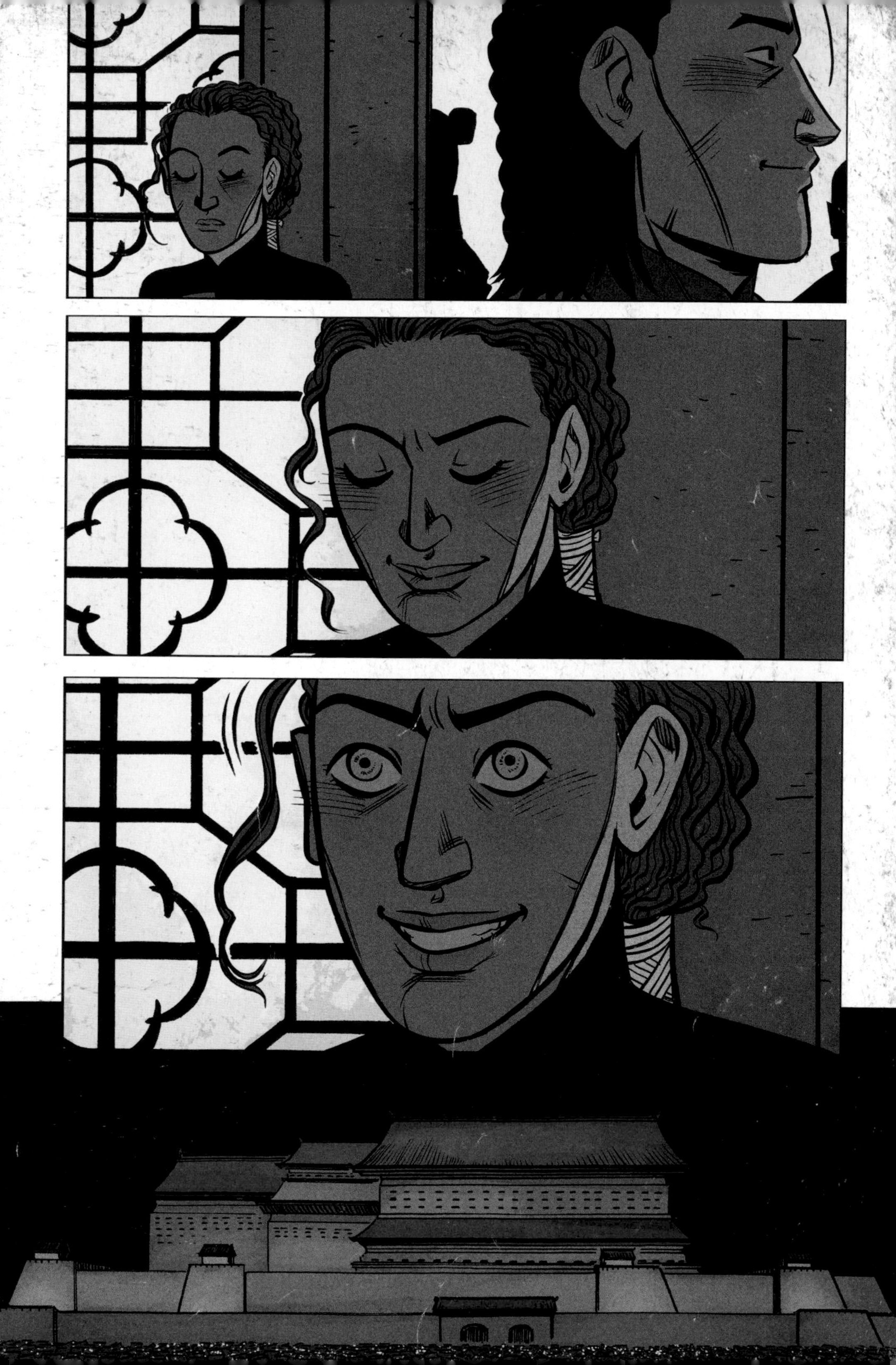

TO BE CONTINUED IN

THE DIVIDED EARTH
BOOK 3 OF THE NAMELESS CITY SERIES

AUTHOR'S NOTE

As of this writing, two books in The Nameless City trilogy are complete, and I will soon begin work on the third, where the story of Rat and Kai and the various characters introduced over the past 450-plus pages will (hopefully) find a satisfying ending. The Nameless City has been an unusual and challenging project for me: It's the first trilogy I've both written and drawn on my own and the first comic I've drawn that has not been set in present-day North America (or its post-apocalyptic future). After two graphic novels set in a modern high school (*Friends with Boys* and *Nothing Can Possibly Go Wrong*), I wanted to stretch my drawing muscles, and I settled on creating a comic with thousands of tiled Chinese rooftops. During my darkest times drawing these two (soon to be three) graphic novels, I may have had one or two moments regretting that choice and longing for the easy-to-draw lockers of a modern high school hallway. But they were only moments. For all its challenges, I've greatly enjoyed drawing the complicated world that Rat and Kai inhabit.

The world of The Nameless City is fictional, but its roots are based on thirteenth-century China. There is no "Nameless City" in history, but I drew from my research on the Yuan Dynasty and the Silk Road to create this vast, multicultural place where Kai and Rat live. Hopefully that research gives their home weight and substance. I have tried to create a world that is visually authentic, if not accurate to historical events of the time. There are differences between the real thirteenth-century China and the world of The Nameless City—the history, the language of its people—but I have tried to ground my artwork in that particular time and place. I am grateful to the historical clothing reference books available at the Halifax Public Library (where I did much of my research before moving all the way across Canada to Vancouver, British Columbia), as well as the online photo galleries of libraries across the US and Canada, all of which were a great asset in the years leading up to the creation of this trilogy. Libraries are, as always, a cartoonist's best friend.

CONCEPT ART FOR

THE NAMELESS CITY

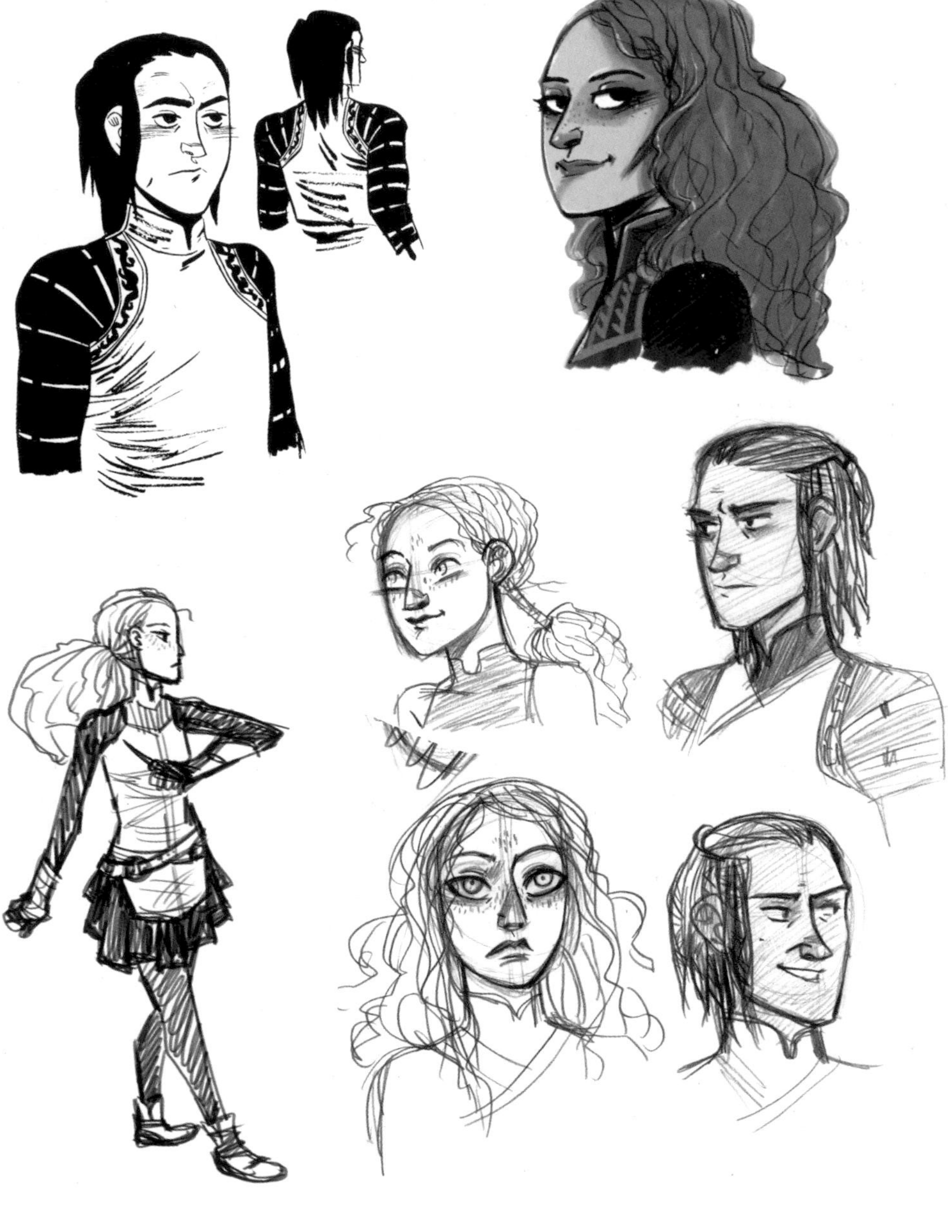

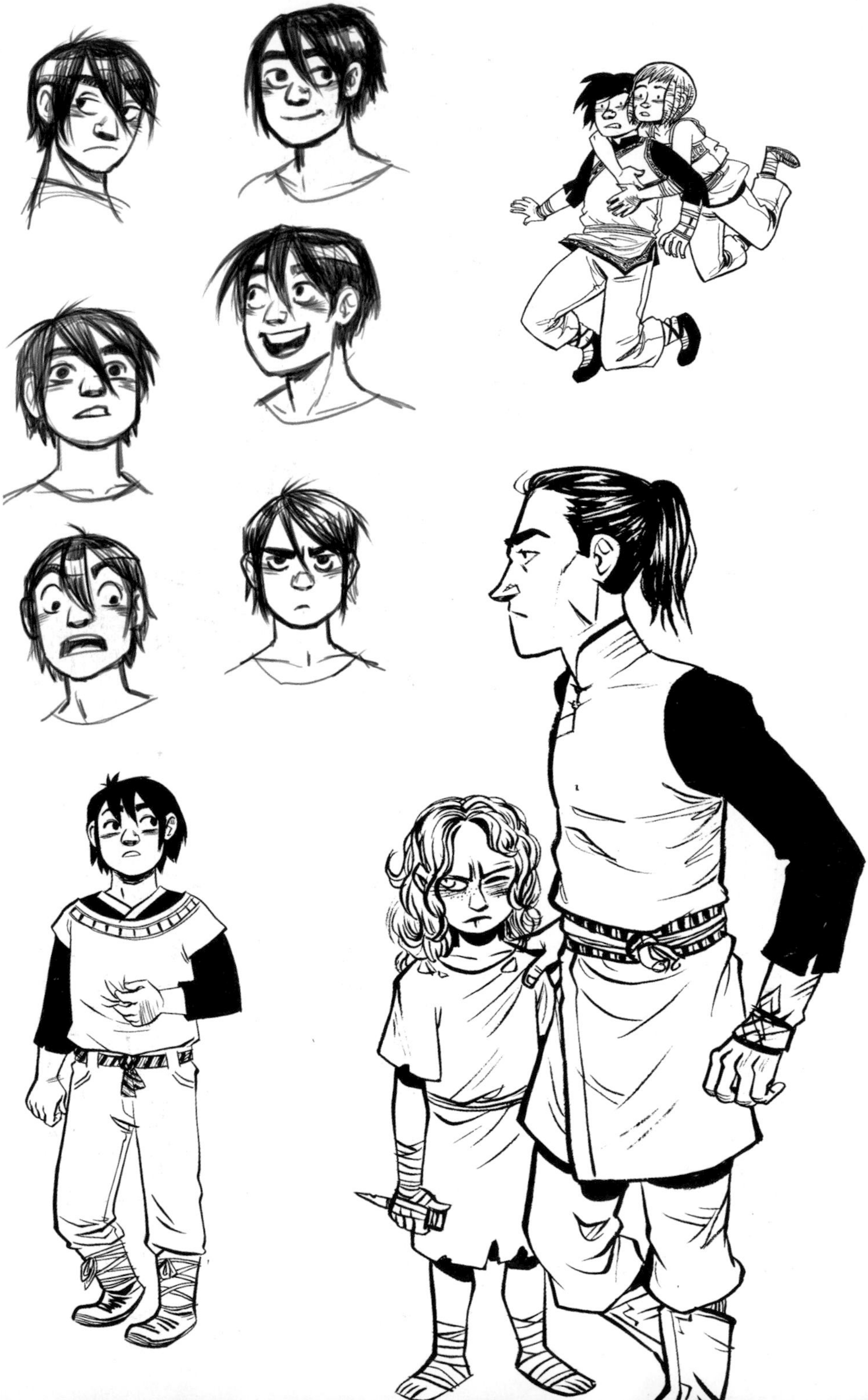

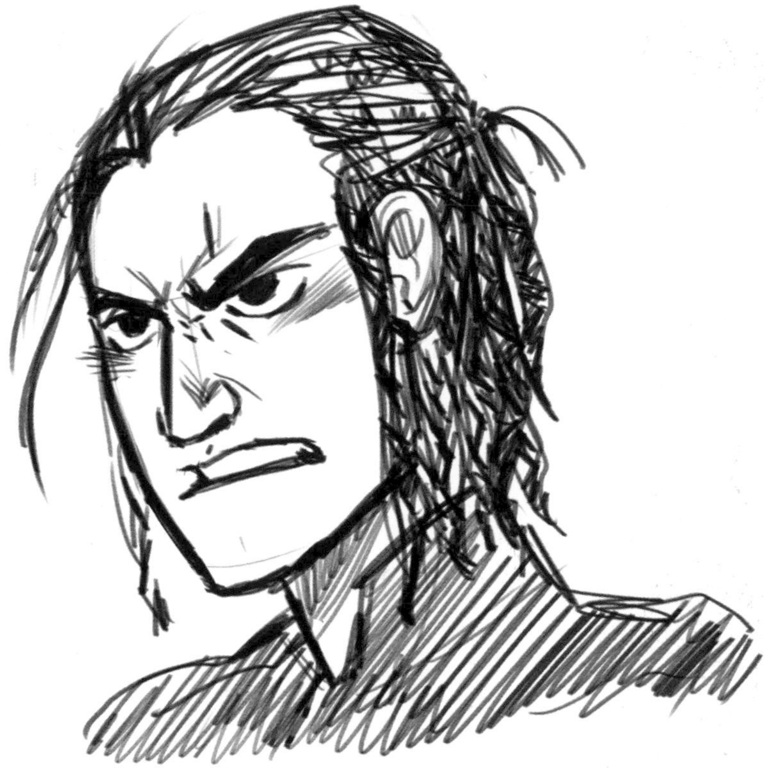
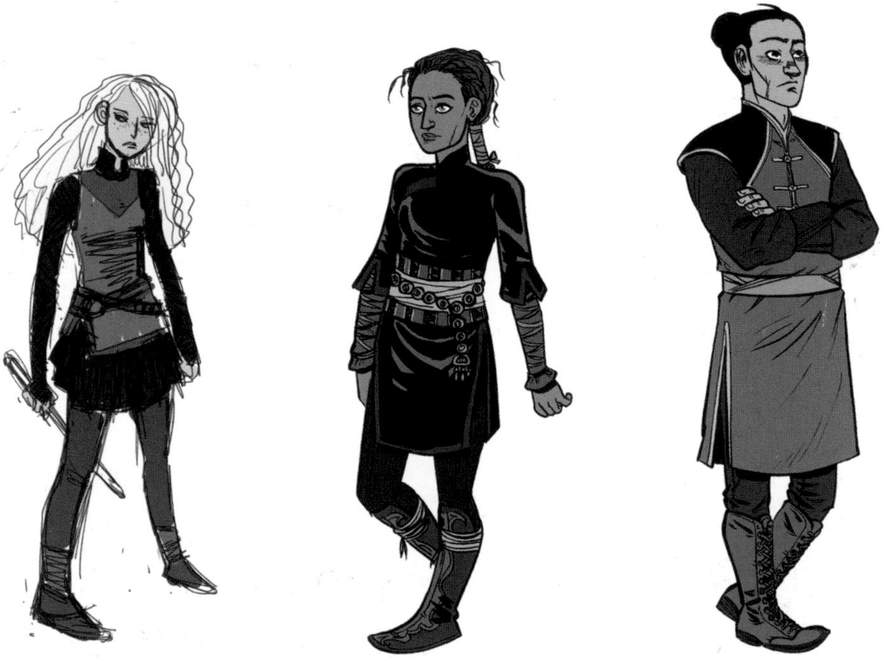

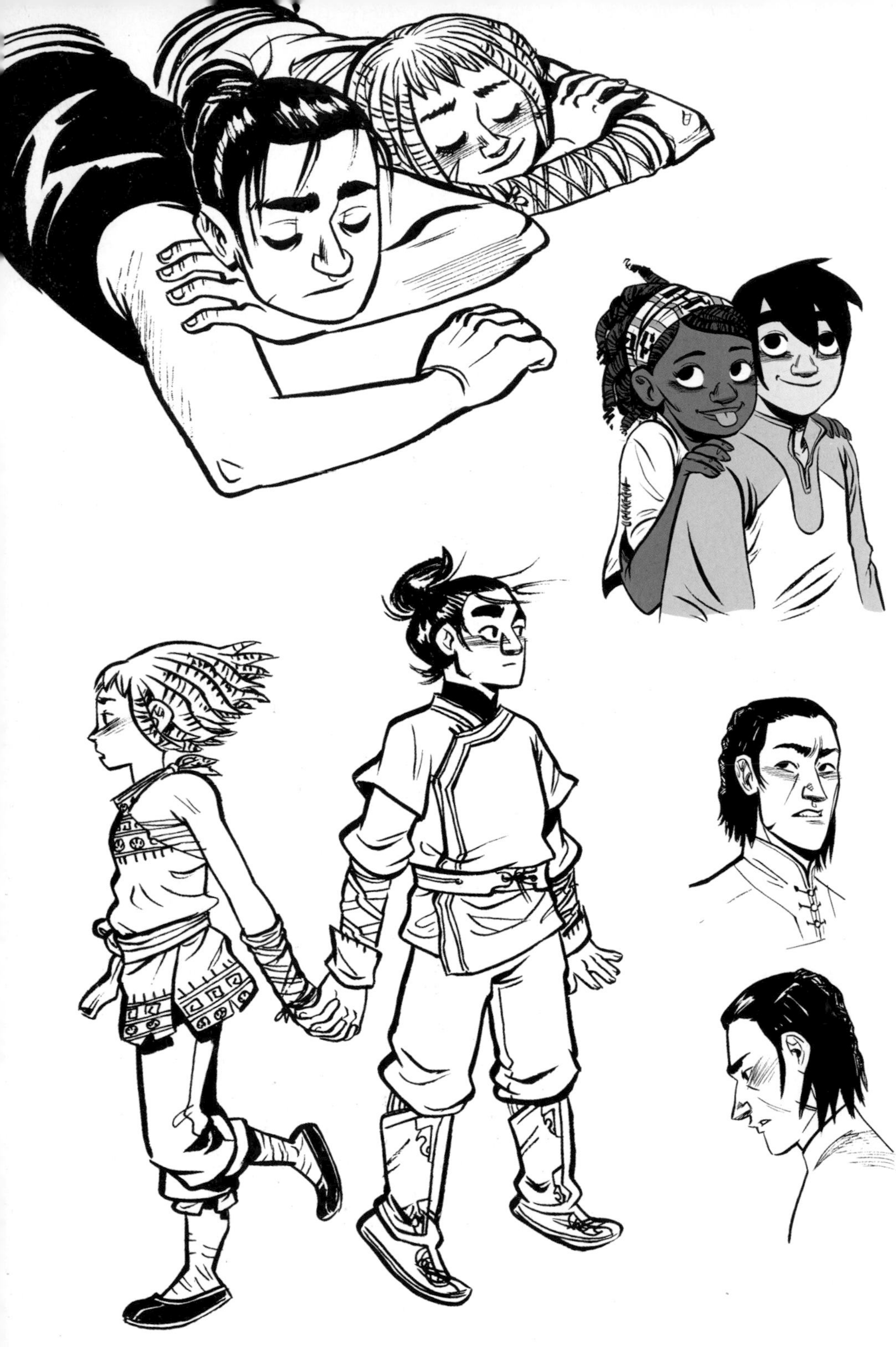

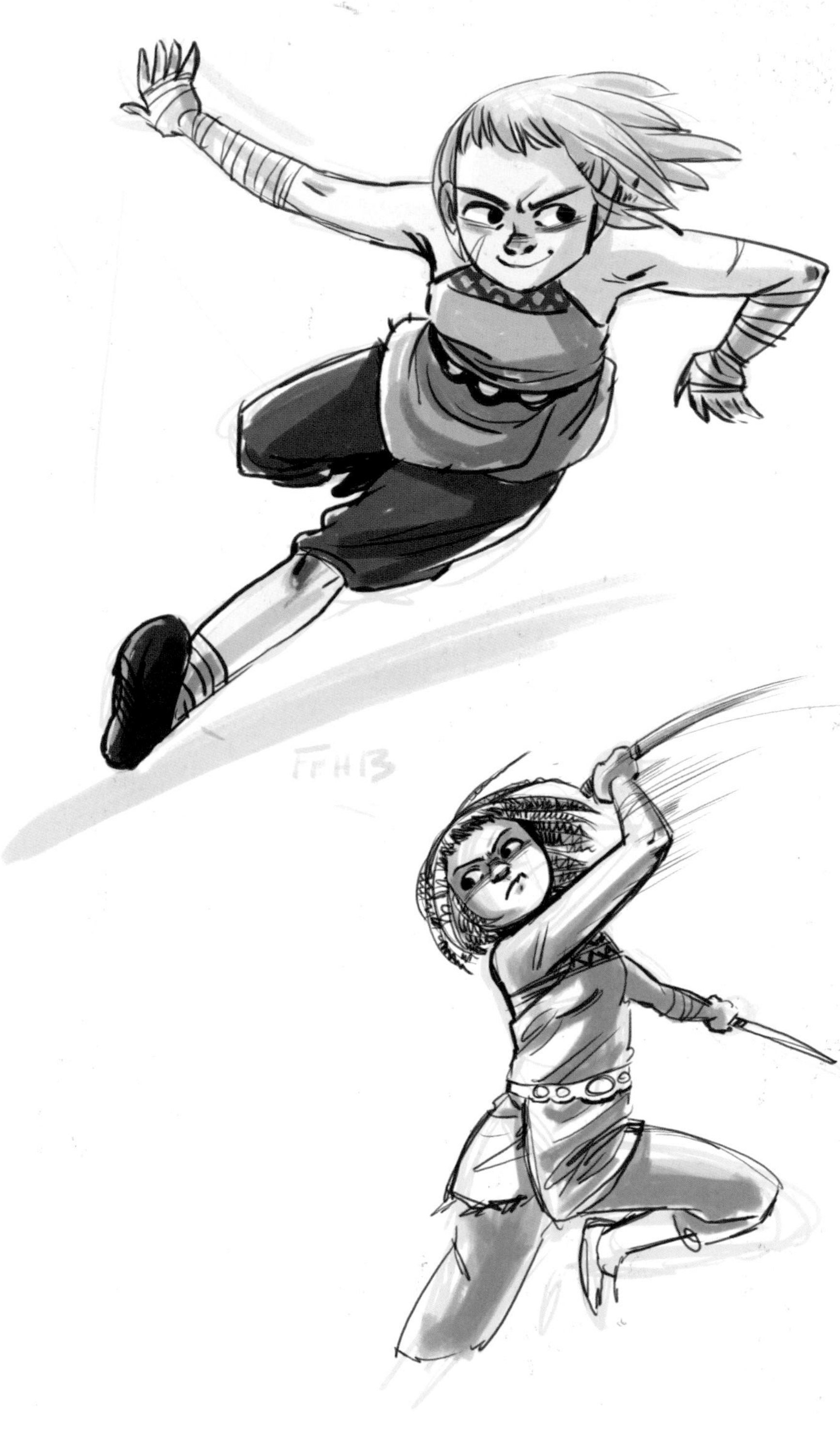
FFH13

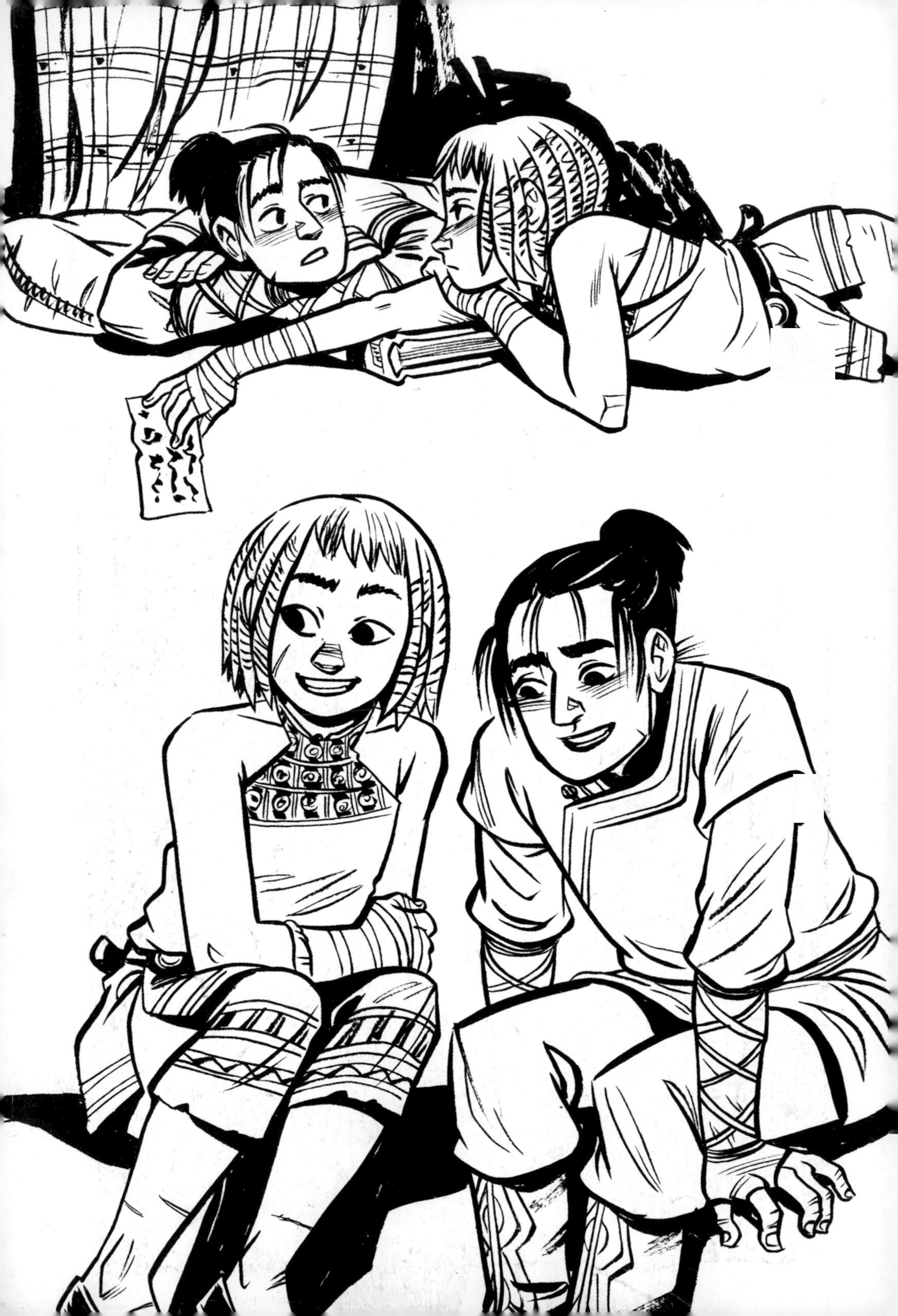

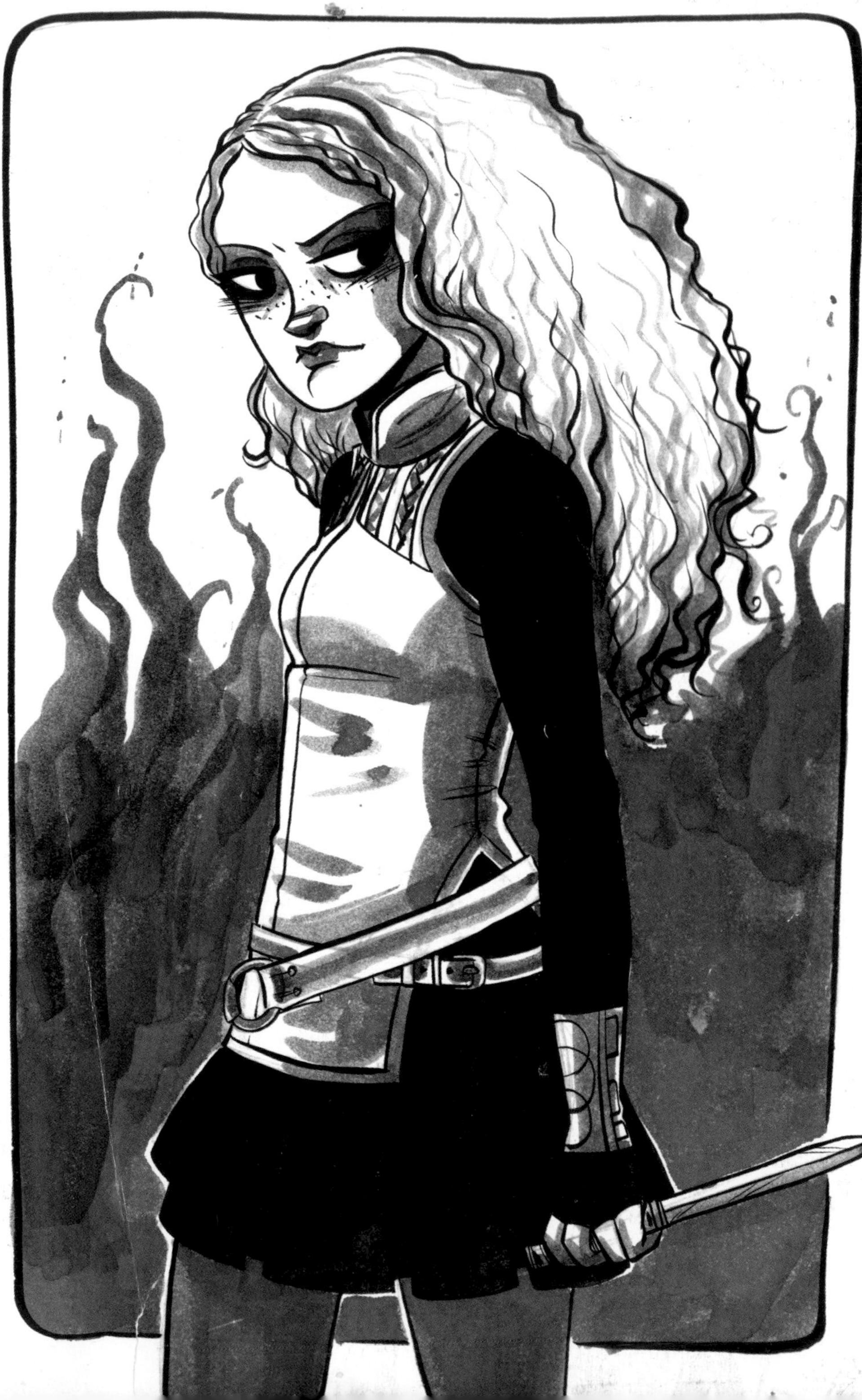

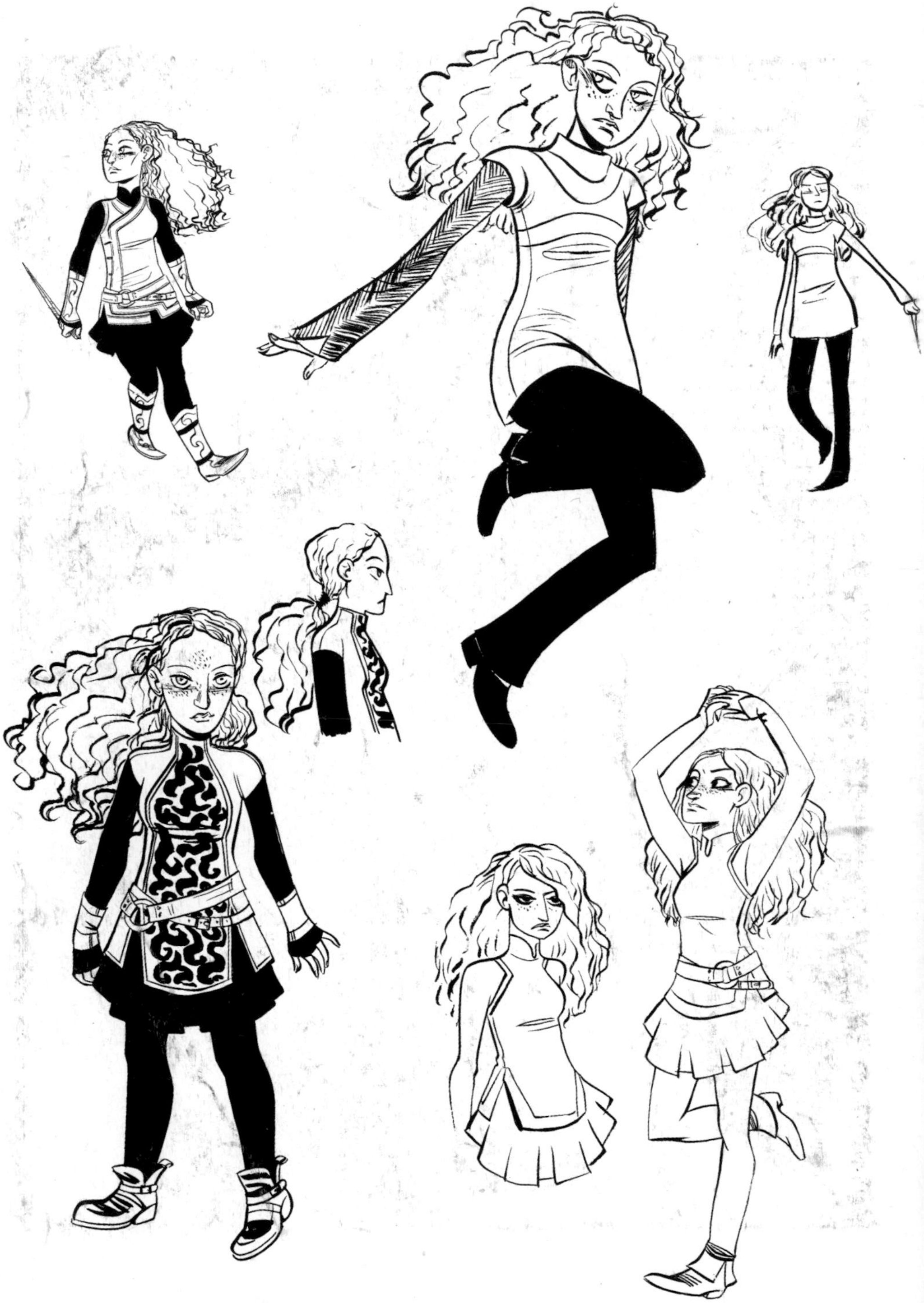

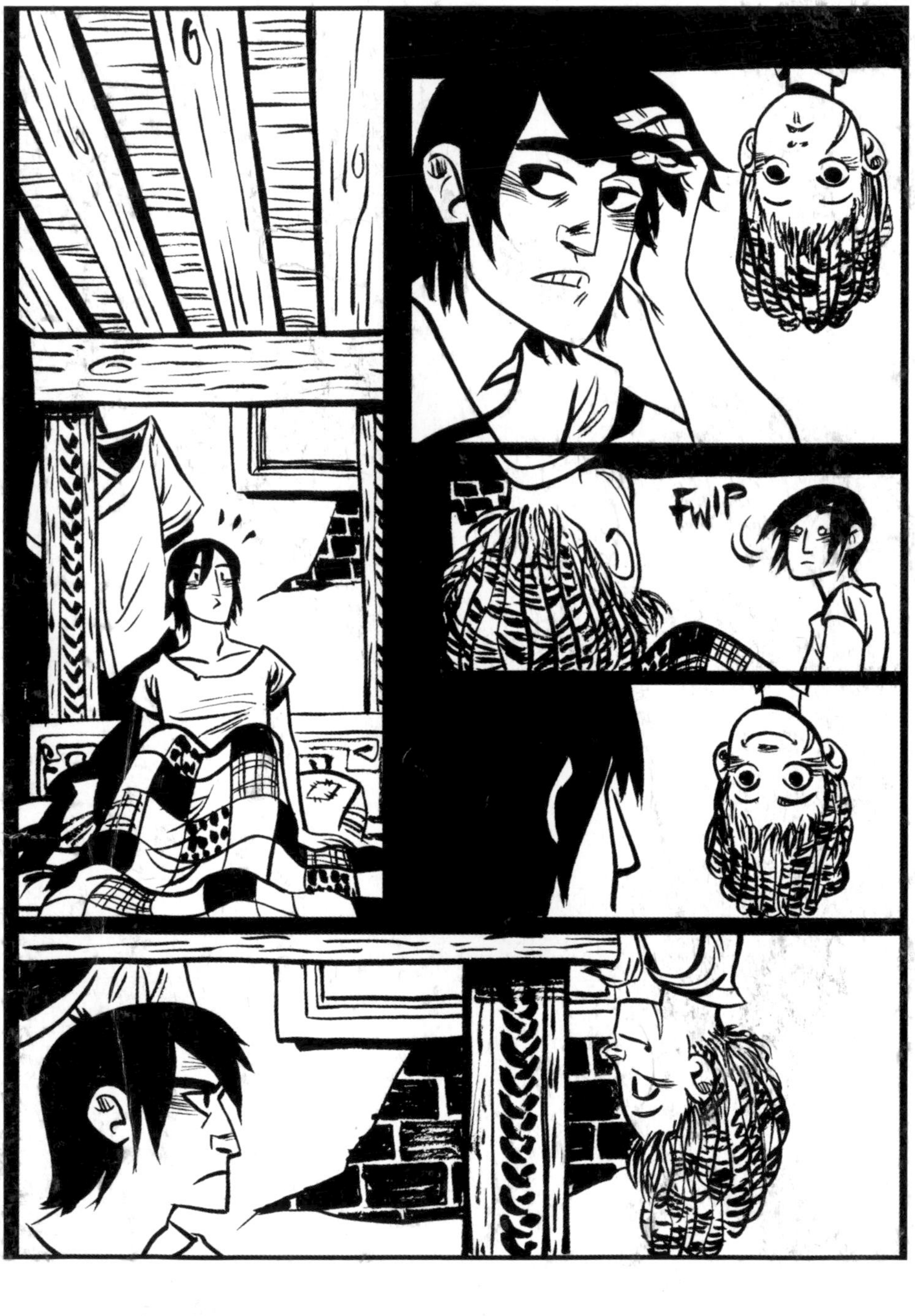
FWIP

Canada Council   Conseil des arts
for the Arts   ·   du Canada

Faith Erin Hicks acknowledges the support of the Canada Council for the Arts, which
last year invested $153 million to bring the arts to Canadians throughout the country.

Faith Erin Hicks remercions le Conseil des arts du Canada de son soutien. L'an
dernier, le Conseil a investi 153 millions de dollars pour mettre de l'art dans la vie des
Canadiennes et des Canadiens de tout le pays.

First Second

Published by First Second
First Second is an imprint of Roaring Brook Press, a division of
Holtzbrinck Publishing Holdings Limited Partnership
175 Fifth Avenue, New York, New York 10010
All rights reserved

Library of Congress Control Number: 2016938731

Hardcover ISBN: 978-1-62672-159-3
Paperback ISBN: 978-1-62672-158-6

Our books may be purchased in bulk for promotional, educational, or business use. Please
contact your local bookseller or the Macmillan Corporate and Premium Sales Department
at (800) 221-7945 ext. 5442 or by e-mail at MacmillanSpecialMarkets@macmillan.com.

FIRST
EDITION

First edition 2017

Interior art colored by Jordie Bellaire
Cover art colored by Braden Lamb and Shelli Paroline
Book design by Danielle Ceccolini
Printed in China by Toppan Leefung Printing Ltd., Dongguan City, Guangdong Province

Hardcover: 10 9 8 7 6 5 4 3 2 1
Paperback: 10 9 8 7 6 5 4 3 2 1

Penciled digitally in Manga Studio on a Wacom Cintiq. Inked traditionally with a Raphaël
Kolinsky watercolor brush.

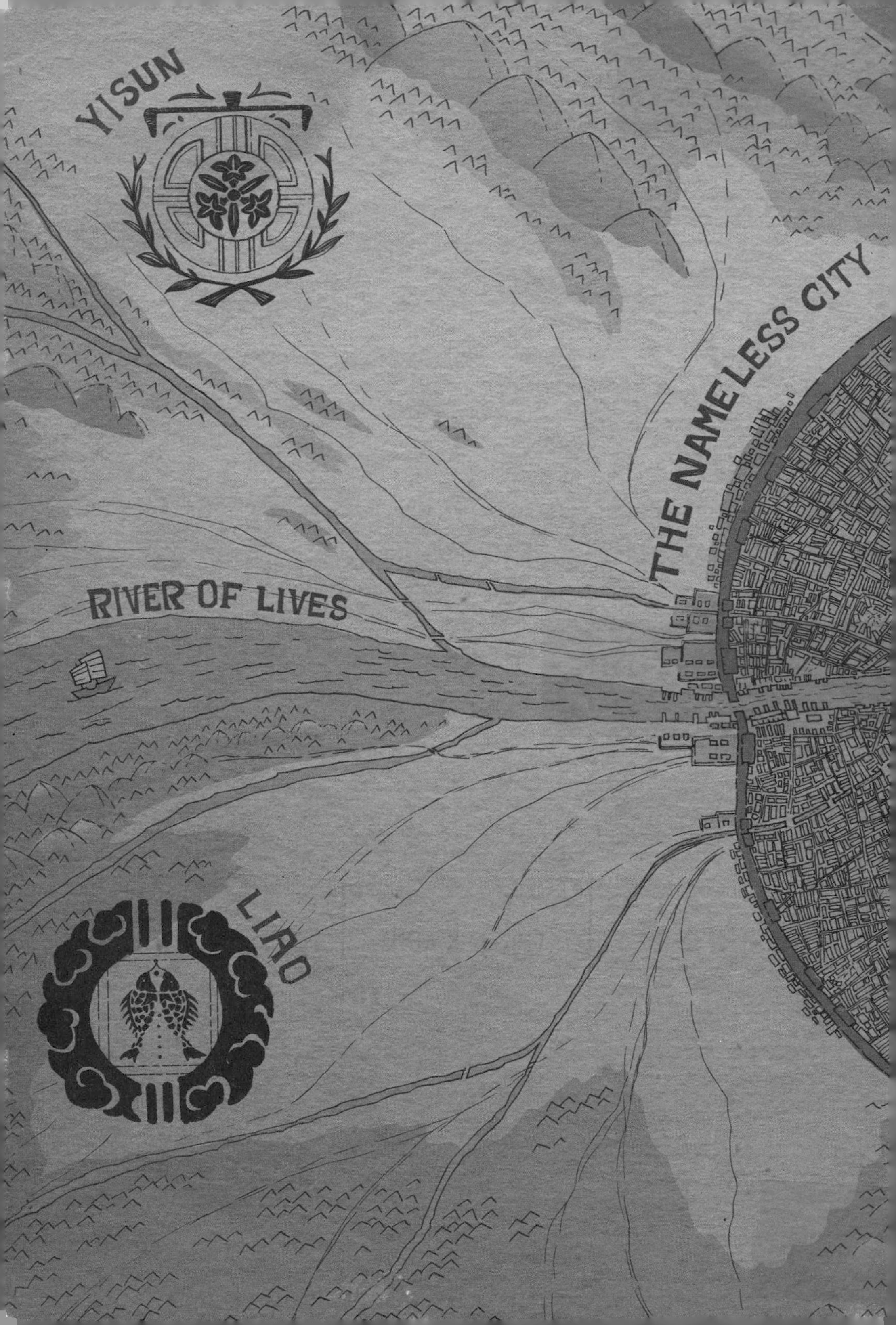
YISUN
THE NAMELESS CITY
RIVER OF LIVES
LIAO